CW01506440

HellBound Books
Anthology of
Extreme Horror

curated by
Samantha Hawkins

A HellBound Books® LLC Publication

Dedication

Horror is subjective. This will always remain a fact. My love for this genre, and you authors, however, is not. I could say so much, but instead all I'm going to say is thank you. Thank you for allowing me to be a part of this arena. I am a better reviewer, curator, and person because of every single one of you amazing authors. You may not know it, but I couldn't have weathered the storm I just came out of, without you.

To James, Xtina, and HellBound itself, thank you for taking a chance on me. Thank you for giving me a reason to stay...;

-Samantha Hawkins, Curator
July/2025

Contents:

Foreword
by
Matt Shaw

If you've picked this anthology up, it's for one of two reasons.

The first reason is that you thought it had a kick-ass cover and knew it would look great on your shelf (I've done this before!). The second reason is you are already a fan of extreme horror and know what is involved with this genre: boundary pushing, graphic, over-the-top, shocking, and almost cartoonish levels of violence and gore (and usually sex).

The exact time of when 'extreme horror' became a notable sub-genre is debatable with some believing it really came into itself in the late 1980s but I'd argue this wasn't extreme horror - this was the 'splatterpunk movement' (the two genres are often confused). Still, the late 80s? I was too busy watching *He-Man, Thundercats, The Real Ghostbusters* and *Teenage Mutant Hero Turtles* (don't go correcting me, I'm from the UK and we weren't allowed to have "Ninja" in the title) but that's by the by. Personally, I was never really aware of extreme horror until I found myself writing it to "upset" a publisher who called me a "Sick Bastard" after reading a book he was looking to publish (Art, co-written by Michael Bray). I saw his message and thought, *You cheeky bastard... I'll give you 'sick bastards',* and I started writing the start of a new book I never intended to finish; ten pages of the most graphic, fucked-up sex, which was interrupted with an old woman bursting into the room and saying, 'Oh for God's sake, put your sister down! Dinner's on the table.'

The 'dinner on the table' in question being a naked man, strapped down while the family's father hacked at him with a knife.

I sent it to the publisher and said, 'NOW you can call me a sick bastard!' He didn't disagree. Also, as an aside, he didn't publish *Art* either because his beta readers warned him against it. This worked out well for Michael and I, though, because we self-published, and the audience loved it.

The thing is, while those ten pages were fucked up, I was having way too much fun writing it and, so, I decided to finish it. I thought of a plot, I thought of some cool twists, and I got cracking - even checking with the publisher if he minded me using the name "Sick Bastards" as the title. He didn't give a shit.

My intention was to self-publish and quietly release it (via Amazon) because I figured I'd most likely get complaints if it fell into the hands of more 'sensitive' readers. At that stage, I didn't have a career and I didn't want to alienate the readers before they even had a chance to get to know me.

Because I wasn't expecting much from the book, I didn't want to invest in a cover, so I ended up designing a really simple one myself: a plain black cover with the title in bold white writing. Along with the title, I also added a warning in red. It stood out really well on Amazon and, twenty-four hours after release, it was number one and going viral.

A couple of weeks after that, I sold the film rights (sadly reverted back to me now) and, a month after that, I quit my day-job. I'd launched my writing career purely by accident and found an insatiable appetite for fucked-up horror amongst Kindle owners.

About a month or so after that, suddenly Amazon was *filled* with extreme horror books from people who were starting their careers. Some were great and still write today and others… well… they no longer write. But *this* was the first time *I* realised 'extreme horror' was a full-on genre in its own right.

*

Unfortunately 'extreme horror' gets a bad reputation. Chief complaints are the writing is awful, littered with mistakes, and nothing but the sordid fantasies of edge-lords who dwell in their mother's basement. I've lost count the number of times I've been called an edge-lord. I've also lost count the number of times I've been accused of living in my mum's basement. At times I wish I *was* living down there because I'd save a fortune in rent. As for the writing being awful, well, that's subjective.

Weirdly, even though this is my full-time career and has been for more than a decade, I don't actually consider myself to be an author. I'm a *storyteller*. My books tend to be on the shorter side (as does most extreme horror). They get to the point fast and throw the shocks at you while telling a fun story. The kind of book you can take on holiday, read by a pool, and then move on to the next. There are *much* better authors out there with their fancy prose and descriptive natures, but that doesn't mean extreme horror writing is necessarily awful (sure, in some cases it can be). It's just not to that person's taste (which is fine).

That being said, what doesn't help the genre is some authors who dabble within it do get it wrong with their stories. By this I mean they abandon the story completely, along with the characters, and literally throw nothing but grossness at the book and - truthfully - this gets boring for the readers really, really fast. These are usually the flash-in-the-pan writers. They see a topic sells like hotcakes and, very soon after, have their own variation of said story (albeit without the 'story'). They literally fill their books with scene after scene of what made the initial book controversial, but without any real reason other than to appear shocking and disturbing. The thing is, for the shocks to really land, the violence needs a point to it. If you don't give a shit about the characters, then it's just stale, desperate writing trying to cash-in on an already successful book. I've seen it time and time again, and I'm sure I will see it many more times. That being said, even without *these* books out there, you'd still get complaints from readers who accidentally read extreme horror without realising what they were getting into.

Only the other day was I cancelled (again) for writing 'child pornography.' They demanded people stop reading my work and said that I was glorifying CP because, clearly, I fuck children in my spare time.

I wish I was joking.

The thing is, the book they mentioned is *not* available on any platform but my own site, and certainly *doesn't* glorify any such activities. It does highlight the topic, though, and makes for a deeply uncomfortable read (not a sexy one, thank you). But to find the book, you need to go on my site and ignore all the warnings. That's what this reader did: they found my site, they saw the book, they read the blurb, they read the warning, they would have read the further warnings within the first few pages, and yet *still* chose to go ahead and read it. Then, when done, they went straight to social media to call me out (via an anonymous post, I hasten to add).

Now, CP is, obviously, a taboo subject. The book was kept off Amazon for two reasons: Amazon would ban it outright (it's been banned in Australia from where customers tried to get it shipped to them from my store, only to have it seized by customs), and I wouldn't want such content falling into the wrong hands. It was intended for *my* readers who wanted to push their own boundaries and triggers, but extreme horror can also feature 'normal' violence between adults and still, when in the wrong hands, can cause great upset / uproar.

For example: I've written books where women get hurt, so, apparently, I'm a misogynist. It doesn't matter that, in the majority of my books, it's the women fucking the men up. The reader saw me hurt a fictional character and then went on a crusade to tell all who'd listen that this was the type of person I was in real life.

Sam West is a misogynist, too, because 'he' also wrote books in which women were murdered. The only issue with that being Sam West is actually a woman. but that doesn't bother such people once they get a bee in their bonnet. If they're going to gun for someone, they don't care about anything but their own beliefs. Hell, they're even happy to straight-up lie about the authors in an extra effort to prove their point the authors of these books are bad and should be locked up.

Again, from my own experience, I have even been accused of being a wife-beater – something my father-in-law laughed at when I told him: 'She'd kick the shit out of you.' True, that. Had the person who made the video been in the United Kingdom, I would have sued, but to sue in America? I can't be arsed (yet) because, a lot of the time, these inflammatory remarks are *also* written by people who are seeking clicks and likes on their content. With that in mind, really, they should be thanking such authors as I for their 'toxic writing' as it gives them something to bitch and moan about. Personally, I prefer channels which push the works they *love* – but what do I know?

Now, as stated, a lot of extreme horror does actually come with warnings. My own books do, when I know the content is 'out there', because I *don't* want people reading it who aren't fans of the genre. Why would I want them to read it and get upset? I don't want to trigger people who aren't looking for such content, yet even with these warnings front and centre, people still buy them and are offended. It would be nice if we could find a way in which these books could be sold without falling into the wrong hands, as we *want* to make *fans* of the genre uncomfortable and, better yet, disturb them. And we want to do so without the sensitive readers accusing us of being evil sons of bitches who belong in prison.

*

Love it or loathe it, extreme horror isn't going anywhere. It does come in peaks and troughs, though; in that, some months, it's really popular and then in other months, not so much. I actually write in many genres but always circle back to extreme horror and splatterpunk (SP has more of a social commentary within its story) because it is where my main audience is. Also, in times of stress, it's *fun* to write such content because you can let loose and set aside realism in favour of some disturbing stories with over-the-top scenes, which are great for venting stress from real life. It's therapeutic to write just as, for some, it's therapeutic to read and - yes - I'm very aware how fucked up that sounds.

The important thing to note is not all content will be for you. You might even enjoy extreme horror as a whole but find certain titles are just too far out of your comfort zone, and that's perfectly fine. So long as the work is kept in the realms of fiction, we can enjoy *what* we want, *how* we want.

Writing or reading extreme horror does not make us monsters.

With that in mind, I hope you truly enjoy this collection!

Matt Shaw 2025

The Interview
Matt Shaw

The author shifted his weight in his seat, bored of the interview already and wondering why he'd accepted it. There was hardly anyone in the audience, the interviewer clearly knew nothing of his work or accomplishments and he was in danger of missing his favorite show on the television.

Out of politeness, while the interviewer searched out their next question from a sheet of scribbled notes which looked as though they'd been complied by a two-year-old, he forced a lackluster smile. The red-faced interviewer, clearly aware she'd lost both the man she was interviewing and the watching audience, umm'ed and err'ed while scanning the page, completely oblivious to the fake smile being presented.

"Okay. By your own admission you write some pretty graphic content." She laughed. "I'm almost scared to ask this question but where do you find your inspiration?"

There was a wicked glint in the author's eye when he answered in less than a beat, "Oh, inspiration is never far."

Even now, he was feeling inspired to write a gruesome torture scene; something really fucked-up where an irritating woman decided to position herself too close to the wrong man. Within pages she'd be abducted and from there?

He'd start with some cruel jibes about her weight and looks, playing on her insecurities, then he'd put a few paragraphs in where he'd beat her black and blue before finally feeling sorry for her and fucking her good and hard because it was clear she needed it.

And a nice plot-twist for those who like such turns? The characters would end up falling in love and raising a fucked-up family together. The fact that, in his head, the female character shared a startling resemblance to the interviewer was neither here nor there. Another coincidence being that, in that quick-thought plot, the male character would beat the female character in a way similar to what he so desperately wanted to do to the interviewer now.

Why the fuck did they ask for this interview and not properly prepare for it?

The author, Simon Jones, had been invited to a small book group held in the town he lived in. When he said "yes", he hadn't realized how small it actually was. That was his mistake, just as they should have done more research into who he was; he could have done the same for them.

From the moment they first greeted him when he entered the community hall—*a fucking community hall*—it was clear they'd not read his work and seen the actual content. They had only invited him because his name was all over social media at the moment with people talking about his latest book but had they stopped to actually watch the whole video, they would have quickly realized they weren't talking about it for the "right reasons".

The only reason his name was being thrown around was because these online accounts were calling for his cancellation.

The group was mostly made up of wannabe authors. They spent most weeks talking about their books without actually ever writing them. They liked getting authors in to discuss their own works because they believed it might offer them inspiration to finally pick up a pen for themselves but it rarely worked that way.

Especially when the authors were being as difficult as Simon was; not that he'd initially intended to be an ass. He'd come to the meet with all good intentions and had only really lost interest when he realized how useless they were and, yes, he knew everyone had to start *somewhere* but, they couldn't have been more ill-prepared if they'd tried.

Still, from the desperate look on the interviewer's face, he knew he had to give them a little more so he continued, "Honestly inspiration can come from anywhere. Ever watched a film and wished it had ended a different way? Congratulations! The end you just imagined? That's the end for *your* new book. Now all you need is to build a story around it. Or maybe you've overheard something interesting from a conversation in a coffee shop? Nice one.

"You now have a couple of characters for your story… The trick is to not fall into the trap of walking around, lost in your own little world. Keep your eyes open and you'll be surprised how inspiration can come. Oh, and keep a book by your bed. A journal, or something, in which you can write your dreams. Never… *Never* think to yourself, *That's a good idea, I'll make a note of it in the morning.* I guarantee, by morning, you'd have clean forgotten about it." Careful not to just talk to the interviewer, he directed some of his response to the audience but—fuck—if they weren't all braindead-looking morons.

"That's some good advice, thank you." She continued, seemingly finding her next question in the time taken for him to answer, 'And what about research? How long do you spend researching a topic before you begin writing?'

Simon couldn't help but laugh; not because the question amused him but because he wondered how they'd fare had he answered truthfully.

THE LIE

'I don't tend to write books which require research. I'm not that kind of author. My books tend to just need an active imagination, something I've had ever since I was a little kid.'

THE TRUTH

"Ssh... Ssh... It's okay... It's all right. We're finished for now," Simon said quietly as he scribbled down his notes from his afternoon's entertainment. He wasn't sure if *she* had heard him, given her incessant crying. He didn't know why she was making such a song and dance about it.

He'd not hit her *that* hard; just hard enough to fully appreciate how it would feel and sound to crack an eye-socket; not too dissimilar to the sound of a thick piece of wood splintering. The noises she was making—a person would think it was as painful as the time he took the garden sheers to her large toe. A little pressure and *snip*. The blades cut through the bone with surprising ease and—this little piggy went to market...

He turned back to the naked, bound woman and gave her already swollen cheek a tender touch. Sore, she flinched at his touch as he said, "I have to pop out later. I'm not sure how long I'll be. I don't think I told you but there's a local book group looking to interview me about my work in the local community hall. Quite exciting, isn't it? Although, not sure about the location. Could have been somewhere a little more glamorous but, oh well. And you never know, it might even lead to more sales, which would be nice."

He put the lid back on his pen and closed his journal. "Then, when I get home, I'll do a bit of writing and then maybe we can spend a little time together?" It wasn't just violence he offered. He offered *love*, too, whether she wanted it or not. A cuddle, a kiss, a tender touch and more "intimacy" than he'd ever experienced with anyone else.

Such time together didn't bring her physical pain, he was careful of that, but - there was plenty of *emotional* pain whenever he penetrated her. He paused a moment as a thought crossed his mind; neither of them had eaten anything so far. "Before I go, I can make you a sandwich if you want?" The older woman continued to weep through both fear and pain.

*

"I think that's the problem with my own writing," the interview continued, seemingly satisfied with his answer. "I tend to get too bogged down in research." It wasn't the first time she had referenced her own writing; another reason why he wanted to kick her in the cunt. Were they there to discuss his work or what she was failing to write? He smiled sympathetically while simultaneously hoping they were nearly done so he could get back home.

"I'm sure you'll figure it out," Simon said, trying to sound as friendly as possible but ensuring she got the hint he didn't want to engage in such discussion. He thought he'd been pretty clear with his initial answer being that he didn't tend to write books which required research so why she would then try and expand on the conversation was beyond him.

It was clear from the woman's face she'd expected a little more help with her problem than what was given. Her cheeks flushed with embarrassment, knowing she'd made a fool of herself.

She cleared her throat and hastily moved on to the next question. "Can you tell us a little about your current project?" This was another question which annoyed Simon. Why would an author willingly divulge information about their new book to a room full of people all hoping to write their first? Ideas spoken so freely were easy to rip-off; something he'd seen happen before, although, thankfully, not to him. Anyway, there was only one person he shared his stories with while in the writing stage.

THE BETA "LISTENER"

Some authors used beta readers; trusted people who'd get an early read of a finished—sometimes unedited—piece of work in exchange for feedback. Such readers had the potential to be useful to an author as it gave the writers a chance to amend their work before it was released. The *problem* with beta readers was that *everyone* wanted to be one. Or rather, they wanted a free read which had the added bonus of not being readily available yet.

The issue was, just because they'd said "yes" to offering themselves up for an early read, not all of them came back with feedback. They simply took the free read and disappeared, only to ghost the authors when they reached out.

Another problem was that some clearly didn't understand the role of a beta reader and would give lackluster feedback along with lines of, *I liked it.* While it was always nice to hear a book was enjoyed, such feedback didn't help the author when it came to improving anything.

None of this was to say that all beta readers were bad; there were some great ones out there. It was just hard finding them.

Simon didn't bother with beta readers after hearing the depressing stories from other authors who'd posted they were seeking such people only to be let down by them. He figured it was a headache he didn't need. He was also very aware he was his own best beta reader because, unlike others, he actually wrote his books for *him*. The fact he'd struck it lucky and found himself a readership was nothing more than a fluke. As well as his own opinion, Simon also had a beta listener.

Every morning he'd go into the spare bedroom and sit on the edge of the single bed in there before reading what he'd penned the previous night. His listener lay there and listen, quietly. Her tears would only come when he'd explain where the story was going next and, more specifically, how he was going to use her to ensure he wrote *realistically.*

"She fucked him over in college and he bumped into her years later, purely by chance. There's going to be this great scene where he fucks her with a broken glass bottle. The only thing I don't know yet is whether it would be better to have it in her pussy or ass. What do you think?"

"Please... Let me go..."

"No. That's not part of the story. I feel that would be somewhat anti-climactic." A sudden burst of enthusiasm and he added, "Oh and... He could throat fuck her with whatever's left of the bottle, too... She could drown in her own blood as he stands over her, laughing."

And then she'd be crying. He knew he'd struck gold with the final 'fuck you' of the book because of the tears as he started imagining other readers having the same reaction although, in his head, these tears would be of joy. They'd be *happy* the poor guy had finally got his revenge after all these years. Or, to think of it another way, *closure*.

"That's it," he said with glee. "That's the ending… well, *almost*. So what do you think? Does the bottle need to be in the pussy or the arse? On the one hand it would clearly be worse for women, feeling their insides getting ripped and cut with a broken bottle but the arse would be just as unpleasant, right? And then, that's something for the *male* readers to feel too because, let's be honest, the men probably won't feel too squeamish if it's dealing with a vagina…" When she still didn't give him an answer, he asked, "Should we go for a practical?"

*

Simon paused a moment while searching his mind for a suitable answer. After a few seconds he said, "I *can* tell you it's another extreme horror and it will be due for release in about two months. Oh, and it's brutal." He smiled. That was enough. They didn't need to know the exact plot details although, again, it was clear from the interviewer's face she wanted more. Something Simon had learned long ago though: You *always* leave them wanting more.

Also, giving them more would have likely turned them away from his work. From the looks of those in the audience, extreme horror probably wouldn't have been their first choice in reading material. Hell, listening to conversations they'd been having prior to the interview starting, they'd probably have been better off finding a romance author to interview.

"Well I'm sure others will agree, it all sounds very exciting and we look forward to reading it when it comes out." The bitch couldn't have sounded less enthused if she tried. Still, not wanting to come across as an asshole, Simon forced yet another smile.

"Okay before we start to wrap things up,' she turned her attention to the audience and asked, 'does anyone have any questions for Simon?"

At least she got his name right. Simon looked to the audience. A couple of them were sitting there with entirely blank expressions on their faces, clearly bored and not listening to a damn word he'd said throughout the whole thing.

Another was sucking on a boiled sweet and had been for the duration of the interview, stopping only long enough to rattle it around her cheap dentures. It had been real hard to ignore the noises and pretty much took Simon his all *not* to snap at her and ask her to shut the fuck up. It took even more to *not* snap her fucking jaw. He smiled at the thought of it hanging off her skull. He already knew it was a tough crowd and such a reaction would have done nothing to endear himself to anyone.

Just as both he and the interviewer were starting to think there'd be no questions, a lone hand went up at the back of the room. It was a little old lady with purple rinse to her hair, thick rimmed glasses and enough lines across her face to tell a story of their own; she'd lived a hard life.

The interview pointed to her as though it would be possible for the old lady not to know it had been her who was about to be addressed. "Yes. Betty. You have a question?" While the interviewer was clearly excited that someone was engaging, Simon was less so. Had their been no questions, they could have wrapped things up and he could have been on his way. Still, all being well it would be something quick and easy. Even better? It wouldn't prompt further questions from the others.

Betty, a sixty-three-year-old who'd had dreams of writing her own book for at least five minutes, didn't bother to stand. Rooted to her seat, she called out, "Why do you hate women?" The question had come out of the blue.

Simon was used to such questions in the online space but, here, he'd figured he would have been "safe" from them. It wasn't just Simon who was taken aback by the unexpected question, either; the interviewer looked just as flustered.

"I'm sorry?"

"Why do you hate women? From what I read about you, apparently all your work is written solely to degrade and humiliate women so, why do you hate them so? It's a fair question."

And another smile forced. "The majority of my readers are women," he said. This wasn't a lie but, when he discovered this for himself, it was a surprise given he'd presumed most of his readers would have been guys who were into horror.

He didn't know why so many women read his work, nor did he understand why—of those—some liked to send him explicit photos, not that he was complaining. He just presumed they were dealing with trauma or had dark fantasies they could live out through his writing. Whatever the reason, whoever the audience, all he knew was, such content sold and, for him at least, was pretty well reviewed by people who'd actively sought out such material. Simon said, "I don't *hate* women." And he genuinely didn't, either. "I love women."

Betty was a cunt though.

A KIND BEDSIDE MANNER

Cutting through the outer thigh with a sharp scalpel was very similar to slicing into a thick cut of ham. Simon wasn't exactly surprised by this but did feel a little guilt as he cleaned the wound and glued it shut. Hindsight was screaming at him that he probably could have just purchased a thick slice of ham to test as opposed to cutting her but... At least he knew for sure now. Also, it wasn't only hindsight which was screaming at him. She was screaming too now that the adrenaline from the initial cut had worn off leaving behind only the painful sting.

"It's okay. It's *okay*. Look… all closed up again," he said reassuringly as he dabbed the glued wound with a clean towel. "Good as new. Just breathe through the pain… *Breathe through the pain* and I'll fetch you some pain relief." He leaned down and gave her a kiss on her pale cheek. "You did well. Very helpful."

His comforting words offered her no such comfort but it didn't stop him from saying them—it never did. She was being a great help, ensuring the realism in his book was on-point, both in the way the wounds occurred and the way the character reacted to them. She deserved his kind words and *more*. He gave her another kiss on the cheek. 'This will be the best book yet,' he said.

*

Betty continued, "Are you not worried writing content as you do, others might not be encouraged to try it for themselves?"

It baffled Simon how idiots could come to such conclusions but he knew it wasn't *their* fault. It was the media who tended to push such narratives. For a while, especially in the nineties, they often made a habit of linking real-life atrocities to fictional tales. One such case was the brutal torture and murder of Jamie Bulger; a young boy abducted from a shopping center by two older boys.

The press linked the killing to the films *Braindead* and *Child's Play III* which resulted in the movies being banned for a short period. In conversations where people were quick to blame horror for what happened in the real world, Simon would argue that if people had murder in mind, they didn't need a book, game, film or even piece of music to trigger them into going ahead with it.

Sooner or later they would respond to the darkness within regardless. "If someone is capable of murder or animal cruelty, they already have that in them. No normal person is inspired to go and lash out because of a story." In short, even if there was no such genre as horror, there would always be *real* horror in the world. "I have had messages from people before though—Victims—who said they were grateful for my work because it helped them process their own trauma."

"I don't see how that works."

Simon laughed. "Neither do I but who am I to argue? If they say it helped them then good." He added, "I've never had a message from someone telling me they feel inspired to go and rape someone because of a book I've written..." And he laughed. "Although I did once get a video of a woman masturbating. The message that went with her video was something like, *The main scene in the last book... Look what you made me do.*"

Betty had a look of disgust on her face. Clearly she wasn't impressed.

"At the end of the day, my work isn't for everyone and that is perfectly acceptable. We all like different things. That being said, it's never okay for you or anyone else to judge others for their reading material or accuse the authors of such content of glorifying and encouraging violent acts toward people. The majority of the readers know what I do is fiction."

"And the minority?"

Simon shrugged. "I've been writing for a number of years. Not once have I ever been linked to any real-life crimes so..."

The interviewer was aware this line of questioning was most likely frustrating their guest so was quick to put a pin in it. "Does anyone else have any *other* questions?" Betty didn't wait to hear. She picked her handbag up from beneath the chair and made her way to the exit. It didn't matter how Simon would have answered her. To her, he'd always be a misogynistic asshole.

Simon was fine with that. From experience he found it better when such people walked away. It was better for them and led to a quieter life for him and while a few did walk away, there'd always be others who would seek out such content.

"No one else has any questions?" The interviewer gave the room another quick scan. No one made themselves known to her. "Okay well... Finally, do you have any parting words of advice you could share with the group? For those looking to start their own book?"

Simon nodded. One thing he'd always considered himself to be good at was giving advice.

FRIENDLY ADVICE

Simon entered the spare room with a jam sandwich on a plate. It wasn't exactly gourmet food but given the bruises on her face, it was better to have something soft and easier to eat. He set the plate down on the bedside table next to where she was bound. Despite being tied, the plate—and a glass of water—were within easy reach.

"Just chew carefully, it'll hurt less." In case she couldn't tell what it was already, he added, "It's a jam sandwich so should be nice and soft... Easy to manage after..." After he'd previously knocked some of her teeth out while researching how hard he had to bring the hammer down for such an accomplishment.

As it turned out, 'not too hard' was the necessary force to crack and splinter a tooth, even dislodge it a little but more force was needed to actually knock it—with a rip—from the gum. There was a reason why dentists would twist and pull instead of simply hitting.

He did wonder whether age played a part in how easy it was to knock a tooth out. The older a person was, the easier they were to bruise and damage compared to those who were younger and with more 'bounce-back'. Could it be that the older a person was, the more wear and tear they had, the easier it was to dislodge their teeth? The only way to *really* know the answer was if he had a younger person to experiment on to. The only real disappointment being, there was no one he could currently think of to fill this newfound vacancy in his workforce.

One day, maybe.

"And don't forget to drink, too. You need to stay hydrated."

She pulled on her restraint and winced. It had cut into her skin. "I know you can't undo it and I'm not asking you to but could you loosen it just a little. *A little*. I won't try anything but…" She tried to get her sandwich if only to prove how awkward it was. "I can't reach."

"I can't remove it," he said.

"No. I know. Just… loosen it a tiny bit so I can reach without it cutting into me." She pulled on the restraint again to show him what it was doing.

He hesitated a moment before, with some reluctance, nodding. "Just a little. It'll still be tight but… a little." Without waiting for her to say anything, he walked over and re-worked the knot to give her a fraction more space. It still looked too tight to slip out of but at least it wasn't cutting into her flesh anymore. "How's that?"

"Thank you."

*

"Start with something small. A short story or a novella. A lot of people fail when writing because they jump straight into a novel and get themselves bogged down. If you finish a short, you give yourself confidence for something bigger. And don't get too wrapped up in editing, either.

"Yes you will need your work edited but I've known some wannabe authors who've never released anything because they keep going back over their work over and over... Just get it written and *then* worry about editing. And, finally, keep in mind this isn't going to be something you bash out in a day or two. It will take time to perfect your story and that's fine.

"There's no time limit other than the ones we impose on ourselves. The trick is to be patient and not put too much pressure on yourselves." It was the usual line of advice he gave to everyone who approached him about writing and, as far as advice went, it was sound for those who cared to properly listen and take it onboard, something which not everyone did.

Those people would ask for advice and then seemingly do everything they could to ignore it, which frustrated the hell out of Simon because he *hated* wasting his time.

"Thank you for that." The interviewer continued, "And thank you for coming to talk to us. I'm sure I speak for everyone here but we truly appreciate it."

THE LIE

"It was my pleasure."

THE TRUTH

Simon followed the interviewer's lead and stood while the few audience members half-heartedly gave them both a round of applause. He made his way off the stage, using the steps at the side while the interviewer gathered her belongings together.

As Simon gave the audience another nod, he made his way to the exit just as two uniformed officers stepped in. His heart skipped a beat when they noticed him and made their approach. "Simon Jones?"

"That's right."

"We were wondering if you could accompany us to the station to answer a few questions."

"A few questions? May I ask what about?" He already knew. He'd loosened the wrist restraint too much and she must have gotten free. He also knew this wasn't a request from the lead officer but more of a demand instead; no doubt worded more delicately to save him some embarrassment from those behind who were watching, curious to know what was happening. Guilt written all over his beetroot face.

"We've had a complaint…"

For the benefit of the spectators, he tried to play innocent. "A complaint? Against me?"

"HER"

With the restraint loosened ever so slightly, Simon returned to his previous conversation. "Please do make sure you eat and drink something, though. You need to keep your strength up." A quick check of the time on his wristwatch. "I'm not sure how long I'll be out for," he said, "but I doubt it will be late. Do you need anything else?"

She shook her head.

He smiled at her in much the same way a true friend would smile at someone they'd known for years. "I'll see you soon, okay?" He didn't wait for her reply. He stepped from the room with a final, "Love you, Mum" and closed the door behind him. She immediately started struggling against the now-loosened wrist restraint.

*

The officer nodded. It wasn't just *any* complaint either but a very serious one that officer didn't really want to go into in front of anyone else. He simply said, "From your mother."

That fucking bitch.

The Umpire Strikes Back
Joe Pasquale

LOCATION: Mortuary in the town of Carlton – 2km from Melbourne, Australia.

TIME: Day 6 of the Test Match, Australia VS England. 1.35 a.m. precisely.

O *h, fuck me… What's going on?*
I don't know how long I've been here… I just know it's been a while… I can still see clearly, yet I know my eyes are only half open…

When I say I can see, I mean I can make out shades of darkness and light – it all keeps flashing by in a dull, blurry mess above my head, like clouds passing the sun… I think I'm in a room with strip lights and ghosts wandering about…

What the fuck *is wrong with me?*

I'm here, lying on my back without a fucking clue, and I hear the irritating buzzing of the lights as neon gas gets excited in its cigar-like tube and fluoresces. And I can't remember a fucking thing...

I hear the ghosts' voices. Muffled. I can barely make out what they're saying, so I listen harder. It's something about... a tree stump?

I can't move any part of my body. I can't say anything. But I can hear and I can see....

I cry – but I don't shed a tear or make any sound at all.

TIME: 1.40 a.m.

My silent sadness is interrupted by the noise of a thick, heavy zip being undone. The sudden intrusion of light blinds my half-open, still eyes as the ghost opening the zip turns out not to be a ghost after all....

It's a man.

He speaks.

"*Fuuuck*... Oh, Jesus H. Christ on a fucking stick... what the fuck is *this*?" His voice is thick with an Australian accent.

Oh, dear God, I think I'm in a body bag!

I'm naked. I can't move my head to see what's going on, but there's a small magnifying mirror just in my eyeline.

I see two men: one is dressed like a surgeon, the other wears the pale blue scrubs more of a hospital porter. I also see a large piece of bloodstained wood protruding from my chest – it's pale brown and about 2-foot long.

The surgeon opens up the body bag all the way down and steps back to scan me from head to foot.

"Is that a fucking *cricket stump*?" he asks the porter.

The porter nods sagely and pulls out a pack of cigarettes. He taps it on the palm of his hand, and one of the filtered cancer-tubes pokes its head out. He puts it to his lips and sparks up the flint from a Zip lighter he conjured from thin air.

The surgeon looked to me to be some 30 years older – at *least* - than the porter. I put him at probably in his mid-sixties. He has mad professor hair – a lot like Doc Brown in *Back to The Future* – and a wrinkled, saggy neck that reminds me of a turkey's wattle. I can tell the younger man, the porter, is a waster, an air head, just from the way he talks – or *doesn't,* as the case seems to be.

Illiterate wanker

Even dead, I can tell there's nothing going on behind his eyes except for illegal drugs and fucking.

"You can't smoke a cigarette in here," Doc Brown snaps. "It contaminates the body."

"He's fucking *dead,* isn't he?" The porter protests; the name tag on the left breast of his bland scrubs informs me his name is Gonzales "Not like he's gonna get lung cancer, is it?!"

How can I possibly be dead?

I can hear every word of what the two are saying. I can see them. The acrid stench of bleach in the room is burning my nostrils... how can that happen when I'm not even breathing? My chest isn't going up and down with even the shallowest of breaths, my lungs aren't taking in oxygen and releasing carbon dioxide....

So... how am I smelling the fucking bleach?

With a smoky snort, Gonzales stubs out the cigarette on the stainless-steel table upon which I'm lying and slots it behind his pierced ear. Then, he reaches into the breast pocket of his tunic and pulls out a tightly rolled doobie.

"What about a touch of the green stuff?" Gonzales says, wafting the white paper cylinder under Doc Brown's nose.

The old surgeon scowls and says, "Look – just let me get this underway. Then we can fire that up. I want a clear head for this because I wanna know what's going on here.

Once I've opened the stiff up – maybe then we can kick back and have some fun."

Gonzales tuts and pops the doobie back in the pocket it came from.

TIME: 1.50 a.m.

"So, what happened to this poor bloke?" asks Doc Brown.

"Oh… this is *so* fucked up." Gonzales tells him. "You're not gonna believe this."

"*Really*?" says Doc. "Try me – I'm all ears… hold on, just give me a sec' to get this fucking stump out."

I watch the doc with the wild, white hair snap on a pair of rubber gloves. Then, he grasps the wooden stump sticking out of my chest with both hands….

He pulls.

I feel my back arch and lift off the cold trolley as he tugs.

"Stubborn fucker, ain't ya?" he snarls at the stump. Then he pulls on it again – after getting a tighter purchase.

It doesn't budge.

"D'ya wanna put some gloves on and give me a hand instead of just gawping, ya dopey Muppet?" Doc Brown isn't impressed by the stoner's inaction.

"Yeah, sure." Gonzales sniffs. "But, please, don't call me a Muppet… I fucking *hate* those felt bastards."

The doc keeps on tugging away as Gonzales saunters over to a small cardboard box filled with white latex gloves. Pulling one out, he blows into it and then pulls the inflated mitt over the top of his head. I watch him in the mirror as he does a pretty good chicken dance behind the doc's back.

Doc Brown spins around to slap the porter about the

head. "Stop fucking about and help me – or get the fuck out of my mortuary!"

Looking like his feelings are hurt, Gonzales removes the glove from his head and snaps on a fresh pair – on his hands, this time.

"What do you want me to do?" he asks the doc.

"Stand behind him and hold his shoulders down," Doc says. "I'm gonna climb on top –"

Gonzales snorts out a laugh. "You dirty old bugger," he whispers to himself as he rests all his weight onto the top of my arms.

Ignoring the comment, the doctor climbs onto the gurney and sits on me with his scrawny arse just below my rib cage. I can see Gonzales' face level with mine and the look of disgust on it when the pressure of the doc's weight pressed upon my abdomen forces the dead, foetid air out of my lungs in a long, slow rasp which squirts blood from my mouth onto the porter's lips and chin. For good measure, I fart loudly at the same time.

The porter recoils in horror, wiping my dark blood off his face, and the doc laughs his ass off.

"Ha! Serves you fucking right, Brainiac," Doc Brown chuckles. "You might wanna put a mask on. Now, get back on his shoulders."

Gonzales wipes his face with a fist full of wet wipes, which sit in a gayly patterned dispenser on a small table next to mine. He puts on his mask and gets back to holding me down; this time, with his face leaning away from mine.

The doc then puts all his strength into retrieving the cricket stump from my rib cage, his pale old face turning quite red.

I let out another loud fart.

I'm not breathing, but even I can smell its vile odour.

"Was that you or him?" Gonzales giggles as he gags on my fart's foul stink.

"Shut up, Gonzo." The doc snarls.

"Don't call me Gonzo," Gonzales shouts back. "I'm *not* a fucking Muppet! I told you – I fucking hate Muppets!"

"Fair enough," Doc Brown grunts as he finally yanks the stump from my chest. "There you go, ya stubborn bugger." He passes the stump to Gonzales. "Wrap it up in the paper roll over there and put it on the table. I think the police'll wanna look at it later."

Gonzales does as he's asked as the doc fingers the hole in my chest.

"Well, he was one lucky bugger, I'll tell you that much," declares the doc.

"Why's that?" asks Gonzales.

"Missed his heart by about half an inch!" The doc laughs raucously at his own tasteless joke.

Gonzales joins in the laughter, but he clearly doesn't know what he's laughing at.

I feel nothing. I felt no pain when they yanked the stump out of me. Well, I'm dead and pissed off now… does somebody want to explain to me why I'm dead and how this is happening?

TIME: 2 a.m.

The doc picks up a scalpel from the silver side tray and slits the shape of the letter Y into my chest: shoulders to the top of my breastbone, top of my breastbone – avoiding the hole in my chest – down to my belly button.

That done, Doc Brown peels the skin back to reveal my ribcage. He starts picking out fragments of splintered rib bones nestled in the crevasse of my chest with a pair of fine-nosed tweezers.

"So…" the doc grunts. "What's the score here? D'ya know what happened? Who did this to the poor guy?"

"Well," Gonzales says, and I can see he's excited at being able to tell the story.

"The copper that came in the ambulance with the dead guy said –"

"Wait a minute!" The doc interrupts. He picks up a surgical hacksaw. He dons safety glasses and begins sawing into my sternum.

"Fuck!" Gonzales snaps. "D'ya wanna know or not?"

"Yeah, course I do," the doc tells him. "I'm just getting to the good part now."

I feel the teeth of the saw grinding and gnawing away at my bone. It's jarring my whole body and making my vision shaky, especially with half-closed eyes. I see the enjoyment on the doctor's face, beads of sweat running down his brow to be absorbed by the mask covering his face.

"There." The Doc seems pleased with his efforts. "Now, watch this… you're gonna love it." He places the tips of his fingers along the line he's just cut into my chest. Then, he pushes down to widen the gap…

Doc Brown cracks me open like a goose egg to reveal my internal organs.

"Tadaaaaa!" he shouts, displaying my guts to his sidekick with a theatrical flourish like he's just performed an astonishing magic trick.

Gonzales pulls his mask down and mouths *WOW!*

"I think it's time we fired up that special candle of yours," The doc says.

Needing no further encouragement, the porter pulls out the spliff, lights it, and takes a long, hard draw. He holds the smoke in his lungs for a few seconds before coughing and choking for the next minute. "*Whooooa!* This is strong shit," he splutters.

"Fucking amateur," the doc chastises. "Give it here."

Gonzales passes over the joint – he's still coughing and

spluttering, his eyes watering.

The doc takes it from the porter's fingers with the tweezers, pulls down his mask, and places the joint gently between his lips. I watch his eyes close as he sucks on it slowly, taking the smoke deep into his lungs. Then, eyes still closed, he smiles gently as the smoke escapes from his lips with no effort. "Wow. This is some *fucking good* gear," the doc says. "What is it?"

"Dunno," Gonzales tells him with a shrug. "I found it in the dead guy's pocket."

The doc has started to sing. Gently, softly, he's singing the opening refrain to *Bohemian Rhapsody*: *"Is this the real life? Is this just fantasy? Caught in a landslide, no escape from reality. Open your eyes, look up to the skies, and see..."* Grabbing my eyelids, the doc pulls them wide open....

I see it in his horrified face as my eyes shock him back into the room and the job in hand.

"Fuck!" the doc exclaims. "Look at them!" He pointed at my face with a trembling finger. "His eyes are *all* black – all pupil and no iris... look ... black as the Devil's arse!"

Oh, this is good. I'm loving this.

I watch as Doc Brown passes the spliff back to Gonzales.

TIME: 2.16 a.m.

"So, what did the copper say? I'm all ears." The doc picks up the scalpel and begins systematically cutting my organs free from the housing of my cold, dead body. I say cold, but I feel no actual temperature. I don't feel the chill from the air conditioning unit that's buzzing away in the corner, nor any warmth from the doc's breath on my pallid skin.

For his part, Gonzales just keeps on puffing on the joint as he recalls the story of my strange demise. To be honest, *I'm* just as interested in finding out what my story is – at this point, I'm still none the wiser; I simply can't remember a thing.

"Okay…" says Gonzales. "So, apparently, our dead guy here was watching the cricket match this evening – according to the news, it's been rained off all day. So, it's a nighttime Test Match – us versus the Pommies – and we were well in the lead: 102 in front with 6 wickets to go. We were pissing all over the bloody Poms! So, this guy… *this* guy here… this poor fucker here…." Distracted, Gonzales pauses. "What's that?" he asks the doc.

"It's his liver." The doc places my liver gently into a large stainless-steel bowl. "Do keep going."

"Isn't that much bigger than normal?"

"Oh yeah, its massive. Fucking heavy as well. It's full of blood – more than I've seen in a liver before. Just look at it – it's the size of a fucking bagpipe!" The doc picks my liver up out of the bowl with both hands. Squeezing the end of it between his finger and thumb, he chuckles as my thick, black blood squirts over Gonzales' previously spotless tunic.

"Fuck, Doc!" Gonzales squeals, still puffing on his spliff. "This was clean tonight!"

Not bothered one bit, the doc plonks my liver back into the bowl. "Carry on, Gonzales, I'm still listening." He then proceeds to slice out my spleen and kidneys as the porter picks up the story.

"Anyway," Gonzales says. "So, this poor fucker is just sitting there enjoying the cricket, when suddenly the umpire goes fucking mental. He's screaming and shouting some fucking nonsense about evil, the end of days, the Dark Lord – shit like that – and then runs to the centre of the field, grabs one of the stumps, and runs toward the boundary. Then the crazy bastard launches himself into the public stand and stabs this poor fucker right in the chest with the stump. Kills the poor bastard stone dead."

Fuck yes. That's it. It's starting to come back now. I'm beginning to remember....

"So," asks the doc. "Is this guy a pom?"

"Yeah, I think so." Gonzales says.

"Well then, he fucking deserved it!"

They both laugh uproariously at my misfortune.

Fucking Aussies – no class.

TIME: 2.19 a.m.

I watch as the doc once again plucks the spliff from Gonzales' lips and takes a few more tokes on the barge before placing it on the side table.

"What you gonna do now, Doc?" the porter asks.

Doc Brown answers with one, simple word: *"Brain."*

Grinning, the doc pulls the mask back over his mouth and picks up a small circular saw; it reminds me of the kind you'd buy at B&Q, only shinier. Deftly, he cuts around the top of my skull and removes it by twisting slightly as one would a child-proof medicine bottle. As I feel every part of it, I imagine it's like taking the top off a hard-boiled chucky egg.

Once again, I felt nothing but the vibration of blade on bone and smelled stink of burning skull from the friction of the stainless-steel saw.

Most peculiar.

Next, Doc Brown gently removes my brain from its protective housing. He holds it up in front of Gonzales like some gruesome trophy.

I begin to get dizzy: the room spins, my eyes are losing vision. I feel faint

No! Don't black out now!

Thankfully, the dizziness starts to pass after a few seconds as I pull myself together – which isn't easy, considering my spleen, kidneys, and liver were in a bowl and my brain was in Doc Brown's gnarly old hands.

"What do you think?" the doc asks his underling.

Gonzales' mask is still under his chin. "Oh… oh… I think its lovely."

"Then lick it," demands the doc.

"What?"

"I said… fucking *lick it,* you Muppet." So saying, the doc pushes my brain into the porter's face.

With great reluctance, Gonzales touches my cerebral cortex with the tip of his tongue.

"Don't *play* with it!" The doc seems angry. "Fucking *lick* it, or you're next." He picks up his bloodied scalpel and holds it to Gonzales' neck.

Terrified, Gonzales starts licking, which makes even me feel nauseous. They're tiny little flicks of the tongue at first, like a snake sensing its next meal, and then the licks get stronger, harder, until he's lapping at my disembodied brain like a dog licking its own arse. Blood had coagulated within the folds of my brain, and the porter laps up the juices oozing from it.

"That's it… that's it." the doc coos his encouragement. "Good boy… *good boy.*"

In all the excitement of the foulness taking place, I see the doc has accidentally nicked the side of Gonzales' neck with the scalpel's keen blade. Looks like he might have caught the jugular – slightly – and blood oozes from the cut, flowing steadily. It's dribbling down his neck to soak into his scrubs. Every beat of the young man's heart pushes more blood from the tiny wound, and neither of the sick fucks notice.

But *I* did.

Both Doc Brown and his porter friend are now leaning over the gaping hole in my chest and licking my brain right in front of my face, lapping and sucking on its juices in some nasty, perverted frenzy.

Then it happens.

A single drop of Gonzales' blood drips from his neck and into my opened chest. Straight on to my exposed heart...

And then... *then* it all comes thundering back.

I remember who I am.

I remember what *I am!*

My heart begins to beat. I feel the nerve endings of my skin again, the muscles in my arms spring to life, and I feel so immensely *powerful.*

Lifting my hands to the doc and the porter's throats, I tear at the soft flesh of their necks with savage grace; my fingers rip open their arteries with ease to let their blood flow into the cavity of my chest.

Shocked, in agony, Doc Brown drops my brain; it lands in my body cavity. It's quite weird, but at the same time, it's funny to see my brain laying there in the middle of my body.

I know it won't be a problem, not now my strength has returned. Sitting up straight, I pop my brain back into my empty skull and put the top of my head back on. Then, I slip my kidneys back into place, along with my liver, spleen, and any other odds and sods Doc Brown had taken out. I don't bother seeing if they're all in the right place – they will sort themselves out all in good time.

TIME: 2.45 a.m.

I sit there for an age, literally pulling myself together, gathering my thoughts – and then one thought pops into to my mind over all the others….

The doc was right – I was very lucky the crazy umpire missed my heart by a mere half an inch, what with me being a vampire and all.

End

The Umpire Strikes Back was first published by HellBound Books Publishing LLC in Joe Pasquale's collection *Of Mice and Wolfmen* in 2023:

https://hellboundbookspublishing.com/miceandwolfmen.html

Goreslut

Taylor Z. Adams

The ring light hums a soft, barely audible whine. I sit cross-legged on the blanket—pink, plush, the one that looks good on camera. My thighs are oiled just enough to catch the light. Everything's clean. Framed. Perfect.

"Hey bunnies!" I say, smiling into the webcam. I always open like this. It's tradition now.

The chat starts crawling. Hearts. Tongues. Emojis. A chorus of usernames calling out for me.

"Poppy's looking FIRE tonight!"

"Got the blade again, hun?"

"Let's see that cute little neck"

I've never told them my name. They call me Poppy because the site makes them. RedPoppy was just a throwaway handle, something soft but dramatic. I picked it two years ago and now it's who I am. I don't mind it, not really. I've never gotten used to hearing it instead of Emma. But it's who I am now, at least for a few hours a night.

I shift my shoulders, let the robe slide open just a bit. Thigh, a hint of lace. After a few minutes of teasing, I start getting into the meat of the show. I run the knife down the inside of my arm—just tracing, not breaking skin yet—and lean into the mic.

"Tell me what you wanna see, bunnies," I coo. "You know I'm good, but I can be better."

The chat lights up. A flood of usuals:

"Scratch your tummy, Poppy!"

"Knife on your neck maybe??"

"The belt again, baby! Please!"

"God, you're all so impatient tonight," I tease. "I love it!"

I grab the belt from the hook on the wall. Soft, broken-in leather. I thread it around my neck slowly, like a ritual, keeping my eyes half-lidded, lips parted.

"Just a little?" I ask them. "Or should I go until I start seeing stars?"

Hearts explode. Tips hit. Encouragement rolls in like waves. I play along, pulling the strap tighter, feeling that pleasant fuzz creep into my skull. But this time, I misjudge and accidentally go on a little too long.

Fingertips numb. Tunnel vision. Static. When I fumble with the buckle, panic pulses through me. I yank it loose and fall off-frame, coughing hard, lungs burning like I've swallowed heat.

"Oh damn, princess!"

"What a good slut!"

"Should have choked longer, bitch!"

The usual.

Angel_Bite tipped $500

Angel_Bite: *"That was incredible. You're the most beautiful girl I've ever seen."*

I blink.

The number doesn't feel real. Way more than I usually

get from one person. I fumble to sit back up, hair in my eyes, throat raw. I laugh—half choked, half flustered.

"Oh my god. Angel_Bite?" I say, eyes scanning the username. "That's… Jesus, that's so generous. I don't even know what to say."

I stare into the camera. Try to flash a cheeky grin, but it feels weirdly honest this time.

"You're gonna make me blush, babe. Seriously."

My heart's still rattling, but not just from the belt now. There's a strange lightness behind my ribs. A kind of warmth that doesn't come from tips alone.

***

Next night, he's there before I even go live. The second I turn on the feed, the first message I see is:

Angel_Bite: *"Hi again. I've been thinking about you."*

I laugh, brushing my hair behind my ear, already smiling. "Well, well. if it isn't my new favorite bunny!" I say. "You thinking about that little blackout?"

I pause, trying to seem coy—a little innocent—running the knife down my thigh.

"Or was it something else?"

Angel_Bite tipped $400

Angel_Bite: *"Would you mind cutting a little deeper for me tonight? I bet you'd look ethereal."*

The message hangs there. My fingers tighten around the handle. *Ethereal?* That's a new one. I keep my smile on, but my throat goes dry. Usually I just tease with the knife.

Gentle.

Leaving an array of tiny chicken scratches to titillate the audience. Any blood drawn is usually an accident—a happy accident for the fans, but an accident.

But $400?

I can work with that. Seems like the kind of guy I'd wanna keep as a regular, too.

"You don't waste time, huh?" I say, laughing lightly. "I usually ease people into that sort of thing."

I shift, adjusting the camera angle slightly, framing just my hips, the curve of my thigh. I feel my heart rate picking up a little bit.

"Alright," I whisper, more to myself than the camera. "Just a little."

I press the blade in and drag it in a horizontal line across my leg—not just a scratch this time. It bites. The sting shocks me. Real, sharp pain. I wince and nearly drop it. Blood beads up fast.

The chat explodes:

"HOLY SHIT"

"Yesssss!"

"God, you pathetic little slut!"

I see a couple viewers leave. No one I recognize, probably just a few people either checking me out for the first time, or the people just here for the gentle stuff. No love lost, it happens. They're usually not the type to tip well anyway.

Angel_Bite: *"My goodness, you're exquisite. Radiant."*

Angel_Bite: *"You've never looked more alive."*

I run my fingers through the blood, spreading it across my thigh like paint. My voice shakes, but I keep talking.

"You really like seeing me like this, don't you?" I ask softly, eyes low. "All this blood?"

Angel_Bite: *"Of course I do. You're glowing. You're so beautiful."*

***

The next night, I don't even get through my warm-up before I notice it. New names in the chat. Not just one or two—more like a dozen. They don't type in all caps. No one's asking for feet or calling me "slut." They're quiet. Polite. Tipping in small, frequent bursts, like they're trying not to startle me.

"Hi Poppy. You're breathtaking."

"First time here. You have something special."

"You look like a painting."

Someone tips $30.

"Thank you for being so real."

It throws me off more than the occasional creeps ever did. I brush my hair behind my ear and lean into the mic, trying to stay in character—but something's shifted. I feel... watched but not devoured.

Admired.

"You guys are being soft tonight," I tease, twisting the belt slowly in my hands. "What happened to all the filth?"

A few hearts float up. Then a name I know appears:

Angel_Bite tipped $600

Angel_Bite: *"The new ones missed something. Can you show them how beautiful you look when you don't breathe?"*

I stare at the message. It doesn't feel like a command. Just a polite request.

I wrap the belt around my neck. Tighter this time. Faster. I don't test it first—I just pull.

My vision narrows almost instantly. There's a static rush in my ears, like ocean waves in reverse. My body panics, but I stay in it. I keep eye contact with the camera, jaw slack, fingers trembling, instinctively gasping for air.

The chat lights up again—but different this time. Not what I'm used to seeing.

"You look like a goddess."

"I've never seen anyone so serene."

"You're perfect like this."

I hold until my vision blooms white, then release. My whole body crashes forward. I land half-off the frame, coughing, gasping, snot running down my lip. No one signs off. Tips roll in. No one's freaking out from how far I took it.

It's the opposite:

"So strong."

"That was transcendent."

"You're an artist, Poppy."

I push myself back into frame, breath ragged. My skin's flushed, my chest heaving. I look like I've survived something.

I smile.

I'm used to praise. I'm used to being ogled. People tell me I'm sexy, that I'm hot. But no one's ever told me I'm beautiful until I stopped breathing.

***

I lose track of time more often now.

Not in a dramatic way. Just… in little pieces. I forget to eat. To respond to texts. I fall asleep with the ring light still on. Streaming feels like the only thing I do that leaves a mark. It's not even the money—it's the structure. The schedule. The routine. I get on, I perform, I get told I'm incredible. That I'm beautiful.

It feels nice.

Angel_Bite tipped $200

Angel_Bite: *"Could you show us more of your ribs? If that's okay?"*

I stare at it longer than I mean to.

I've been losing weight anyway—unintentionally, at first. But I like how it looks. My hip bones are sharp. My waist photographs better.

"Yeah," I say to the camera, smiling like it's nothing. "Yeah, I can do that."

I sit back on my knees and lift my shirt, slow and

deliberate. The chat goes quiet for a second—then erupts:

"You're unreal."

"So elegant."

"You're like a beautiful marble statue, Poppy. Expertly carved."

I laugh a little, rubbing my hand over my ribcage. I don't think of it as starvation. It's just… control. It feels good to be good at something. To have something they love.

Angel_Bite: *"Thank you. That was wonderful. I'd love to see even more of them"*

I tilt my head, thoughtful.

"You want to see more?" I ask, curiously. "I guess… I could maybe lose a little more. Just a little. If that's something you'd like."

The hearts start immediately. Tips drop in waves.

"You're already perfect."

"We'd love to see if you want to share though!"

"Only if you want to, Poppy."

"No," I say. "It's okay. I want to."

"We love you, Poppy!"

The shows get quieter. Not boring—just calmer. Fewer requests, more watching. My audience knows what they're there for now. They come to see how far I'll go, but they act like they're there to protect me. Like they're taking care of me while I bleed for them.

Sometimes someone new joins and asks for something crude. The regulars shut it down before I even have to say anything.

They're protective now.

Gentle.

Territorial.

I don't need to mute anyone.

They handle it.

Angel_Bite tipped $1000

Angel_Bite: *"If it's not too much… I'd love to see you thread something through yourself. Like a needle. Just a little. Nothing dangerous. Only if you want to."*

I stare at the message.

I look at the chat. No one panics. No one calls it out.

"That could be beautiful."

"I'd cry if she did that."

"She's strong enough."

"Poppy, you'd look amazing!"

I nod.

"I think I have one," I whisper.

I go to the drawer and take out a sewing kit I bought for fixing lingerie. The needle is thick. Maybe meant for upholstery. I choose a red thread and tie it in a loop. I hold it up to the camera.

"Perfect."

"So elegant."

"We're here."

"We love you."

My stomach feels warm. Like praise lives in my belly now.

I decide to do it on the side of my stomach. Just under the ribs. Where there's still a little softness left. I pinch the skin. I sterilize the needle with a lighter, shaking as it glows orange.

The thread dangles.

I look at the camera.

"Tell me I can, bunnies," I say.

"You can."

"You can."

"You can."

"You're safe."

"You're beautiful."

"We're here."

I press the point against my skin and push.

The resistance is sharp and sudden. My body tries to jump away from it, but I hold myself steady. The needle punctures. A second of shocking pain, then a strange pop as it slips through the layer of flesh.

I moan.

It's not sexual.

A neat loop of red. Flesh threaded like fabric. Blood beads at the entry and exit. The skin puckers.

I do it again. A second stitch, beside the first. Then a third. Three loops. Bright red thread in pale pink skin.

"Do you like it?"

My stomach throbs. The skin's inflamed. The thread is tight. I feel lightheaded.

I press a finger to the top stitch and pull. The skin lifts. The thread digs in deeper.

"Leave it in."

"Please don't undo it."

"There she is."

"That's our girl."

"You're perfect."

Angel_Bite tipped $1000

Angel_Bite: *"Can we know your first name? If you feel comfortable? I think we'd all like to know who our perfect woman is."*

I freeze for a second. Not out of fear. It's just... strange. Personal. No one's asked before. Not seriously. My heart races a little—not in the scary way. It feels like being asked to dance.

"Emma," I say. Quiet, like I'm still testing how it sounds out loud. "My name is Emma."

"Emma. That's beautiful."

"Perfect."

"Our Emma."

"She's real."

"We love you, Emma."

***

It comes in a white box. No return address. Just a black ribbon and a small envelope on top.

"RedPoppy, our beautiful Emma.
For your devotion
~Angel_Bite"

The stream's already live when I open it. I hadn't planned anything special tonight. Just blood. Breath. Bone. But the box is sitting in the background, and the chat starts asking.

"What's the present, Emma?"

"Did someone send you a toy?"

"Could we please see?"

I smile, pretending I hadn't planned to.

"Alright," I say. "Let's see what my favorite bunny sent me."

Angel_Bite: *"Aww, you're too sweet, beautiful."*

I open it slowly, like it's a ritual. The ribbon comes off easy. The box creaks when I lift the lid and then I still.

Inside is something wrapped in satin. Dark stains soak the fabric. The smell hits before I touch. Like something left in a sink drain in summer. It's the kind of smell that clings to your sinuses. The kind of smell that gets deep inside of you.

I reach in, hands shaking slightly and I unwrap the satin. I was expecting a dildo or something, that's usually the type of gift someone sends me for my shows. I knew my new fans would send me something special, something out there, but I didn't expect this.

It's an animal's penis. Not some silicone recreation, an actual, severed penis. I can't tell what kind of animal it belonged to—possibly a dog? That's my best guess. The cock is thick at the base, tapering to a curved point that looks bruised, crushed flat near the tip. The surface is green in patches, bloated, blistered, flaking, veins like a spider-web across the shaft.

The skin is peeling in places. The flesh at the base is ringed with stiff wiry hair, matted with a yellow crust. A gelatinous clear-pink fluid leaks from a split down the side, coating the shaft and pooling at the bottom of the box. It reeks of spoiled lunch meat that had been sitting in a hot car for months.

I gag. I retch. My throat seizes. I turn off to the side, knocking the box upside down. The severed cock lands on my lap and I vomit. Bile and half-digested broth splash onto the floor, the acid burns my throat as it comes up. My stomach keeps spasming even though nothing is left inside of it. I wipe my mouth with the back of my hand.

The camera catches all of it.

Angel_Bite tipped $2000

Angel_Bite: *"This was made just for you. Please don't feel pressured to use it. Only if you want to."*

My hand hovers over it. Slime seeps from its tip in long, stringy drips. My inner thighs are sticky just from holding it there. It feels like it's almost weeping.

I stare at the screen, breathing through my mouth.

"I–I don't know if I can."

"You don't have to!"

"It'd be so incredible, but we'll love you no matter what!"

"We'd never love anyone more than you, Emma!"

"N–no," I muttered. "I'll… I'll do it. For all of you."

"We don't deserve you."

"You're perfect."

I guide it down.

It sticks to my fingers. The fluids have gone tacky, halfway between pus and glue. I angle it downward, and it makes a thick, wet pop as the trapped gas shifts inside. The skin slides slightly around the meat, like a balloon pulling away from whatever's inside it. There's a deep black spot at the base where it's starting to collapse inward–soft to the touch, like a sponge soaked in gore.

I press it against my sex. It squelches.

I gag again, coughing as the smell of rot mixed with my fluids cling to my throat. My cunt pulses—fear, rejection, warning. My body knows it doesn't want this. It knows it's not supposed to be touched by this thing.

But I push anyway.

The head forces its way into me with a pop. Soft in places, like bruised fruit. The cold stuns me. Not cold like ice. I can feel the walls of my pussy already warming it up. All the gore and unknown ooze find their way into my body, sticky decay, milky discharge all fill every inch of me and spread.

Something wiggles. Something beneath the surface of the dildo. Something I didn't notice before that didn't make itself known before it wanted to come out and play until my hole devoured it. I feel one of the writhing things burst.

My insides convulse. I scream.

"Holy fuck, Emma."

"You spoil us.

"You're so divine like this. Angelic."

I push deeper. The shaft collapses in places, tissue bursting a rotten sausage. One side splits, leaking a thread of blackened red gelatin down my thighs, catching on the open wounds I had made. I slide it further in and feel the slick tear of muscle detaching from gristle. The thing makes a wet groan inside of me as more gas escapes and air forces out through a pocket in the base.

My cunt clutches it. The walls ripple around meat that isn't meat anymore. I can feel the decay leaking deeper with every thrust. The smell blooms inside me. I can almost taste it.

I scream again—not in pleasure, not even in pain. Just sound. Raw, visceral sound. I claw at the blanket, thighs shaking, the rot slicking down my legs, into the carpet, into everything.

I cum.

I don't want to.

My body doesn't ask.

My vision white-outs. I seize. I arch. My muscles pull tight around the thing, locking it inside me. I feel a tendon snap. A cavalcade of pink liquid and dark chunks pour out of my hole. My body shudders and dumps fluid across my thighs, my calves, my blanket.

"That was the most incredible thing I've ever seen."

"Oh my God, THANK you, Emma."

"You're perfect."

"You're SO perfect."

I collapse sideways, twitching. The dildo slips from me with a noise like wet plaster peeling off tile. A slurp. A splat. It hits the floor and lies there twitching with rot.

I'm still crying. Sobbing.

But I'm smiling, too.

"Thank you, bunnies. Thanks for showing me so much love."

Angel_Bite tipped $1000

Angel_Bite: *"We love you so much, beautiful."*

***

Angel_Bite sent an address in the chat. No note, no explanation, no tip.

Angel_Bite: *"We're ready for the next step if you are."*

The chat got excited.

"We're ready if you are!"

"We love you, Emma!"

The door to Unit 2C was already unlocked and I set up my camera and ring light to start my stream. Inside, the apartment is bare. Gray carpet. Off-white walls stained at the corners. A single ring light hums on a tripod, positioned to face the mattress on the floor. The mattress is draped with white satin sheets, pulled tight and tucked at the corners.

He's already lying on it.

Naked.

Male. Late 40s, maybe older. Skin bloated, discolored. Greenish around the neck, purplish down the arms, yellow at the chest. The abdomen is distended, glossy. The groin has been shaved. Someone took care to arrange the limbs— arms resting at the sides, fingers curved inward slightly, legs positioned to hold weight. The face is frozen in partial slack: lips dry and cracked, one eye open, the other sunken, tongue stuck to the back of the teeth.

There's a tube jammed into the base of the penis, seemingly inserted from the urethra to help it hold its erect shape.

The chat's buzzing:

"We're here."

"She made it."

"She's ready."

"Emma, we love you."

I undress by the door. Not for show. Not for drama. I fold my clothes and place them in the corner. I walk across the carpet barefoot, the fibers stiff under my soles.

The corpse's chest rises and falls slightly as gases shift beneath the skin. A pocket of fluid bulges at the armpit. Small red splits line the thighs, stretched too far for too long.

His flesh is still alive with motion. Maggots swarm beneath the curve of his belly. They bubble in the fold of skin above his hip, fat and wet and squirming. A few trail along the inside of his thigh, leaving a glistening track behind them. One nestles in the corner of his left eye socket. Another pulses in and out of his nasal cavity with each shift of the gases in his chest.

The eye that remains is cloudy, veined with burst capillaries. It stares through me.

I mount him, one knee on either side of the bloated pelvis.

The sheets are damp.

The penis is erect, gray, and coated with a thin film of waxy residue. The foreskin has split and curled back on one side. The veins are dark blue. A yellow crust has dried where the shaft meets the body, thin pus bubbles having bloomed at the slit.

I spit into my hand and smear it across the shaft, causing something to wiggle its way out from the urethra and onto the back of my hand.

It doesn't help. The texture isn't slick—it's rubbery and uneven. The skin separates from the core slightly as I push. I press it against myself. The smell rises again, warmer, richer. A ripe mix of decay and dried feces.

I gag. I retch. Only for a brief moment.

"She's giving everything."

"We love you."

"It's okay, Emma."

"Let us see."

I guide the head to my cunt and push down. The pressure is immediate. My skin fights back. The shaft bends beneath me, the skin slipping slightly around the stiff interior. I grind downward. It presses in with a pop and a rush of fluid.

Something inside me gives.

I lower myself fully.

The shaft spreads me wide. The friction peels at the rawness already there. My walls clench reflexively, and I feel the shaft give a little, warping inside me. Slime oozes out around the seal of my thighs. It runs onto the mattress in slow, mucous ropes.

I feel the penis skin tear. I feel it come loose in patches. Some of it folds in with each motion, curling like cooked fat, folding into the slick heat inside me.

Maggots are on my knees now. I feel one on the back of my thigh. I feel another near my calf. One brushes the underside of my breast, cold and squirming. I don't brush them away.

I grab his jaw and press our faces together.

His lips are chapped, open just enough to show the purple-grey of his tongue. There's something white crusted at the corners.

I kiss him, anyway. His teeth scrape my lip.

"Thank you," I whisper as I ride the rotting, erect cock. "Thank you for helping me with this."

Air pushes from his mouth with each thrust—a weak wheeze that smells like spoiled yogurt. His chest is soft under my weight. I dig my fingers into the sternum and feel the cartilage shift.

I start to cry again. Tears run down my face, over my chin, into the open mouth beneath mine. The camera stays focused. The viewers stay present.

"She's glorious."

"She's more than human now."

"You've become something divine."

"You're love, Emma."

"We see you."

"You are perfect."

"We love you."

I ride harder.

The shaft is failing. Each push floods me with fluid, black and yellow and slick with decay. My cunt is raw and torn. It doesn't matter.

The bed creaks. The body gurgles. My hips stutter, and the orgasm rips through me without warning.

It feels like vomiting in reverse. A purge. A full-body

collapse inward.

I shudder, eyes open, pupils wide.

"There she is."

"She's perfect."

"Thank you."

"Thank you."

"Thank you."

I slide off him.

The shaft leaves my body in pieces. The outer skin stays lodged inside, peeled like a glove. I drag it out with two fingers. The rest follows: pulp, paste, fluid, worms. It spills across the bed in wet strings and black jelly.

I lie beside him and place his hand on my breast.

"Thank you," I whisper again. "You're just like me."

"Rest, Emma."

"We're still here."

"You're everything we dreamed of."

"Our Emma."

"The perfect woman."

***

My skin is translucent in the light.

Bones frame everything now. Elbows sharp. Ribs counting themselves in the mirror. My thighs don't touch when I sit. The bruises never go away anymore. My blood doesn't clot right. The last time I bled, it took almost an hour to stop.

They just call me "Emma" now.

Never Poppy.

Just Emma.

They know me.

They don't tip anymore.

I don't let them. I took the donation bar off the overlay.

"This is why we love you."

"She's selfless."
"Perfect."
"The most beautiful woman I've ever seen."
"She's free now."
"She's doing it for love."
I start preparing.
I shave everything. Arms. Legs. Head.
I scrub my body raw in the shower until the water runs clear.
The stream goes live at midnight.
No music. No talking.
Just me, in front of the camera, kneeling on the pink blanket. The ring light reflects in my eyes. My ribs twitch every time I breathe.
I hold the rope in my lap. Coiled. Clean. Bleached white. There's a knot already tied at one end—perfect.
The chat scrolls slowly, steadily:
"She's glowing."
"This is holy."
"We love you."
"Thank you for everything."
"You're so brave."
"Perfect, perfect girl."
He chimes in.
Angel_Bite: *"No, the perfect woman. Our Emma."*
I smile.
"I've never felt more loved," I say.
I step onto the stool.
I loop the rope over the beam.
I slip the noose over my neck. Adjust the knot behind my ear. Tighten it gently.
"You're beautiful."
"This is love."
"Ascend."
"We're with you."

"We'll never forget you, Emma."

I close my eyes.

I jump.

The rope snaps tight.

My legs kick once. Twice. Muscles fire. My bowels release. I feel heat run down my thighs, then nothing. Blood vessels burst behind my eyes. My tongue swells.

I can still faintly make out the chat as my vision fades.

"You're so strong."

"She did it."

"You're free now."

"We love you."

"She's gone."

"She's perfect."

"Thank you."

The last thing I feel is the rope creaking above me.

The last thing I see is:

Angel_Bite: *"The most beautiful thing I've ever seen."*

How to Go Cold Turkey on the Coldest Night of the Year
Priyanuj Mazumdar

My first Thanksgiving is tonight, and I'm excited to break the voodoo that has surrounded my appetite of late. Food has been the only source of joy for as long as I can remember, but now, even the thought nauseates me.

Maybe, a Thanksgiving meal cooked by Helen will do the trick. Since I moved to rural Minnesota last December, my ghosts and I have resided in a modest ten by ten bedroom in a sprawling Victorian house.

Steeply pitched roofs with church-like finials, painted brick exterior and iron railings, wraparound porches with spindle work—it stands tall and solitary with acres and acres of uninhabited land around—the nearest neighbors at least a mile away.

My landlords are an elderly White couple, spirited and affectionate, but mildly racist. In the way that most rural Minnesotans are. They mean well. Helen, a housewife and retired nurse in her sixties, keeps my late cheques a secret, even forgoing my rent on a particularly barren financial month.

Harold, a farmer and medical store owner and at least a decade older than her, gives me a ride to and back from the city every Tuesday and Thursday, where I teach an introductory literature class at the University of Southern Minnesota as part of my post-doctoral duties. But there's one strange thing about them: whenever I'm in their company, people refuse to meet my gaze, but when I am alone, even strangers wave at me.

It's been snowing since morning, and I slip twice on my way to the turkey house. On my way, I stop at the wooden shed that shelters seven cats, and the adjacent shed filled with farming machinery—two tractors, plows, harvesters, and hundreds of bottled chemicals. Living this far away from the city makes me delirious sometimes. But rent is cheap. For a broke student surviving on a teaching stipend from a state university, that's priority numero uno.

Harold and I hover around the turkeys. He points out the fattest one and signals me to lure it away from the other turkeys with corn. Once it's far enough from the rest, I grab its legs with both my hands. Fucking hell, it's so much bigger and heavier than it looks.

The bloody thing flaps its wings violently, hitting my stomach and knees with so much force I almost drop it to the ground. Outside, Harold waits behind a long, stainless-steel table with a large killing cone, three knives, shears, buckets, and a hose.

I huff and puff to Harold, placing the turkey on the table. It flaps its wings with more desperation as he turns it around. I have never watched a turkey get butchered. When my father would take me to the butcher shop as a kid, I would turn my head the exact moment the knife swung in the air.

As Harold gets ready to slaughter, my breathing turns heavy, head dizzy, sweat surfacing on my skin. Then a drop of blood splats against my right cheek, mixing with my sweat like poison. Red blood. Malicious blood. Futile blood. I want to throw up.

I walk away. Watching a bird getting eviscerated is bad enough, but a bird that I put on its deathbed? Fuck no. I hold my chest, hunching forward, puke, puke, puke. Blood colors the snow red.

#

My parents passed away from Covid last year. Underlying heart issues. Lack of beds in the hospital. Delayed admission. Too late. Since then, I have maintained a secluded life, fending off the need for human connection, telling myself it would only bring more grief. Since I moved here from India, Helen and Harold have become my proxy parents.

In return for all their generosity, I look after the cats and work at the turkey farm on the weekends or when Harold is at the store.

The first time I went to see the turkeys, my chest split open from my skin. The four feet creatures, all huddled together, stared and screeched at me, triggering my Ornithophobia. Housed in a long, spacious barn the size of a football field, we feed the turkeys a diet of mostly corn and soybeans, a ploy to make them gain weight rapidly.

I don't remember when my fear of the big birds became tamable. But the repetition of exposure to fear does something, I guess. I mean, if I was afraid of clowns and worked in a circus, my first day will be hell.

By the third month, a lot less so. On nights I can't sleep, I walk to and back from the turkey house. In the lull of the night, shrill, throaty yelps reverberate eerily. But some days, it's the only thing I hear. It's not like I don't enjoy the quiet, but sustained silence makes me hear things—and when there's nothing to hear, my mind invents them.

At two in the afternoon, Helen knocks on my door, inviting me to join them for Thanksgiving dinner. Downstairs, ornate rugs and tapestries and vintage furniture adorn vibrant, expansive rooms—a stark contrast to my dreary converted bedroom. Mounted deer heads stare into your soul as you enter the living room, mutating and multiplying over time.

On the white, oval dining table, a feast awaits—sage and sausage stuffing, green bean casserole, roasted sweet potatoes, mashed potatoes, brussels sprouts, cranberry sauce, pumpkin and pecan pie. And the turkey. Skinned butterflied roast turkey with gravy. The turkey I killed.

"We have been waiting for you," Helen says. She sits on one side, Harold on the other, both smiling at me, wrinkled skin stretching loosely.

"This looks fantastic. Are you expecting someone else?"

"No. It's all for you," Harold says. Their smiles linger for a few more seconds, then stop abruptly. I make my plate with some stuffing, casserole, sprouts, and the two kinds of potatoes.

"You guys aren't eating?"

"No. It's all for you," Helen says. She has always been an excellent cook, so I gulp down everything in minutes, then a second helping, adding some pie and cranberry sauce this time. "Do you want me to serve you some of the turkey?"

"No thanks, Helen. I don't feel like having turkey."

"Nonsense. A thanksgiving meal isn't complete without some turkey," she says, slicing a big portion and putting it on my plate. "You probably never get to have turkey in India, you poor thing. Eat as much as you want."

Like I said before, they mean well. I stare at the white meat, then at Harold and Helen, trying not to throw up. Taking a deep breath, I stab at it with my fork and shove it down my throat in one swift movement. The turkey tastes cold. I want to go to the bathroom and pour bleach into my throat and gurgle and gurgle until I can't taste it in my mouth.

"You are a big boy. You must be fed well. Take some more," Harold says.

"I really can't. I'm full," I say.

Harold ignores me like I ignore red flags, dumping another big portion on my plate. A drumstick, reminding me of the turkey's legs that I held with such venom. I don't know how far I am from puking, but I clear my plate somehow. When I get up, Helen stops me, putting her hand over mine. "That's it?"

"I'm sorry, but I absolutely cannot eat more, or I'm going to—"

"It's just that—I made all of this for you."

"I get that, but—"

"We haven't had a guest for Thanksgiving in so long. Not since Michael died." Helen's eyes shift left and right in rapid succession, lips quivering with each word. "We had that Chinese student once, didn't we? How long ago was that?" Harold puts his arm around Helen, looking miserable.

Michael, their only child, died in a fatal shootout with a park ranger many years back. Harold, who was also out hunting, survived, but lost his left arm from a gunshot wound infection. Harold still blames himself to this day. He told me once, "I don't have a missing arm. I have a missing son."

"One more serving?" Harold says, and I nod. He slathers some gravy on top of the turkey. I close my eyes, put the meat to my mouth, and chew on it as fast as I can, using as much saliva I can produce. It tastes even colder. "Okay, I'm done."

"Not so fast."

I feel a hand on my shoulder. Harold and Helen stand over me, pinning me down.

"What—what are you doing?" I say, kicking my legs, trying to stand. They grab an arm each and push me against the chair, my bones creaking. I can't move. For their age, they are surprisingly strong, restricting me easily.

"You ungrateful boy. We are being so nice to you, trying to feed you. And you are throwing tantrums? You will finish this turkey," Helen says as Harold breaks the meat with his bare hand, dips it in gravy, and puts it to my mouth. I refuse to open. Helen punches my stomach, and Harold jams the meat down my throat, gravy smeared all over my nose and cheeks. "Chew, chew. Good boy," he says.

My brain shuts down, only registering the food funneling into my stomach. Cold, cold turkey down my throat, bloating and poisoning my stomach. "Done," Helen says, clapping gleefully. "Now was that so hard?"

I grit my teeth, trying to hold back anger. "Can I go now?" I say, my words slurring.

"Of course," Harold says. He puts his hand in his pocket, pulls out something, and holds it over my nose and mouth. Total blackness.

#

When I wake, I don't recognize where I am. From the faint lightbulb in the distance, the only thing I can make out are the brick walls. My head hurts, arms ache, body burns. Light cascades in from a gap in the roof, beams colliding into a series of arches. Cobwebs hang from the dusty ceiling, nails poking from each side of the wall.

A toilet seat is on one corner, and an open fridge on another with a kitchen sink inside. What the fuck is this place?

"Hey."

"Oh my god." I scream, jumping at the sudden voice.

A young boy sits on the opposite side, his frail frame leaning against the wall. Both his hands are raised above his head. But they aren't chained or cuffed or tied. They are nailed to the wall, thin lines of dried blood dripping down. I close my eyes. Open. He's still here. This isn't a nightmare. Not one I can escape, anyway.

"You okay?" the boys says meekly.

"Who—who are you? How did you—where are we?"

"I don't know where we are. But I have been here forever," he says.

"Forever? But—"

"Listen to me, you can still escape."

"How?"

"Your hands are still free. Your legs are still free. Go, run, get out of here."

"I don't even know where I am," I say, glancing at his hands from the corner of my eye. They are surprisingly still, but the veins are so visible it makes my stomach churn.

"I can help," the boy says, breathing heavily. "Go down the staircase. To your left, there will be a hallway. Keep walking down that way. When you see a door, open it. There will be three more doors next. Walk through the right one. Make *sure* you walk through the right one.

"And then you will find a smaller door. This door isn't full size, so you gotta bend down, kick it open, and squeeze yourself out. And then run and run and don't look back."

"How—how do you know all this?"

"Like I said, I have been here forever."

"Why didn't you try and escape, then?"

"I tried. But it was too late for me. It's not too late for you."

I have a million questions swarming in my head like the flies above me, but the fear of dying in this disgusting, revolting place takes over. Getting up takes both my hands and all my strength.

In the right corner of the room, a small staircase hides in complete darkness. I take one final look at the boy and climb down the stairs. My head is spinning, nausea invading every fiber of my body. I stumble around, using the wall for support, almost falling over a couple of times. Walking has never been this hard even when I have been drunk out of my skull.

The solitary window at the end of the hallway reveals a murky late evening sky. Dim, somber lights cast long shadows on the ground of what looks like an abandoned field. Bitter wind blows violently, smashing into my face, penetrating the pores of my skin, numbing me. I try to close the window, shivering violently, but admit defeat to the force of the wind. It's only November, but this feels like the coldest night of the year.

Where the fuck am I? Why can't I recognize this fucking place? Could this be where the screams were coming from that day? I have been hearing things in this house ever since I started living here—taps on the walls at night, slams on the ceiling, scratching on the floor. Nothing unusual.

This is an old, old house with wooden interior and flooring—when everyone's asleep and I need to go downstairs, the floorboards creak with every step. But last Sunday, I heard high-pitched cries that sounded humanlike. My first instinct was to blame it on my nightmares. But I heard it again a few minutes later. And then they stopped. I decided to let it go. For the sake of my sleep. For the sake of my sanity.

Near the window is a wooden door. This must be the one. It's harder to open than I anticipate. Taking a couple of steps back, I run into it, slamming it open. Fuck, fuck, fuck, my shoulders hurt like a bitch.

I keep walking in the darkness, nursing my arms, taking slow, cautious steps to avoid crashing into something. Three white doors in the distance. Did he say the right door? Or the left? I check each one—locked, all of them. A small, red cross marks the right door. This must be the one. I take a few steps back. Breathe. Running into the door at full speed, it bursts open, and I fall face down into blue vinyl flooring.

Blinding lights from all directions stab at my eyes. Icy cold air bites my skin. Strong antiseptic smell combined with something burning. Every inch of the blue-plastered room is filled with stainless steel tables, defibrillators, monitors, ECG and anesthesia and God knows what other machines.

Two beds in the middle, and—*oh my god*. Suspended along one side of the wall are severed heads of dead people, each encased within a transparent glass block. Eyes peeled off. Lips scarred. Hair shaven. But skin in perfect condition. All boys, all young, all colored skin. I get up and turn back. This can't be where I'm supposed to be.

"Look who it is," Harold says, appearing in front of me—dressed in a green surgical suit, face covered by a white mask, scalpel in hand.

"Ha—Harold?" I look the other way, and Helen walks toward me with a tray of surgical instruments.

"Surprise!" They both say in unison, yellow teeth exposing sinister smiles. My eyes are on the verge of popping out, too shocked to comprehend what I'm seeing. This would put my most terrifying nightmares to shame.

"Darling? Look how confused the boy is. Should we explain what's going on?"

"Yes, darling."

"Would you like to do the honors?"

"No darling. I like the way you tell it."

"Aren't you sweet? This one thinks I should have become a writer," Harold says, grinning at his wife, and for a moment, they are the old couple who took me in like a son, fed me, made me believe in tenderness again. "Son, let me tell you the secret to a happy marriage. Enable your partner's passions."

"That's right," Helen says.

"Now, why don't you come and take a seat here?" Harold points to a solitary banquet chair on the other side of the room—black, with a red cross painted across the middle. I stay glued to the floor, immovable, paralyzed, unable to swallow the unpalatable hostility.

Harold grabs me by my sweater collar and throws me to the chair. "You know my dear boy Michael died ten years ago today. It was Thanksgiving Day," he says, staring into the distance, lips forming a somber smile. "He wasn't killed by no random park ranger. He had a hit on him."

Harold's entire face changes from absolute lunacy moments back to almost human. "I had a longstanding rivalry with this guy. Business rivalry. Used to be my best friend growing up, too." Harold shakes his head, attempting to hide his bruises. "The bastard threatened me several times that if I didn't fold my business for good, he would harm my family.

But I refused to comply.

"I am a red blood American. I don't take no orders. So, I decided to dig up dirt on him. And boy did I find a minefield. He was an illegal alien. Came to this country illegally. So, I told him that if he didn't leave me, my business, and my family alone, I was going to expose him. Two days later, one of his men killed my son. Straight headshots. But really, I killed my own son."

My heart sinks, sharp pain infiltrating my chest. I forget where I am and what's going to happen to me. Watching Harold's face—a portrait of devastation, it's hard to not choke up. The pain of losing someone you love is understood only by the most ill-fated of people.

"I killed the piece of shit a few years back and it felt good. But not for long. It didn't feel enough. It was my son, you know? A piece of my heart, my soul, my entire life," he says, thumping his chest. His eyes water, but he wipes it immediately.

Helen keeps the tray on a small desk by the chair and holds her husband's hand. "Taking one life didn't feel enough. So, every Thanksgiving, I take another. The life of an illegal alien. The life of someone with the same skin color my boy was killed by. We are nice people, kind people the rest of the year. We do good for the community. But once a year, we need to do what is right for us."

"Please don't kill me," I say, my voice shaking like tremors, all sympathy evaporating. I want to tell him I'm in this country legally, so killing me would defeat the purpose of his mission. But I know better than to contradict him, to point out the fallacy in his twisted logic.

"Look, son. It's nothing personal. It wasn't personal with any of them," he says, pointing at the preserved heads of the boys he killed. "But I like staring at them knowing they can't stare back."

"We have loved having you. But our hospitality ends today. You do too. The best thing for you now is to cooperate, and it will be a painless death," Helen says.

"How did I end up here? I entered the door on the right," I say to myself, but Harold overhears me.

"You met the boy, didn't you? He is the neighbor's kid. I pay him a hundred bucks for every person he lures into this room. See, I'm getting old and can't carry you over this far. Neither can Helen.

"Not to mention I'm down one hand. So, he brings you to the room upstairs, then manipulates you into walking here voluntarily. I mean, he could bring you here directly, too, but the kid's a drama queen. He used to do off-Broadway, you know. Got a solid future ahead of him. Don't you think, darling?"

Helen nods.

"Please, don't kill me. Please. I have never done anything to you. Please, I swear I won't tell anyone. Just let me go." My voice cracks into a pathetic whimper, lump the size of a massive tumor in my throat.

"It's too late, son. You are already poisoned," Helen says.

"What?"

"Why do you think we fed you the entire turkey? You are going to die either way. Now would you want a slow, painful death or a quick, painless one?"

"That can't be true." I fail to hold it in longer, tears streaming down my parched cheeks, the magnitude of betrayal consuming me more than anything else. I can't believe I trusted these people, considered them family, confided in them on the coldest of nights.

How can two people, two perfectly sweet and considerate people, flip a switch and turn into this? Am I so dim-witted that I never saw any signs? No wonder my mother used to tell me, "The world is going to chew you alive and spit you out." People go cold turkey all the time. But going cold turkey on your humanity?

"I never lie, son," Helen says. "We have been slipping appetite suppressors into your food over the last couple of months, so your body weakens and eating an entire turkey becomes torture in itself."

"What?"

"Okay, enough chit-chat. Let me put this on you," Harold says, tearing open a transparent packet and pulling out a breathing mask. He pushes my head back, places the mask over my mouth and nose, places one strap over my head and the other at the top back. "Helen here is going to administer some anesthesia that's going to help you fall asleep, okay? You know she used to be a nurse, right? You won't even know you are dying."

Harold turns around and keeps his scalpel on the stainless-steel tray and Helen moves toward me, smirking. So, this is how it ends? In the hands of these two old, fucked up, racist, treacherous pieces of shit. Everything I have been through, everything I stood my ground for, everything I fought against—all fucking meaningless.

Everything I want to be, everything I know I can be—gone. I came to this country to find myself. But instead, I found two psychopaths whose shady hospital room will house my last remains.

No. In a split second of red-hot, frantic fury, I feel something kick inside me and I kick Helen's legs with bone-breaking ferocity, utilizing the deep groves on the sole of my snow boots.

The tray crashes to the floor with an ear-splitting noise, my legs stinging from impact. I pick up the scalpel and Harold turns around. He charges at me, and I shove the pointed side into his eyes, on target on first attempt. Blood and fluids ooze out like a fountain, Harold stumbling to the ground, screeching in agony. I scream along, the sight more horrifying than anything I have seen in my life.

Helen chokes me from behind. I cough, cough, cough, energy in my body draining, the temporary burst of impassioned anger dissipating. The room becomes fuzzy, my eyes starting to shut down. No, fuck this bitch. I throw a blind punch to my back and then another and then another and it finally connects and Helen screams, letting go of me.

I cough and spit and spit and cough as she nurses her bloody nose, and stick the shovel into her thighs, using both my hands to penetrate it deep, deep into her flesh.

A deafening cacophony of tormented screams ring around the room. Helen lies flat on the ground, but Harold gets up, covering his right eye. I head toward the door, pushing it open. Limping through the hallway, a trail of blood follows me, but I run and run and run until I see the window again and jump through, splattering blood all over fresh, velvety snow, and I trip and fall but get back up as snowflakes fly into my eyes and spill more blood and I run and run until I can't breathe.

The turkey house appears in front of me, Harold's voice echoing in the distance—chilling screams possessed by murderous anger, "I'm going to kill you, you brown piece of shit."

I quietly enter the turkey house. In the darkness, I can't see anything. Neither will Harold. Covering my nose to block the overpowering stench, I crawl along the ground, following the faint squeaks of turkeys.

As I find a hiding spot in their midst, my throat tightens, stomach aches, ribs threaten to burst open. I spit and cough, cough, cough blood onto the ground. Red blood. Malicious blood. Futile blood. I roll across the dirt, holding my stomach, vision blurring, body giving out, an army of turkeys looking over me like I am meat.

The End

Eddy Long Legs
Gabriel Giddings

To my partner in crime, with a mind as wild as mine –
Phillip Joubert. As without you, all this would be
impossible.

Chapter I

A blond kid sat at the desk. His head a smashed melon. Newest victim. Number nine or… eleven, depending what he did to the mum and toddler I saw in the *psychopath's* living room before. Now, less timid with my observation into the life of the *demented freak* who lived in the complex across the street.

I knew what he did to them.

Smoking my fifth cigarette. Chewing two nameless "Xanax" tablets. Letting the sharp, chemical, gritty, taste numb my pallet as I take a final drag of my cigarette. Oddly, there wasn't one in my fingers anymore. Patting about the grid of the fire escape, checking my coat pockets. Nothing. Vertigo hit me. Soon I was in my living room.

The old couch was icy. The coiling ache inside my gut twisted against the cool muggy mock leather. Thumping started. It rocked my brain like a pinball. I gritted my teeth. It was *him*. *He* was battering cats against his walls; taking the strays he had gathered like the fuckin Pied Piper, gripping them by their scruffs and bludgeoning their fragile emaciated bodies to his walls in a bid to paint the flaking apartment walls of his inner sanctum where he casually killed kids.

Evil bastard.

I turn over on my back, the ungulated thing entwined around my spine. Its waxy body pressing on my hipbones. Hungry, gaping, fanged, cunt maw... chewing into my core. Thick dick arms with hooved le—

"Ed!" Banging shuddered through me. Sitting up, bubbly bile silk shot out my nose.

"Open up!"

Before I could think, I snapped, "Go way!"

The banging on my apartment door didn't stop. She *was* a relentless little bitch.

"You don't open this goddamn door now, I'm gonna go *SWAT* on it!" she growled.

My disjointed body made it to the door, somehow. I undo the latches and locks.

"*Jesus...*" her blue hair reminded me of a tiny tropical bird. Piercings just about everywhere. In one of my band shirts she had commandeered. UK flagged leggings that gave her a total punk pixy platform boot glory. A greasy paper bag in her hand.

"...Torri-Bird,' my voice sounded spoken through a mouth filled with cotton... stuffed with a ball gag. Swallowing dryly, I got back to the couch.

"Ed..." Torri's voice was strained, "why don't you answer your goddamn phone? You look... terrible. *Fuck*. I shouldn't've moved out." A greasy cardboard container appeared on my lap. The long slimy worms twisted within. Feasting on the bits of flesh and moldy vegetables soaking in shiny grease. A ball of worms. Worms having a ball.

"Why you laughing?"

I had no idea I was. Two tablets on my dead tongue, my hand automatically went to the bottle of gin on the cluttered coffee table. Unable to swallow, it just burned the inside of my mouth.

"God, *no*, stop! *What the fuck* did you just take?"

The gin-fireball squelched down my throat. Torching the open sores all the way to the passenger within my non-existent gut. The calcified seminal foetal nightmare relished the drink. Labia blooming open the vaginal maw to absorb the nectar within me.

"I'm f-fine."

Her eyes were on me. The badly done black eyeliner framing her silky brown stare travelled my body. I hated that. *I know* I'm an *alien creature*. It was broken into me when my father sent me to ICU.

His fury to what *disgusting monster* I was, made me trace my fingers over the lumps on my ribs. Feeling the wires. Ha. I was only in boxer-briefs and grotty once-pink robe. Skeletal legs winding as the moniker I had been given throughout my childhood. Fuck my long legs.

"You *ain't* fine!" She was in my face. If she touched me, I would spontaneously combust. The congealed *thing* whin breaking out of my hosting corpse. Birthing itself from my scarecrow body. It was bound to happen. *Due.*

Her tiny hands on the sides of my face shocked me to bolt back. Worms flew everywhere. Balls of intestinal worms. She leaned over me. Humming, "just breathe… how many pills you take?"

Unable to get out from under her. A scream trapped in my chest. The thing in my core yearned for her. Not me. Wanting to grow. Pleading to feel whole again. To feel filled. A hollow parasite.

Only when Torri slapped the piss out of me did I return

to the present. She wasn't fucking me. Her enormous pulsing cock was not ripping my insides to shreds. Relieved... and disappointed.

"Fuck's *sakes*! Where's your goddamn keys?" she growled.

On the floor. It was a shock. Bones clattering. I didn't—

Chapter II

He ran after the car as it sped away. Silent. He screamed on mute. Sinking to his knees in dramatic agony of losing Big City Girl.

"Eddy Coburn?" was crooned beside me. The man was almost as round as his glasses. Bold with a grayed beard. In a white coat in the overly white sterile ward. His tag read *Dr. Burns*.

My mouth was stuffed with a ball gag, straining my jaw. My body was numb.

Paralyzed.

Despite knowing it was my panic disorder that nuked me, it felt as if I was tied down. All sorts of equipment against the walls. Every item designed to inflict pleasurable-pain on the victim, and dominant power on the sadist. Vomit rose in my throat. I felt it bubble in a flood of tadpole sperm excrement that the thing within me released when excited.

It began pulsing in my core. The murky congealed arms pushing two tiny dicks behind my navel. Overly excited to *feed*. Despite the obscenity, I became hard as a rock.

Paralyzed.

Catatonic.

Stuck in the utmost freeze response, which allows me to feel nothing done to the skeletal husk that hosts the cystic tumour of countless *dominant* masterful donors.

"Can you hear me, Eddy?" Doctor Burns loomed his hulky body over me, staring in my eyes with his beady little blue irises. I gave a slow blink. It was all I could do.

"Why ain't he talking, Doctor?' Shockingly, it was my mother. The tall lean Romani-American woman had her big sunglasses. Thick Tennessee accent.

"He's coming off anesthesia, Misses Coburn. Rest assured, he'll be dandy in a beat," Doctor Burns informed, chipper in a dour tone. "Was this a robbery? Poor boy." I was a man in my mid-thirties but go off, I guess.

"Yes… *yes*," my mum lied, as usual, "on… on our street. He was on his way home. Three uhm… men attacked him… for his phone." That was a partial truth. But the three men were my father and he found my conversation with Martin.

It was quite *personal*, the unrestrained mind of a teenager chatting with a love interest. If Martin was real or not, if we would ever have met in the park, if he had a Prince Albert or not, was all up in the air. My father was a fervent Catholic, and I was Satan.

He attempted to exorcise the demons with a bat and reinsert Jesus with his fists.

Amen.

I didn't lose consciousness. I felt my ribs cave, gagged on blood. I was going to drown in the pain. My arm shattered. Leg snapped in three places. Wondering how I was still alive after the bat hit me square in the face, amounted to watching my mum cover for him.

She did so with the cops and welfare as well. Sending me off to go live with my blind aunt in Liverpool. Never leaving her manor. Studying the one thing that made sense in my life. Physics. Mathematical formulas. Numbers. There were no variables. Nothing hidden. Always a solution I would inevitably find.

Coming back to the present was quite a leap, Torri-Bird was standing beside the bed. Not my mother. The doctor was a woman. Blonde and lean. *Dr. Oakley*. They were having a conversation about me—over me. I had no broken bones… that I was aware of. Just complete paralysis and a raging hardon.

"… here for the night. Conversion disorders are quite rare. Do you know if he was professionally diagnosed?" the doctor asked my best friend. "That's a neuro atypical panic disorder if I am correct? Almost like micro seizures?"

Ha-ha. Close but no biscuit, Doc.

"Yes. He was. Along with some… other things. All… mental. Edward had a… bad childhood accident, Doctor." Ran over by a father-shaped redemption-bus.

"Well," the doctor stared down at me as if I was a weird bug, "when he is deemed stable, he will be released to the psychiatric ward. Perhaps his medication needs some tweaking.

Suicidality is quite common in those who misuse prescription drugs and the trauma of your loss."

Unable to scream, I just blink. Mentally bashing my fist into her overly white teeth. Ramming the drip rod down her throat. Choking her with the elastic drip cord. Recently, since the guy in the building across form me began slaughtering children, prostitutes, and random animals, I was beginning to have violent fantasies. And I hate *nonconsensual* violence.

"Alright, doctor," Torri agreed. Distantly, I felt something on my hand. As if I had been sitting on it for an hour then tried to feel something. She was holding my hand tightly.

I wondered if it was possible to transplant the congealed semen foetus into her uterus. Having a general understanding of female anatomy, in a medical sense, I knew I could transplant the congealed little bastard into her womb. Would she be a better host than me?

Probably.

I had a thing for blondes. Maybe my cunt-mouthed, dick-armed, goat-legged, waxen, cystic seminal fetus had as well?

The only sensation was in my groin. It felt as if a hellhound had my dick in its jaw. Gnawing on it like a sinner's femur at the gates of hell.

Unfortunately, doctor-fertile-uterus left. Leaving me alone with Torri in the hospital cell—room.

Whatever.

An ad for car insurance was on the overhead TV. Muted. A man with a mustache loved saving money.

"Ed?" she was hazy. A tiny blue haired punk pixie I befriended as she was the worst barista I ever met. Fucking up a simple café latte and popping the cap on wrong for the scalding milk to melt my hand.

I had a hypersensitive skin condition all my life, which makes basic shit a hassle. Having hot milk on my hand felt like magma. The manager dismissed her. I went to the restroom and ran cold water over my hand while listening to a businessman piss like a racehorse.

Imagining him pissing in my mouth calmed my nerves enough to commence with my day. I found her outside. Sitting on the curb. Makeup smeared. I sat beside her. My freakishly long legs crooked like a fold-up chair. She began apologizing again before I gave her a cigarette and invited her to my apartment that evening to come listen to my collection of old CDs. She soon began dating…

"Ed?" there were tears in her eyes. Streaking her raccoon eyes down her pixy cheeks.

"I… I… I let the academy know you're taking some time off. Professor Hawthorne understands. He says you should've taken time off sooner. Your doctorates ain't going nowhere," a weird pressure on my hand again as she squeezes.

"Not," I managed, "going to, nut house," been there, done that. Helped me absolutely nothing besides having a fling with a hot schizophrenic in the shower. He believed I was his nephew "Scott" while fucking me, it didn't bother me until said "Scott" came to visit and he was a seven-year-old autistic kid.

"No. You gotta, man. You're *reckless*. You take all kinds of fuckin pills and don't eat. You look like *death*. I *ain't* gonna lose you, too." She was furious.

My mouth twitched.

"You *wanna* die? Tell me *now*, Ed." She sneered through gritted teeth down at me. It was a difficult question.

"I wanna go home to... Nyx... Torri." She looked stunned, "Nyx died last year, Ed. She had cancer, remember?" My black rescued cat I had for six years did die of glaucoma. I had taken her to the vet many times with one false diagnosis after another. They only knew she had advanced cancer when I paid for an autopsy. The three of us mourned her. Me, Torri and...

"No... no... I'm going home," forcing feeling back into my legs. Who knew what that psycho from across the street was doing in my apartment while I was not there? *Disgusting* things. Licking my damn plates, the *weirdo*. With his breeder breath. Pube-laced teeth. I felt sick just thinking of his pussy-juice saliva on my nice silverware.

"Ed."

She shook me. It felt like an earthquake. "You're *staying*," she insisted.

"No." With my core alone (and the help of the thing growing inside me), I sat up, "Going home."

"I'm gonna get you sanctioned!" she growled behind me, "you're a *danger* to *yourself*."

My dead hand entered the hospital gown. I try to feel

the thing inside me, but it never wanted me to, it always just feels me.

"*Ed*," she was in front of me now. So small. So angry. So *simple*.

"Stop this shit," she grabbed my shoulders, fuck but she was way stronger than she looked, "ain't letting you go, *too*." She sobbed, "You're... all I have, you selfish *motherfucker*!" fury and agony made a strange combination.

Placing my spindly hand on her shoulder, in a bid to comfort or push away, "I'll be fine, Torri-Bird. I just... went a bit overboard. I got shit to do."

"What? *Drugs*?"

"And you're one to judge?"

Revolt, pain, confusion, and sorrow. Something stopped her from slapping the hell out of me right there. I wouldn't blame her. I would slap myself on every given opportunity just to feel something.

"*Really*? I'm *clean*!" her voice hitched in her throat. The eye tattoo in the middle of her birdy neck bobbed.

"Get out my face, Torri. I'll take the time off. I'll cut down on the drinking. Take only the pills I need... and maybe get another cat," I mused.

"No. You'd be *dead* if I didn't come by earlier last night. They pumped your stomach. Flushed you. There's a chance you got permanent brain and heart damage." My care was so miniscule that I almost told her that a bit of damage to something that's become obsolete meant as much as breaking a window on a factory due for demolition.

"You gonna drive me, or should I get an Uber?" I say, twitching my toes to get my feet working again. My body was so long and skeletal that the entire gown hung open. Exposing much more of me than it should.

I only realized because Torri looked at me oddly. She

had never seen me naked before, even living in the same two-bedroom flat with me and… she lowered her eyes. She was bisexual. Which is why I introduced her to… and they had a three-year relationship that was like an ox-waggon on coke.

Being stared at by her, of all people, like a freakishly long skeleton with a dick, just brought it all back. Me and (say her name goddammit) had so many fights about how close we were. Maybe Torri had a *thing* for me? She was like a sister to me which made this moment awkward and… somewhat *refreshing*.

I have in my thirty-something years never been with a woman. Kissed one, but she tasted like spring onions. I wondered if Torri would be able to feel what they had put inside me? I should probably give it a name. I felt the toothy cunt mouth gnaw inside at my guts, wishing Torri had a big fat cock to fuck me and shut the little bitch up.

Maybe she did?

"Ed," her UK tights touched my long bony knee on the side of the bed, 'we gotta be there for each other. I… I… I miss her so much," her tiny hand fell on my skeletal leg, "I miss you, too."

I never thought about fucking Torri. She was *childlike* compared to me. It was odd for my warped, dazed mind to make out if I fancied her or not. *Nope*. Not at all. I ain't the schizophrenic guy that fantasizes about fucking his kid nephew while balls-deep inside an anorexic masochist.

Same principal.

Through, she would look good strung up and power drilled by a fuck machine.

Damn, I wanted a drink. Or four Xan tabs. Or a fat line of coke. Anything. I'd probably huff gasoline just to get *this* as far as possible away from me.

Torri, with her fairy hands and mini pixy face leaned closer to me. I smelled her. She reeked of sweat, candy apple perfume, and the odd bleachy smell girls get when emotional. The thing I wanna call it 'Scott', lurched in my stomach and I promptly vomited a frothy gurgle of come in a wild gush down my chin.

"*Fuck*!" Torri seemed to wake from whatever she was thinking wanting to kiss me. Grabbed a bit of the starched hospital blanket and wiped my face. "Must be more stuff they pumped you full of to get the pills out." Accepting her conclusion, even though it felt like a bukkake drain in my mouth.

"Look," she tried to get my attention back, "it's just *us*. I need you just as much as you need me. I loved her, too. You know that."

Spitting a glob next to her platform boots onto the linoleum, I hacked my throat clear of Scott's excitement in my guts, "Yeah. Get the doctor. I'm refusing treatment."

Chapter III

She drove me in my shitty old Ford back to our apartment. It was late afternoon. Not like it mattered. All I thought of was my stash of mystery pills in the cabinet behind the kitchen sink. "I'm taking the keys. You're not leaving the apartment until I know you're good enough not to wander into traffic."

She took a drag of the blunt. Belphegor was thundering from the speakers.

My eyes linked to her bee sting breasts bouncing free below my loose shirt. It hung off her. Exposing her birdlike shoulders. A weird noise emitted from my rotting gore. Her eyes met mine.

"What?" she handed me the blunt, tailgating a U-Haul at a red light. I take a deep drag of the pungent mix. relaxing back in my tattered passenger seat while running my hand up and down my leg to try and gain more sensation. My nerves were wreaked. Dull. I either felt too much, or nothing at all.

In a bolt of hellfire, I shocked all the way through my spine and up to my airy head when her doll hand rested on my long skeletal thigh. Her black nail polish a bit less cracked off than mine.

"You falling asleep?" her voice had no emotion. It felt good after a while.

"I asked you not to talk about her," The words leave me like the cloud of thick weed vapor. She missed a gear and my car choked a shudder into the underground parking area. Removing her hand left me feeling empty again.

Even Scott stirred.

Disrupted. Both dick-legs hard and desperate for her kiddie hand behind my navel. She parked in my spot. Cut the engine. Turned to me. I knew what was coming.

She slammed her lipless dry mouth into mine. Her tongue darted inside. I just sat there. Electric. Her childlike hand gripped my dick in a vice. "I know you wanna," she moaned in my mouth. "*Fuck me*, Ed."

My hand went up to her throat. I did what I always wanted to. Choked the living shit out of her. Crushing the side of her head into the window. She looked terrified for a few seconds, then leaned over and bit the absolute hell out of my lower lip. My blood tasted divine.

She flipped both legs over to me. I stopped her halfway and forced her down on the gearshift. She squirmed. I ripped her UK tights off. Forcing my old Ford's gear stick up her ass. Being the considerate guy I am, I spat some thick frothy come in my palm and slathered the lever head slick before making her sink down on it. She exhaled a high-pitched scream as the Ford's gear knob impaled her tight virgin ass.

She was holding to my shoulders in a death grip.

Gritting her teeth as she exhaled weird angry screams. "You fuckin *bastard*!" she growled in my face. Her body was fighting, but her eyes not. She gave me the look of *more*. I sunk her down for the lever to permeate into her lower intestine enough that she was skewered on the gear box.

I gripped her throat, leaning her back and forth. Making my old Ford gear-fuck her. She began jacking me off with her kiddie-strong hands. Trying to get me to fuck her cunt along with my car. I was weirdly flexible. It was possible. But *nah*. I was good, thanks.

The sultry aroma of blood and shit was mouthwatering. I wondered how the hell she was bleeding, then felt her cunt slit was sticky slick with period blood. She was trying to speak but it was all just a rap of cusses and random insults.

I pulled the string. Popping the tampon out her mousy bold cunt. She had a darling skull tattoo on her pubic mound.

Taking a long drag of the blunt, I exhaled the smoke in her gasping maw. She moaned. Jacking me off viciously, but she might as well be twiddling my toes. Popping the tampon between my teeth. I gave the soggy spongy blood-soaked material a few chews, sucking it dry, before leaning into her mouth.

She began cussing viciously. Deeply impaled on the gear lever. I shoved my mouth into hers. Forcing the tampon as deep as possible down her throat.

Now, she was trying to rip my dick off. Good luck with that. Felt *odd*.

Leaning down like an anorexic arachnid crane, I tasted a cunt for the first time. The blood *sent* me. She moaned so loud the whole apartment block must be hearing her at this point. Tongue-fucking all the blood I could out of her.

Neither me, nor Scott, wanted it to end. The incredible

hunger took over my entire body. Biting into the thin fleshy flaps covering her gaping fuck hole.

Torri now screamed in a growing howl. Moaning in horrified ecstasy.

Rocking her hips for my mouth and her impalement. When there was no more blood left - I reached behind her and popped open the central locks.

Torri gasped. "*What... fuck... no! Come back! Don't stop!*" she screamed in a guttural growl.

I lick my lower lip, "Nah, I'm good."

She knocked me a solid shot to the jaw. I gripped her throat, leaning her back. Her petite body being demolished by the gear lever in her gut. I spat blood-froth in her face,

"Really want *more?*" I sneered as she was losing consciousness. As she was passing out, I let go and opened the passenger door. Maybe I might not have stopped soon enough. Not risking killing my best friend.

"You *sick* fuck! I hope you *die* in your fucked up *sex cult*! She *killed* herself because of *you*! My girlfriend *killed* herself because of *you*, you sick fuckin *bastard*! Burn in *hell*!"

Gladly, sweetheart.

Lurching my long body toward the stairs, I fall against a car.

The alarm went off.

I tripped to my knees, then dragged and crawled back up to my feet until I gained enough mobility to reach the stairs that will take me to my apartment.

Fuckin mad.

Chapter IV

Biting open the bottle of nameless pills, I sit on the kitchen floor. I manage to break the seal. Popped three in my mouth and just lied on the floor. I smelled the guy from across the road's spit and Torri's cunt-blood on everything.

Neighbor Guy had taken over my house by claiming everything like the damn five-year-olds he kills.

Probably fucking my cancer riddled cat's corpse like a black, furry flesh-light. Maybe her small stiff body was also pregnant with a sentient cystic sperm tumour? That made me somewhat connected to her again.

Wherever she was. I jacked off, imagining my dead cat wrapped around my aching dick. Coming over my emaciated stomach.

Scott was *happy*.

My body was turned inside out. The little bastard, Scott, was having the time of his pustulating parasitic life. Snippets of Master Remmi picking me up off the kitchen floor. Spiking me with something he cooked up over a candle while talking in reverse.

The man in the opposite apartment's lights were on. Six little children were standing in a line to be shaven and given ice cream. He shoved a little girl's face in the next kid's ass and had them shit down her throat. It was unfair that they didn't get it in cones with sprinkles, the evil sonofabitch.

"You good, Eddy?" Remmi was so sweet. I loved it when he cared. My body had shut off. I was paraplegic due to the insane amount of drugs in my system and the natural knock-out response my brain surrendered me into when in delicious shock.

All I did was breathe occasionally. Hear. Feel. Taste. Smell.

Remmi was a big guy with honest eyes and a caring affinity for me. I just wanted a hug most of the time. Staring up into his enchanting eyes as he played with my longish filthy black hair while I was being cut in half by a partition. On my back on a cold iron table. My lower body in a different dimension.

"Relax them long legs, Eddy-baby," he crooned down at me, leaving me in the dark kink dungeon's reverse glory hole. Incredibly long legs. Sticks they manipulated in the "other dimension" beyond the partition halving me. Stuck in my hollow shell. Being filled relentlessly by God only knows what on the other end. A great place for men who wanted to fuck something without a face. Something unique.

A long-legged anorexic freak.

Gagging on frothy come as the fetus had been satiated, and sprawled on my filthy bed back in my apartment. Frothy coppery microscopic tadpoles caked down my throat and clogging every artery. Remmi smiled down at me.

"Told you, baby," he ran his hand through his silky golden hair, "I got you. You're mine. Did good tonight. When last you eat?"

"Do you love me?" gurgled from my throat. Her ethereal shape stood beside the closed door. Long, cascading, black hair poured down to her slender shoulders, to her synched waist.

"What kind a question's that?" Remmi burst out laughing. "Sure. Whatever. Yeah. You do it for me, alright?"

"Then why'd you... *do it*?" my words were like the last of my sick will leaving me. She didn't turn to me. Didn't move. Just a dark silhouette of what had once been.

"Do what?"

"I miss... you. So... fuckin much." Tears couldn't come. My hand dug at my hard stomach. Somehow there had to be a way in to get the thing out. It was fat. Fed to the brim with come, piss, and shit that was still caking my pallet. It wanted something more. Something... *real*. Like a *big* tampon or an ever-bleeding cunt.

"You talking to the walls?" Remmi chucked deeply. Rubbing my skeletal back. "Come on, baby, don't go loopy on me now."

"Miss... you, sis," broke from my throat.

"Hey, focus,' he spat in my face, a sign of his endearment. "Come say goodnight to me. Jessie's almost home from her sift. You *want* me, baby?"

I hummed a non-answer. Licking his thick spit from my lip.

"You make me *wild*," he growled as he took my arm—knowing I was basically paralyzed—dragging me to the bathroom in my apartment. He dropped me in the middle of the dark bathroom. Gently.

She stared at me from under the bathroom cabinet. I had no idea how she could fit under there, but her Victorian goth style rendered her as the perfect vampiric queen of the damned. Being the social reject that I was, a UK immigrant, born in Tennessee to gypsy parents, I was just as much as a living abortion as she was believed to be.

We drew close. An unspoken bond where the most were said in complete silence during lunch breaks at Boston University. She was an enigma. Eventually she agreed I was one to her as well. She opened up to me that her life had fallen to the point where she lived in the backroom of a man who had her pay for her lodging by fucking him once every month.

She had been disowned by her conservative family for being a prolific atheistic wiccan and sapphic. Having a place of my own with the inheritance my aunt had left me and no worries of student loans due to having a physics scholarship, she moved in with me.

"You and me against the world." She had a small tattoo of a daddy longlegs spider on her wrist below a semicolon. In the same fashion, I had a cartoon romantic ghost covering one of my many self-inflicted scars.

We were united against this fucked up world. I introduced her to Torri and they hit it off. Torri's bright punk spunky attitude to life brought something back in her that she never had. We were complete. Until… she wasn't under the cabinet. She wasn't in the apartment. She wasn't in Vermont. She wasn't in America. She wasn't on fuckin earth anymore… and I basically raped Torri with my car for her period blood.

Eventually, Remmi got bored with fucking me. My bones clattering on the tiles with every thrust as he poked the stuffed malignant tumor that was on the verge of exploding in my core. He flopped my long body over like a living corpse. Squatted beside me on the tiles and took a shit. Grunting like a pig. The smell made me ravenous.

It spurted beside my ear. I got hard as a rock when he coated his dick with his shit. My Master has ties to the mob, that's all I knew. And a doctor wife with three brats. He kept grunting stupid porno comments as he shoved his shit-caked cock down my throat.

Consciousness was a blessed curse.

Chapter V

The sun rose as I lied on the fire escape. Waiting. Knowing he was going to wake up soon and execute the terrified Jewish boy standing below his window. Gas chambers and human experiments. Piles of shoes that the victims wore before entering the chambers, before removing the gold from their teeth. The tumor inside my guts rolled and boiled up to my gullet. Unable to swallow.

I rubbed the crusted shit from my nose, incapable of taking my eyes off him. He was… *awake*. He stood in the window. The first time the *evil sadistic bastard* was staring straight at me. I stopped breathing. His eyes connected across the massive five-story drop to his. He did one thing, and one thing, only.

Slowly shook his head.

My body reacted out of some internal instinct. I got back onto the fire escape from outside the railing. I staggered back, then fell through my open window and just lied there. In only a filthy shit, come, piss, puke covered gown. It was once pink. Now I bled on it as well, adding to the miasma of fluids and madness as my head twisted.

I should be down *there*. The pavement. *Why am I inside?* Curling up beside my sofa, I laughed, hugging my freakishly long legs.

A rhythmic thumping called me. Polite. Not Torri's bashing. Not Remmi's punching. Just a polite knock. I rolled over onto my spine. It dug into the floor. I felt every vertebra try to break out my skin.

Time for the birth.

The tumour couldn't be inside me much longer. It was thrusting. Scott was fucking me on the inside. Cock arms in my liver and cunt maw fucking itself with my pancreas.

Another polite knock.

I pulled myself up on the side of the couch. The cut on my arm tore to expose bone. The cuts on my legs exposed bone. What I was to the freakshow of sadistic anorexia-kink men who wanted to see more and more *bone*.

That was all I had.

How I bought my pills. I popped two in my shit crusted mouth, swallowed it with a mug of curdled coffee from the end table. Reaching the door, I leaned against it urinating myself, as pregnant women do. It was blood, but same principle. "What?" my voice was strained. My throat a raw wound.

"Uhm. Afternoon, Mister Corburn," he had a deep cadence. Reluctance. A slight Birmingham accent. Perhaps it was the familiarity of that which made me relent.

Opening the door to the man from across the street. A middle-aged *monster* of a *psychotic bastard* who had ruined lives. Huge blue eyes that have seen countless *atrocities*.

He was sick. Depraved. Horrendous, in his brown cardigan and corduroy slacks. Shorter than me, no surprise there, most people were. Salt-and-pepper hair. I was momentarily stunned. He looked so fucking *normal* for all the shit I *knew* he did.

Creepy bastard.

He clutched a flat cap in front of his chest.

"I… got your name from the groundskeeper. Fifteen B. I'm Samuel Davenport, and I'm sorry for your loss. I heard what happened."

He was sincere.

I asked the only question to the man that had seen it all happen that I could, "Did… she look scared when she fell?"

Samuel Davenport blinked, seemed to digest the question, "No. Peaceful."

"You… saw it. Why *did* she? Why did Alice jump?" for the first time, tears broke free in front of the man I hated most. Who saw my failure to be there for my sister. Who failed her even worse by staring at her demise from this reality to pavement oblivion.

Samuel Davenport shook his head, "Not for you to die like this… What you do in here is… disturbing. Maybe I can help? I'm a child psychologist, but I specialise in trauma."

I smile a bit, tears streaming, shit caked in my teeth, "Yeah? You *kill* kids, kittens and… lick my shit when I ain't here. You a shrink? Ha. Figures."

He didn't look insulted, "Uhm. No. Perhaps I could… help you. May I come in?"

I felt the switchblade in my revolting pink (once fluffy) night gown. The tumor thundered inside my gut as the man stepped closer and hugged me tight. Relaxing my long sickly body in the arms of the man who maybe, or maybe not, had witnessed her decent to nothing.

I had him.

Digging the blade deep between his shoulder blades as I pulled him inside my apartment web.

I was *starving*. The struggle was over quickly. One less evil in the world. Eating for the first time in days. Old floppy cock marinated in shit I squeezed fresh from his slippery sick guts. I came in his gauged-out eye with delight. Slurping piss straight from the source to down four more tablets.

My Master Remmi will clean this up. Only fair to ecstatic Scott, and I, that he does his *Masterly* duty.

The door opened. I glance up into the barrel of a Glock. Torri's expression was unreadable as she slowly shut the apartment door behind her.

"Hey, Torri-Bird," I fiddle with a piece of flesh stuck in my teeth with a long blood-sticky finger. The gun pressed to my forehead felt itchy.

Her black-smeared doe-eyes, take in everything. They turn from shock, to horror, to... intrigue. "You... *what the fuck*?" She lowered the Glock. Staring at the dead psychopath I was straddling. Castrated, gored, skinned - it was a beautiful shit-blood-flesh buffet on the floor.

"... you... oh, my *god*," she exhaled, but didn't shoot me or run out. Unable to look away.

I took her tiny hand in my spiderlike fingers. Evenly pull her down to her knees beside me. Enter the corpse's chest cavity, our hands entwined.

I whisper in her ear, "... friends?"

She begins moving her doll hand in the mess of lacerated organs, blood and gored shit. Exploring the feeling. "Only if I get to do to *you* what you did to *me* in the fuckin car, Ed," she sneered, still gripping the gun by her side. Molding the intestines with more force.

I exhale a hoarse laugh. "Of course."

The fun had just begun.

Luster

Dave Davis

Mickey felt like the luckiest man alive. They say if you love what you do for a living, then you never really work a day in your life. Well, being that he loved both knives and photography, it couldn't get any better than earning a decent salary serving as a photographer, and sometimes contributing columnist, to a popular knife enthusiast magazine.

The digital age made this vocation even dandier: the electronic publication allowed more global exposure and access, not to mention the capabilities of modern media modalities, while the continued printing of old-school glossy magazines concurrently, enabled retention of the tangible materialistic aspects that many devotees of the rag still relished.

Along those lines, Mickey was cognizant of the fact that with digital camera utilization, he was permitted to revel in the productions of his work, since no time was wasted on the tedious chore of developing old-world film, as an unavoidable necessity of the craft; therefore, allowing more time and energy to be focused solely on the exciting hunt and purview of knives, and incorporating the art of photography, for exquisite portrayal of the tipped treasures.

The absence of time consumption, or obligatory space allocation for extinct film processing, allotted Mickey more extensive freedom to pursue his hobby, as well. And if you're considered blessed, to have your job involve your favorite things, what does it make you, if your hobby also revolves around the exact same?

Although his position with the edgy publication necessitated some travel, Mickey wasn't overly burdened with such requirements, and for that he was thankful, as again, return to his hobby ambitions came more readily. Fortunately, he just so happened to be situated in the prime location for his occupation(s). You see, Mickey lived in southeast Texas. And although it can generally be stated that 'everybody loves knives,' it is a greater certainty in the Lone Star State.

No difficulties came about identifying opportunities to collect material for the blade-love media. When there weren't large knife shows or conventions, there were blade sport competitions, self-defense seminars, tactical knife combat courses, and various other exhibitions.

Outside of scheduled large-scale events as such, he could make use of the myriad museum specimens across the state as features. Heck, everything from frontier knives, to cavalry sabers, to prison shanks, and Ranger blades could satisfy avid consumers for volumes to come.

Don't forget the infamous Bowies! The early coffin handle variety was his favorite of those, by the way. To keep things interesting, readers even appreciated articles showcasing EDC (everyday carry) models and blade patterns of the everyday folk, or BBQ cutlery brandished within the knifist community, of which the regular subscribers felt akin, and we ain't just talkin' 'bout the workin' edged tools.

Don't get me wrong, knifers like to let their sharp friends get dirty, but they also keep around some more revered items, which are for ogling and fondling only. On that note, more than a few hardware stores off the beaten track housed huge displays of countless sharp and shiny accoutrements as a surprise boutique for the collectors of folders and fixed blades alike within their walls.

Round all that out with the occasional show-and-tell interview featuring special forces operators' preferred trusty steel companions, and Mickey had plenty of material to work with, right in his neck of the woods.

Now, about that *hobby*. The current age, and his locale also suited that. It may be surmised that those of his disposition had easier pickings in the days of hitchhiking and obliviousness to his kind.

But the prevalence of mass migration and human trafficking throughout his region overrode and nullified any newly gained advantages over the past. Undocumented or desperate individuals were plentiful. Even the most desirable 'participants' for his hobbyist endeavors were readily accessible. No, Mickey didn't have to settle at all; he was able to have his pick of the litter.

Mickey ignored the whimpers emanating from around the threshold of his open-doored computer room, as he applied the finishing touches to the captured scene upon his screen, of his beloved side art, which he was modulating to his pleasant satisfaction.

The finalized imagery brought an insuppressible smile to his dry lips, upon appreciating how perfect editing of the hues and lighting, captured the reflective edge's bevel and recipient flesh just perfectly, dazzling his mind. As the audibly mounting anguish of his awaiting company began to disturb his focus, Mickey cursed to his anticipatory audience, "Goddamnit…I'm trying to concentrate!" before turning his head to announce more loudly down the short hallway, "Don't worry, you'll get your time to shine! I'll be there in a second!"

Pleased with the new submission to his fetish collection, Mickey took a sip from his coffee mug resting on the terminal table, clicked 'save,' then closed the private art portfolio file. *Next model*, he thought, while rolling his chair away from the monitor, and retrieving his faithful camera off the desk as rising to stand.

The consummate professional readied his photography instrument while making the short jaunt down the hallway toward his involuntary specimen, ever-ready to catch the wonderous visual potentials in totality, even from first impressions. Oh, especially those initial reactions!

As Mickey stopped within the 'game room's' threshold, camera aperture already aimed, his mouth fired first, "Hope you're feelin' photogenic today…"

In distress, and bondage, she was a beauty to Mickey. Her already quivering limbs and luscious assets, accelerated in pace and amplitude upon eyeing the monstrous example of cold steel that the imprisoner was slowly extricating from his belt sheath, while snapping photos. The surreal situation shattered the 'model's' mind, lending to copious urination and tremoring, as her sight endured the onslaught of repetitive flashing light and edged weapon presentation.

Invigorated with the streaming piss and running make-up now painting his portrait, the studious photographer ensured efficient capture of the provided captive art, letting no glamorous visual escape his entrapment.

After some ambulatory pics were acquired from various vantage points, Mickey fixed the Nikon to its awaiting tripod at an oblique angle within three feet of the twenty-something, nude, brunette. "You're gonna make a *beautiful* addition to my album," the tormentor complimented, while setting the automatic discharge interval of the visual documentation device.

A rapidly crescendoing *"uuunnnhhh"* emitted from the bewildered hostage, now frantically yanking on her bindings, as the scene conductor encroached her personal space, while raising his wide blade to horizontal at the level of her sweat-slicked, spongy breasts.

"Hold still for the camera," Mickey cooed, while elevating the cup of the 'model's' left tit, by levering it with the cheek of his thickly spined knife. The keenly sharp edge of the tortuous tool's belly greedily burst the tender hide just beneath her mammary, as the implement wielder grazed her torso wall during the process of scooping up the tantalizing tissue onto his high-carbon steel, upper-extremity extension.

She instantly froze in place, staring wild-eyed through the sweat-drenched dark hair plastered to her face and neck. The sword in Mickey's blue jeans tried to penetrate the denim fabric, as his visual cortex fired on all synaptic cylinders, readily receiving and engulfing the display of spectacular ocular delights.

Knowing he not only got to witness the exhibit live, but would also own the images for perpetual revisiting, only further pushed him into exquisite euphoria. Mickey took it *all* in: the smeared eye shadow; the disheveled wet hair; the trembling lips; the glistening sweat; the vibrating nipples; the glimmering blade!

The gory glamour glutton never could decide whether he loved the tools of the trade or the torture-ee more; admiring the curves, angles, and reactions of both with equal zeal, he decided he would never have to.

Almost hoarse, the disrobed photography featurette eked out, "What do you want?"

Slowly slipping his left hand behind her neck, Mickey, the metallurgical media mogul, anxious to capture his creation of synergized beauty and barbarism, leaned in and revealed, "Art."

With that, the knife and photography connoisseur withdrew his blade-wielding hand from beneath her breast into an abducted and semi-pronated posture, before explosively thrusting the single-edged drop-point combat knife into the fabulous female's left orbit, completely through to the hilt. The dispatched's dynamite death rattle brought about a rapid conclusion to this photo shoot session. But oh, what a juicy climax!

On a summer Texas afternoon, during the hottest part of the day, Siesta time, while soaking up some AC, sipping a Shiner Bock, and perusing the flesh files within his 'side art' collection, Mickey kept returning to the series of his most recent addition.

He scrolled through the stills repeatedly, scrutinizing his polished work; relishing, and recounting the encounter which rewarded application of his craft and toys. For hours, he reflected inwardly on the melding of his trophy model, metal weapon, and psychopathic mettle:

She's the best one yet! That look is priceless on her gorgeous face. I definitely chose the right knife for that stint. She deserved my favorite SYKCO model. That DB 421's tip made targeting and entry a sinch. And the resiprene grip allowed full penetration through her skull.

Oh, my, this shot of her boobs through the death throws is amazing! The red and white ichor idling down her face makes an excellent combination with her eye shadow and sun tan. That new nifty Nikon sure enhanced the delineations. I hope my new Busse Hell Razor II arrives soon; I don't wanna have to spring for catering on the hot tamale waiting her turn for the next photo shoot...

In Temple, Texas, on a Tuesday, Mickey was burning up. That wouldn't be too atypical, but the climate wasn't to blame. On this temperate afternoon, sickness could only steal claim, for too long had lapsed since this deviant had paid the Devil his due. The sudden encephalopathy had not occurred previously, at least not nearly to this severity.

Faint traces of tinnitus and increased intracranial pressure seemed to turn up, 'round about the time he was on the hunt. But never, had the symptoms come on so rapidly, and reached such intensity, with such crippling effect. Although he was pretty capable of putting two and two together, readily able to discern what this was about, a voice, unrecognizable as self, resounding from deep within his psyche, cleared up any confusion on the correlation, *Slay her!*

Earlier in the day, the sleazy steel junkie spied a much too tempting sorority slut. She wasn't interested in the services Mickey was providing, nor the activities being conducted at the college agricultural conference, and just happened to be there with her hick boyfriend.

No matter, the demon saw her image and wanted to capture her soul on film. The photo fiend was parched for deviltry, desiring an end to the recent drought. His travel and assignment schedule hadn't slacked up any, but the herd of whoredom that once seemed so plentiful, was all of a sudden lying low, as if the prey knew it was hunting season.

However the sparsity came about, apparently his needs weren't following suit. On the contrary, his devilish desires operated in an inverse relationship. Anguish for cutting flesh and clicking pics only climbed, as the resources receded. Mickey (or part of himself) promised himself, *I'll find her*, to which an appreciable abatement of his symptomatology was awarded.

Now he just needed to make a stop at the sorority house, before leaving town. He may have been poaching, but Mickey knew of one dingbat duck-face that was gonna get whacked.

Tailing the hot-tail was simple. She apparently had taken her own swanky ride to meet her boyfriend, and led the stalker straight to her lair, driving through the small town in oblivion. A few dozen feet back from the Bacchic driveway, Mickey could see a few vehicles parked about, but detected no activity, save for the bimbo's entry.

Liking the view of the hunting plot, he exited his vehicle and shimmied closer for a better peak. The common area of the sorority house sported large bay windows in the outer perimeter walls. 'Blondie' seemed to be alone. Her 'sisters' must've all been attending events outside of hickdom (*or* playing *in their rooms*, he inwardly giggled).

Upon realization of this most opportune scenario, a rush of excitement became just too much to bear. Glimpsing the bubble-butt blonde consumed the action photographer with inspiration. Chronicling her immaculate pain was imminent. His blade free of its scabbard, the maniac was unleashed. Mickey gently tested the front doorknob.

It was open, *dumb blonde*.

And so, morbid lust pervaded.

Later that night, while relaxing from his road trip on the couch, the knife aficionado scrolled through the recent album additions attained from his roadkill. These memorializations weren't exactly up to Mickey's standards; he would rather have been able to abduct the bitch (Alexis was her name; he only discovered this by the thin cursive gold necklace documented in the slaying series; he didn't notice it during the 'melee'), use his best photography equipment, and take his time; but beggars can't be choosers.

He didn't want to come out of there empty-handed, so, his cellphone camera saved the day, allowing him to now savor the moment. Hovering over one of the pics, Mickey had to laugh out loud, *never thought I'd be doing that*, he mused. *Wonder if irrumatio qualifies as necromancy.*

He never got a reply.

In his Temple frenzy, fraught with blue balls and blued steel, anxious to completely satisfy his fetish without interruption, the knife diviner let all hell break loose. Like fate, Mickey walked right up to the airhead and pummeled her eye with his knife's extended-tang pommel. The porcelain doll collapsed to the floor, *where she belonged.* Extricating a pound of flesh from the skirt was easy (off her big-assed behind), and the beheading just…happened.

The knife just felt *too* good, and he was feeling just *so* virile. Seeing as how her eye socket was already prepared, sticking his pecker in there, well, only seemed natural. The POV must've been amusing, because Mickey smiled, and smiled, and smiled.

Reflecting on his exploits into the evening, the devotee of desecration fondled the hefty cleaver of his most recent desires, admiring how the chopper had made equally quick work of the carving duties thrown in its path. The snuff pig similarly ruminated on how the blonde wasn't nearly as spicy as the Latinas, but the change was nice, especially from the dry spell.

Having enough of the visual stimuli for now—It was never enough!—Mickey went to the kitchen and withdrew a gallon-sized zip-lock baggie from the fridge. The optics had always been the most desirable, the most satiating. But this day, this time, the urge to satisfy more tactile sensory input seemed needed, to fill his dopamine prescription.

He gently compressed the contents between his fingers, before turning the package over to continue scrutinizing and palpating his trophy. Though it was immediately tempting to taste the Temple treasure, Mickey replaced the rump roast into the icebox for another time. See, the vile butcher had already unwittingly sampled the specimen when he went berserk in the Greek palace.

Once again, his sweet and sinewy photo collection elucidated what he might otherwise miss out on, for reminiscence sake, anyway. (Though always a willing actor, some blackouts couldn't be denied.) Let the evidence show, that Mickey is one nipple macerating nympho. *Already had titty tartar, better try the buttock...braised*, he amused himself while shutting the cooler's door.

A few days later, the only thing that made a big-booty-ho's butt-meat taste any better, was the news feed Mickey was glued to while gustation ensued. It made Mickey downright giddy to discover (not *too* much to his surprise, though) that the buffoons in Temple didn't have a clue.

No leads, no traces, no video footage, no eyewitness accounts; zippo! Due to the markings left behind by a precision cutting instrument, wild animal attack could be ruled out (*ha,ha*). While his cranial nerves seven and nine were transmitting pleasurable impulses from his fantasy conquest, his frontal lobe mind (or wherever it exists) beamed in the synaptic radiance of knowing he was nowhere on their radar.

The authorities proximate to the sorority house of slaughter, were convincing themselves some ultra-violent gangbangers were headed South, and just leaving casualties in their wake. The local Sheriff had only this to proffer at the miniature press briefing, in order to give the sense of some kind of justice, or security: *"Bite marks and semen found at the scene were cataloged and will be compared with all registered criminals."*

Mickey understood this to mean the elected law enforcement agents were already giving themselves a pass. The traffickers were already being run out of the country, what else could be expected of them? Indigestion wouldn't ruin this homecoming queen choice-cut. No, with a pleasantness throughout, the cannibal's vagus nerve took it from there, ensuring optimal absorption of the spoiled brat's gluteus maximus.

Sweet dreams of savage artistry accompanied his nutrient assimilation. Its sustenance satisfied, the devil's DNA continued its orphic marching orders.

A few years down the road, Mickey's road trip duties dwindled. That suited him fine, as he'd gotten his fill of honkies abroad, and the more alluring chicas had gradually returned to his stomping grounds (or otherwise somehow just reappeared), en masse. What didn't sit well with him, was the associated reasonings for his reduced travel agenda.

The knife community wasn't what it used to be. Although Mickey was certain knives would never leave culture (just look at the gastro geeks), the scene was certainly shrinking. He didn't bother trying to understand if modern offerings of the technological age competed for their potential customers' loyalty, if it was just a generational divide, if the firearms industry was sponging up all the discretionary funds of sportsmen, or some hybrid semblance thereof.

All he knew, felt in his bones, was that he was on the chopping block. Although some anxiety stirred within his abdomen, he couldn't assign it to fear, for the only adjoining thought was, *then I will be free!*

At this point in Mickey's 'career,' multiple federal and local law enforcement agencies had been collaborating on apprehending a suspected interstate serial killer. It took quite some time for the realization to hit them, that they were dealing with such an accomplished sexual sadist.

After all, murdered and mutilated hot mammas weren't that atypical across the great states; and use of a knife was nearly universal, not only because the tool was typically readily accessible, but because the dominance-lusting usual suspects liked their action, and reaction, up close and personal.

One may perceive that necrophilia and cannibalism aren't quite as taboo as the general public had been led to believe, since the authorities didn't consider a solitary culprit, a lone wolf, a solo sadist, until a pattern arose. Maybe if Mickey had rotated regions, and sampled the carcass queue more completely, he wouldn't have prompted such interest in his exploits.

However, when the bite marks where more than thirty girls' mammary ducts had been liberated lined up, a multi-agency mission was mounted. The deceased's ever-present defleshed rearends, his mastication act's morbid mate, only solidified his calling card. Yeah, admittedly, Mickey never altered the ritual he so loved, once initiated in Temple.

Except for the skull fucking part; that fit of nigromancy never resurfaced, and he had no interest in psychagogia, or jiuji, or anything else with his vanquished *Vogue* models. What he wanted from them, he already took.

How many sarcomeres of prime skeletal muscle had the demented one devoured? How many nubile nipples had the warped one wrenched free of their supple mounds? The detectives scowled at the crime scene and autopsy photographs scattered amongst other investigatory evidence strewn about their large conference room desk, disgusted at the irregularly scooped-out breasts and butts before them.

("Are you a butt man, or a boob man?" Mickey was once asked in youth; he didn't get it.) Mickey knew his handy work was gaining a grander audience after mainstream network news outlets began showcasing his case.

Mickey also knew the investigators weren't getting near the glory, nor the glee, that his real-time reels revealed. Only *he* was graced with the brilliance that permeated the point of view on his footage. And that luster, only the blade could project. Oh, so many blood baths in paradise!

Those baptized in butchery had their tunnel of light substituted for a polaroid flash; their Jacob's ladder whittled away, the blade leaving only brutal descent into an infernal pit of carnage. Mickey's gullet served as sarcophagus for samples, the remainder of their mortal coils cast to waterway or ditch entombments. (Somewhere along the way, he decided just leaving the corpses where they lie after shooting action sequences abroad, wasn't such a good idea.)

Even though he had always been more discreet and cautiously thorough when 'shitting where he eats,' the mounting investigation was making him feel commensurate climbing pressure. To his demon, there was no effect. The only pressure it was feeling, was that which was brewing in its loins, owing to the kill-fuck-taste rest interval.

Though the gap had steadily been narrowing, the drive of bestial barbarism only blossomed. Heck, the carnal exercise was approaching super-set status. Seeing the writing on the wall, Mickey didn't wait for the inevitable; he promptly called his employer and offered his resignation. Now, the demon could take on his true form. Serving no master but himself. Seen by none, except for the poor souls to whom he revealed himself. Everywhere, and nowhere. His only burden now: the tower of luscious keepsakes infused in 'film.'

Knowing they were closing in, Mickey's singular purpose gained momentum. His only modus operandi: curate as much cold cunt charcuterie as possible, before he was stopped. Cutting ties with the knife community only made him more untraceable. The college-aged-corpse connoisseur had no intentions of surrender, nor retreat.

He wasn't going to prison: no starlets of his persuasion

could be found there to lust after; the iron corridors too, absent of luscious steel luster. He would rather die with his boots on, than lick heels.

On a fine hunting-weather afternoon, Mickey was beseeched by an authoritative voice while crossing the street. He barely registered the commands boisterously emanating from the dark-suited, heavy-set man exiting an unmarked vehicle, "Stop right there. Put your hands up!" The detective (already burdened with hypertension, obesity, and diabetes) had to suddenly scramble for his sidearm when, to his astonishment, the would-be detainee launched into the would-be apprehender's immediate space.

Initially surprised at his lucky break in spotting the notorious necro-nibbler, total disbelief washed over the habitual homicide investigator, who was thrust into the front-row seat of this blade ballet. His mind just couldn't believe what his sensory organs were telling it: Mickey had given the career criminal catcher a master class demonstration in the art of iaido.

Despite his years of carrying and training with his service pistol, he received a snap-cut to his throat from the lunging assailant, before he could even draw his piece. Whether Mickey had just cut the slash a little short in his haste, or the recipient had too much fat, or there was just no stopping the conditioned motor program, inherent to the policeman, once the neural order was sent, a muzzle report responded to the silent strike.

Mickey was instantly deprived of any follow-up combos to correct his contact mistake, since the 9mm counterstrike from his opponent vaporized his central command center. There would be no more headshots for this vanity vacuum; open casket viewing was no longer optional.

A few weeks down the road, after all the fanfare,

awards, ceremonies, dinners, news and podcast interviews, and other special treatment for the 'world's worst serial killer' catcher had petered out, Detective Trace found himself pulling out that little memento again.

That one polaroid, that somehow slid into his pants pocket instead of going into the evidence locker. ("I don't know how you do it, having to see that…stuff all the time," he heard his peers proclaim in his memories; "See no evil, hear no evil, speak no evil!") He didn't know why he absentmindedly sequestered the photo at the time. They surely didn't need it, with the mountain of damning digital data; and the perp was extinct, anyway.

He justified the involuntary act in his mind by asserting that the concrete evidence of vehement violence would keep him vigilant. That the macabre evidentiary material would remind him of his duties, and that the seemingly surreal, was all *too* real.

Those silly excuses vanished into thin air quicker than they developed, left only by a rapidly roaring seduction from the svelte sinew showcased in the splendid slaughter scene. Unable to deny the arousal, nor his slick, stiff shaft, Trace set his plans in place.

So, while awaiting his first opportunity to continue the tradition, for unlawful carnal knowledge he'd been deprived, the detective studied the photo still.

How illustrious!

No Pain, No Gain

Paul Lonardo

Antoine was about to hit the locker room for a shower when a massive shadow engulfed him, along with half of the gym. He thought the place might be closing early for some reason and the owner was shutting off the lights – but then he caught sight of the walking mountain of a man with a chest of chiseled marble, bulging legs like boulders, and arms as thick as the trunks of giant sequoias. He made Arnold Schwarzenegger look like Pee Wee Herman.

A perpetual smile was fixed above a square, rigid jaw. His blond hair was thin and long, flowing to his shoulders to accentuate an enormous neck and traps any bodybuilder would envy. Antoine self-consciously brought his right hand up to his own neck, one he'd once been so proud of, and it felt like he was gripping a pencil.

The giant was wearing a tight tank top that was stretched so thin it looked like it might rip apart at the seams. It was black with red block lettering that read, BODY BY BRANKO. On the back was the definitive bodybuilding and all-purpose male maxim, SIZE MATTERS.

Antoine couldn't take his eyes off the guy. It took him several moments to notice that there were two people in tow behind him, a woman with an expensive camera and a man carrying lighting equipment. They were like twin moons pulled into the orbit of an immense planet.

Antoine was watching the crew set up their equipment in front of the T-REX BODYBUILDING sign at the back of the gym when the owner came out of his office. Rex, a former bodybuilding champion, looked like a child next to the colossus in the tank top. As the two shook hands, Rex handed a folded sheet of paper to the man, who stuffed it into the black fanny pack around his waist.

Antoine strolled over and stood beside Rex, who observed the photoshoot with a prideful grin.

"Who the hell is that, Rex?" Antoine asked.

Rex didn't take his eyes off the muscle man as he posed and flexed for the lens, curling the heaviest dumbbells like they were nothing.

"That's the guy who's going to put T-REX back on the map," he said. "It cost me quite a bit to get him to come in and sit for a couple photos, but this ad campaign could put me in position to open that second location I've always dreamed about."

Rex seemed to avoid looking directly at him. He was wearing dark sunglasses, something Antoine had never seen Rex do inside, but he didn't think anything more of it. "Yeah, but who is he?"

"His name is Branko Zoric."

Antoine scratched his head. "I never heard of him."

"Well, he's not exactly from around here."

"A guy that big wouldn't go unnoticed. Not in the bodybuilding world."

Rex leaned in close to Antoine and spoke in a

conspiratorial whisper. "He's supposed to have come up with some new training method. You should meet him. I'm sure he could do something for you if you ask him."

This immediately grabbed Antoine's attention because it was exactly what he needed. One last shot at the big time before it was too late. It had been a half dozen years since he won a competition, and he hungered for the respect and adulation that—for him—could only be achieved standing on the top tier of the stage after winning an event.

He may have been past his prime, but he thought he had something left. Over the past couple of years, he had lost everything in the pursuit of reaching that level of success. His wife wanted to have kids, and after five years she couldn't wait anymore so she divorced him. She got the house and his Corvette. He moved into a small apartment and drove a Kia.

Having Branko walk into his life at that time was a sign of better things to come, Antoine thought, and he had to go for it. He couldn't afford not to.

When the gym owner walked away, he shuffled gingerly with a waddling gait. Antoine attributed it to an aging weightlifter doing a little too much on the squat rack, and then he waited until Branko was through and the small crew had everything packed up before making his approach. He stuck out his right hand and introduced himself. "Antoine Rivera."

"How do you do?" The man spoke with a heavy Eastern European accent and took Antoine's hand, along with part of his wrist as he shook it. "Branko Zoric."

"Sorry to intrude," Antoine began, "but as a fellow competitive bodybuilder—though certainly I'm not in your league—I have to say your physique is amazing."

"Thank you, but I have to correct you, I don't compete professionally."

"On behalf of bodybuilders everywhere, thank you,

because you would win every competition you entered."

Branko laughed good-naturedly.

"What I mean is you deserve a lot of credit and respect for your work ethic," Antoine continued. "I, for one, can appreciate it, and that's why I must ask if you can teach me how to develop my body the way you did."

Branko sighed deeply. "I'm afraid I can't do that."

"I tried everything, and nothing is working for me. I've been killing myself in the weight room. There's nowhere else I can turn. You've obviously come up with a phenomenally effective workout regimen I simply must try."

Branko shook his head definitively. "I just couldn't in good conscious recommend it for anyone." He turned to leave. "I'm sorry."

In a bold move, that surprised himself, Antoine stepped directly in front of the enormous man, blocking his path. "Please. I beg you. I'm desperate. I don't have anything else. Please."

Branko sighed again. "It's not that I don't want to help you, but my training method is …unorthodox. It's not for everyone. You'll gain the extra size you want, but at a considerable hardship."

"If I could get anywhere close to your size, it would be worth it, no matter what I had to endure."

A smile played at the corners of Branko's mouth. "I really shouldn't do this," he said as he removed a business card from his fanny pack and handed it to Antoine.

It read, BODY BY BRANKO, and listed a downtown address, but no phone number or email. "Meet me tomorrow at 1 PM." He walked away and the floor seemed to tip in that direction.

Antoine was so excited he almost fell over.

***

The next day, Antoine arrived at the address ten minutes early. He thought he might actually be in the wrong place, because rather than a gym he found himself in an abandoned industrial park.

He strode up to a random door and peeked inside. To his surprise, it opened when he tried the handle. Entering, he wandered the maze of corridors until he spotted Branko inside one of the suites. He wore nerdy glasses and a white lab coat. If this was some kind of disguise, it wasn't working, Antoine thought. The guy was simply too big to be mistaken for anyone else.

The colossus saw him and waved.

Antoine entered the suite and peered around. "So, where's the weight room?"

"There's no gym here." Branko smiled. "I offer something completely different. As I told you yesterday, I'm not a professional body builder."

Antoine gazed at the lab coat and nodded in understanding. "You're a scientist, aren't you?"

Branko didn't say anything. Instead, he smiled that gigantic smile once again.

"Let me guess, you've probably done work for the government."

Branko wagged a finger and offered a conspiratorial smile. "That's not something I am at liberty to talk about."

"I knew it," Antoine said. "All right. So, maybe you were once involved in a secret experiment for muscle gain that you're not supposed to disclose. Not to worry, I promise I won't tell a soul."

"Covertness is very much my stock-in-trade, Antoine. And while I do believe you, I must ask you to sign this." Branko produced a tri-folded document and presented it to Antoine.

"Is this one of those nondisclosure agreements?"

Antoine asked as he unfolded the single sheet of paper. He squinted, holding it at arm's length, trying to focus his eyes. He didn't have his reading glasses, and it was impossible for him to make sense of the small, cursive handwriting penned in spidery red ink.

"It's a standard release form," Branko told him.

"Where do I sign?"

"Anywhere is fine."

Before Antoine could ask for a pen, Branko had one in hand. It produced the same red ink, which soaked into the paper upon contact.

Branko scooped up the document, blowing on it to hasten the drying process, then stuffed it into a pocket of his lab coat. "Just one other thing, Antoine. You also need to know that while the results are guaranteed—you'll achieve all the size you desire, and then some—it's not going to last forever."

"Well, nothing lasts forever, does it," Antoine chirped.

"Follow me." Branko led Antoine into a room around the corner. Everything in the room was red, the floor tiles a slightly deeper shade than the plaster walls and ceiling. The light from the single overhead fixture was dim, which made the room appear even smaller than it was.

The only items inside were a small cot, adorned with red bedding, of course, and a mop sitting in a bucket of water. A metal grate covered the drain in the middle of the floor.

Those details put together evoked a primal fear reaction in Antoine, and for the first time he questioned if what he was about to do was worth it. Then he looked at the incredible size and girth of the man in front of him and his doubts evaporated.

"For true growth, it's not only muscle you must tear to allow it to repair and grow, but you must also break down bone. *That's* the secret to achieving the ultimate size and strength."

Antoine snorted in amusement. "How do your break down bone?"

On cue, a bald, man, equally as large as Branko, head shining in the dim light, strode in. His skin was honeyed, almost every inch of which was covered in tattoos, including his thick, veiny neck. He gripped a sledgehammer in one hand.

"What's that for?" Antoine asked nervously.

"Don't worry," Branko said with a cocksure grin. "When you heal, you'll be bigger and stronger than you ever thought possible."

"What do you mean, *when I heal*?"

"Is there any area in particular you want to work on?" Branko ignored Antoine's question. "If you don't mind me saying, your calves are a little disproportional. We'll fix those later."

In the blink of an eye, Branko grasped Antoine in a firm chokehold.

"What are you doing?" Antoine shrieked, completely immobilized.

"Just relax."

Tattoo Man approached and stood in front of them.

Antoine's eyes widened with terror as Tattoo Man raised the hammer over his head. All Antoine could do was scream as the broad, steel head of the hammer swooped down.

The initial impact on Antoine's upper right arm instantly shattered his humerus; the pain was unlike anything he'd ever experienced before, which included broken bones, torn tendons, as well as a bout of kidney stones. The agony was savage, and it washed around his entire body like a pain tsunami.

Tattoo Man continued to swing the hammer like some perverse Thor, striking Antoine in the chest, upper and lower legs, and shoulders; Antoine's screams for mercy went ignored.

Like tree branches being snapped in half, pink-white shards of splintered bone ripped through Antoine's skin all over his body. Cartilage and tendons were pulverized by that unrelenting hammer as the blood spilling from the gaping wounds spattered the walls and puddled upon the floor. It appeared to disappear at once, absorbing into the interior of the room like the red ink into the contract Antoine had signed – it was as if the room itself was *drinking* it.

After what felt like an eternity of pain, Antoine's nerve endings reached the point at which they could no longer transmit to his overloaded brain. Not that he no longer felt the impacts, he just wasn't sure where he was being struck.

"Be sure to get those calves good," Branko instructed Tattoo Man with a fond smile.

Antoine heard snippets of other comments made by the two men as he was being bludgeoned, but their voices slowly faded into the gray haze of pain. His suffering was overwhelming, and, mercifully, his body began to shut down. As Antoine drifted into oblivion, the last thing he remembered was Branko pissing on him and laughing heartily.

Antoine didn't expect to survive, and with his last fragments of consciousness, he actually prayed he wouldn't. But he *did* awaken, and to his surprise there was no discomfort at all.

He did feel profoundly different, though.

Antoine knew he was in the same room. He lay on his back staring up at the red ceiling. He didn't want to move, fearful he was paralyzed. He had to gather the courage to look down at his lower half, expecting to see a mangled, broken body. What he saw instead made him wonder if he was dreaming. He wore a black singlet, and not only did he appear to be unmarred in any way, his legs were easily double the size!

The door to the room opened and Branko entered, a fat smile on his face.

"Is this Heaven?" Antoine asked.

The big man laughed. Only Branko did not seem so impressively big anymore, at least by comparison.

Antoine was almost his equal.

"You can move," Branko assured. "Go ahead."

Slowly, Antoine lifted his torso upright, swung his impossibly muscular legs to the side, and eased his bulk off the cot. He gazed down in wonderment at the bulging veins in his arms, chiseled abs, rippling pecs, and breathtaking quads. Turning his right leg out, he flexed his calf muscles and cackled with delight at their incredible size and definition.

"You're pleased with our results, I take it."

"I'm sorry I doubted you." Antoine grinned back. "I feel like a million bucks."

Branko nodded in satisfaction. "Hopefully, your new body will earn you the $20,000 prize money at the NPD competition tonight."

Antoine snapped his head up at Branko, looking away from his body for the first time. "That's *tonight*? I haven't missed it?"

"Not yet," Branko told him. "But you'd better get going."

***

There were a ton of big guys at the competition, but none bigger than Antoine. Everyone was amazed by his size and definition. He won so easily it was almost embarrassing; as a result he was invited to compete in the Eastern Regionals.

And just like that, everything changed for Antoine, not just his body but his entire life. He enjoyed his newfound celebrity, and all the perks that went with it, including the beautiful Jamaican fitness model he began dating. He worked hard to get ready for the Regionals, excited about his future for the first time since he was a teenager when he picked up a barbell for the first time and took up bodybuilding.

Antoine was the favorite to win the Regionals and eventually go on to compete for Mr. World in Las Vegas the following spring. Then two days before the show, he woke in a cold sweat. He sat upright in bed for a moment, feeling strange but unsure what was wrong. He was alone; Chandice was due to return from a photoshoot that night. His gaze fixed on the trophy he'd won at the NPD Invitational before he caught sight of his own image in the mirror atop the dresser.

"Oh, my God!" The words caught in his throat.

Antoine didn't recognize the person staring back at him in abject horror, but when he moved, so did the skeletal figure in the looking glass. He peered down at his body, hoping it was an illusion of some kind, like those mirrors in a funhouse that distort everything. It looked even worse to the naked eye.

It was his body all right, but without any muscle mass to speak of. It was pretty much the weedy physique he had in high school before he ever started lifting.

Panic gripped Antoine, his heart began to race. "This can't be," he cried out. He jumped out of bed and just stood there for a moment, not knowing what to do. His first thought was of Chandice, and what she would say if she saw him like this.

He was glad she was away, but he had to do something fast – his only chance was to find Branko.

Scrambling quickly to get dressed, Antoine found none

of his clothes fit; he left home swamped by a T-shirt ten sizes too big and holding up the waistband of the smallest pair of shorts he could find.

Antoine raced to the industrial park in the hope of finding Branko. He managed to locate the same suite, but this time it was completely empty. The red room looked the same, only with that awful sledgehammer resting on the floor; no Tattoo Man wielding it. Frustrated, Antoine wanted nothing more than to tear the place apart, and in a fit of rage he reached for the hammer...

To his profound dismay, however, Antoine found he was unable to lift the damn thing.

"Brankoooooooo!" he screamed out his frustration.

"Back for more?"

Spinning around, Antoine saw Branko standing in the doorway with that big, smug grin on his huge face.

"What the fuck happened?" Antoine fumed. "Look at me!"

"I did say it wouldn't last," Branko said. "And you signed the contract." He produced the document out of thin air and flipped it at Antoine.

"What's this?" Antoine asked after examining it more closely. "I can't read this."

"It would be surprising if you could. It's Latin," Branko informed him. "And that's your signature right there. *Antoine Rivera.*"

Antoine's frail body stiffened with rage. "Who the fuck are you?"

"You know who I am." Branko gave Antoine a sinister sneer.

The contract burst into flames in Antoine's hands and was gone.

In that same instant, Tattoo Man entered the room wielding an even larger sledgehammer than the one Antoine had been unable to even pick up off the floor.

"No." Antoine shook his head in defiance. He refused endure the agony of that hammer and the cruel indignity of being a toilet for the devil just for a short-term favor. Even if it meant never getting that magnificent body back. "I won't… *can't* do it."

"Have it your way," Branko said as his body transformed before Antoine's eyes. His flesh withered and turned black as soot, brittle, like it had been seared in the hottest of furnaces. His eyes sunk into their blackened sockets to become dark, empty holes. Then, Satan laughed, and a disgusting, sulfurous stench poured from his gaping maw.

As Satan promptly disappeared in a billow of thick, black smoke, Antoine knew first-hand that the devil was real; It was not something he would ever have believed if he hadn't seen it for himself. Even if Satan's visage had merely been a manifestation of his own mind—it was *exactly* the way he'd always pictured the Fallen Angel— Antoine knew he was responsible for allowing such evil into his life in the first place. He got the impression Lucifer would look different to everyone, conjured into existence by the human imagination, which didn't make him any less real.

The other thing Antoine inherently understood was that souls are inalienable and cannot be separated from an individual, let alone *sold*. Even the signing of a hellish contract inked in blood could not make such a transaction biding, whether done unwittingly or with full knowledge and consent.

It became clear to Antoine that Satan wanted something from him in exchange for the gift of substantial muscle mass, however brief it had lasted. Satan's only goal, or course, was to inflict misery and pain upon people, and trick them into doing his bidding.

And that gave Antoine an idea.

***

Over the following months, Antoine worked hard to gain back at least some of the size and strength he'd been given, although he wasn't able to get anywhere close to where he'd been even before his pact with the devil. Chandice left him, but that was all right, she'd just proven to him how shallow she really was.

Antoine walked into an empty T-Rex's shortly after closing. He carried a gym bag at his side, but he was not there to work out. His stride was awkward as he struggled to maintain his balance, thanks to the weight of the bag. He headed with purpose straight to Rex's office.

Rex, wearing his trademark dark glasses, sat behind his desk with his laptop open. He looked up in surprise when he saw Antoine.

Antoin closed and locked the door behind him, then strode up to the desk and stopped. He placed the gym bag on the floor. "What does he look like?" he asked Rex.

Rex was nonplussed. "What does *who* look like?"

"Satan. What does he look like to you?"

"Are you crazy?" Rex was dismissive, annoyed.

Antoine reached across the desk grabbed Rex's sunglasses off his face.

And found himself staring into empty, black sockets that promised to drag him into the darkest pits of hell itself.

With great difficulty, Antoine forced himself to look away and, bending down, he unzipped the gym bag at his feet. He pulled out the hammer secreted beneath the towels and gym clothes within.

As he raised the weapon, Rex pushed his chair back against the wall behind him and stood, ready to flee, but there was nowhere he could go.

"What the hell are you doing?" The alarm in Rex's

voice was sweet, sweet music to Antoine's ears.

It took all the strength Antoine had, but he managed to wield the hammer with enough force to strike Rex hard and fast in a flurry of blows. The first strike created a dull, wet, *popping* sound as it cracked Rex's skull like a fairground coconut and spun him around.

Blood spattered the wall behind Rex, turning it into a Jackson Pollock canvas. And, as he screamed in terror and agony, the next blow made a direct hit to the back of his neck. Cervical vertebrae shattered, Rex was silenced in an instance; he dead and on the floor before Antoine stepped around the side of the desk to bash in his head and face until there was nothing left but a crushed mess of flesh, skull, and brain matter.

Perspiring, exhausted, Antoine straightened up and gazed down with a sense of triumph at what he'd done. The gym owner had clearly made his own covenant with Satan and had set up Antoine so he might continue the devil's work. The gym owner got what he deserved, in Antoine's opinion, and Satan had corrupted a soul. As far as Antoine was concerned, the diabolical ledger was balanced in full.

Antoine dropped the hammer into the bloody pulp of Rex's head and strutted out of the gym feeling a whole lot bigger in stature than ever before.

Of Flesh and Kin
Anthony Ferguson

Visiting Gramma Annie's farm was somewhat of a family tradition. Some of my earliest memories were of lying on the carpet in that sitting room that never seemed to change as the years passed. Surrounded by Ma and Pa, Gramma and Pop. Same tired ornaments, same dust-tinged framed photographs. Think I might even have said my first words at Gramma's kitchen table. Probably something along the lines of, "Not the goddamn meatloaf again!"

I still went along with it in my teens, even though it had grown a little tiresome. Well, except that one summer when I hit my teens and discovered Pa's secret girlie magazine collection. In the following years, no matter where he moved his dirt rag stash, I'd always sniff it out like a horny bloodhound.

But I moved past that. Couple of years went by and I had been lucky enough to make some friends and discover the sensually and spiritually stimulating three dimensional delights of real girls. Sometimes I even brought one along to the farm, but this one summer I was on my lonesome again, so a break from the city seemed like a fine idea. Breathe in that country air.

Back then of course it wasn't just Gramma's farm. Pop Chet was still around before the tragedy that took him away. I'll get to that a little later. Pop was Ma's dad, so when my own father suddenly left us for "that other woman" as Ma referred to her, when I was sixteen, the visits continued.

Pop was a fine figure of a man and someone I always looked up to, literally; he stood over six feet tall and was battle hardened by military service. Something I admired but did not aspire to. Always ready with a friendly word of advice on almost any topic.

Taught me a lot about the animals he kept around. Sheep, cows, and of course, his favorite, the pigs. He was a cheeky old coot as well. Often passed a wry comment about any girls I might bring to the farm, always delivered just out of their earshot but not mine, accompanied by a sly wink. Even if I didn't quite get the meaning in my tender years, I understood the implication with all the hormonal rage of a pubescent boy.

The one topic Pop never discussed was his time in the service. Gramma would tell me on the quiet he had nightmares from the some of the things he saw out there in that war in Iraq. It was a place with a funny name I had never heard of till I got curious and looked it up.

Chet never talked about the war, and any time anyone would bring it up he would go all quiet and angry and sort of curl up into himself. I tried to broach it with him as I got older, like any curious kid would, but nothing doing. Even the time I found one of his old medals. He just snatched it back and hid it away again. To me it was like finding an ancient treasure. A piece of a terrible history I could only imagine, but the look of horror on Pop's face burned itself into me, because it was twinned with another unexpected expression—that of shame.

But the farming he loved. Gramma used to marvel at how he would throw himself into it. She hinted at it being his way to work out all his pent-up anger at the world and its wars. Sometimes she would pull out the photo albums and show us some of Pop and his war buddies, but I noticed none of those buddies ever came to visit, nor even call.

Pop did most of the work himself, Gramma pitching in where she could. He cultivated the small amount of crops and tended to the animals. As I mentioned, the pigs were his favorite. I remember one time I was about eleven, and Pop took out a big copperhead with his axe. Thing must have been six feet long. Anyway, he picked the still twitching body up on the end of a rake and bid me follow him to the pig pen.

"The beautiful thing about these porkers, son," he said with a gleam in his eye as he tossed the dying snake into the pen, "is that they will devour anything, bones and all."

The following rush of muddy trotters, excited squealing and feeding frenzy backed up his words. I can still hear his low chuckle as he watched the pigs do their stuff. I saw the glint in his eyes, which stayed with me for years after.

It was that and other little things that struck me as odd but were shuffled aside and ignored at the time, but all added up in the long run. Like when I took Nancy, one of my high school sweethearts, to the farm on a weekend stay. Separate rooms of course, though Gramma had no inkling what we got up to in the middle of the night. Pop, I'm not so sure.

On the Sunday afternoon I had been mucking out the stables when I returned to find Nancy perched on the end of my bed. She was all wound up like an alarm clock.

"Nance? What's wrong?"

I got nothing out of her for ten minutes, but I could see

she was visibly distressed. Her eyes were wide open and she was shaking. Eventually, after much cajoling and sympathy, she came out with it.

"He cornered me in my room."

"Who?" Though I didn't want to believe it, I knew who the only other *he* around the farm was.

"Your grandpa," she said.

"What did he do?" I asked, terrified of hearing the answer.

She shook her head, prompting me to fill in the empty spaces. "Did he touch you? Did he hurt you?"

Another shake of the head. "Not exactly... He said I was a fine-looking little filly, and I'd be pretty ripe for saddling up and riding soon enough... but it was the look on his face that scared me most. It made me feel dirty."

"Nancy, I—"

"Then I tried to get around him to leave the room." She cut me off, so I clammed up.

"At first he moved to block me, laughing, then he stood aside and let me pass. As I ran by, he slapped me on the ass. It really stung."

As you can imagine, the rest of the day and the supper that followed was mighty awkward. Nance avoiding Pop's gaze, and barely touching her food. It made me angry, too. I was determined to confront him, or say something to Gramma, but when the opportunity arose, I just couldn't do it.

That was it for me and Nancy, too. She ghosted me the next week and barely spoke to me again. Can't say I blame her, either.

Things carried on as they do. After Pa left, ma found religion and spent a lot of time either in church or doing churchy stuff. By the time I hit my college years, I was left to myself a lot. Not that I minded. I had dalliances with several girls, normal stuff, nothing too serious. Ma still insisted on visiting Gramma, especially after Pop's terrible hunting accident. She had lost her father, but being a good person, she felt an obligation to make sure her mother-in-law was doing alright.

No way Gramma could keep up the physical side of the farm, so most of the animals were slowly sold off to market, even Pop's beloved pigs. The crops fell by the wayside too, but Gramma got by on Pop's army pension.

Ma and I got on just fine. She loved me well enough as her only child. The only time we had anything approaching a major disagreement was the time she found a pair of women's panties in my room. I heard her hollering and came running, to find her holding them at arm's length, face white as a sheet.

I'll never forget the look she gave me, a blend of malevolence and fear.

"Where did you get these, Taylor?"

I explained, my face turning a shade of crimson. "They're Tammy's," one of my dalliances from a local youth club.

"Please tell me you did not steal these off a wash line."

"What? No, Ma. She... she left them here one day. I was meaning to give them back to her but kept forgetting. Then we broke off."

Ma looked me up and down, trying to probe for a flaw in my story. Eventually she backed down and thrust them at me.

"Just get rid of them." She retracted her arm before I could take the offending item, which to my shame I realized I had never washed. "No, I'll do it. Just..."

Ma sat down hard on the edge of the bed and pulled me down next to her. For my part, I was just relieved she hadn't focused on the fact as to why Tammy had been removing her panties in my bedroom, so the lecture that followed took a sharp turn from the one I was expecting about godliness, purity and fidelity.

Ma took a deep breath and tears formed in her eyes.

"Ma, what's wrong?"

"You got me worried, son. I only hope what you tell me is true. You see there are some men… who make a habit of taking stuff off women to keep. God knows, some of them even wear them. Men with things wrong with their minds. Sometimes, even men you might be close to. Folks who you never realize till too late that they have another side to them, a darker side."

We stared at each other.

"Pa?" I asked. Swallowing deep.

She shook her head slowly. "No, not your pa. He was a different kind of asshole, but he wasn't a pervert. Just a regular adulterer. Trust me, I'd know."

A look of understanding passed between us. No words were necessary. There was only one other dominant male figure in our lives.

Which brings me back to the present day in this fine long summer. Class was out and I was going quite well in my ambition to become a psychologist. I had a growing interest in the machinations of the human mind and had become a keen observer of other people. If that's one way of saying I'm a nosey bastard, I apologize in advance.

Ma insisted I go check on Gramma and spend a few days on the farm. She had some church charity drive event happening, so reluctantly, I shoved a few belongings in my pack and headed out there. Ma dropped me at the bus station, which got me to the nearest town, and I easily hiked the two miles out.

Gramma seemed happy to see me, though I had started to notice a certain hesitance in her, the hugs getting less intense as I got older, but I put that down to her acceptance of my approaching manhood. I don't think it had anything to do with religion for her, as I never heard her say anything about God, nor were there any icons and whatnot around the house.

I had also sensed a growing tension between her and ma on our last couple of visits too, the more ma disappeared into the arms of the church.

It got worse after Pop's accident.

Pops loved his hunting out in the miles of woods surrounding the farm. Mostly for deer and rabbit, which often appeared on the menu at the dinner table. He would set traps in the woods for the rabbits and occasionally, around the perimeter of the farm, for the foxes that would bother his chickens.

It was one of them contraptions that did for the old man one day out in the woods. Seems he stepped into one of his own traps, stumbled, and shot himself in the face with his own gun. Being a solitary man, pops always hunted on his own, like he did most things. Never met a man who liked his own company as much as Pops Chet.

Now what struck me as odd, was how a man like him, with all his military training and experience with woodsmanship and hunting, could come to step into one of his own traps. Gramma explained it as he stumbled or tripped over something, or he had an episode. The old man had an issue with a dicky heart, took the pills for it with him everywhere. Maybe, Gramma said, he had a turn and that set him off kilter.

The medicos sort of backed up this version of events, as it transpired the old man had a heart attack right around the time he shot himself in the head. Definitely not a suicide, everyone insisted, as he just wasn't that sort of guy. Never suffered much from depression, or any of those other mental issues experienced by war vets.

Yet there was just something that didn't sit right with me, and I think Gramma had begun to sense it, too. She had warned me off going out wandering in the woods, on account of Pop's traps, she said, even though the state troopers had done a sweep and cleared them out. She also warned me about wolves, though I never saw any out there.

Yes, I did go out of course, curiosity always got the better of me. I visited the spot where pops died and observed the mementoes left there by Gramma and Ma. Ma was upset, but again, I couldn't help but notice a certain hesitance in her mourning, and I harkened back to the chat we had when she found the panties in my room.

It was my inquisitive nature that also drew me to Pop's big shed down the far end of the back yard. It was a place always forbidden to me as a kid. Being full of dangerous chemicals and sharp tools being the reason given, which I never questioned of course.

But as I grew older and stronger, I felt it calling to me, in the same way my deadbeat Dad's girlie mags somehow called to me in my younger years. The shed seemed like a harbinger of the forbidden, a place that held secrets to be discovered.

Gramma was certainly keen to keep me out of there, that's for sure, which only made my itch scratch even worse. She put a big padlock on the door, much like she hid away most traces of the old man, even the family photos on her walls. Made her too upset, she claimed.

The lock was no deterrent to me, as my probing soon discovered a loose panel around the side of the shed, toward the back, half hidden by an out-of-control blackberry bush. A hidden wasp nest hindered my progress at first, and I wore a few of their angry stings before I dealt with them.

Eventually, I squeezed my way into the forbidden zone. The skittering of tiny insectile feet accompanied my egress, and I was careful where I put my hands as I gained entry to the inner sanctum. The only light came from the sun, peaking through the cracks in the warping wood paneled walls, and coming through the one grimy, web encumbered window perched high up on the back wall, until eventually I bumped into what I at first thought was a trailing spider web, and jumped accordingly, but turned out to be a light cord hanging from the ceiling.

I tugged gently on it and the big space was flooded with the luminescence of a dim bulb. It revealed a room surrounded by grimy shelves filled with the usual implements gathered over a lifetime by a self-sufficient woodsman. Garden tools and mechanical items, lots of bottles filled with indeterminate liquids.

A wooden bench with a vice and grinding wheel set in it, which still worked, as I ascertained when I flicked the switch and set it in motion. Pretty impressive overall as I had been told that the old man built the whole place with his own hands.

Another thing that struck me was the odd smell that seemed to permeate the structure. A mixture of mold and grease and something else. Something a bit like copper. I was trying to picture where I knew that smell from when I heard it, the faint but distinct sound like a rattle.

"Shit!"

I wheeled around and saw flash of something slithering beneath the legs of the shelves across the clear middle part of the shed. Without taking my eyes of it, I slowly reached beside me for a conveniently placed shovel, one of pop's collection of spades and digging implements.

I whispered a quiet prayer of thanks to the old man as I backed up away from the edges of the benches. That's when my I stumbled as I heard a crunch and something splintered under my trailing foot. I almost fell but managed to right myself as the rattler slid out from its hiding place and moved menacingly toward me, as if sensing a threat.

"Christ almighty!" The snake raised its head and let off a warning rattle. Relying entirely on instinct or self-preservation, I leapt aside as it lunged and somehow planted the spade down right on its upper back, not far from the head.

The serpent thrashed and rattled in anger, its tail whipping that rattle around and I almost flinched as it struck me several times on the legs, but my inner resolve made me lean in even harder on the handle of that spade. I drove the rattler's head firmly into the concrete floor, again silently thanking Pops for his resolute handyman skills.

Adjusting my body and planting both feet firmly on the ground. I leaned in with all my weight and slowly felt the scaly flesh and sinew of the snake give way. The rattling grew angrier and more intense as I bore down with all the energy of a youth in his prime, until I separated the head from the body. The head lay still while the body rolled and thrashed away, but I knew the battle was won.

My first instinct was to get the hell out of that place, lest there were other nasties hidden in the dark, but then I remembered the splintering sound that had almost taken my balance away from me, and I turned to the small recess in the ground.

For some reason, Pops had left a small section of the floor unconcreted, and dug a small space into the earth beneath, which he had covered with the panel my foot had gone through. No doubt the wood had rotted away over time.

Checking my surroundings for any other serpentine threats, I dropped to my knees and pulled the broken cover away to expose the small recess in the floor. Seeing something sitting down there in semi-darkness, I reached a hand in tentatively and lifted it free.

The dust made me cough as I brushed the detritus off the cover of a musty hard backed scrapbook, a journal of sorts. I took it across to the bench beneath the window where Pops had installed a lamp. Thankfully, the globe still worked.

I prized the book open to a random page and felt a chill run down my spine. I flicked through several pages of scrawled heavy black text, but it was the drawings that accompanied them that sent a chill through me. Obscene renditions of female bodies. Anatomical diagrams and dissected body parts.

I held the book up closer to my disbelieving eyes.

That's when the polaroid photographs fell out.

I picked them up with shaking hands.

"Jesus!"

"Taylor!"

The sound of Grandma's voice sent my heart slamming upward to my throat like a carnival ride. For a moment I thought she was there in the shed with me. As I swung around, I realized the voice had come from outside.

"Shit!"

I stuffed the book back in the recess and quickly pulled the broken board back across. My heart pounded in my chest as I heard Gramma moving about somewhere outside in the yard. I hoped to Hell she didn't have the key to the padlock afront the shed or she would catch me red-handed before I could cover my tracks. It wasn't so much the guilt of invading this space where I had been forbidden to go, but the horror of having Gramma find out what her late husband, my grandfather, had been up to. I had a brief and absurd flashback to my fear of the old man catching me with his girlie mags.

The images held in those old photographs burned into my mind and a felt bile rise in the back of my mouth. Gramma called again, but thankfully, her voice came from further away. Relief that she hadn't found the loose board at the rear of the shed flooded through me, and I waited there on my haunches with the dead rattler for several minutes, until she stopped calling.

***

"There you are. Where did you get to?" Gramma asked as I let myself in the back door.

"Just went for a little walk, to take in the country air, Gramma," I said, not entirely convincingly, as I was still processing what I found in the shed.

"Not in them woods I hope."

"It's ok," I was glad to move the direction of the conversation away from the yard and the shed. "There are no more traps out there. The sheriff's office took care of that."

"Yes, but the wolves, and maybe even bears."

"Never seen any around these parts, and besides which, I'm a good runner," I gave a nervous laugh, as Gramma looked me up and down, unconvinced.

"You okay, hon? You look a little peaky."

"I'm fine," I replied a little too quickly. "Got a touch of a cold coming on, maybe."

"Mmm. I got some hot soup that'll fix that up, quick. Just make sure you wrap up when you're out and about. The weather's turning."

What I really wanted was to get to my laptop to do some investigating and assuage the thoughts now nagging at me like a brain worm. Thank God I had ignored Ma's entreaties to leave it behind and take a complete break from my studies.

After supper and some awkward small talk, I watched an old sci fi movie on tv and waited from Gramma to take herself off to bed. Like most older folk, she was always up as the cock crowed, and it literally did around these parts, and exhausted by the early evening.

I watched out the side of my head as her eyes gradually slid down like a set of rickety old blinds, and she made her excuses and shuffled off to her room. I waited another half hour till the old house grew quiet, except for the crackle of the old wood fire, and the sound of insects and whatever else might be crawling inside the walls, trying and failing to maintain focus on the plot of the old black and white movie on the set. The old place was only one level, so Gramma was down the hall, and me in the spare room only two doors away.

Satisfied that she would be safely ensconced in whatever dreams old folk had, probably revisiting the happier days of youth. Though given what I had found in the shed, I began to wonder just how happy a younger Gramma could have been, if Pops was anything like the monster who produced that journal and took those Polaroids.

Fingers itching, I fired up the laptop and started researching the history of the county and the surrounding areas. I had snuck the Polaroids, seven of them, into my pockets before leaving the shed. I wasn't sure why, but something compelled me to hang on to those awful images of slain women.

I laid the photos out on the bedspread as grisly reminders of my task. Now I pored over the Internet for old murder cases. Not as easy a task as might be imagined in a country like ours, with so many stories of serial murder, but eventually, I was pretty sure I had the case I was looking for.

The number of victims matched, and the locales were within reach of the farm. Not too close to arouse suspicion, I guess, given the killer had never been apprehended. The only bit that threw me was the sobriquet, *The Shoe Fetish Slayer*.

This particular killer had a thing for women's apparel, and in particular, high heeled shoes. Could this have been Pops? I had a mind to go back to the shed and do some further investigating, maybe even right now, when I heard it… a noise beneath my feet.

I sat frozen in anticipation, waiting for further sounds of movement, and pondering where they could possibly have come from. When no further noise emanated, I started to think. The house was partly raised, so there could be a small crawl space beneath it.

Then it slapped me in the face. A basement. Could Pops have dug a basement to the old place, and if so, was someone down there now? I waited another few minutes and given there had been no further bumps in the night, I quietly let myself out of my room. I stood and glanced toward Gramma's closed door, listening for any evidence of movement or night rumblings, though I had never heard her snoring in all my visits to the farm.

Satisfied I was alone in my midnight perambulations, I made my way through the dark house searching for an entrance point to a sunken room which may or may not exist. Lucky, I had packed my little torch as a matter of habit. I was about ready to give it up when my light happened to flick downward in a built-in laundry cupboard. There, half hidden beneath a mop and bucket, was a circular handle, and as I traced around the perimeter, a square recess cut into the floor signifying an entrance point.

Half terrified of being caught, but also morbidly curious, I edged the bucket aside and gently pulled on the handle. The lid gave way with a slight creak which gave me pause, but nonetheless revealed a set of wooden steps, descending into pitch darkness.

Cautiously, I squeezed my frame through the gap, shutting the closet door behind me but leaving the lid ajar, and edged my way down the twelve steps, counting them as I went. Thankfully, once my feet hit the packed earth floor, I found a handy light switch and flicked it on.

The sight that unfolded before my bleary eyes stunned

me. Yet it was not quite the horror I had expected. No desiccated corpse hanging from chains from the ceiling. No pile of old bones. Instead, a neatly arranged space, with ordered shelves and hangers strewn with clothing.

However, closer inspection soon confirmed my worst suspicions. The clothes hanging on racks were female garments, and there, on the opposite wall behind me, a rack of high heeled shoes. It was these I approached, imagining the worst, like finding a pair of severed feet, all shriveled skin and jutting ankle bone, rotting inside a set of souvenired footwear. Nothing of the sort awaited, however. If anything, the shoes had been well preserved.

Head spinning, I turned my attention to a desk on the side wall looming in the shadows. I tentatively made my way across, dreading what I might find, but driven by the compulsion to know everything about Pop's dark secret.

There were two drawers in the desk, which I opened to find more scrawled notes, which seemed to contain address and drawings of locations on a map. I pulled the Polaroids from my pocket and fingered my way through them with disgust, noting the abject terror on the faces of these hitherto anonymous women, dressed in flimsy lingerie and high heels, bound and gagged and in some cases, trussed from the ceiling.

Their limbs pulled akimbo, wild hair strung with sweat, and tear-filled eyes tore me inside, imagining their terror as they bargained and pled for their lives, hoping against hope.

Pushing them aside, my eyes fell upon a dark object sitting atop the desk, covered in grime and cobwebs, an old-style film projectors. A chill ran through me. Gazing at the blank space on the opposite wall, and noticing an 8mm reel still sitting in place, I found the switch. Swallowing deep, with hesitating fingers, I flicked it on. It whirred into life and a six-foot image unfurled on the wall.

"Oh Christ, Pops!"

There he stood in the grainy footage, in all his ghastly glory. Pops in middle age, craggy but still an imposing battle worn figure, with a shock of cropped dark hair, grinning into the camera. Dressed head to toe in lingerie and wearing high heeled women's shoes, before him hung a gagged and squirming young woman, equally attired. I thanked the gods there was no sound, the camera lowered to reveal his naked lower body and his obvious state of arousal.

That was when I heard a noise behind me.

I swung around to be confronted by Gramma, standing across the packed earth floor at the foot of the stairs.

"We need to talk."

***

The whistle of the old steel kettle brought my spinning mind back to earth. I had a hundred questions to throw at Gramma as she poured us a steaming cup at the kitchen table, but I knew at this point I would be best placed to shut up and let her tell the story.

Gramma sat and eyeballed me through the steam rising off her mug.

She sighed. "He was a monster, Taylor, as I'm sure you've figured out by now."

I listened in shocked awe as Gramma poured out her tale of woe, with certain highlights sticking in my fevered mind.

"It started way back before he went off to war. I came home from the store one day, and he mustn't have heard me come in. That was the first time I caught him… wearing my under garments and a pair of high heels. He was looking at himself in the mirror. At first I let him explain it away, as curiosity and whatnot."

I studied her face, as her eyes dropped to the floor, mouth pulled down in a scowl.

"Then later I noticed some of the shoes that appeared in the closet weren't mine. He told me he had taken to buying his own stuff, and to mind my damn business. I just wanted to be a good wife, so I tried to understand. Soon after that, he bought that damn projector and took to making me dress up in stuff he would buy, lingerie and fancy shoes, and film me as I paraded around the room for his pleasure. Then he would make me film him all dressed up. He turned it into some sort of game."

She looked at me at this point, but it was fleeting, a look of shame.

"When he went off to the war, I thought it might stop. I hoped he would get it out of his system, but it didn't stop... it got worse. He came home a different man, more sullen and silent. He moved all his stuff out to that shed and bid me to mind my own damn business once again.

Then came the first girl."

"Gramma," I interjected. "You knew about that?"

"Yeah, I knew alright. Despite the music he was playing out there in that shed, I heard the girl scream. I banged on that door and hollered like Hell till he let me in, and I saw... oh God, I saw."

Grandma sobbed a little here, and I put my arm around her shoulder.

"You don't have to tell me anymore if you don't want to. I looked it up online."

"No, I need to tell it, boy. Get it out of my system.

"I don't know where he was getting the girls from. Hikers maybe. All of 'em so damn young. He would make them do what he used to make me do, dress up and parade around, before he... you know."

"Why didn't you try and stop him? Why didn't you go to the sheriff?"

"I couldn't! He threatened me. Told me the war had done things to him that I couldn't understand. I tried to run, but he laid a hell of a beating on me. Said I would end up like them if I ever tried to leave.

So, it went on, for years. His collection growing. Until one day he stopped, when he got too old for it. That's when he turned back on me to work out his anger. Till I couldn't take it no more."

Gramma paused, staring dead ahead, not looking at me, and that's when it hit me.

"Gramma... you shot him? That weren't no accident, was it?"

"I had to do it, Taylor, for me, and for them, all those poor girls."

I let this sink in and we sat there in silence for a few moments.

"But, now, Gramma, we have to tell. We have to! To give those girls' loved ones some closure."

Grandma lunged at me and grabbed me by the collar in both liver spotted hands, her eyes bulging.

"No! We can never tell. I couldn't take the shame it would bring on this family. Think of yourself. Think of your mother, Taylor. It would kill her. Please swear to me you will never tell. Promise me!"

I swallowed but gave her my word, and we sat and finished our lukewarm brew. The coolness of the coffee matched the coldness running through my chest.

The next day, I sat on the basement steps and watched her pack the shoes and garments into a box. Helped her carry it out into the yard where she set it alight and watched it burn. I forgot about the projector, but later while I was returning from the woods, I caught sight of her carrying it out to the shed, where she locked it away.

***

It was my last night at the farmhouse, and I lay in bed, tossing and turning, running Gramma's confession over and over in my head. I was deeply troubled as to how I was supposed to keep this nightmare bottled up inside me, like Gramma had done for years. I tried to think of poor Ma, and how the truth would destroy her.

More so, I thought over my own romantic history. Sure, while I wasn't by any means a violent man, I had nonetheless treated a lot of my girlfriends poorly, using them only for gratification, never thinking of them as emotional beings. A period which culminated in Ma finding one of my incipient panty collection. While I thought of it as a harmless teenage kick at the time, with the knowledge I now held of my own kin, I could see where that sort of behavior might lead if left unchecked.

As I was running the narrative back over and over, a sudden thought hit me. Gramma said he would make the girls dress up and parade around while he filmed them before raping, killing and dismembering them. The parts that didn't go to the pigs he would dispose of in the Holyoak River, over in the next county, she said. Some of which were later found. Why would he do that? Run the risk of having them found? Was he taunting the police? Did he want to be caught?

But what struck me was… how did Gramma know the intimate details of what Pops was up to?

A moon the color of bone shone down as I crept toward the shed once more. Using my secret loose board entry point, I pushed my way inside, waving a piece of birch around as I pulled the light switch, in case any nocturnal crawlers lurked unseen in the darkness.

Dull light flooded the room. The headless rattler corpse had gone, but I thought nothing of it. The projector sat atop the wooden bench, where Gramma had left it. An 8mm reel still sat in place.

A growing sickening feeling rose in my gut as I flicked the switch again. The home movie picked up where I had left off. The trussed-up girl struggling and yelling. A much younger Pops, in his prime, with his member swinging around in the air. I thanked God there was no sound, or if there was, I had no intention of finding the volume control.

Pops looked around mid-forties on the film, which seemed about right, as these killings went back over forty years. I wasn't sure what I was looking for, but then pops turned his head and addressed someone across the room.

Someone holding the camera.

The camera moved in toward him, and then it was placed on a convenient bench to take in the whole scene. A figure stepped into view alongside Pops, similarly clad in skimpy lingerie, stockings and high heels.

My hand shot to my mouth. I stared in disbelief even as I heard the shed door creak open behind me.

"I told you to stay out of this, Taylor."

I turned to where Gramma stood in the doorway, pointing a shotgun at me.

"I told you to let dead things rest. Why can't you listen, like a good boy?" Gramma sniffed away a tear, but the shotgun stayed firmly trained on me.

"You knew, Gramma. You knew all along. Why?"

"It was just fun to us, boy. You'll never understand. It was my way of staying close to him. Them little bitches never meant nuthin' to me. Most of 'em were godless runaways, got what they deserved."

"No, Gramma." Now I felt the tears coming.

"We were so good together." I saw her eyes flit beyond me to whatever was happening on the projector screen. I had no intention of looking.

"Then why did you kill him, Gramma?"

"That son of a bitch grew ornery once we got too old to

play our little games, and he started taking it out on me. I warned him to stop, but he took to me with his fists one time too many. Now, Taylor, like I said, you gotta let it go, let sleeping dogs lie."

I shook my head. "No Gramma… it ain't right. Those girls didn't deserve what you did to them. They got families who got a right to know."

Gramma cocked the trigger and shook her head.

"No, Taylor. I can't go to prison at my time of life. I'm sorry."

I realized too late she was going to pull the trigger.

"No, Gramma, please!"

A shot rang out, sending a flock of nightbirds screaming from the trees. I shut my eyes and opened them, looked down at my body. Saw and felt nothing. I looked up at Gramma. She smiled at me as a streak of blood oozed from her mouth. She spat out her false teeth, all bloody on the ground, then lurched over on top of them.

I looked past where she stood through the open door to where Ma stood holding the handgun I had given her for her last birthday.

***

The whistle screamed on the kettle, and Ma poured as we went over our story again.

"Did you know all along, Ma?"

"No, not exactly. I always knew something wasn't right, but I never put my finger on it. I never took to her, your Gramma, but I didn't imagine it would be as bad as this. Those films, Jesus."

"What was wrong with Pops, was it the war?"

She took a sip and eyeballed me through the rising steam of her cup. "I'd like to say it was, Taylor. That would make it easier, but there was always something wrong with

Daddy. I knew it growing up. I'll tell you the story all in good time. Right now, I think we have a very important phone call to make.

I followed her to the old telephone hanging on the sitting room wall.

"I'm glad I didn't turn out like him, Ma," I said, half hoping to at least convince myself.

She didn't turn. Her shoulders heaved in a sigh as she reached for the landline.

"You're nothing like him, Taylor. Nothing at all."

I looked beyond Ma's head, out the kitchen window, where a yellow moon hung like a lantern in the black night sky, and in the distance, I heard it, the howling of wolves.

Transplant
James H Longmore

The pain was excruciating, yet there was nothing she could do to get away from it. Her assailant had administered a muscle relaxant shortly after having spiked her margarita with Rohypnol back at the bar, what felt like a thousand years ago. They had also given her some kind of painkiller, because, despite the searing agony she was suffering through, it was still disproportionate in comparison to what her assailant was doing to her body. Surely that was a sign of compassion; perhaps she had a chance of getting out of this alive after all?

The keen, cold blade of the scalpel glinted as it traced its way down along the faint, white line that ran the length of the paralysed girl's sternum. A thin, red line appeared a fraction of a second after it; fat, crimson beads of blood popped out from the hair's breadth slit and trickled down along the outline of the girl's heaving ribs.

She tried her best to scream, fought in vain against her useless body to wriggle, shift, fight, anything – but it simply wouldn't respond, even when her torturer peeled back the *flawless, alabaster skin that covered her chest and cracked her sternum wide open with a hammer and chisel.*

The rush of cool, still air caressed her exposed lungs and beating heart, a weird, alien sensation that transcended even the agonizing pain that wracked her body and had her mind begging for the merciful swiftness of death.

But even that grim luxury evaded her; the combination of powerful drugs that swilled around her powerless body conspired to maintain consciousness, and she was all too aware of the fact she was being dissected like some ultimately dispensable lab rat.

She looked up into the eyes of the person who was destroying her young body, unable to discern if they were a man or a woman, young or old – all she could make out in those cold, dead eyes was something that had ceased to be entirely human a long, long time ago.

A strong tugging, pulling sensation in the exposed organs of her chest, the sharp snipping sound of precise surgical scissors, and the girl found herself staring with disbelief at the pink, spongy flesh of her own lungs as they were held aloft like some sick, twisted trophy, and all she could think of was the opening scene of The Lion King.

She suffocated to death in the end, her failing brain screaming out for the oxygen so cruelly denied following the deft removal of her lungs, her hollowed out chest cavity filling with thick, viscous blood as her heart twitched and shuddered to a complete, final standstill.

*

"What the hell, Joe?" Detective Bob Lyle growled at his partner, "how can you be eating in here? Especially *that*?" He nodded down with disdain to the fat, greasy burger clutched tightly in his partner's hands, a bunch of slippery onions attempting to escape the fat-sodden bun, like the freshly spilled innards of some exotic sea creature.

"I'm hungry," Jonah – Joe to his colleagues – Pemberton replied through a mouthful of half-masticated burger, "and I'm sure she won't mind any." He pointed in the general direction of the corpse that lay spread out and mutilated upon the motel room bed, not phased in the least by the blood soaked mattress and wide, gaping hole in the girl's chest.

Lyle grunted and stalked around the motel bed, his OCD screaming at him that the bed sheets had been less than crisp and starched white before the majority of the young girl's blood had soaked them through, transformed them into a sickly shade of dark crimson. The M.E. had put the time of death somewhere around three in the morning, which meant the poor girl – Lyle guestimated her age at somewhere between nineteen and twenty-three, and that was one piece of detective work Lyle was rarely wrong about – had laid there for the better part of ten hours before being discovered by the motel's one and only housekeeper. The woman, a plump, squat Mexican lady by the name of Guadalupe was still hysterical and was being babysat out in the motel's grubby reception office by one of the beat cops who'd first attended the call-in.

"It's pretty gruesome, Bob," Pemberton stated the blindingly obvious before taking another huge bite at his burger. Somehow, he managed to capture the errant onions in his gaping maw and all but consuming an entire third of the sandwich in one fell swoop.

Lyle treated his partner to his very best Eastwood squint; there was just something about the guy's undisguised glee at the gruesome crime scenes they were forced to attend that made him more than a tad uneasy; Lyle often mused that had Jonah Pemberton not become a cop, he would most likely be out there slaughtering the innocents himself for his own nefarious kicks. Still, with just two more months before the glorious days of retirement, it was far too easy for Lyle to brush Detective Pemberton's ghoulish lasciviousness to one side – just eight short weeks and the man would be somebody else's problem.

"No sign of sexual assault," Lyle said, he always did his thinking out loud. "And the M.E figures she was drugged up to the eyeballs while the perp' did this to her, although we're gonna have to wait for the tox' report to confirm precisely what he used on her."

"You think she was still alive when he cut her open?" Pemberton said as he peered into the gaping gore of the dead girl's chest, at the splintered sternum, and the once beating heart that now lay quite useless and shrivelled up in a slick pool of coagulated blood. "Jeez, that must have been painful," he snorted and pushed the remainder of his lunch into his fat face.

"Looks that way," Lyle replied, disgusted still further at the glee etched on his partner's face; somebody just died here, and in the most horrific way imaginable, *and* she was still in the damn room – was the man so hardened after his six long years in homicide as to have no reverence at all? "She coughed up a lot of fresh blood," Lyle continued, pointing at the dead girl's pretty, blood spattered face, "she'd have to have been alive for that to happen."

"Reckon she was *awake* when he took her lungs out?" Pemberton said as he gulped down the last of his meal, his throat bulging quite alarmingly as the burger slid down. He let out a quiet, gassy belch that wafted across the corpse, and Lyle smelled the sweet stink of grease and onions over the dank, earthy smell of copper and innards that emanated from the dead girl.

Lyle was about to chastise his partner's crassness when his cell phone rang out. It played a stark, tinny version of

Yakkity Sax – Lyle absolutely loved Benny Hill, considered the comedian to be the pinnacle of sophisticated British comedy – which, given the circumstances, beat Pemberton's gleeful insensitivity at the murder scene hands-down. Flushed with embarrassment – he could have sworn he'd switched the dammed thing to silent before he came in – Lyle stepped into the cramped en-suite bathroom that reeked of disinfectant and stale pee.

"Hello?" he barked into the phone without glancing at the caller ID.

"Daddy?"

"Oh, hi, Sweetpea," Lyle's demeanor softened – his daughter, Tina, may have been a sophomore college student, but she'd always be his sweet little baby girl who'd once upon a time *loved* unicorns and Disney Princesses. "It's not really a good time to –"

"I'm calling to remind you that it's Mom's birthday on Saturday," Tina insisted, "I hope you haven't forgotten."

Lyle huffed. "Of course I haven't forgotten, Tina," he grumbled, "how could I possibly forget my own wife's birthday?"

He had forgotten, of course, just like he did every year – in fact, had it not been for his daughter's annual reminders since the tender age of eight, Lyle's marriage would have long ago gone the same way as so many of his colleagues' at the Precinct.

Tina's light, breezy laughter echoed out through the phone. "Okay, Daddy, that would be a first, but as long as you remember we're taking her out for dinner."

"Luigi's," Lyle butted in, "same place as last year." It was, in fact, the same place as *every* year.

"It's her favorite."

A familiar shape appeared at the bathroom door, outlined by the warped frame and its yellowed, peeling paint. Pemberton tapped at an imaginary watch on his wrist, eager as ever to press on.

"I really gotta go, sweetie," Lyle sounded flustered – he was always the first to admonish cops for taking personal calls on the job.

"Sorry – bye, Daddy,"

"Bye, Tina, and don't forget to take your meds."

Tina's sigh was so loud that even Pemberton heard it. "I'm twenty-two, Daddy, I don't need reminding."

Lyle knew full well that the reminder was superfluous; Tina had been fastidious in keeping up with her immunosuppressant meds since the operation that had saved her life at the tender age of thirteen. But, it made Lyle feel like a good father, and in some ways he hoped it kind of compensated for all the times he'd not been there for his daughter as she'd grown up.

Before Lyle could say *bye,* Tina had hung up.

"All done, Bob?" Detective Pemberton grinned at Lyle, the sheer delight on his chubby, grease-stained face all too plain to see. He'd not dare say anything to his fiery tempered partner, of course, but he sure as all hell was going to wear that holier-than-thou attitude for the rest of the day.

Lyle nodded sheepishly. "Yeah," he said quietly, "let's get out of here."

*

Tommy Rydell was still very much alive when his eyeballs were plucked from their sockets.

"*Pleeeese!*" his voice, high and shrill, was soaked up by the verdant foliage of the dense woods that surrounded him, closing in on his terrified form like some dark, smothering, malevolent creature.

The person sitting astride Tommy on the damp, mossy ground was heavy enough to render him entirely helpless, no matter how much the terrified boy wriggled and fought. His hands, trapped beneath his attacker's sharp, bony knees, felt numb beneath the weight, his trapped wrists feeling as if they could snap at any moment.

"I'll do anything you want!" Tommy pleaded, "just please don't kill me!" He stared at the face that hovered above him, into the cold, staring eyes that burned out from behind the dark gray ski mask. There was a glaring halo of sunlight around the featureless head, created by a persistent shaft of light that sneaked through the canopy high above, and in Tommy's frantic mind, he thought his assailant resembled some kind of evil angel.

If his attacker wanted to do sexual stuff, that was quite alright with him; hell, he was thirteen and all bets were off as to where Tommy Rydell got his kicks; there was just no need for all the brutality and overriding promise of an untimely death.

Tommy had been out stalking around the woods – a popular destination for the older kids who craved a little alone time – as he did most weekends. There was just something special about sunny Sunday afternoons that just screamed *make out time!* Tommy would sneak around the concealing shade of the trees and overgrown shrubs, find himself a frisky couple of high schoolers, make himself comfortable and settle down to enjoy the show. Sometimes, if he was really lucky, a courting couple would get *really* carried away on the soft, leafy ground, get completely naked and go through all of the bases like they were going out of fashion – it was one heck of a way for Tommy to get his sex ed.

Something flashed in the harsh beam of sunlight, reflecting the radiance directly into Tommy's face, it was a cold, metallic glint that hurt his eyes. "*Owww!*" he complained, screwing his face up and twisting his head from side to side – wondering just why the person who pinned him so resolutely to the ground had gone to all the trouble of bringing along a dessert spoon.

The burning sensation the glaring sunlight triggered in his eyes had Tommy crying, and streams of hot, salty tears ran down his wobbling, pock-marked cheeks to sting at the open acne sores that marred his otherwise handsome features. It brought back to him the dreadful memories of the seemingly unending pain he'd endured back in first grade, when they'd removed the bandages from around his head at the hospital and his Mom and Dad had told him that it was all for the best and he'd be able to see properly for the first time in his life.

He'd had to wear those spectacles with thick, heavy lenses that looked like they'd been fashioned from the bottom of those old style Coke bottles and made him the target for so much merciless teasing – if he'd been called *Mr Magoo* once, he'd been called it a thousand times! But, his folks had been right, and once the post-op pain was gone, Tommy's world had become a whole lot clearer – although he could still remember well the times when the whole world had been nothing more than a thick, syrupy white blur.

A pressure on his eyelids, strong fingers prising them open.

"*Nooooo!*" Tommy squealed, hoping against hope that somebody would hear him and come running to his aid at the very last minute, just like they did in the action movies he devoured on a Saturday night.

"Stay still, kid," the gruffness of the voice startled Tommy; this was the first thing his attacker had said since jumping him in the clearing.

"Please let me go," Tommy snivelled, and bubbles of thick, clear snot oozed from his nostrils, "I promise I won't tell anybody –" Unable to do anything else but snivel and plead, Tommy stared up with his forced-open eye at the concealed face, painfully aware that his bladder had let go, with his bowels threatening a similar protest.

And then, all Tommy could see was the spoon.

He yowled like a stuck pig as the spoon slipped between his eyeball and its fleshy housing, the curved edge making its way around all the way to the back of Tommy's socket. Bright, white flashes of startling light set off in his head as the concave metal nudged at the delicate wiring of his optic nerve; it was like Fourth of July and New Years going off in his brain all at the same time.

It was a peculiar feeling for Tommy as the spoon scooped out his eyeball, he got a kind of wibbly-wobbly view of the trees that held sentry above him, much like the camera shake effect they put into the found-footage horror movies in an attempt to make them appear authentic. Tommy felt all too well the tugging, tearing sensation around his eyeball as the thin muscles that held it into place gave way to the harsh probing of the cold metal spoon. And then, his assailant's face grew closer, closer still and Tommy could feel the tepid afternoon air rushing into his denuded eye socket, and the warmth of sticky fluids cascading down his face and into his hair.

"Dammit," that gruff voice again, and Tommy felt his eyeball pop like an overripe fruit and warm, viscous fluid spattered onto his face to invade his shrill scream with its thick, cloying taste

Then, all went black and Tommy felt powerful, insistent fingers prising open his other eyelid.

*

"There are a lot of similarities in M.O.," Detective Lyle lectured Pemberton, his brow furrowed as he thought out loud, "to the Ranier case that came in last month." He pointed to the veritable gore fest of crime scene photos he'd pinned to the battered old cork board on his office wall – no point throwing good departmental money away on a new one, not this close to him walking out of the Precinct for the final time – the victim's mutilated corpse splayed out upon the blood soaked, king-sized bed in glorious technicolor.

After enduring the ghoulish start to his day, it felt good for Lyle to be back in the dingy confines of the precinct, bustling with activity, filled with cop's chatter and where the coffee was thick and black like molasses and tasted like armpit.

They didn't have a name on the missing lung gal as yet, which Lyle found frustrating, she'd used a fake ID to book the room at the motel, and paid in cash, clearly she didn't want anyone to know where she was.

"The liver guy?" Pemberton threw in.

"Yeah, the liver guy," Lyle huffed and tapped a well-chewed fingernail against the photograph of the unfortunate young lady with her chest cavity yawning wide open like some hideous, gaping maw, the pink-white of her split sternum and ribs poking through the ragged meat of her torso, her heart sitting forlorn and deflated amidst her ruined flesh. "Both victims were drugged, but still most likely conscious. Both had one major organ removed – the weapon in both cases is still unknown." Lyle took in a deep breath as he recalled the M.E. telling him that, in his considered, professional opinion, the killer had torn the poor girl's flesh apart with his bare hands while she'd watched.

"So, if it is the same guy, what's his motivation?" Pemberton asked, still accustomed to going through these things by the same old book he'd devoured at the training academy countless years ago.

"Damned if I know," Lyle grumbled. "Could have Mommy issues, quite possibly some junkie out of his tree on Bath Salts or some such – or could be just your plain old, run of the mill lunatic." The detective leaned closer to the board to peer into the dead girl's chest, doing his best to ignore the way in which her no doubt once delectably perky breasts lay flopped either side of her lifeless body upon the bed, still attached by torn flaps of pale, flawless skin. "Perhaps he's building another person piece by piece, from the inside out?"

"Like Frankenstein?"

"Yeah," Lyle said, "or maybe he's eating his way around the human body, one major organ at a time." Thomas Harris had a lot to answer for, the detective mused, with his damned fava beans and nice Chianti.

"So, what do we do? Wait for the psycho to kill again?" Pemberton stood up, his old wooden chair scraping loudly upon the office floor.

"Unless we can pick something out of this goddamned mess, that's just about all we can hope for right now," Lyle told his partner. "We should pull the files of all murders with personal possessions or body parts missing over the past ten years – there may just be something in there."

Pemberton's sigh was audible; by *we*, of course, Lyle meant him. And there'd be a hell of a lot of homicide cases fitting that description, since pretty much *all* serial killers took some kind of trophy home with them.

The door burst open, a ruddy faced, rookie cop stood framed in Lyle's doorway, looking decidedly uncomfortable in her freshly starched uniform, her not inconsiderable chest heaving as if she'd just run a marathon.

"Did they not teach you to knock in basic training?" Lyle snapped, annoyed at having his all too ephemeral train of thought broken.

"I'm sorry, Sir," the cop panted, her pretty face reddening still further, "but I thought you'd want to know straight away." She glanced across the cramped, dusty office at the seemingly random array of ghoulish pictures displayed upon the board above the detective's paper-strewn mess of a desk.

"Know what?" Lyle asked.

"They just found some kid wandering around Devil's Woods with his eyes missing," the cop told him. "He said somebody popped 'em out with a spoon."

*

As it turned out, Tommy Rydell was less than useless as an eye witness – an unfortunate turn of phrase, of course – as he was wildly hysterical, bordering upon downright loony-tunes by the time Lyle and Pemberton arrived at the hospital. The medics had done an efficient job of patching the kid up, his empty eye sockets padded out with cotton balls and gauze, his head wrapped around with a thick swath of bandages that made Lyle think of Boris Karloff.

"Are you sure you can't remember anything at all about the person who did this to you?" Pemberton asked Tommy for what seemed like the thousandth time – the cop was nothing if not persistent.

"You're going to have to leave now," the skinny, sour-faced doctor sounded most insistent. "Tommy needs to rest."

"She took my eyes!" Tommy screamed again, his voice piercing, so desperately high that it fair hurt the ear drums. *"She took my new eyes!"*

Lyle ushered his partner from the tiny, stark white hospital room. He cast a cursory nod in the doctor's direction, expecting at the very least an upturned corner of his thin-lipped mouth by means of a *thank you*.

Nothing.

"She?" Pemberton whispered to himself.

"What was that?" Lyle said.

"The kid said *she*," Pemberton scratched at the two-day old stubble that prickled his chin. "His attacker was a woman?"

"It's possible, I guess," Lyle said, "but the boy hardly knows what day it is. Until the shock and the pile of drugs they've got the kid on wear off, we'd be best keeping an open mind on that score."

Pemberton gave a sage nod. "You're probably right, boss."

"There was something, though," Lyle added as they made their way through the intricate maze of hospital hallways. "He said his *new* eyes," he pondered. "What do you make of that, Joe?"

"Like you said, the kid was not in his right mind –"

"What say we do some digging around murder cases involving transplant patients?" Lyle thought out loud once again. "And find out of the Rydell kid had ever had an eye transplant."

"I don't think that's a thing, Bob," Pemberton corrected Lyle, even though he knew damn well the senior detective hated it when he played the pedant. "Something to do with not being able to reconnect the optic nerve, I think – they do transplant corneas, though…" he added the last part to appease the thunderous expression that clouded Lyle's face. "I'll start digging the second we get back to the precinct."

*

"Take a look at this, Bob," Pemberton squinted at the grainy computer screen that perched precariously upon his partner's desk – since the budget cuts, they'd been forced to share the temperamental Dell, so old that it still ran Windows 95.

Lyle leaned across the desk, his reading glasses clinging to the end of his greasy nose, a beige case file clutched in one hand, stale pastrami on rye in the other. He peered over his spectacles, and Pemberton's shoulder, at the fuzzy, badly copied newspaper article displayed in all its monochrome glory on the screen.

"Three weeks ago – it was over in Los Angeles, but the vic' had a kidney taken." Pemberton read from the article. "The victim actually survived the attack and the removal of the organ, but died a week later from an MRSA infection he caught at the hospital."

"Ironic," Lyle grunted.

"They chalked it up to organ farming," Pemberton continued, "happens a lot in LA, apparently; they sell human body parts off to the rich folks."

"Maybe that's all it was, then."

"That's what I thought, but look…" Pemberton scrolled down the page, the screen moving downwards with jerky, pixelated movements. "At the bottom," he said, pointing to the article's penultimate paragraph.

"He was a transplant recipient," Lyle said, his voice oozing from him like a diseased whisper. "Nine years ago; the perp' left the old kidneys behind."

"They leave the sick kidneys in place when they transplant in new ones, unless they're cancerous, of course," Pemberton recited what he'd learned from Gray's anatomy – his wife made him sit through the show, even though he hated it – it was pretty much all they had in common since he made detective. "They just plumb in the new one next to them."

Lyle slicked back what remained of his thinning, silver hair. It felt greasy, weary, and he honestly couldn't remember the last time it had seen shampoo. "That could be our man," he growled, "maybe the heat got too much for him over there."

"Or woman," Pemberton said, "Rydell said –"

"– I know what the kid said, Joe," Lyle snapped. "We need to find out exactly when he had his eye transplant – or whatever the hell it was – and same goes for Ranier and the chick with the lungs."

Pemberton studied his partner's face, recognized the look of consternation that dwelled there, like a dark cloud hovering over a grim landscape. "You think this might be the same killer?"

"I'm leaning that way," Lyle said. "And I have a hunch," he sat back in the creaky old chair that had been with him through most of his twenty years as a detective, "and a bad feeling about this."

"Didn't know you were a *Star Wars* fan, Bob," Pemberton attempted to inject a little levity as he returned his attention to the computer.

Detective Lyle cleared his throat, and it sounded like a snarl. "I'm not," he said.

*

"I already told you, Detectives, you'll have to get a warrant," Doctor Christoph Pena informed the two surly looking cops who had stormed into his office without so much as a by-your-leave.

Lyle pulled a face, he was pretty damn close to flattening the doctor's thin, pointy nose – world renowned transplant surgeon or not, the man was still an obstinate prick. Since they'd discovered that the guy in LA, Rydell, Ranier, and the lung gal – turned out her name was Sheralyn Braxton, she was all of twenty-one when her life was so brutally snuffed out – had all received their spare parts from the same donor a smidge over nine years ago, Lyle knew they were in a desperate race against time if they were to prevent more death and bloodshed; the murderer was escalating, the time between kills shortening exponentially.

"In the time it would take to obtain a warrant – and we *will* get one – somebody else could die at the hands of this manic," Pemberton tried his best to guilt the good doctor into compliance, but to no avail – the medic remained quite steadfast.

"All we need is the list of names of any other recipients of organs from Jake Cooley," Lyle added, fighting to keep his temper. "Who the hell is that going to hurt, *doctor*?"

It had been easy enough to find out the name of the donor of Tommy Rydell's replacement corneas, since his family had made a big gesture out of thanking the Cooley family for their brave altruism – Jake Cooley had been nineteen years old when he'd gone ass over teakettle through the windscreen of his drunk mother's Corvette. There'd even been a big splash in the local papers, complete with a grainy picture of a chubby Tommy Rydell, aged four and change, with his eyes bandaged up in what Lyle thought was an eerie foreshadowing of what was to come.

The doctor wavered slightly, and Lyle thought he was about to give in. But no. "Do I have to remind you about doctor/patient confidentiality, Detective Lyle?" He looked down his pinched nose at the cop, as if studying some much lower life form.

"Can you at least tell us what other parts of the Cooley kid were donated?" Lyle growled. "Unless of course, the confidentiality you're hiding behind extends to the dead."

Doctor Pena snorted his derision at Lyle's sarcasm. "It does not," he said, grabbing a pristine sheet of pink-tinged paper from the pad on his immaculately ordered desk. He scribbled studiously for a minute of two, before handing the note to Pemberton, a deliberate snub to the older cop who hovered at his shoulder.

"Oh, sweet Jesus," Pemberton said, glancing down at the spidery scrawl that seemed almost feminine; there were nine items on the list.

*

"He's not here," Dr. Pena's assistant insisted, her immaculately made up face reddening beneath the stern scrutiny of the two cops, her ruby red, bee-stung lips pouting like she was about to cry.

"Listen, Miss – Johnstone –" Lyle read the gal's nameplate that sat precariously dead center at the very front edge of her desk, as if it were plucking up the courage to jump. "We have a warrant, and we need to speak to Dr. Pena, so unless you would like to take a trip to the station to chat to us about obstruction, I suggest you hit the button on your intercom and let your boss know we're here." He leaned across the desk to better intimidate, hands planted firmly in front of the terrified assistant, fingers splayed wide.

"H-he left straight after you this morning," the ever-professional Miss Johnstone explained, "and he never came back – I had to cancel all of his appointments and surgeries for the day."

Detective Pemberton eyed the door to Pena's office, noting that there was no light to be seen emanating from the thin crack between it and the polished floor, even though it was already eight at night – either the good doctor liked to sit and work in the dark, or his assistant was telling the truth.

"Is it unlocked?" Lyle asked, following his partner's gaze.

"Yes, but –"

Even as Miss Johnstone began her protest, Lyle was already on his way towards the doctor's office door, crossing the office with long, purposeful strides. "We don't have time for this," he snapped, by means of an apology, "show her the warrant, Joe."

Pemberton slapped the warrant on the secretary's desk and followed Lyle into Pena's office, admiring the grain of the expensive door on his way in – Brazilian Mahogany, unless he was otherwise mistaken.

Lyle sat himself down in the doctor's plush, leather chair with a satisfied groan, the chair was a million miles away from the battered old thing in his office, and his ass felt like it would never want to leave. He fired up the expensive Mac on Pena's desk and stabbed at the intercom with an impatient finger. "What's the password on this thing?" he growled, enjoying the luxury of not having to shout through the door at the top of his voice like they had to back at the precinct.

"I-I don't think I can tell you that," the harangued assistant replied, her voice cold and tinny through the small speaker; she sounded dangerously close to tears and Lyle almost felt sorry for her.

"*Must* we go through this again?" Lyle harrumphed, his finger pressed so hard on the little red button that his knuckle turned white. "We *could* get another warrant, but that would mean disturbing some poor judge out of hours, which really won't go well for you in court – and all the while, there's a killer out there planning his next outing and your stubbornness could well cost someone else their life." Lyle laid it on thick, the poor woman was close to cracking as it was, and he figured that just one more push ought to do the trick. "So, unless you want *that* on your conscience, I strongly suggest you –"

"Jake Cooley," Miss Johnstone blurted out, her voice choked with tears, "lowercase, all one word."

The two words smacked Lyle square in the face, sent his mind spinning in a dozen directions. "Seriously?" he growled as he tapped the doctor's password into the little gray box in the center of the computer screen. He shook his head slowly as the computer whirred to life and there, set as the screen's wallpaper, were the happy, smiling faces of the late Jake Cooley and his exceptionally pretty mother.

It didn't take Lyle long to find what he was looking for, his doggedness at keeping himself abreast of ever-evolving technology never failed to pay off. Pemberton, for his part, wandered around the spacious office, his footsteps silenced by the outrageously thick pile of the beige carpet, poking his nose into the tall, metal filing cabinets that were dotted about the place.

Lyle looked up from the Mac, his face glowing a ghostly white in the screen's light. He pressed the intercom once more. "What happened to the Cooley file?" he barked, imagining Miss Johnstone jumping in her seat at the sound of his voice.

"It's there, under *donors*," the woman replied. She'd composed herself since her earlier breakdown and now sounded cold and detached. "All of the donor cases Doctor Pena worked with are in that folder."

Lyle scrolled down the list, then up again, his keen eye registering that the cases stretched back nine years, the earliest of which was one *Cooley: J*. He tapped on the name again, as if opening the file a third time would somehow, and miraculously, yield a different result.

It didn't.

The file was empty, nothing more than a standard form, each field a virgin white, not so much as a checked box or a note.

"There must be a backup paper file for Cooley," Lyle scrutinized each of the filing cabinets as he posed the rhetorical question to the ever-patient Pemberton. "Could you –?"

Pemberton beat his partner to the punch, yanking open the top most metal drawer of the cabinet closest the picture window – he figured the view across the parkland would be spectacular during the day, but for now it was just cool, still blackness. "It's not here, Bob," he announced, somewhat predictably, "looks like he took it, though." Pemberton rifled through the neatly arranged taupe files that hung suspended within the drawer, making doubly sure that *Cooley: J* had not simply been misfiled.

Lyle let out a huge, weary sigh and leaned back in the chair. His eyes flicked the length and breadth of Pena's PC screen, as if in the vain hope that the information that had been so diligently wiped would magically dissolve back into view. Jake Cooley had been the newly qualified Doctor Pena's first donor preparation, which quite possibly explained the weird attachment the guy had with the kid, quite possibly akin to a cop's fond affinity with his first department-issued firearm.

Unless…

"We gotta go," Lyle barked, jumping from the chair, his knee joints complaining with twin pops that sounded like firecrackers going off. "Get Pena's address from the girl, now." And with that, he marched from the office and towards the elevator, with Pemberton hot on his heels.

*

It hadn't been difficult to extract Dr. Pena's home address from Miss Johnstone; by that stage in Lyle and Pemberton's second visit of the day, she was pretty much broken and just wanted to go home.

"Nice place," Lyle said, looking up at the wide expanse of the Pena house's limestone brick façade. The house, nestled cosy at the far end of an exclusive, gated community estate, was colossal, bigger than some of the exclusive country house hotels that Mrs. Lyle liked to frequent. "I guess I chose the wrong career," he snorted, a wry smile playing about his lips.

The doctor's house was dark, quiet, yet the black Carrera sporting the vanity plates that sat motionless in the driveway suggested that Dr. Pena was home.

Lyle drew his gun. Pemberton followed suit, and the two cops made their way towards the front door in silence, their footsteps swallowed up by the impeccably trimmed, damp grass of the lawn.

"You ready?" Lyle whispered, one hand resting upon the huge brass door knob, the other aiming his Glock at the thick wood, at chest height.

Pemberton nodded, his own gun raised; he'd worked with Lyle long enough to know that the man would merrily kick the door in if it was locked, and to hell with waiting for the backup they'd called for to arrive.

The knob twisted smoothly in Lyle's hand, and much to his surprise, the heavy wood of the door eased open with nary a creak. With a cursory nod at his partner, Lyle slipped inside Pena's house, his slim frame swallowed up by the darkness that dwelled within. He knew that he really ought to have announced their presence, but something deep down in his seasoned cop's gut advised to the contrary, and Lyle was too long on the force to ignore it.

Pemberton wrinkled his nose at the smell that wafted down the long, sweeping staircase. It was an earthy, rank odor, with distinct undertones of something unpleasantly chemical; quite unmistakably the vile stink of death. He tapped Lyle on the shoulder and pointed towards the stairs, indicating that they should make their way upwards – it would be a while before the acrid reek registered with the older cop, his sense of smell had been all but destroyed by years' of heavy smoking back in his younger days. Pemberton fished a small penlight out of a pocket and clicked it on, the narrow beam of yellowish light illuminating the intricately patterned carpet that adorned the sweeping staircase.

Slowly, carefully, the cops made their way to the upstairs of Pena's mansion, alert eyes searching for traces of movement within the inky shadows, ears pricked for tell-tale sounds that may give away any inhabitants.

The hallway at the top of the staircase led off to both the left and the right, stretching away into the lightlessness like some infinite corridor. Following his nose, Pemberton peeled off to the right, the stink growing stronger with every step, and by now, he could see that Lyle's nose was crinkling. Pemberton figured they'd be discovering the doctor's body behind one of the myriad doors that his torch lit up – he hated suicides, there was just something about those who took their own lives that yanked hard on his soul, killing it off one small piece at a time.

The third door down on the left, Pemberton paused, sniffing the air like a well-trained tracker dog. He shone his mini flashlight at the door handle, gun poised, with Lyle close behind him. He hesitated; something wasn't right, his heart pounded hard and heavy in his chest, so much so that he wouldn't have been at all surprised if his partner was hearing it.

"Open the damn door already," Lyle hissed in Pemberton's ear, startling him. The cop popped the penlight between his teeth, reached out, and opened the door.

Lyle gagged as the fetid wave of stink hit him full force, the bile rising up from his guts to leave a burning trail all the way up his gullet. He gulped it down, fighting the nausea that washed through every corner of his body. He'd been in the presence of corpses before, many in advanced stages of decomposition, but never in his life had he smelled anything that bad – it stank to high heaven of putrescent flesh, thick, congealing blood, body wastes and the sharp tang of chemicals; he dreaded Pemberton's inquisitive light revealing the source of such an unearthly stench.

With trembling hands, Pemberton directed both the thin light and his weapon towards each corner of the room in turn, ascertaining that they were in a teenage boy's room, adorned as it was with posters of the Texans, Britney Spears, Katy Perry and Miley Cyrus. There was an office chair, a twin bed, and a modest, brushed aluminium writing desk, home to a thick laptop, and laying next to that, as if tossed there carelessly, was a thin, card file that Pemberton thought he recognized.

"Oh, sweet Jesus," Lyle gasped as Pemberton's light hit the bed, illuminating the ghastly figure that rested atop expensive cotton sheets that were stained dark with the ghoulish effluvia that had oozed from it.

The cops stepped gingerly towards the body that lay in the center of the bed, its withered arms by its sides, discolored bare toes pointing upwards.

Fighting against every instinct he had to turn tail and run, Pemberton played his penlight's beam over the desiccated corpse, lighting the atrocity up one ruined piece at a time.

The body had been young at the time of death, Lyle took a guess based upon its height and the Pokemon boxers it wore that the guy had been no more than mid to late teens when he'd shuffled off his mortal coil. His body had been sliced open; gray flaps of emaciated skin draping either side of the body cavity like old, discarded shrouds, to reveal the body's innards.

Glistening wetly amidst the shrivelled viscera that lay deflated and slack inside the corpse's body, the black-red liver shone out in stark, ghoulish contrast, as did the gray-pink loops of neatly arranged intestines, along with the collapsed lungs that nestled within the cracked open rib cage. A kidney lay next to the liver, disconnected from the arteries and veins that should feed it, yet looking somehow *fresher* than the rest of the body.

There were patches of skin here and there, an upper arm, one thigh, a section of the peeled torso, still pinkish, yet turning blotchy as if it, too was rotting. The kid's face was adorned with seemingly random scraps of graying skin stretched taut over uneven the bumps of once prominent cheekbones – as if someone had tried their best to rebuild something irreparably damaged. The unforgiving gleam of Pemberton's light flashed across the corpse's eyes, the cop gasped and staggered back into Lyle, feeling the hard metal of his partner's gun jabbing hard into his spine. One of the corpse's eyes was sunken, oozing, like it had burst, but the other sat proud in the opposite socket, a thin black thread of catgut snaking from its edge, the silver curve of a surgical needle dangling at its end, the eye itself glassy, whole and staring…

The lights blazed on, temporarily blinding Lyle and Pemberton, and mercifully blotting out the horrifying vision of the corpses' fixed, dead eyes. The cops spun around on pure instinct, guns aimed, fingers on triggers.

"Don't shoot!" a terrified voice cried out, *"please!"*

Doctor Christoph Pena stood in the doorway, hands raised, tears streaming down his pinched, pale face.

"What the hell is this?" Lyle demanded, his eyes still smarting from the harsh light.

"She made me do it," Pena sobbed, "I didn't kill anybody, I promise I didn't. She just wanted her son back."

"This is Jake Cooley?"

Pena nodded. He glanced across at the ruined corpse, his eyes red rimmed, shame shadowing his wan features. "I married her after –" the doctor faltered. "After her husband left her, he blamed her for Jake."

"She married the surgeon who took her kid apart?" Pemberton threw in. He clicked off his penlight and sauntered across to the desk, flicking open the beige file that lay next to the unopened laptop. "That's kinda morbid, don't you think?"

"Grief makes people do strange things," Pena offered, as if that was any kind of excuse.

"Like murdering innocent folks so you can reassemble your dead kid?" Lyle growled, his hackles up.

"I didn't kill anybody," Pena protested, "I just –"

"– stitched the parts back together," Lyle growled, "doesn't make you any less complicit, *Doctor*," the cop all but spat out the last word, as if it was a sour taste upon his tongue. "So, where is the delightful Mrs. Cooley?"

"It's *Pena* now," the doctor corrected the cop, as if the detail really mattered.

"Bob," Pemberton interrupted, "you got to see this." He plucked a page from the file on the desk, scrutinized it, his brow furrowed.

"What you got there, Joe?" Lyle kept his gun pointed at the doc's chest, one move out of place and he'd more than welcome the opportunity to blow the sick bastard to Kingdom Come.

Pemberton waved the flimsy sheet of hospital issue paper at his partner, his face so drained of color that he all but resembled Jake Cooley's sorry remains. "It's Tina –"

Lyle's cell rang out, the jolly Benny Hill theme tune a disturbing juxtaposition to the ghoulish circumstances in Pena's house. Without thinking, Lyle grabbed the phone from his pocket, answered the call.

"There's somebody in my apartment, Daddy," Tina's terrified voice squeaked through the miniscule speaker. "I'm scared."

"Stay calm, baby girl," Lyle fought to contain his own panic that rose up from the pit of his stomach. "Did you call 911?"

Tina sobbed, her voice a trembling whisper, "Yeah, but she's in my apartment right now, she keeps saying I stole her son's heart, but I don't even know anybody called Jake – I'm hiding in my closet."

"You stay there, sweetie, you're gonna be just fine…" the words died in the cop's throat; he'd never felt more helpless in his entire life.

And then, Tina Lyle began to scream.

The End

Transplant first appeared as *Carnal Harvest* in the anthology *Schlock, Horror!* Published by HellBound Books Publishing LLC in 2018.

https://hellboundbookspublishing.com/schlockhorror.html

Show your Work
Keith Durocher

"I've never developed a taste for blood clots – or gotten over the smell. They say you can get used to anything. Not so. The soft, chewy texture; the taste of pennies; the acrid fust that sticks to the back of the sinuses – these remain distasteful to me. It's like the worst possible version of toffee; you get this shit stuck between your teeth, and it's all stringy, too?

"I hear some guys talk about how great cannibalism is, that nothing beats the fatty meats of 'long pig' rendered oh-so-tender in a bone marrow broth, but honestly? It's greasy and bland, little more than a delivery vector for the spices you'll inevitably need to hide the wretched flavor."

I'm sitting in my mesh-backed office chair, warming up a well-practiced lecture. With its rollerblade casters and extra firm lumbar support, I feel like I'm sitting on a throne from which I hold court over my little domain of murder.

It's encrusted with a gummy cake of bodily fluids, sure, and layer upon layer of sweat, grime, blood and tears. But aren't all the greatest seats of power throughout history built upon a foundation of the same?

In front of me sits a glistening young man. He's nude save for the black hood I've gifted him, and he's thoroughly tied to a much less ergonomic—but much more robust—heavy wooden chair. The arm rests are long and wide enough that his hands don't dangle over the ends. His legs are parted and tied at the ankles, knees and groin, exposing his shrivelled, uncut manhood.

His well-defined chest heaves with the heavy breathing of terror. In this setup, a slight slope in the stained concrete to which his seat is bolted leads to a rusted drain cover. Occasional wet burps and belches of unhappy plumbing interrupt our conversation.

"I doubt I'll ever forget the first time I tried to consume one of my victims. It feels like a lifetime ago now; what was once a thrill has long since crumbled into ash. Most of my memories of those heady early days are like that – fingerprints on abandoned handrails. I used to have a passion for killing; now it's just something I do. Rote butchery. Banal assassination.

"Where was I? Oh, yes, eating the flesh of a victim. All the greats did it: Gein, Fish, etcetera. Pretty sure Lucas claimed to have done it, too, but who believes a single thing that fucking inbred hick ever said? Regardless, it struck me as a rite of passage as well as a potential avenue for cadaver disposal. 'Goodbye for now, faceless drifter. The next time I see you, you'll be much smaller and flushable.'

"The lead up was all anticipation and mounting glee. I chose head trauma, so as to preserve as much meat as possible, carefully draining the fluids into tubs, and I was almost reverent with the fillets and cubes for stewing. All that effort, and the payoff was abysmal. The worst soup I'd ever had. No amount of bouillon cubes could cover that dreadful taste."

A single wire dangles from lazy staples in the wooden

crossbeams above us, a clear bulb giving off harsh light and heat. None of these new LED-style smart bulbs. Oh no. That would never do. I zealously covet my slowly dwindling supply of good old fashioned incandescent filament bulbs. One must have certain standards when one is creating an aesthetic. Not that my guest can see the stark contrasts of shadow cast by this aggressive little wire encased in glass.

I'd decided early on I wanted his experience to be pure, unspoiled by whatever he might perceive too soon, so I made sure the hood was secure. Sewn from blackout curtains, I was aiming for that "executioners victim" look you see in movies. It meant he missed the tableau, the full display of my instruments, but perhaps I might give him that vision as a final touch. We'll see how my mood strikes me.

"After that stew, I tried to get creative with it, you know? Always chasing that gimmick for the history books. We can't all dress like clowns or rail our mothers severed neck stump, but we seek out new horizons all the same. So I put my blender through its paces; I thought maybe I could get away with some kind of purée or pâté – perhaps even a mousse.

You ever try to aerate flesh to make a delectable, whipped spleen? I don't know what I was thinking. I mean, the thought of head cheese has always made me gag, and what I wound up with was… a meat-smoothie, I guess?

"Realistically, all I had to do was add gelatin and it would have been indistinguishable from that post-war 'delicacy.' But nope; I had to admit defeat. I just couldn't sort out how to make cannibalism palatable. Alas, it was clear I wasn't going to get tagged with any 'the vampire of' or 'the beast of' suffixes."

I leaned back with a weary sigh and looked around. This kid fancied himself an apex predator, a demon lurking in the hidden places of the world. It was my job to teach him how far off the mark he was at this stage of his budding career.

But where to start? Wood plane on the shin? It was a satisfying experience when the skin caught just right, peeling off the bone like the skin of a banana. Again though, that hood. He'd miss the show. Plus, I'd really done a number tying him to the chair, and leaning over to work the tool would play hell with my back. So, I'll save that for later.

Oh! Pliers and bamboo wedges. The classics never go out of style. I got up and selected my most reliable needle-noses.

"Now, what was I saying? Oh, yes, I guess that's good news for you though, right? Well, no matter how this turns out, at least you can rest easy knowing your grave won't be the result of some greasy defecation. No, I won't be eating you. When you put out those ads, you spoke of unforgettable experiences. I'm sure being turned into shit fits that description, but let's be honest, its not like you'd be aware of that journey. Seems like a waste. Literally, am I right?

"So, we'll focus on what you can appreciate. The tactile rewards of a whole new sensation. It's what you wanted, correct? To learn? Or was it to teach? To be frank, I kinda skimmed what you'd written, so I'm fuzzy on the fine points.

"Now, you're about to feel a little pop. Don't be surprised."

As I grabbed his left index finger with my pliers, he tried to flinch away, but I was an old hand at this – pardon the pun. With a smooth motion born of confident repetition, I thrust a six-inch length of sharpened bamboo sliver up under his nail bed and as far into the digit as it would go.

I chuckled at his screams, muffled as they were by the gag and the hood. It wouldn't have mattered much even if I hadn't taken these precautions. My lair was isolated and quite soundproof. It's serial murder 101. Let nothing escape – no sights, sounds, smells, or victims. Keep it all inside. His howls brought me back into focus.

"Oh, I know, I know. It's bad, right? You're doing well, though. You really are. Just seven more to go. You keep truckin' li'l soldier; it'll all be over soon."

I finish the job with banal efficiency. It's routine now. Even the pine-oil in the Dettol I pour on his wounds doesn't bring me joy anymore. I used to love that scent. My lair is cliché to the point of absurdity, like I used horror movies as a paint-by-numbers decorating guide.

But I could never abide letting the place smell bad. Cleanup is a chore, but it's also the most necessary of my evils. Given enough repetition, though, it becomes an albatross around my neck. Just like killing has become. Torture, murder, dispose; torture, murder, dispose. Rinse and repeat.

Maybe I should grab one of those old punch card machines they used in factories and really lean into the motif. I could have dull water cooler conversations with myself while taking a breather from the acid baths: *"Those fumes today. Am I right?"* Perhaps even some cubicle farm partitions to complete the illusion.

"Now, I know you're probably thinking, 'What kind of lesson is this? You're just torturing me!' Well, you know how writers say 'Write what you know?' Well, that goes for us, too. Murderers should know the pain they plan on inflicting.

Any time you think, 'Hey, I'm going to shove six-inch splinters in this guy's fingers,' you'll know precisely what it feels like, how brutally effective it is. You're welcome.

"Listen, I'm going to give you some space now, all right? I can tell you need time to come to terms with this little lesson – and I need coffee. Believe me, I can be quite the *monster* when I haven't had my robot juice. We wouldn't want that, now, would we? So hold tight, and we'll resume shortly."

I left him down there, screaming and sobbing into his gag. He was in no immediate mortal danger, so I had room to be leisurely. I got my moka-pot brewing and gazed out the kitchen windows over the fields surrounding my little castle. Quiet and isolated, snowy and serene on the outside.

Not so much on the inside. Every inch of everywhere in my home covered in kitsch, from the macabre to the merely quaint. Mid-century psychedelia, gruesome freakshow oddities, heavy patina antiques. Some people find minimalism calms their minds. I've never understood that. Don't let me think – ever. Blind myself with stimulation, keep the visual cortex occupied – always. It might look like a hoarding nightmare, but it's intricately curated. There's a process.

I finished the ritual of brew and considered the man I'd captured. I'm drowning in clichés – my own by choice but also those of this poor moron. He'd intended to capture me, the immortal predator stalking easy prey. Arrogant, stupid, inexperienced. I'd seen through his veiled codes almost immediately. "Dangerous daddy seeking students willing to learn how far they can go." I mean, seriously.

What he thought of as clever metaphors and innuendos, I saw as clumsy and blatant fumbling. Might as well put up flyers around town that read 'I plan on killing the first kid stupid enough to call this number.' The first lesson to teach him was that the dark web can always get so, so much darker. Where I stalk, it's a city of broken razors. Around any corner, you might face your fear – only to find it's much bigger than you dreaded.

It took little more than a week to get the measure of the kid and his abilities. He thought himself a master murderer, the embodiment of his media icons. A Dunning-Kruger Hannibal Dexter, with all the ego and none of the wits. Setting up a trap to snag him was laughably easy. A few choice messages exchanged, the phrasing tweaked to make me sound sufficiently naive. Convince him I was a barely legal twink seeking a dominant Zaddy.

All these new blood killers, always leading with their balls. None of them have worked the streets for their victims – and it shows. It falls on our shoulders—the venerable elders—to pass our knowledge to the younger generations. Those who can, do; those who can't, teach. These days, I feel like I can't do this anymore.

I poured more black blood of the earth into my mug – a big red ceramic devil's head with spring-mounted googly eyes, and descended back into the hell of my own making.

"You know, I was just thinking about everything and nothing, kid, and you know what your first mistake—What the hell?"

My soundproofing was indeed efficient. I hadn't heard the rhythmic thudding of his struggles as he jerked his entire body with enough force to pull the bolts loose. He was lying on his side now, still securely tied to the chair. That couldn't have felt good. I set my mug down and squatted by his head, the hood now partially up and exposing the gag in his mouth, traceries of blood and drool leaking from it.

"Impressive. But that can't be comfortable. You in a hurry? You might as well relax because we still have a lot of ground to cover. Here, let me help you back up. Now, don't be a dick and wiggle around like bait, all right? Last thing I need is to put my back out. If you make this hard on me, I'll drive rail ties through your feet, straight into this floor. Don't test me."

As I sipped my coffee and considered my options, an idea came to me.

"So, what was I saying? Oh, yeah. Your first mistake. It's a simple one, made by all of us at one time or another. It's thinking with your dick. There's an ocean of reasons to want to kill indiscriminately, but I can tell you right now, when you're substituting murder for fucking, you're setting the clock on your own capture. I mean, look how easily I caught you. That is absolutely because you let your cock think for you."

While I was talking, I fashioned a wire noose out of clothing hangers, secured it to an overhead beam, and set it around his neck.

"OK, I wouldn't advise trying your little dance again, you'll just garrote yourself. So, stay still and don't interrupt me.

"Fuck, I lost my train of thought… Oh! Right. See, most of the guys who get into this—a few women join our ranks from time to time but mostly it's us lads—are fundamentally cowards. Sexually frustrated and weak. Dress up like a clown, go after little boys, or waste gas looking for hookers to end. You know what they all have in common? Besides flappy little todgers? They all got busted because they were thinking with their hard-ons."

I strolled over to a stained bench and grabbed a wooden stool covered in deep gouges. Then I took a moment or two deciding between cleaver or ball-peen. The latter won out, if only for the irony of its impending use. Then I grabbed some tongs and came back to him, slamming down the stool. I had made it specifically for this purpose, and it was exactly the right height to act as an extension of the chair.

"They all seal their own fates. They all end up serving life sentences, or they fry, or they get shot up with the state's needle cocktail…" While I was speaking, I grabbed his member with the tongs and pulled it forward. "So, if there's any one thing you take from this experience today, it's this: Don't. Kill. For. The. Sake. Of. Your. Dick," I said, punctuating each word with an emphatic and savage hammer blow.

There's a fine line between tenderizing meat and simply obliterating it. The ball made short work of his peen—ha!—and he screamed at an inhuman pitch. He thrashed, trying to get away from the source of the pain, but only succeeded in choking himself on the wire. I kept to my business, vaguely disinterested in the chunky spray of spongy meat wetly sputtering off the surface of the stool.

He passed out—as I knew he would—and I got to the task of wound care. I wanted him dickless, not dead. At least not yet. So with methodical ennui, I unhooked the wire around his neck so he wouldn't strangle.

Then I bound a tourniquet around the ruin of his crotch and busted out the blow torch. Surviving this was possible, although the cauterization wasn't going to do any favors to his love life. Not that I much cared. I was supposed to be his underage victim, after all. This was the 'find out' stage of fucking around.

I would have gone back upstairs to make a late lunch, but I couldn't be sure when he'd return to consciousness. My little trick with the wire only worked if I could monitor his actions. If I left him like that, there was entirely too great a chance that he'd strangle himself to death. Wouldn't want that, so I grabbed my mug, put on some Lustmord, and got as comfortable as I could. I've never regretted installing a decent sound system down here, and the oppressive droning ambient was always the perfect complement to this little pit I'd created.

Why was I doing this? What was the point? I'd asked myself that question with increasing frustration many times over the years. Other killers spoke of compulsion—an all-encompassing drive—but I'd never felt that. Not the way they described it.

They'd say they'd lost control of themselves: *"For heaven's sake, catch me before I kill more!"* Others would talk about acting out fantasies. But most of them were garden variety cowards inflicting their impotence in the most pathetic way possible.

Of all the names, the one I felt most connected to was Panzram. *"I wish you all had one neck and that I had my hands on it!"* Now that was a sentiment I understood. I'd always felt like I was born to murder the world, but I lacked the ballyhoo for politics and the discipline for military service.

So how else are you going to kill as many people as possible? Some things, I guess, you just have to learn to do with your own two hands.

As I got older, the magma of that hate, once always bubbling beneath the surface, hardened into jagged rock, then crumbled into char and ash. It remained in my psyche now as little more than crystallized resin coating the substructure of my veins.

No passion for death now, just torpid malaise and the crotchety bitterness of habit. Feeling nothing was deceptive because you didn't feel *numb,* you felt nothing *good.* But it's still all too easy for despair to creep in, settling into your aching joints and clouding your vision.

I glanced over at the kid in the chair and felt a flash of fury and envy in equal measure. I hated him for his stupidity and youth; I hated him because he was me. I wanted to hurt him because I wanted to feel pain. Better that than nothing. For all my scorn of cowardice, I'm plenty lacking in courage myself.

As decisions slowly began to coalesce in my mind, I thought about what was to come. No matter how many times I've attempted to acclimate to the aftermath of murder, the 'after' just never quite lives up to the 'before.'

Corpse disposal is such a goddamn chore.

The chainsaw, the woodchipper, the meat-grinder, the freezer, the furnace – all necessary tools, but all incredibly messy and inconvenient. If only cannibalism had been to my tastes. Eat, shit, and die – the circle of life.

Well, I guess it would be more like "die, eat, and shit," but we quibble over semantics. It was a moot point, anyway. Why couldn't I stop thinking about eating meat?

Ah, right. I skipped breakfast.

The kid stirred, moaning fitfully as consciousness flickered about his skull. There was a good chance of delirium from the mauling and the seared meat where his genitals used to be, but I wasn't about to hook him up to an antibiotic IV drip.

Let him enjoy the oneiroid psychosis while it lasted. It's not a trip most people can claim to have experienced, and he did go on and on about that sort of thing while we were setting up this little adventure.

"Hey, you awake? Bet that feels fantastic, doesn't it? I mean, you're in for a lifetime of sitting while you piss, but that's more polite and evolved, anyway. Writing your name in the snow is overrated, don't you think?

I kid, I kid. What's a little ball-busting between friends? Too soon? Gallows humor, son. Gotta be able to laugh in the face of death. Smile through the bleeding."

His moans of pain and sorrow were growing louder, more insistent, rising to interrupt my monologues. Don't interrupt me when I'm on a roll, damn it.

"Hold tight, kiddo, I'm going to give you something to take the edge off. Don't go anywhere. I know the ticket price was for the whole seat, but for what's coming? You'll only need the edge!"

I chuckled bitterly. This is what it's come to. Dad jokes to an unappreciative audience. I went rummaging around my various toolchests, looking for my first aid kits. You generally want to be well stocked on the essentials in this line of work. I dug up a few morphine autoinjectors and killed his pain.

"There we go. That's better, isn't it? Now, listen; initially, I had planned much more for our little adventure, but I have to level with you. I'm not getting as much out of this as I'd thought I might. Sure, we've had some laughs, shed a little blood, maybe even learned a few things.

"But I'm bored and I don't think you're listening much at this stage. It's kinda bringing me down. So, I'm going to leave you some cliff notes and call it, I think. I hope you don't mind."

I grabbed an X-Acto knife and got started. There was a finite amount of space to impart what wisdom I could, but determination set in. Meticulously, I carved out an extensive litany of murderous laws across every inch of his skin. The commandments of blood, pus, and gastric juice: *"Thou shalt revel in flesh." "Covet neither fornication nor fame." "Worship no other gods before dismemberment and excoriation."*

I mixed Dettol and uncut betadine to cleanse the gore and trigger an anti-microbial apocalypse. The morphine kept him insensate enough that I could complete my task. In order to get to his back side, I'd had to cut him free from his chair and lay him down. The process took time — and the excessive bleeding didn't help. Had to be careful that he wouldn't bleed out, though.

Work quickly but get it right.

Once I'd covered him in words of power and wisdom, I gently set him into my comfortable chair. It was an incredibly difficult process, owing to his almost totally dead weight and the slipperiness of his body.

Finally, I pulled off the hood. What a face. I wanted to kill him so badly, to give in to the base impulses driven by my envy. He was young and pretty, whereas I was old and jaded. Dark hair and angular bone structure gave him an architectural look that would serve him well—if he lived through what I'd just done to him.

Finally, once he started lolling his head back and forth and gently moaning in mounting pain and not mere delirium, I made good on a decision I'd made without really realizing I'd made it. I guess I'd been thinking about it the whole time. I really have been on autopilot, just phoning in my psychopathic spree killing over and over. Well fuck you, Charlie.

I went upstairs, grabbed some cardboard, scrawled a last message on it, and then descended back to my domain… for the last time. I laid out all the tools of my trade on the various work surfaces, displaying them prominently. Like a proud hoarder, but with surgical steel and other implements of destruction.

Finally, I tied the cardboard around my neck, grabbed the hood, and tied my legs to the chair formerly occupied by my guest. It would have to be handcuffs for the hands; nothing much could be done about that. Once my ankles were secured, I pulled the hood over my face and cuffed my hands behind myself.

"Wake up, you little shit, you have work to do!" I barked as loudly as I could from under the hood. It was time for me to learn. The last words I'd written, which would be the first he would see, were simple: "Final exam. Show your work."

The Janus Experiment
Ronan Grey

They told him the rules.

"Your role is simple," a voice said. "You are Subject A: the torturer. He is Subject B: the test body. If he screams, the experiment resets."

There were other things—something about stress environments, pain thresholds, empathy decay—but it didn't matter. Only the red light in the corner, and the weight of the scalpel in his hand.

Day 1:

There were no clocks in the room. No windows. Just a stainless-steel table, and a single camera in the corner with a red eye. The walls were off-white, stained faintly at the edges. Subject A stared at the man. Subject B was chained to the table. Neither remembered how they got here.

A speaker crackled. "Begin."

The room was cold—no windows, just concrete walls and more stainless-steel fixtures. The slab stood in the center. Subject B was already restrained, naked, bleeding slightly from the wrists where barbed cuffs bit into his skin.

The cuffs tightened each time he moved.

Subject A was chained to the wall. He could reach the tools, and Subject B, but not the door. A tray had been left for him: a scalpel, clamps, a cloth. No instructions yet, just the knowledge he already carried—if Subject B screamed, it would all start over. There were no time limits. No safe words. Just pain, silence, and the constant gaze from unseen eyes behind the glass.

Subject B hadn't spoken yet. Neither had Subject A. When Subject A had grazed B's arm, just to see if he was real, B had flinched. He was real. That was the part Subject A wasn't prepared for; he was supposed to hurt someone real, who probably had a family who loved him.

Subject B looked at him with confusion, fear, and maybe even pity. Subject A told himself he would start with something small, just enough to test Subject B's threshold. But he couldn't do it. Instead, he sat in the corner, watching the red light on the camera blink.

They knew he hadn't begun.

Day 2:

The room felt noticeably colder on the second day. Subject A woke to the clatter of the tray being replenished—fresh cloth, a new scalpel, and a bottle of antiseptic that burned the air with its sharp scent. The restraints on his ankle had been tightened during the night; his skin was tender where the metal pressed.

Subject B watched Subject A with vacant eyes, waiting. There was no anger in his gaze—only exhaustion and a quiet, persistent dread. Subject A levitated his hand near the tools, hands shaking so badly he had to clench them into fists. He stared at the scalpel, willing himself to pick it up, to do what was expected. The camera's red light blinked in the corner, patient.

He tried to speak; nothing came up other than mumbled unfinished sentences. Instead, he reached for the antiseptic, dabbed it onto a piece of cloth. He pressed it gently to one of Subject B's wounds, more an act of care than cruelty. Subject B flinched but didn't pull away.

Minutes dragged by. Subject A's mind raced with excuses—maybe if he waited, they would change the rules, or someone would intervene. The experiment was pressing down on both of them; it was inescapable.

He set the scalpel down, unable to bring himself to make another cut. The stillness between them grew dense, punctuated only by the sound of their breath and the distant, mechanical hum behind the walls.

Subject A sat back against the concrete, head in his hands. The chain rattled as he shifted. Guilt stabbed its teeth deep into him, it felt sharper than any blade. He had failed the test—whatever it was—but he couldn't bring himself to hurt someone who looked so achingly human.

The day passed in agonizing increments. Subject A did nothing but wait, paralyzed by indecision and fear, knowing that eventually, someone would come. And when they did, he wasn't sure who they would punish first.

Day 3:

By the third day, the rules had changed. The tray that usually arrived with food and water was empty—except for the tools. No explanation was given, but the message was more than clear: participation was now a condition for living. Subject A's stomach ached with hunger, his mouth dry and heavy. Subject B looked even worse—pale, lips chapped, eyes sunken with exhaustion and thirst.

The camera's red light seemed more illuminating than before—unrelenting. Subject A's hands trembled as he reached for the scalpel, not out of obedience, but out of desperation. He glanced at Subject B, searching for some sign of permission, or forgiveness, anything. But Subject B only shuttered his eyes, as if bracing for what was to come.

Subject A made the first incision, shallow and slow, across Subject B's upper arm. Blood welled up, and Subject B's jaw clenched, but he did not scream. Subject A cleaned the wound with the cloth, hands clumsy and hesitant, to minimize the pain even as he inflicted it. He whispered an apology, barely audible.

The tray was replenished an hour later: a small bottle of water, a single piece of stale bread. Enough to keep them alive, but only just.

Subject A forced himself to eat, guilt churning in his gut with every bite. Subject B refused his share, turning his face away. He would not make this easy.

As the day dragged on, Subject A found himself caught in a cycle: inflict pain, receive sustenance, feel shame, and repeat. The line between torturer and victim obscure with every passing hour. Hunger gnawed at his will, and the idea that he was now involved in the victim's suffering rested over him like a wet, heavy cloak.

Day 4:

The scalpel digs slightly further into Subject B's torso, parting flesh with repulsive ease. Subject A starts dragging the blade down in a jagged line all the way to Subject B's lower abdomen. Blood gushes from the long cut.

Subject A peels the skin and tissue back, inch by inch. The muscle under is raw, twitching, and glistening red from the harsh lights. They kept pumping blood into him, refusing to let him die. They fill him up with blood, forcing new blood through a body that's being dismantled piece by piece.

His heart hammers, as Subject A tears him open. Blood

splashing everywhere, pooling beneath the table, the blood splattering across Subject B's arms and face. He never makes a sound, just stares at the ceiling—eyes wide and empty.

Then, suddenly, he screams. A raw, animal cry that shreds the air, echoing off the walls. The room falls into stillness. Even the machines seem to pause, the only sound being his scream. The door bursts open. A group of men swarmed in, masks covering their faces. They dragged Subject B away, only leaving a trail of blood and skin behind.

Now Subject A is alone.

Day 6:

They brought Subject B back. What was left of him, at least. His body was a patchwork of skin stretched taut over jagged, uneven stitches; he was bruised and swollen, seams leaking pus and syrupy dark blood.

The smell of infection was insufferable. He should be dead, but his chest still shook with each breath, a wet, rattling gasp that bubbled through the blood in his throat. His eyes peeled open like old paint flaking from a wall. They were glassy and unfocused, but alive. Somehow, alive.

They told Subject A what came next. The voice was cold and clinical even merciless; it cut through his mind like knives: Cut off his fingers and toes. Swap them. Fingers for toes. Toes for fingers.

Subject A's hands shook violently, the scalpel nearly slipping from his grip. He forced himself to look at Subject B's hands; his fingers twitched; his nails rimmed with dried blood, with skin mottled and bruised. Subject A's stomach gurgled, bile burning the back of his throat as he imagined the blade cutting through flesh and tendon, the crunch of bone. He gagged, a body wracked with dry heaves, but nothing came up.

He pressed the scalpel to Subject B's finger. The skin split with a wet, obscene squelch, blood was welling up instantly, pouring over trembling hands. Subject B jerked. Subject A sawed through the joint, the blade scraping and catching on bone, until the finger finally tore free with a nauseating pop. Blood spurted in thick, pulsing jets, splattering across Subject A's face, soaking his clothes, pooling on the floor in sticky, spreading puddles.

As he moved to the feet. Subject B's toes curled and trembled, the flesh was softer, the bones were smaller, but the blood was just as relentless. Each cut was worse than the last, the skin parting, the muscle tearing, and the bone snapping with a brittle, stomach-turning loud crunch. The room reeked of rot, the air with the sound of Subject B's sobs, and Subject A's own panicked breathing.

When he finally began the disgusting job of swapping the toes and fingers, he forced the toes onto the mutilated hands—the flesh resisted with might, the blood trickled and spurted with every movement. His vision had blurred with tears, spinning like a roulette wheel. The horror of what he was doing was about to consume him whole. His hands were slick covered in blood, trembling, and useless, caked with bits of skin.

Day 7:

The speaker crackled to life overhead, its voice cold, slicing through the murk of rot and exhaustion "Proceed to dental modification," it commanded, each word sharp. "Remove all teeth. Replace with available materials given to you on your tray—nails, screws. Begin now."

For a moment, he could only stare blankly at the weak body on the table, at Subject B's slacked jaw and the chipped teeth from clenching. His own breath came in stress-filled bursts. He wanted to speak up, to beg for some different task, but he knew better. The threat of punishment was always there, behind every order.

His eyes wandered to the tray of instruments. Among those scalpels and forceps were sporadically arranged rusty nails and screws. The fasteners sat dully under the harsh lights, making his stomach turn.

He stared again at Subject B's mouth: cracked lips, discolored teeth, and swollen gums. The very image of wrenching each tooth out, of driving metal through living flesh, sent his hand into such a tremor he nearly dropped the scalpel.

But the voices waited still. The red eye of the camera blinked. The air was stained with the scent of decay, and every breath tasted of old meat. Subject B lies motionless on the cold metal table. His hands are swollen, purple and black, the skin around the stitches puckered and angry. The pus at the seams oozing slowly, and pooling in his palm like thick yellow sludge.

Subject A stood above him, the scalpel trembling between fingers slick with sweat and blood. Somewhere inside the wide frame of the camera, the red light glowed— cold and steady. Half of Subject B's cheek had gone soft; the skin sloughed off in greasy yellow chunks-as if it were rotten fruit.

The exposed muscle shone raw and wet. Subject A fought the urge to retch as he scraped away the necrotic flesh and snagged on gritty bits of cartilage, with his scalpel. Every stroke was slow, methodical, and deliberate. The voices were constant. They drill into his skull: "Replace the teeth. Use what's at hand. Nails. Screws."

Subject A's hand trembled as he pried open Subject B's jaw: the lips were cracked, leaking pus at the corners. He fumbled for the dental pliers, gripping a molar slick with blood and saliva. The tooth resisted, rooted deep, but he twisted and wrenched until it ungrudgingly popped out with wet crunching, pouring blood out from the socket, thick and dark, dripping down Subject B's chin in viscous streams.

One by one, the teeth are ripped out of the jaw: incisors, canines, molars; each one tearing free with a fresh spray of blood, their roots accompanied by shreds of nerve and gum. Subject B's head lolled truly vacant now, a deep, guttural whimper broke free. The sockets gape as one, raw and naked; and the gums being shredded pulse with every labored breath.

Subject A reached for some rusty nails and screws, their points dulled with age and dried blood flecks. He aligned one with an empty socket; its tip shone bright under harsh light. With a trembling hand, he pressed it inside the bleeding hole, then smashed it with the handle of a scalpel; the nail went in with a sickening crunch, splitting the gums and driving into bone. Blood spurted, flecking onto Subject A's face.

He repeated the process, forcing nails and screws into each empty socket, the metal scraping against bone, the gums tearing and splitting with every blow. Some nails had bent, others drove in crooked, but he kept going, hands slick and shaking, vision blurring with tears and sweat. Each new "tooth" jutted at a grotesque angle, transforming Subject B's mouth into a jagged, metallic maw.

When he was done, Subject A stepped away, chest heaved, hands smeared with blood and bits of flesh. Subject B's mouth was a wreck—lips ripped, gums frayed, rows of nails and screws sticking out of the jaw like the teeth of some corroded, mechanical animal.

The experiment is still asking for more, but at the moment, the voices are silent, and only the sound of ragged breathing and the slow drip of blood can be heard in the room.

The voice came again, crackling through the speaker: "Remove necrotic tissue in the femoral region. Replace as needed." No feeling. No tone. Just a cold command. Subject A followed. He incised, scraping at Subject B's thigh, unveiling muscle, tendons, and bone. Blood collected dark and thick on the table. He suctioned it away, the tube gurgling.

Subject B's eyes stayed open, glassy and blank. He did not blink. He did not move. Subject A wondered if there was still something inside—whether Subject B was a man, or just a shell that kept him alive by the tubes, wires, and the unbearable pain.

Subject A's body struggled as well. He felt pain in his back because of standing for a long time. His wrists were bleeding and raw where the chains had been biting his skin. Hunger was like a sharp pain in his stomach that never stopped. He was unable to recall when he last ate or slept. He was like a person who dreamt even though his eyes were open—flashes of memory in his peripheral vision.

He saw Subject B, laughing once, before this nightmare. He saw his own hands, stained with blood, again and again.

The work was over. The camera gave a blink. The voice went mute. Subject A stepped away, breathing heavily, his hands going through an uncontrollable numbing. He wiped them on his apron, thus making blood, filth, and dirty spots appear.

Day 9:

Subject A's body was a collection of bruises, sores from chains, and skin cracked and raw from dehydration and malnutrition. His eyes were wild, bloodshot, darting nervously as if the shadows themselves might reach out and drag him under.

Subject B laid on the table, more corpse than man now. Lifeless limbs, tubes, and dried blood. His chest rose and fell in faint gasps. Subject A moved with precision, his hands slick with blood and antiseptic.

He was a surgeon, caretaker, and prisoner all at once—trapped in a grotesque cycle of destruction and repair. Today's task was worse than the last: he must replace a joint in Subject B's arm, a procedure that required cutting through fragile tissue and exposed nerves.

As he worked, the unseen voice sputtered through the speaker once again: "Faster. No mistakes." When Subject A got cold feet, the restraints that hugged his wrist and ankles tightened their grip, sending jolts through his heavy limbs. Hunger and exhaustion nibbled at him for what has felt like forever, but there is no break.

The punishment was inevitable and brutal.

Blood pooled beneath the table, dark like meat gone bad. The sterile room had transformed into a chamber of horrors—machines whir, and tubes hiss. Subject A's mind fractured further, slipping between reality and delirium.

Day 10:

Subject A's behavior was no longer merely different—it had radically changed, as if Subject A was emptied out, and now it walked around wearing someone else's skin. The practice of the morning begins as always: harsh lights flicker on, the tang of blood floated in the air, and the camera's red eye blinked awake.

But Subject A did not move with the practiced, mechanical precision that had defined his previous days. Instead, he stood at the foot of the slab, hands slack at his sides, staring at Subject B's ruined form with a gaze that seemed to look straight through flesh and bone, into some distant, unreachable place.

He was slow to respond to the first command. It was like his mind was somewhere else, dragging behind him. His fingers hovered above the tray of blood-lusted tools, twitching, tapping out a silent, irregular rhythm. He picked up a scalpel, then put it down. Then he did it again. His lips moved, forming words. Sometimes, a low mutter escaped him, fragmented syllables, half-remembered orders from previous days.

Subject A's eyes flicked to the red eye in the corner of the room, then looked away. He wiped sweat from his temples, even though the room was cold. His breathing was shallow and quick. He began the day's procedures, but his focus was gone.

He paused often, the scalpel hovering above exposed tissue, as if he had forgotten what came next. He ran his fingers along Subject B's stitched skin, tracing the seams with a kind of idle curiosity, then suddenly recoiled, as if burned. He rubbed his temples, digging his nails into his scalp, muttering, "Not me." over and over until the words dissolved into a wet, choking cough.

The voice crackled through the intercom, sharper than before: "Continue. Do not deviate. Efficiency is survival." The words seemed to deflect off Subject A, barely noticing the noise that has become regular. He glanced at the speaker, his chapped lips curling into a faint, grim smile, then he returned to his work with a jerky motion.

He cut, but not with the usual care. The blade sliced too deep, and blood welled up like rusted oil gushing from a torn engine. Subject B did not scream but squinted hard. Subject A stared at the wound, mesmerized. He dipped a finger into the blood, smudged it across his own forearm, then wiped it away with a shudder. His hands shook, but not from fear.

From emptiness. From exhaustion. From something else entirely maybe.

At times, he simply stopped. He stood over Subject B, breathing the fetid air. Minutes passed. The camera's light seemed to get brighter then slowly dimmer. The intercom hissed, but Subject A did not move. He was somewhere else—lost in thought, or hallucinations, or the endless, ringing quietness that had taken root inside his skull.

He began to talk to Subject B, voice low and urgent. "Do you remember?" he whispered. "Do you know who I am?" Sometimes a laugh escaped his raspy throat, a dry, broken sound. Sometimes he wept silently, tears falling through the dirt on his face. He leaned close, saying something that couldn't be heard to Subject B. The overseers watched, their voices more insistent. "Continue. Do not stop. There is no end."

Subject A obeyed, but each movement was more uncertain. He became more deranged by the second, thread by thread, sanity fraying in the sterile light. The experiment continued. He had become someone—something—else. The room was silent, except for the breathing of Subject B and the periodic tapping of Subject A's fingers against the blood-covered metal tray.

The camera watched.

Day 11 Incident Report:

At 16:57, the facility containing Project Janus was plunged into sudden, absolute darkness. The surveillance monitors were black, fluorescent lights died, and the red glow of the camera winked out. The only thing left was silence, the technical teams scrambled to diagnose the cause: a catastrophic overload, triggered by the demand of the blood pumping apparatus.

The last frozen image captured before the blackout

showed Subject A, unmoving, hunched over Subject B's exposed abdomen. His hands clutched ropes of intestine, blood soaking his apron and hands, pooling beneath the slab in slow, viscous waves. Subject B's skin was corpse-pale, lips parted, eyes fixed on nothing.

For over two hours, the chamber remained sealed and unmonitored. Attempts to restore power failed, the backup generators flickering and dying. Staff claimed to hear faint, wet noises, something dragging, slithering, the metallic scrape of instruments against tile. Others refused to approach the chamber, paralyzed by fear that grew with every passing minute.

At 19:00, the lights came back to life. The cameras flickered on, revealing a scene that seemed frozen due to the outage. Subject B lay motionless on the slab, he didn't move, not even a twitch, his chest was still. No signs of life seemed to pick up on the monitors. His blood had dried in dark streaks across his torso and pooled beneath him in a chunky red halo.

Then, at 19:01, Subject A moved. He climbed atop Subject B's body, his face a mask of manic determination and exhaustion. In his fist, the scalpel. Without hesitation, he plunged the blade deep into the side of Subject B's neck, sawing back and forth with a frenzy that bordered on the inhuman.

The scalpel tore through skin and muscle, sending pulsing arcs of blood spraying across Subject A's hands, his face, the walls. The crimson torrent drenched the floor, splattering the camera lens.

At 19:02, the emergency alarm screamed. The response team burst into the room, voices raised in urgent commands. Medical personnel rushed to restrain Subject A, to revive Subject B, but their efforts were futile. Subject B was gone, he had no pulse, no breath, no hope of recovery.

Suddenly, at 19:04, Subject A flared into violence. He tore free from the hands that held him, launching himself at the nearest nurse with the bloodied scalpel. His movements were wild, and animalistic, his eyes rolling with rage. The blade flashed, catching flesh of medical personnel, drawing screams.

Hell erupted; staff scrambling, slipping, falling, the alarm drowning out their cries. Calls for lockdown were shouted through the halls. Security barriers slammed shut. The experiment was terminated, the facility plunged into emergency shutdown. The chamber doors sealed, trapping the aftermath inside.

Day 12

After the first restoration of power, an emergency bulb cast a harsh, pulsating lighting in the corridors. Security personnel had weapons drawn, quietly moving about the building. They found surgical instruments littered like breadcrumbs and bloody handprints smeared all over the walls.

Some rooms had become so cold that frost had formed on the glass. The thought of being alone was horrific. Narrowly pressed against the wall, eyes evasively darting toward every flicker of dark light, the staff would literally cling to one another. Others said they saw a figure— barefoot, all covered in blood, and jerkily moving around.

The intercom, once used for clinical orders, now spat static and the occasional, distorted fragment of Subject A's voice: "Not me…" over and over again. Sometimes it was a whisper, sometimes a howl, sometimes stretched into a sound that was not quite a word at all.

The mainframe logs showed erratic surges, as if something was feeding on the building's power, draining it from every circuit. The doors to the chamber where it all began sat still, peaceful almost. No one dared to open those doors. No one wanted to see what might be on the other side.

The experiment was over. The order had been given: suspend all operations, secure all personnel, and contain Subject A at any cost. But as the night wore on, it became clear the facility was no longer a place of science or control.

Day 19

The operating room had turned into a shrine of agony. The floor was a hideous scene, there were severed limbs twisted at impossible angles, jagged bone jutting through muscle, and fingers curled into claws as though their bodies had died trying to escape. Desperate handprints and arterial sprays were streaked across the walls.

The heads were crudely hacked from their bodies, staring blankly from pools of blood, their mouths agape in silent screams for help.

At the center of this massacre, the Torturer stood over the man who had once controlled everything: the overseer, the head of the experiment. Stripped of his authority and his clothing, he was simply nothing more than another trembling body. The overseer's wrists and ankles cinched tight in barbed cuffs, like his previous victims.

Each twitch sent fresh streams of blood trickling down his limbs, the metal biting deeper with every movement. The Torturer leaned close, voice slick with reverence and mockery.

"Subject A, my beautiful disaster," the overseer rasped in awe. "I remember when you couldn't even lift a scalpel—you've become everything they feared. And oh, how I adore that."

The Torturer's eyes were wild, bloodshot from the

restless nights he spent in that chamber, the madness within sharpened to a lethal edge. In his hand, he had a ravenous blade that shined with a glow in the light.

He moved with a slow, meaningful menace; he made sure he was saving every second of the anticipation. The overseer, once the observer, was now the prey—the subject. With a violent yank, the Torturer tore away the last pieces of clothing, exposing bare skin.

He knelt close and pressed the blade to flesh. Superficial lines bloomed red, blood welling up and trickling down the overseer's body. Each cut was a cruel stroke, the Torturer's gaze never leaving the blood trails he created.

He forced the man into grotesque, and agonizing poses, muscles screaming in exhaustion. Whenever the man stalled or gasped for air, the Torturer sliced his torso; these cuts got deeper than the last, crueler; he refused to grant even a moment's respite. Blood pooled beneath the overseer, as pain blurred the edges of reality.

The Torturer watched, a twisted, sickening smile playing on his lips, the torture was feeding on the suffering of the man who had once watched him through the camera. He hummed an tuneless melody, his breath hot and erratic against the overseer's skin. His attitude shifted without warning: still one moment, then exploding with frenzied violence the next. Between the fits, he leaned in, muttering a mix of broken meaningless words.

Without hesitation, the Torturer dragged the blade across the man's thigh, carving a jagged, gaping wound. Blood poured down the leg, pooling on the floor. He forced his fingers into the raw incision, digging through muscle and sinew until he touched bone.

The pain was blinding; screams tore from the man's throat as the Torturer methodically peeled the skin from his legs, exposing the glistening tissue beneath. He paused only to meet his victim's gaze, his eyes flat and unfeeling. "Screaming breaks the rules," he murmured coldly, before returning to his gruesome work.

The overseer was secured upright against a vertical operating table, vision shrouded by a tight blindfold. His jaw was forced wide open by cold, unyielding metal hooks. Suddenly, a jolt of agony erupted as a tooth was wrenched from his mouth with pliers. Before he could recover, rough hands seized his tongue, threading a fishing hook through its flesh. The sharp pull on the line forced his head to twist and follow, helpless to resist.

The Torturer loomed at his side. The overseer's jaw ached. The flavor of copper was rich in his mouth from the gaping socket where his tooth had been torn free. Blood dribbled down his chin, dripping onto his chest.

He tugged the fishing line, wrenching the head at a grotesque angle, making the neck strain and burn. There was no scream—the pain too sharp, the mouth too full of blood and metal. The Torturer jammed his fingers into the mouth, prying open another tooth with forceps, rocking it back and forth until the roots tore away with a sickening crunch.

Nerve pain exploded, searing hot, as blood spurted and mixed with saliva, running down the overseer's throat.

The Torturer lowered himself, dragging a scalpel along the gums, that separated flesh from bone while making slow, intentional incisions. The blade scratched against the enamel and jaw, the vibrations rattling through the overseer's skull. The Torturer carved a flap of gum, then peeled it back, exposing raw, glistening bone. The overseer's body convulsed against his restraints.

The Torturer let the blood pool, then scooped it with his fingers, smearing it across the man's cheeks and forehead. He said something frantic and unintelligible, he wasn't finished. The Torturer grabbed a dental elevator, wedging it between another tooth and the socket, twisting until bone cracked and splintered.

Shards rained onto the chest, sticky with blood. The overseer's vision was swallowed in total darkness, the coarse blindfold pressing into his skin like sandpaper. Deprived of sight, every other sense screamed into the void—each nerve ending raw, ripped open, begging for the smallest relief.

The Torturer's movements were almost clinical, but there was wildness in his breath—a pleasure in the suffering he inflicted. The overseer was nothing but a body to be opened, a mouth to be ruined, flesh to be torn and bled. Time ceased to exist in that room.

There was only pain, the wet sound of metal in flesh, the taste of iron and salt and the smell of something rotten. The Torturer became a shadow—sometimes close: breathing, humming, sticky hands on the man's face; sometimes far, footsteps echoing in the darkness. Sometimes he spoke, sometimes he only muttered to himself, words melting before they could be understood.

He cut the man's cheek, peeled the skin back, slow, humming louder. The overseer saw nothing, but felt everything—air stinging the rawness, the urge to scream or sleep or simply vanish.

The Torturer murmured something. "No screaming," the man repeated in his head, over and over.. He could no longer feel his hands. He tried to wiggle his fingers, nothing. Maybe The Torturer had taken them. Maybe he was only a mouth now, ruined and bleeding, waiting for the end.

The Torturer pressed something cold against his forehead. "Almost done," he whispered, or maybe he didn't. Maybe the pain was all that was left. And in that room, the Torturer finished what the overseer had begun—turning the architect of suffering into its final, most broken victim.

When the blood stopped flowing and the last shudder faded from the ruined body on the slab, the architect of the project was reduced to so much torn flesh, his ambition and authority was erased in red. The Torturer stood over him, hollow-eyed, the rigid scalpel slipping from his gore-slicked fingers.

Nothing announced the experiment's fall. No scream. No cold order. Only the arrival of what had always been promised: violence. The same violence that cradled its birth. All that remained was the aftermath—a room painted in failure, and the knowledge that in the end, the experiment had devoured everyone who touched it.

The Nordsolen
Galo Romero

On a winter day in 1932, as the sun rose, I crossed the gangway onto the M/S Nordsolen carrying my personal effects in a canvas sack slung over my shoulder. The Nordsolen was a break-bulk vessel manned by a crew of thirty. Launched in 1912, under the Norwegian flag, the ship wasn't elegant like a passenger liner, but its practical design served a purpose: built with five cargo holds, the ship could transport freight weighing 5,000 tons.

By midday the Nordsolen left the Port of Oslo on its way to the North Sea. I took my first post on the main deck for watch duty. As I leaned over the bulwarks, I expelled a diaphanous frosty breath and watched the drifting chunks of ice as the ship plowed through the frozen waters of the Oslo Fjord.

My chest heaved and gulped the cold Norwegian air. Tears formed as I beheld with glazed eyes the green hills and valleys of the land of my birth, as if this was to be the last day I would ever see them.

#

I shared my living quarters with our boatswain, a jovial ginger named Anders Schulman. Anders and I were the only unlicensed personnel invited to eat with the officers. This was an honorary membership bequeathed to us for our many years of devoted service to the Nordsolen: a privilege both envied and vilified by our fellow seaman.

Later that evening, amid the pungent aromas of cigar smoke and alcohol, I learned the Nordsolen had abruptly set course to London. As we ate what our cook called his gastronomic specialty, Anders asked my anticipated question: "Why London, Captain?"

The sonorous voice of Captain Reidar Goransen, the hawkish and stern commander of our merchant ship, succinctly replied, "To retrieve a very special item and ship it to New York City, into the waiting hands of a museum curator."

Anders queried, "What kind of item?"

"A sarcophagus."

Anders kept the chatter going, "What's a sarcophagus?"

Captain Goransen stoically replied, "A coffin."

"Dear God!," I grimly uttered.

Chief Mate Nils Ohlin fixed his disapproving eyes on me and said, "Jonas, where's your Viking spirit? Didn't you once say you were a direct descendant of Erik the Red? Tell us, were your ancestors also there when his son, Leif Erikson, discovered Vinland?"

"No, I never said that. I said one of my ancestors was on a Viking ship, a colonist in…"

Second Mate Olof Moen growled, "Erik the Red? More like Jonas the Meek! His ancestors were probably thralls."

I saw a sadistic glee in Nils eyes as his words dug

deeper, "What's the matter, Jonas? Don't like coffins? Do the dead spook you? Will I need to tuck you in at night and leave the lamp light on?"

The mess room erupted into laughter. I lowered my head and stared at my food, as humiliation and a creeping dread drove a searing knife through my appetite.

Anders childlike curiosity led his mouth, "So, Captain, who's the stiff in the box?"

"Do you really want to know?"

Anders nodded. "Yes, we're all curious to know. Tell us a story."

Captain Goransen wiped his mouth clean on a cloth napkin. His eyes narrowed as he rubbed his chin, which was buried under a black cropped beard. Inexplicably, he appeared overcome by a sudden sorrow until he smiled and spoke, "Have it your way."

With an air of gravitas, Captain Goransen quickly downed a shot of vodka. He puzzled over the empty glass in a brief moment of silent reflection then violently threw it over our heads, across the mess room.

It hit a wall and shattered upon impact. A pronounced hush settled over the once boisterous group. Our startled faces washed onto him with rapt attention. He leaned forward and looked us dead in the eyes as he spoke, "The sarcophagus contains the remains of the High Priest of a sadistic cult who worshipped the storm god of ancient Canaan: Baal, 'Giver of Life', son of Dagon.

"As legend has it, the High Priest and his retinue conspired to kidnap the three sons of the Ugarit King and murder them on the night of the Syrian full moon. They schemed to drink the blood of the eldest son, eat the flesh of the second, and burn the last child, as sacrificial offerings to Baal.

"In return for these sacrifices, the high priest and his followers sought wisdom, invisibility, and immortality.

This diabolical machination was leaked to the Ugarit King by way of a spy who whispered into the king's ears, 'They have built the high places of Baal, to drink, eat, and burn your sons as offerings to Baal.'

"The King of Ugarit, mad with rage, sent an army to destroy the Baal temple and slaughter its congregation. Baal's worshippers were massacred in a bloodletting that is legend, save for the High Priest who was brought to his knees at the foot of the King's throne. For the pleasure of his eyes to witness, the rabid ruler instructed his soldiers to remove the High Priest's evil heart.

"As this vengeful deed was done, the Ugarit King, in an act of blind hatred, read arcane words from an ancient parchment: *'Never again will your body follow the laws in which we mortals live by. You are forever reduced to a creature of the night: not alive, nor dead; a creature that is both a plague to man and to thyself; a parasite feeding on the blood of the innocent. Never again will your eyes gaze upon the golden radiance of daylight: if ever thou attempt such, may the burning rays of the sun deliver you screaming into oblivion in a burst of hellfire. You are forever cast out as a demon in the service of Baal.'*

"The High Priest's bloodied corpse and still beating black heart were placed within a sarcophagus. A warning, written in cuneiform script, in the ancient Ugaritic language, was inscribed on each side of the sarcophagus. It reads, *He who lies within is neither man nor beast, but a demon servant of the Temple of Baal. His evil heart and wicked soul remain immortal, contained within this stone prison for all eternity. Break not this sealed lid, for to do so is to unleash onto this world, the darkest plague.*"

Captain Goransen's fierce black eyes measured each and every one of us. He mesmerized our frayed fraternity into a mindless stupor; his recondite knowledge proved too much for our simple minds.

No one among us swallowed or drank, nor stole a breath, or spoke a word. The fog of uncomfortable silence mercifully lifted when he spoke again, "In the spring of 1928, in what is now known as Ras Shamra, a Syrian farmer ploughing land accidentally discovered a catacomb. Local authorities and French archaeologists determined the site as the Necropolis of Ugarit. A few years later, many excavated artifacts made their way to London, including a sarcophagus. The very sarcophagus we are to transport to New York City: The Sarcophagus of The High Priest of the Temple of Baal."

The captain produced a cigar and pocket cigar cutter, cut the cigar tip, placed the cigar into his mouth, lit it with the strike of a match, deeply inhaled, leaned back against his chair, and let out a long puff of smoke. He flicked cigar ash into a glass of water, studied the floating ashes, and waited for some kind of reaction from his captive audience.

Nils was the first to come to. He poured vodka into a shot glass, raised it to eye level, and did his best to mimic a pirate, "If any man here be afraid of sea monsters, ghosts, or things that go bump in the night, let him whimper in the dark and hide behind the skirts of little old ladies as we courageous pirates prowl the seven seas in search of the perfect plunder!"

Once more the officers behaved in fraternal fashion, laughing as they raised their drinks, insouciantly toasting to Nils. I kept my glass on the table, petrified by an icy chill that crept up on me like a pall of doom.

#

The next morning, under heavy fog cast from the Thames River, our crew, aided by stevedores from the Port of Tilbury, had hoisted the sarcophagus onto the Nordsolen. It was packaged in a thick wooden crate labeled fragile. We stowed it in cargo hold no. 5: the aft hold.

Captain Goransen ordered it cordoned off, isolated from the other freight, and lashed by rope to four iron rings bolted to the floor to ensure minimal damage in the rolling waves of the ocean. I stood staring at it, loathing its existence, and wondered if there was any truth to the legend.

With the sarcophagus onboard, the Nordsolen left the port of London on course to New York. The weather was cooperative, as were the unseasonally calm waters of the English Channel, which seemed to embrace our ship in an inviting manner. And yet I was still bothered by an all-oppressive gloom: a gloom rooted in cargo hold no. 5.

#

As an Able Seaman, I was assigned a nightly four-hour watch. It was my duty to patrol the ship for any signs of trouble. At the stroke of midnight, I began Middle Watch armed with a flashlight and a cylindrical-shaped tin whistle. After I patrolled the forecastle, the main deck, and the bridge decks without incident, a nagging curiosity led me to cargo hold no. 5. I entered the aft access hold and climbed down the hatch ladder into the hold.

As I squeezed through a narrow passage of crates, boxes, and casks, I heard a heartbeat echo through my ears. Was I mad or was the combination of darkness and salty air getting the best of me? I convinced myself what I just heard was my overworked imagination, so I pressed on. I took a half step before I came to a jarring halt. On the far side of the bulkhead, revealed in the cone of my flashlight, was the crate housing the sarcophagus.

With trepidation, I approached the crate with my flashlight in one hand and my whistle in the other. The crate shifted, scraping plywood against the steel floor, producing a grating sound like the sharp talons of a predator tearing flesh.

Aghast, I dropped my whistle as I sprang behind a wall of boxes and cowered. My ears followed the tin body of my whistle rolling away in the darkness. Rising bile coated the inner walls of my throat. Beads of cold sweat slithered down my brow.

I barely held onto the flashlight with trembling hands, but my terrified fingers wouldn't release it for the stark dread of being plunged into an obsidian abyss. I heard plywood rasp once more and felt the floor move under my feet, synchronized to the undulating waters of the North Atlantic Ocean. The ropes and iron rings the crate fastened to, held it in place.

I closed my eyes and let out a sigh of relief. I stood, braced my back against the bulk of a heavy box, and readied my flashlight. A disembodied heartbeat echoed once more. I made a mad dash for the hatch ladder, climbed the rungs for dear life, and never looked back.

My relief watch, Ordinary Seaman Sebastián Reynaldo Reyes, a young, gangly, bronze-skinned fellow from Lisbon, whom I suspected was the illegitimate child of Captain Goransen, discovered me curled up on the mess room floor. It was apparent I ended middle watch prematurely and sought refuge in a bottle of vodka. I bribed Sebastián to keep his mouth shut with cold cash and the promise of cigarettes. He smirked, pulled me up to my feet, slapped me on the back and let out a laugh.

Much of the next morning, I spent hidden in my cabin avoiding my fellow seamen by pretending to be ill. The crew was not aware of my dereliction of watch duties. I was grateful Sebastián was a man of his word.

It was late in the afternoon when I emerged from my cabin. As I turned to the bow, on the horizon, I spotted five streaks of black and purple clouds which resembled the skeletal fingers of a dead man's hand. This was an omen, a celestial warning, which had to be linked with the destiny of the Nordsolen and the heretical cargo it carried.

I speculated the hand was forged from the North Atlantic waters by vengeful gods to capture, sink and drag the Nordsolen into the lowly ocean depths toward a murky grave.

I ran up to the bridge deck to alert the captain. I flung the door open and burst into the wheelhouse, panting and sweating.

Chief Mate Nils Ohlin looked at me and snickered, "Well if it isn't the little thrall. What's the matter, Jonas, are the dead still troubling you?"

Captain Goransen's brow furrowed. "What's the meaning of this, Jonas? I gave no order for your…"

"Forgive me for my haste, Captain, but we are all in mortal danger!"

"Danger? What do you mean?"

"Danger from the evil which lurks in the bowels of this ship!"

"He's gone mad!" Second Mate Olof Moen exclaimed.

"I am not mad! Can't you see? On the horizon, the gods are ready to bring us down, to crush and drown us all unless we release to them the remains of that blasphemous being we carry in our cargo hold!"

Captain Goransen approached me and, with two gorilla-sized hands, held me in a vise clamped at my shoulders. "Jonas, calm yourself. It's just a coming storm. We've been through them before."

"It's not just any storm. Darkness will soon engulf this ship unless we do something about it. We have to get rid of it… jettison into the ocean!"

"Jonas, there's absolutely nothing to fear. I promise you."

"No, Captain, you're wrong! The Nordsolen is doomed

unless we dispose of it. We must cast it into the water and let the ocean do with it what it wills!"

Captain Goransen turned to his two officers and barked a command, "Nils, Olof, escort Jonas to sickbay. He is to remain there under medical supervision until he is fit to resume his duties."

I protested, "But sir?"

"Jonas, go with these men, for your own sake."

"No! Can't you see?"

"Jonas, this is an order! Nils, Olof, take him off my bridge! *Now!*"

Flanked by Nils and Olof, who held me firmly at the crooks of my arms, they ushered me into the mouth of sickbay. We were greeted by the startled face of the Nordsolen's doctor, Mathias Jensen, who rose from behind an antique writing desk.

"What the devil is going on?"

With a stiff upper lip, Nils replied, "Doctor, the captain has ordered Jonas to be placed under your care until he's fit to resume his duties."

From behind a pair of gilded Windsor glasses, Dr. Jensen's blue eyes cast a soft radiance. His index finger pushed the saddle of his spectacles up. "Why?"

"This seaman has gone mad. He trespassed onto the bridge ranting and raving like a lunatic. By his conduct, it's obvious he needs a one-way ticket to a straitjacket and a padded cell."

I twisted forward to loosen the grip of my captors. "Don't believe them! It's not true! I'm not mad!"

Olof struggled to subdue me. "Keep still! Don't force me to strike you!"

Doctor Jensen came to my defense, "There'll be no need for that. Unhand him. Give him some breathing room."

"Doctor?" Nils said, taken aback.

"It's alright. I've known Jonas Ludvigsen from the day this ship made its maiden voyage. He's a good man. Trust me; let him go."

Nils and Olof eyed each other and nodded. Olof cupped my jaw with one hand and squeezed it like a lemon. With the other hand, he held up a meaty fist and waved it menacingly as he looked deep into my eyes, "Don't try anything funny, or else! Got it?"

Dr. Jensen brushed both men aside and took hold of my arm. "That's enough!"

He pulled me into the infirmary and quickly slammed the steel door. "Jonas, this is unlike you, causing a commotion on the bridge. What's this uproar all about?"

"You're going to think I'm crazy, Doctor."

"Let me be the judge of that. Now, tell me, what's troubling you?"

Dr. Jensen was right, we had known each other for nearly twenty years, working on the Nordsolen since its maiden voyage when I was just a pimply-faced teenager pretending to be a man. I felt I could confide in him and speak freely of the fate of the Nordsolen. "It's the cargo we carry... that stone coffin... the sarcophagus."

"What about it?"

"There's something unnatural about it... something evil."

"Evil? I don't follow."

"Doctor, I'm speaking about the legend of the High Priest of the Temple of Baal: an ancient evil, made immortal, buried thousands of years ago in Syria, now rests in cargo hold no. 5."

"Jonas, surely you don't believe such nonsense... do you?"

"It's true. That thing's alive. I heard it!"

"Heard it?"

"Yes, Doctor, on my watch duties last night. I heard its

heart… beating."

"You mean to tell me you heard a heart beating from within the sarcophagus?"

"I know it sounds outlandish, but it's all true. You must believe me!"

Dr. Jensen stared at me in much the same way the officers did. It was obvious he didn't believe me. He did not say a word. But I continued undeterred, desperate for him to listen. "And now, Doctor, a storm is on the horizon; a storm created by the gods to stop the Nordsolen from delivering this abomination to New York City. We are all doomed unless…"

"Unless what?"

"…unless we release the sarcophagus into the waters of the North Atlantic. Let it plunge into the murky depths of the ocean where it should remain, forever."

"Jonas, you've fallen victim to the fanfare of a myth… a piece of historical fiction. But it's just storytelling nonsense meant to provoke a scare. None of it is true."

"But, doctor—"

"No buts, Jonas; listen to me. I want you to take off your coat, roll up your sleeve, and lay down on the cot."

"But…"

"Trust me."

I had no choice; I trusted this man with my life. I took off my pea coat and slung it over a chair. I rolled up the right sleeve of my shirt as I eased myself onto the cot. Dr. Jensen rummaged through a medical cabinet. He pulled out a vial and syringe. He approached me with the needle in his hand. "This will sting a little."

"What is it, Doc?"

"It's a mild sedative to calm your nerves and help you rest."

"Sleep?" I exclaimed.

Before I had time to protest, the needle pricked my vein

just below my bicep. I felt the burn of the drug as Dr. Jensen gently pressed the plunger of the syringe.

"You're putting me to sleep?"

"Relax, Jonas… you'll feel better very soon."

The sedative that coursed through my veins quickly took root. I waved my hands and fingers, intrigued by the light trails it created. Dr. Jensen's face and body became distorted, compressing and expanding like an accordion. The infirmary melded into a miasma of coruscating color.

It swirled into a raging vortex and funneled me into a surreal scene of nightmarish design. *From a rocky perch, I lifted into the sky and flew above the shores of Norway—a Herring Gull in search of food. On the horizon, a dark speck appeared against the orange and gold of the sun.*

As I flew closer, I could see it was the familiar shape of a cargo ship. With all my strength, I flapped my wings and increased my speed. Soon I was above the vessel, circling it from a great height, and observed below the odd absence of passengers or a crew. But it was when I completed the aerial circle, that I eventually discovered the very reason for this dereliction; in the ship's wake, the sea was stained a murky red from a long trail of human bodies that littered the path, floating and bobbing… carrion for scavengers. I did not resist as my gull instincts assumed control.

I descended, gliding in a downward spiral, until I landed softly on the chest of a floating corpse. For a moment I waited, curiously studying a man in a blood-soaked uniform, with a familiar bearded face and soulless black eyes which glared vacantly at me, until a wanton and insatiable hunger drove me forward.

I pecked and pulled on his skin, tore flesh from his cheek with my bill, and gorged on his face.

And I ate, and ate, and ate.

#

When my world came to, I blinked several times before my wristwatch told me it was a few hours before sunrise. Through the sickbay porthole, I could see a steady rain was falling. Fully clothed, I quietly rose from underneath the blankets of my cot, grabbed my pea coat, and crept across the dark threshold of the infirmary, ever careful not to disturb my snoring comrade, Dr. Mathias Jensen.

As I made my escape, the damp and frigid winds of the North Atlantic greeted me with a bitter embrace. Lurking in the sky behind purple and gray clouds, the flash of lightning illuminated my surroundings.

I grabbed an axe which was mounted near a fire hose. Raindrops pelted my laced boots as I navigated down to the main deck. The Nordsolen was eerily silent save for the howls of the windswept ocean. I thought it curious I had not seen the light of the middle watch at any given time during my descent. Under the cover of night, I sneaked my way to the hatch cover of cargo hold no. 5.

Seldom do desperate men think through their course of action, employing little logic or reason, but in my defense, there was scant time to prepare or waste.

My on-the-spot plan was simple: remove the protective tarpaulin on the hatch cover of cargo hold no. 5, loosen its clamps, open its telescoping hatch cover using an electric winch, and finally, with the aid of a crane, I was to hoist the sarcophagus up from the hold and drop it into the raging waters of the North Atlantic.

Of course, there was a major flaw in this plan to contend with: even under the camouflage of darkness and the veil of the brewing storm, my actions would no doubt draw attention to the watch and crew who would do their best to stop me. But no matter, I was a determined man, for the fate of the Nordsolen rested solely upon my shoulders.

And sure enough, the conical glow of the light of the

middle watch had forced me to take cover and hide. I opened the access door to cargo hold no. 5 and quickly entered. With bated breath, I gripped the axe with my left hand, and, one-handed, swiftly climbed down the hatch ladder into the bowels of the hold.

I waited in the dark, hoping the watch would continue his round without spotting me. To my surprise, I heard the wheel of the hatch door located on the floor, which led down into the propeller shaft tunnel, squeak and turn. When the hatch door popped open, dark shadows and heavy boots climbed up and scrambled into the hold.

The overhead lights of the cargo hold flickered to life; I crept behind a stack of crates and boxes and hid. Whomever they were, they probably accessed the propeller shaft tunnel from the engine room located in the middle of the ship, walked the claustrophobic threshold of the tunnel in the hull above the keel, which passed beneath cargo holds 4 and 5, and ended at the ship's propellers. But if they were doing a check on the ship's propellers, why would they loiter in the aft hold? I took a deep breath and slowly titled my head sideways to sneak a peek. To my dismay, Captain Goransen, Chief Mate Nils Ohlin, and Second Mate Olof Moen had gathered around the sarcophagus, cutting the ropes that held it in place.

Captain Goransen spoke, "Gentlemen, our time together has grafted a unique and special bond. The countless voyages we have undertaken have given me a profound understanding of this bond, unbreakable save for the specter of death. You have served me both dutifully and faithfully. You are my family. In all the years as your captain, I have looked for a way to repay you for your loyalty."

Captain Goransen laid three crowbars on the crate of the sarcophagus. "I have searched for the secrets which lie beyond man's grasp; a search which has taken me to some of the strangest and most exotic ports of the world. I have held court with wise men schooled in the peculiar ways of the arcane - ancient occult and mystical wisdom, passed down from generation to generation, from a time when the Earth was young and filled with celestial influence. My patience and diligence have finally paid off. You have been summoned to this cargo hold for this very reason. Our destiny lies with what's inside this crate. You have all heard the same calling as I. It cannot be denied."

In all my life, no greater blow had been delivered to my soul with such catastrophic impact. Had my ears betrayed me? I could not accept Captain Goransen had uttered those words. My heart sank deep into a black pit of despair. Any hope which resided in me quickly vanished. I wondered if all this was a nightmare delusion of my own making.

Then the luminous beam of a flashlight and a familiar voice interrupted, "Captain?" It was Anders Schulman, the ship's boatswain and my cabin mate, who entered the cargo hold during his watch duties.

Captain Goransen and his two cohorts calmly turned in Anders's direction. In the cone of the light, Captain Goransen's bearded face glowed in a fevered menace. "Welcome, Anders. We've been expecting you."

"Expecting me?"

Captain Goransen took a crowbar and gripped it firmly in his hands. "The men and I are going to open this crate and take a peek inside."

"Take a peek inside? But I thought we were shipping this artifact to a museum in New York City?"

Captain Goransen approached Anders like a predator stalking an unsuspecting prey. "There is no museum. There is no curator. There is no consignment. I made the purchase. The sarcophagus is mine."

The pitch in Anders voice rose as he mewled, "Yours? I'm sorry, Captain, but I don't understand?"

Captain Goransen stopped a breath short of Anders's face; their eyes locked. "Oh, but I believe you will... in time." The captain swung the crowbar and struck Anders with a vicious blow to the side of his skull. Anders slumped unconscious to the floor.

Chief Mate Nils Ohlin sneered, "What are we going to do with him, sir?"

Captain Goransen crouched over Anders and plucked the flashlight from his splayed fingers. "Anders is a portly fellow. The High Priest will need all his strength. I suppose he will make good as the first sacrifice."

Captain Goransen stood upright and winked at his fellow conspirators. "Gentlemen, grab a crowbar, and let's rip open this crate and commit to our destiny."

I watched, stunned and impotent from that black pit of despair, as the men dug their crowbars into the nails and wooden frame of the crate. Yet in that black pit, those emasculated feelings soon smoldered, kindled, and burned, and gave way to a fire; the eternal fire of a berserker's rage from a Viking ancestor. I emerged from my hiding place, lifted the axe over my head, howled like a feral madman, and rushed in to attack.

The first chop wedged into the wide back of Second Mate Olof Moen. A red haze mottled my face as he collapsed to his knees and then fell chin-first to the ground. The second chop, a lateral strike, found Chief Mate Nils Ohlin. Nils wailed in anguish, stupefied as he gaped at his severed arm lying on his blood-splattered boots.

A follow-up chop to his abdomen soaked his peacoat with streams of blood. He gurgled blood from his open mouth until I put him out of his misery with a fatal blow between his eyes.

I glared at Captain Goransen. "Why, Captain, why?"

"Jonas, I know this is a shock to you, but I also heard the calling. The High Priest has chosen us to join him on his conquest of the world. In return for our loyalty and servitude, we shall be given powers unimaginable, and perhaps the greatest gift of all: immortality. Do you understand?"

"You're insane!"

"My boy, this is a chance for something far greater than mere mortals have ever dreamed of; a chance to walk the earth as Ambassadors to a God… and I want to share this with you, my most deserving member of my crew."

My gaze drifted to the supine body of Anders Schulman. "Tell me, Captain, what do you plan to do with Anders, Dr. Jensen, Sebastián, and the rest of the men aboard this ship?"

"The High Priest will need to feast… and so shall we!"

I gripped my axe and defiantly shouted, "*Never!*"

Captain Goransen scowled. He swung his crowbar and missed. I held up the axe ready to counter-strike but the Nordsolen rolled aggressively. I lost my balance and fell, landing hard on my side, the axe popping loose from my fingers.

Captain Goransen crawled over me, committed to strike. I threw my arms up to protect myself from the oncoming blow. The Nordsolen heaved up on the crest of a monster wave, surged forward, and then the ship precipitously pitched down.

Captain Goransen fought to hold his balance and squandered the opportunity to strike; the crowbar dislodged from his grip. We wrestled for the skinny weapon. His hands groped for my neck and clamped. I clawed Captain Goransen's eyes with my fingernails.

He bellowed and released his noose-grip around my throat. I launched a fist, my bony knuckles landing flush on his hawkish nose; Captain Goransen's head snapped back. Somehow, through the chaos, my ears heard the unsettling squeal of scraping wood. I rolled to avoid the speeding wooden crate.

It flew by and smashed through a wall of crates and boxes, hurling loose freight into the air. It crashed with a deafening explosion against the steel bulkhead of the hold.

Lying prostrate, the thought of having narrowly escaped being crushed to death unsettled me. I rose, shaken, and searched for equilibrium amid the violent pitch, sway, and roll of the ship. As I wiped the sweat from my brow, my vision beheld the sarcophagus exposed amid a pile of splintered wood. When I inspected the wreckage, there was a limp and mangled body pinned against the bulkhead.

Blood trickled down Captain Goransen's grotesquely pulverized face. His soulless black eyes targeted me with stark condemnation. As he coughed blood, in defiance, he managed a wicked grin and revealed bloodstained teeth, and sibilantly hissed these final words, "You're all doomed."

Something stirred within me. I reclaimed the axe and ranted at the sarcophagus, "Blasphemous thing, I will cast you into the North Atlantic where its angry waters will pull you down into the deepest ocean depths, never to see the light of day!"

But as I advanced, terror had once again arrested my courage. The impact against the steel bulkhead had compromised the integrity of the sarcophagus: vein-like fissures branched throughout its stone casing. It shook, threatening to explode as a vapor, like soot, steamed through the branching cracks.

I raised the collar of my peacoat and covered my nostrils, to shield it from the putrid stench of death which filled the hold. The sarcophagus ruptured like an eggshell and fell apart into as many pieces. I witnessed in disbelief as the black vapor formed a trail, looped and coiled and magically coalesced into a corporeal form.

What stood before me not even my worst nightmares could prepare me for. What stood before me was an ancient curse come to life, spawned by the madness of a long-dead king and the dark magic of long-forgotten gods. What stood before me was a living, breathing, monster!

Placed on a human-like face, a pair of obsidian eyes stared vacantly from within cavernous eye sockets. These ghoulish eyes rested above two narrow slits which seem to serve as a nose. Just below the nose, a long triangular jaw was fitted with a ferocious set of short, spiked teeth, topped off with a pair of viper-like fangs.

Devoid of hair, with an albino and leathery complexion, its desiccated skin was pulled tautly over protracted skeletal limbs. Where the heart should normally be, a gaping hole framed by tattered and decomposed flesh, revealed a hollow torso. In the clutches of jagged and fungal-infected fingernails, it held a heart—a beating black heart.

With triumphant glee, it squeezed the heart through the hole and placed the organ back inside the empty cavity. Skin and tissue regenerated: the hole sealed; the unholy heart entombed.

I staggered backward and nearly tripped over the unconscious Anders Schulman. Then, something beyond comprehension took hold of me. I felt two sharp stings followed by hot blood trickling down my neck.

A paralysis neutralized my limbs; the axe slipped from my lifeless fingers. I was lifted. My rubber heels and soles dangled a few centimeters above the floor. I sensed my life essence being drained from me; darkness was occluding my soul. It had me; this abomination had me and was consuming me. I bleated mercy to the gods of my ancestors, "Save me! Please, save me! Don't let it take me!"

My prayers were answered. Upon hearing my pleas for

help, Anders Schulman regained consciousness. Dazed and confused, he rose zombie-like to his feet. In a display of unyielding friendship and courage, he picked up the axe and committed to my aid.

Anders drove the axe blade into the back of the creature. Distracted by this transgression, the demon dropped me to the floor. Stunned and bleeding, my eyelids fluttered in a spastic frenzy, like the flapping wings of wild avians imprisoned in a cage. I covered my eyes to shut them. When I regained focus, my savior threatened the anachronistic and incongruous being with another attack. Anders raised the axe with both hands over his head and released a powerful chop.

It hit the demon squarely on the torso, lodging the axe head deep into its broad chest. Black and crimson streams of blood oozed like sap from a tree. The monster uncoiled a deafening roar and dematerialized into a sooty cloud. The axe fell and bounced before Anders's boots.

He stood petrified. Absolute despair marched over his blood-leeched face. Uncertain as to what to do, perhaps barely comprehending the nightmarish scene played before him, Anders turned to run. I clutched my bleeding neck as the sooty cloud enveloped him.

The blasphemous thing launched Anders off his feet and levitated him into the air. With superhuman strength and speed, it burst through the closed steel hatch cover above, with Anders in tow. In the distance, through the rain-soaked night sky, Anders's bloodcurdling cries could be heard coming from the main deck—the sound forever seared into my memories. Mercifully, my eyes rolled into the back of my skull as I passed out.

\#

Hours later, I awoke lying in a shimmering pool of sea,

rain, and bloody water. I spat out the unpleasant tasting mixture which found its way into my mouth. Radiant streaks of sunlight filtered through the partially torn steel hatch cover: it illuminated my cold form and a shallow area of the hold. I peered up, squinted, and focused my vision through the narrow opening.

The power of the sun burned my eyes. I closed my eyelids for a brief respite, allowing my seared pupils to adjust to daylight. When I reopened them, I beheld a clear azure sky and observed the storm had passed. The ocean was also at rest. All things had seemingly returned to normal until I sat up and gulped a deep breath and was instantly seized by a stabbing ache in my throat.

I reached for the side of my neck, and the bulbous tips of my fingers discovered two puncture wounds and dried blood: that vile thing had violated me; a quiet anger welled up inside me.

I staggered to my feet, weak and wobbly. My clothing was wet and soaked with my own blood. I spotted the axe which Anders used to save my life discarded on the steel floor and grabbed it. A ruddy blood had dried on its blade. I stood shivering in disbelief, until a lapping and sucking sound stole my attention.

Remaining in the protection of sunlight, I trained my ears on the sound. Yet again I heard it: a lapping and sucking sound, as if a thirsty dog was drinking. I fixed my eyes on a section of the hold camouflaged in darkness. Allowing my eyes to adapt to the darkness, I waited patiently to reveal what could not be seen through ordinary eyes.

Slowly, through the fabric of darkness, my eyes discerned a bald, bone-white, slender figure of a man, straddled atop a lifeless body. He rapaciously sucked and slurped on his victim's neck. When he turned his head up to look at me, flesh and blood dangled and dripped from his mouth.

Panic-stricken, I made a break for the hatch ladder. Racing up the rungs and pushing through the access hold door, I stumbled and tossed the axe into the air as I landed on my hands and knees on the main deck. For a fleeting moment, I felt safe in the warmth and protection of the sun, for I knew the creature could not survive in it, until a new, more disturbing horror revealed itself. From the Nordsolen's stern to bow, a trail of bodies littered the entire length of the vessel.

I examined each fallen man and discovered all had their necks savagely torn open and their blood drained from their bodies. Among the dead, I found Doctor Mathias Jensen, Sebastián Reynaldo Reyes, and my cabin mate and savior Anders Schulman, whose body the monster had mutilated the most.

It was apparent the Nordsolen's crew had been massacred last night by the unholy being the captain brought on board, and it was this very thought that triggered my memory of Captain Goransen's final words, which now rang with a prophetic truth: "You are all doomed."

The Nordsolen's engines were noticeably silent, perhaps rendered inoperable by a crew member in a desperate effort to save mankind from that thing. The ship was adrift somewhere in the middle of the North Atlantic Ocean. I felt the combined weight of hopelessness, guilt and despair suffocate me. I dropped to my knees and wept as I begged the heavens for salvation.

But the hypnotic stench of blood and death swirled through the frigid ocean air and invaded my very being. I soon realized a queer hunger pang and sensitivity to sunlight had taken root. I touched my throat and remembered the monster's bite. I rose to my feet with an invigorated sense of anger, courage, and determination, and knew what I had to do.

I removed the protective tarpaulin and clamps on the hatch cover to cargo hold no. 3 and opened its telescoping hatch cover using the electric winch. I reclaimed the axe. Climbing down into cargo hold no. 3, with the axe in hand, I sought the cargo that would aid in the destruction of the Nordsolen: eighty barrels of highly flammable crude oil.

I had twenty pallets to pillage from. Each contained four upright wooden barrels held tightly together by a plywood frame. I struck the center of a plywood frame with the axe blade. The effects of gravity, the motion of the ship, and the weight of the oil barrels collapse the frame.

The barrels tumbled and spilled from their perches. They bounced and rolled freely onto the cargo hold floor. I pried open the wooden lids of the overturned oil barrels, allowing the shiny and viscous black liquid to ooze and spread throughout the hold.

I climbed up the hatch ladder onto the main deck, but the orange sun greeted me like a mortal enemy. Diaphanous vapors billowed and trailed from my exposed skin. My body was slowly burning; my blood and my body had been tainted by the monster's bite.

Undaunted, I used the ship's crane to raise and drop several barrels onto the main deck. They crashed and splattered oil over the deck. I dropped and spilled as much crude oil over the main deck as possible before my arms and legs succumbed to fatigue.

The daylight had waned. I raced up to the second bridge deck to the port lifeboat. I switched on the lifeboat's spotlight and left it's tarpaulin cover on for protection from the sun. I snapped the ropes with the axe and launched the lifeboat from the davits. It landed with a heavy splash. It floated and drifted; its bright spotlight acted as a beacon so I could track it.

Back on the main deck, I placed the axe on the floor as

I searched Sebastián's corpse for matches, for he was a smoker. Sure enough, I secured a box of matches from his coat pocket. I struck a match. The yellow and orange flame lit but was quickly extinguished by a blur.

To my shock, there appeared before my eyes, a naked bald man stained with garnet and burgundy rivulets of blood which had dripped down his mouth and onto his chest. A spectral gray and blue mist wafted from his ivory skin, the consequences of the weakening sunlight slowly scorching his body, but it seemed to have no ill effect on him.

This ancient creature stood observing me most curiously, perhaps confused by this alien world, perhaps aware he was out of place and out of time. His focus descended to the ebony muck at the soles of his bare feet, which stood in a puddle of crude oil.

Hastened, I lit another match and tossed it. But the blur caught the match and extinguished the flame. Without warning, I was on my back, and the creature was on top of me. The demon penetrated my mind with a pair of hyper-dilated eyes. His dripping mouth widened revealing a ferocious set of fangs.

I struggled, using all my fading strength to hold him back. The red sun was setting; its final rays casting a spectacular radiance. I raised my hand soaking as much sunlight as possible; it sizzled and burned. The High Priest tore at my throat and sunk his teeth into me; the pain nearly swept me. My hand finally sparked and caught fire. I dropped it down onto the floor and pressed my flaming fingers and palm into the crude oil.

Fire engulfed the main deck; our black silhouettes were caught in the conflagration. Astonished, the monster withdrew. Seizing the moment, I grabbed the axe, took a wide overhead chop and found his head: it split open like a melon.

The High Priest stood in a bath of flames. Stunned and defeated, he fell backward into cargo hold no. 3 and landed in a pool of crude oil. A massive fireball leapt from the hold and threw me overboard, ablaze. The frigid waters quickly extinguished my body, saving my misbegotten life.

I floated, shell-shocked, until I spotted the trail of light reflected off the waters and swam the distance to the lifeboat. Exhausted and in agony, my skin charred, my clothes burned to tatters, I clung onto the side of the boat and coughed seawater I had gulped.

A monstrous roar erupted from the ship. I wearily turned and watched the Nordsolen spew angry fire and plumes of smoke into the twilight sky. I immediately thought of the High Priest and felt in my heart the inferno had sealed his fate. Satisfied, I wormed through an opening in the tarp cover and collapsed.

#

Sheltered from the burning rays of the sun under the tarp of the lifeboat, I found myself under the spell of an insatiable hunger which was quickly driving me mad. And in my madness, I devoured the unsuspecting seagulls which foolishly landed on the brim of my lifeboat, only to violently retch their bloody entrails.

Unmercifully, there was no cessation to my hunger. But what exactly did I hunger for in this floating coffin? It was not a normal craving for sustenance, no, it was far from that. It was something darker, foul, sinister. Human blood was the substance that would bring cessation to my hunger. Panicked, as I clung desperately to my fleeting humanity, I threw the oars of the lifeboat overboard and pledged myself to the open sea, for the alternative of rowing to land and roaming the world of man as a monster was a far crueler sentence.

The boat drifted for untold days. As my lifeforce waned in the throes of agonizing starvation, I had vivid visions of my ancestors; of the great medieval Viking longships, led by Erik the Red, and the tribe of colonists who followed the explorer.

How wonderous it must have been, to be there on that day when they became the first permanent European settlers, on an island Erik Thorvaldsson named Greenland, to live a life of peace away from the bewildering constraints of modern man.

However, with sacred life comes inevitable death, and the rituals of death: the fire… the burning funeral pyres of my pagan blood, to commemorate the worthy; the brave and the fallen. My eyes now beheld the lighting of the torch… the cleansing fire… the plumes of smoke… the ashes… the spirit… the sky.

Death indeed was inevitable, as death ingloriously took the life of Erik the Red through an epidemic of infectious disease, so too was it about to claim me, through a horrific disease of a demon's tainted blood. Yet die as I might, I decreed my death will come under my terms. I pulled the tarp cover and cast it overboard. The stygian waters accepted it as it floated away: a fugacious token of my existence. I closed my eyes as the ocean gave way to the ephemeral glories of the sunrise… and the cleansing fire.

"Valhalla awaits!"

The Tooth Fairy
Kira Blackwood

Dennie had punched Grisham in the face before either of them knew they were fighting. Her right fist caught him square in the mouth, slicing open two of her knuckles as a spray of bone and blood flew, his face caught in that perfect 'O' of surprise. He spun with the momentum, stumbling. All ninety pounds of her pounced as he lost his balance, knocking him to the ground, her legs pinning his arms to her side. A quick one-two later, and he'd lost consciousness.

"Don't wake up," she whispered her prayer at the altar of his bloody, supine body. "Please just lay still, okay?"

With one trembling hand, she grabbed the pliers from her back pocket. Grisham hadn't wanted to help her. Refused. Said he was gonna rat her out the next day since they weren't at school, and it's a good thing they weren't. This was just another side street full of boarded up windows in a town no one had moved into in twenty years.

She thought he'd be cool. Grisham was always cool. The coolest, even. She didn't like him enough to date him, but she did like him enough to notice the tears dripping off her nose into his blood-gushing face hole. She grabbed his jaw with the other hand, clamping the pliers around one of the teeth.

She pulled. Not hard enough, then too hard, tearing the bone free with the sort of wet squelch that almost made her stomach empty itself onto his face. *Don't puke. Don't puke, you dumb bitch. It'll be so much harder to get the rest.* Plus, he'd probably die of a horrible infection. Even now, she'd be ruining him.

She knew this.

His smooth, dark skin was gonna be so swollen with bruise and inflammation that she wouldn't even recognize him tomorrow. The smile that made the cheerleaders swoon? They were never gonna see it again.

The second tooth came free more easily, a chunk of root still dangling from it. Was she less afraid on this one, or had she just hit it harder? Her hand started slipping a little, soaked thoroughly with fresh, dark crimson. She kept his head turned so he wouldn't choke, leaving a puddle to spread beneath him.

A third was broken, but still, anything was worth taking. All of them were worth taking. If they were good enough for the Tooth Fairy, they were good enough for her.

Raw, pink gum swelled up, already mourning its loss, reaching further into the single gaping cavity like it might claw back what she'd removed. Bits of root dangled free, but beyond a little faint. Though he groaned, Grisham hadn't shown any sign of waking. That could change in an instant. She was going to Ryder pre-med next year. Dennie knew what pain would do to his body—how even in his current state, his body was flooding with adrenaline, attempting to stir him to fight back.

There were two gaps where teeth should've been— where she must've socked him with enough force to send them flying.

"Fuck," she spat. One was an upper canine. The Tooth Fairy *loved* upper canines. A quick glance around, a scramble across the sidewalk, an increasingly panicked ten seconds of fumbling later, and there, thank the gods, she found it. She slipped it into the baggie along with the others. That was five. Back to the pliers. Six. Ten. She kept careful count. One had a cavity.

TF wasn't gonna like that.

She had to keep going. Dennie moved as steadily as she could, trying to avoid hurting him any more than she had to, but everything was starting to hurt and her hands weren't just shaking from fear of getting caught.

But. Oh. Sweet Christmas, jackpot, baby girl. This motherfucker still had his wisdom teeth. They looked fresh and shiny, their alabaster unmarred by the stains most teeth suffered, by years of coffee and fast food and deserts with more sugar than the average slave child could pick in a week.

She was kneeling in the blood pool now. None of her almost-education in medicine taught her whether it was possible to bleed out from your mouth if someone ripped out all your teeth, but no one ever exsanguinated at the dentist, right?

No one ever bolted upright screaming at the dentist either, though. Grisham did exactly that, his cry loud enough to echo across the empty streets, so sudden that she reared back, punching him in the nose with the force of M Bison's psycho crusher.

He went silent as quickly as he'd gone loud, the back of his skull rebounding off the sidewalk with a crack that made her entire body clench. The street was still empty for now, but even this town didn't ignore something like that.

"Screw it," she whispered, wrenching his mouth open and tearing his four wisdom teeth free of their moorings.

They belonged to her now. She deserved them for the trouble he just caused. "Shouldn't have screamed. Sorry 'bout it."

Blood poured freely from his open nose, darker and faster than from his mouth, which now housed two pews of dark, loose parishioners, singing hymns of agony to every nerve in his face, begging the god that was his brain to save them. The scarlet beneath him was spreading too quickly, though. She checked the back of his head and swore at her own stupid stupidity.

A siren rang out in the distance. Dennie was still straddling him so hard and tight you'd think it was prom night, her blue jeans almost entirely red, hands stained, possibly forever, with pliers in one hand and all his teeth in a bag in the other. Might be kinda hard to talk her way out of this if caught.

But… this was Grisham.

She reached into his pocket, knowing she was probably leaving prints all over it and on the emergency function on his cell screen. Once the operator picked up, she fled, leaving GPS to do the rest.

***

Mae didn't give a fuck what her dumb bitch daughter was up to or how she was losing her damn mind. Schizo shit ran in their family. It just did. Skipped Mae, who never once heard God talking to her and didn't talk to him, either.

She never heard much more than the nightly creaks and groans of their old house settling. Her ma had spent Mae's whole childhood whipping her ass with a switch whenever God decided she did something bad.

Now she had gone her whole life without once so much as swatting Dennie for the myriad bullshit she got up to, and what had that gotten either of them? A daughter who kept talking to the walls, insisting she was gonna be pre-med with grades that wouldn't get you pre-assistant night manager at McDonald's.

Whatever.

She'd failed with her firstborn. It happens. Januarius was still normal and fine. He hadn't hit puberty yet. Puberty is where shit goes wrong. He was ten. Had a few more good years before hormones tried to ruin him like they did Dennie.

The brat was mouthy and moody on a good day, sarcastic and psychotic on a bad one, and when her tits came in, it was all over. The only favor Mae did her from that point on was pretend she didn't notice the condoms going missing from her drawer because like fucking hell was she gonna let a grandchild into this world through that particular door.

Dennie had come home in an absolute state the night before, racing up to her room through the back door, but today was Saturday, and she hadn't done a chore in maybe two years, so Mae knew better than to ask her daughter to help with anything.

No sense in waking her.

Such as it was, her daughter didn't drift downstairs until four in the afternoon, her eyes still half-lidded, her skin sallow. She wasn't twitchy like usual, and for that, Mae did breathe a sigh of relief.

In quiet moments, she admitted she only hoped this was all hormones. Maybe there'd be a way to get her daughter back once they weathered the storm. But she was erratic, paranoid, jerky. Early MS ran in their family, too. Mae watched her Pa die. That was way worse than Ma. Then again, she actually liked him.

So it was nice to watch her daughter smile lazily, then just sit quietly next to her brother, watching Januarius play *Street Fighter 6*. Sometimes, Mae caught him looking a little too hard at that Chun-Li chick and worried his time had come. Other times, she could swear she caught Dennie staring, too.

That made her worry less.

Didn't explain the condoms, but if she liked women, Mae would—hopefully—not have to take care of any grandchildren anytime soon.

She busied herself tidying the kitchen while listening to the meaty slaps, punches, and kicks from the next room, soon accompanied by the whine of Jan's voice stringing itself more tense than guitar strings over repeatedly losing. Just before the point where Mae said something about taking a walk to calm down, she heard Dennie start talking, low and soft.

"Hey, buddy, relax. Just a game, right? That's all it is. Akuma is supposed to be tough, but I'm here if you need it." Soft and sweet. Like old times. Before blood, before tits, before the twitching.

Mae peered in, trying to be subtle. Dennie sat next to Jan, and while Mae wished she'd put a bra on around her kid brother, the girl's hands glided over the controller, smooth and skilled. Their mom watched Dennie rock Akuma for two back-to-back perfect matches without ever fully opening her eyes.

"It's just practice and patience, little dude," Dennie said, handing the controller back, then ruffling his hair. Mae kept his short so there wasn't much to ruffle, but he sniffed and wiped his nose on the back of his hand with a smile. "Don't get too stressed about this kinda stuff. I don't want to see your blood sugars go wonky."

On cue, Januarius checked his Dexcom, saying he was still one-twenty, right where the doctor wanted. The boy threw his mom a glance and a small smile. Mae strolled back into the kitchen. Just puberty, she told herself. Just puberty. She'll get through it. They all would.

***

The Tooth Fairy always made Dennie feel so good. Theirs was an old house, you see, and her buddy TF lived in the walls, just above the old dumbwaiter. She met him a year prior when Januarius lost one of his teeth. Literally, lost it running into a wall. Good thing it was loose first. But she was the one to find it and still had it in her pocket when she heard the voice. The dumbwaiter went from her room to the kitchen.

"Leave it inside," had come the whisper, "and I'll leave you some fairy dust. Rub it on your gums to feel the magic."

That was a year ago. Januarius had lost four more teeth since then. The Tooth Fairy gave her a generous pouch of fairy dust for them—a few ounces each—but he was getting impatient. He wanted more. That's why she tried to ask Grisham for help. His dad was a dentist. They could've had a deal. His dad gives him the teeth he extracts, he gives the teeth to her, and maybe she shares a little bit of magic with them.

That's all this had to be.

Dennie wasn't thinking about that now. She laid on her bed, smiling dreamily. The magic had a sweet spot. It made her really sleepy at first, then she was calm and content, then crazy horny. She'd just finished rubbing one out to her double perfect against Akuma. Nothing turned her on like beating the piss out of Akuma.

She'd bought her own copy just to play it in her room so she could whip his ass up and down the screen over and over again. Slaughtering Bison was pretty fun, sure, but knowing she could obliterate the one who haunted so many gamers' nightmares? That was pure ecstasy.

Kristy texted.

She ignored it.

Then she called, which Dennie also ignored. Kristy texted again. Dennie sighed, reading that apparently Grisham was in the hospital. Someone jumped him. Beat him so bad the kid was in a coma. The whole track team was gathered at his bedside, twenty-something almost-grown men openly weeping for their friend.

The freak even ripped out all his teeth. Cops suspected a weird gang-related violence, like maybe he was planning to snitch on someone so they sent a message. Kristy called again, so Dennie answered this time, listening in a blur as her friend rambled about some urban legend about a drifter serial killer who stole teeth because of course there's a fucking urban legend about a drifter serial killer who steals teeth.

Dennie just sat there, counting the rapid slams of her heart against her ribs. She dipped her finger into the bag of fairy dust, rubbing it along her gums, feeling the sweet little bumps and ridged where her own teeth shoved themselves rudely into the soft meat of her jawline.

Her tender gingiva anchored into alveolar bone, working poor propping up the ruling class of her molars, incisors, and canines. Unlike Grisham, her wisdom teeth sat anchored in the soft tissues, encapsulated, refusing to come out. Stubborn brats.

The magic kicks in quick, though. Didn't take long before she hung up with Kristy, forgot about Grisham altogether, smiling at a daydream of being Chun-Li and kicking someone's teeth out.

***

Dennie had a plan.
A strategy.
A routine.

She had everything worked out. Keep her head down, get good grades, get the hell out of this town. The Tooth Fairy helped a lot. She'd been a bright kid, once. After her dad died, she lost a lot of that spark. He'd dropped dead of a sudden heart attack because his doctors said his aching chest was 'sore muscles' and didn't catch myo-fucking-carditis. Ever since high school, she'd slipped further and further down that spiral staircase.

Now, it was all over.

Becoming a doctor meant going to a good medical school. Getting into a good medical school meant going to a good pre-med program. Getting into a good pre-med program meant getting good grades in high school. Now, that bitch Ms. Haggerty ruined it. Ruined her whole ten-year plan over something as trivial as *history*.

The point of this assignment was to craft a five-page analysis of modern American politics and how the current government was shaped over the past fifty years. It was not to go on an extended personal diatribe about how the government is run by "bigots and morons" and "should be abolished altogether." I'm not saying you're wrong or right. I'm saying you have to defend your position in an academic paper. Also, no swearing next time, okay?

A zero.

On the whole midterm paper. That absolute bitch. A zero on something that weighed so heavily she couldn't get above a C in the class for the whole year, and slamming that nail into her coffin the week before winter break? That piece of shit was just part of broken ass system, perpetuating the same injustices.

Dennie wanted to be a pediatric endocrinologist and everyone knew it, so where did this Reagan-body-pillow-humping cum stain get off acting like this?

The beautiful thing about her friend's pixie dust is that sometimes, you just were. Maybe you just were the most intelligent person in the room. Maybe you just *were* happy after days, weeks, months of stress and heartache. Maybe you just *were* a kid again, taking a walk with your father, back before he died.

She'd followed Ms. Haggerty home, watching from outside, rubbed a little magic powder on her gums, and suddenly just *was* standing over that cunt with a meat tenderizer.

"You're propagating fucking inequality against me, you head-up-her-ass, sanctimonious sack of shit," Dennie gasped, her head swimming. The sweet spot had a dark side, pounding and fast and wild. She made sure not to be home if the good times didn't hit right.

Fairy magic was fickle.

"You're some trickledown economic fuck, aren't you? Licking corpo piss off our oppressors boots? Huh? Jackboot bitch, not feeling so truculent now that you gotta look me in the eye while pissing on the grave you dug me, huh, you sack of old dog dicks?"

This was bad. This was really bad. Even as she kicked Ms. Haggerty in the side, she recognized how awful this was, and kicked her again *because* of how screwed she was. There was no coming back from this.

The teach was gonna go to the cops after this, report her, slam her up in a cell where she'd get ladyboned by some gangbanger chick or forced into being a drug mule if she ever made it out. This was the school-to-prison pipeline on steroids.

There wasn't any coming back from this. The magic whispered to her, though. It gave her ideas. Her hands didn't stop shaking, but they slowed. Her mallet hand swung, cracking Haggerty over the face. She'd missed a little. She'd been aiming for the temple to make this a clean kill, but got her orbital instead, shattering the bone. Dennie got lucky, just like with Grisham.

Must've hurt too bad to scream, even though her eye rolled from its socket onto the floor. When the woman pulled back a little and the optic nerve drew taught, *that* was when the 'hurt too bad to scream' transcended to 'wake the dead and summon the devil to my doorstep.'

Dennie wasn't making the same mistake as she made with Grisham. A solid whack to the back of the woman's skull silenced her. It didn't knock her out, somehow, but the sudden concussive force against the cerebellum stunned her harder than a point-blank hadouken. The fact that she could hear her own blood didn't make her dumber, it just made her faster and fast could be sloppy but fast could be good, too.

"The rumors of your death are gonna be greatly exaggerated," Dennie panted, her voice cracking out of her vocal cords. Her mouth was dry. It was always dry these days, same as her eyes. She made a note to see her primary about ordering her the Quest Diagnostic's early Sjogren's panel. Better catch it now before it gave her neuropathy.

"They're gonna think it was a vengeful ex-lover, or a break-in gone wrong, or a serial killer, but really? It was just you, shitting in your own mouth, you insolent reprobate."

Dennie stomped on the dislodged eyeball, squashing it under heel. This was a terrible idea because it was *just* enough liquid for her to slip in, causing her leg to slide out. Teach apparently had enough desperation in her to swing at Dennie's other leg, roaring like an animal.

That, too, was a terrible idea, because it just meant the girl had gravity on her side, lending her even more strength as she spun into the fall, smashing a hole in the woman's skull that nobody could come back from.

That one blow definitely killed her, but Dennie wrenched herself up, swinging again, and again, and again and again and again. Gray matter splattered all over the cabinets, the floor, her shirt, bone fragments stuck into her hands like vengeful splinters, she tasted blood on her tongue and couldn't tell if it was her own.

A pig squeal filled the kitchen, and it took a few seconds to realize it was her own deranged screech, strangled in a throat so dry she couldn't swallow.

Sweating and trembling, Dennie froze, mid-swing. The magic demanded a certain care. The Tooth Fairy required payment. She got up, searched the drawers til she found plastic baggies, then got Haggerty's biggest, sharpest knife, carefully extracting every treasure from that bitch's lying mouth.

Then, once they were stowed safely in her pocket, she went back to swinging.

***

Dennie spent winter break holed up in her room. Mae could hear her whispering to the walls. When the girl wasn't talking to anyone, she was asleep. Sometimes, she went out. Sometimes, she managed to smile, sit on the couch, play games with Januarius, but that was about it. Didn't even really see her eating anymore.

They exchanged gifts at Christmas, like people in America tended to do whether they're religious or not. Simple stuff this year, like last year, and the year before. Since Joe passed. Nothing Dennie opened made her smile. Not really. A mother knows when her kid is faking a smile.

Even as a kid, that girl could've lit a room with it, and when it was real, the corners of her eyes crinkled up, yet somehow, the crinkle made her seem youthful. Full of life and energy. Now, the lack thereof made her seem older.

Dennie wore the same pair of pajamas damn near the entire break. One of the few times she was functional enough to do chores, her sleeves drifted up, letting Mae catch sight of scabs and sores along her arms. Bedbugs? Roaches? Do roaches bite people?

Or…

"You doin' alright, sugarplum?" Mae finally asked, after months of refusing to.

Dennie almost recoiled, like asking conjured a memory of being slapped. Like the idea of being okay bore such trauma that it was safer to cling to misery. Her eyes glistened and lip trembled as she told her mother that yeah, everything was fine.

"You're barely eating. Act like I can't tell how much weight you've lost, but if your jaw gets any sharper, I could use it to dice carrots. Only time you seem to eat is sneakin' downstairs at night to snack on leftovers."

"I don't need food like that, Ma, and I don't sneak it," Dennie scowled, rolling her eyes, her hand jerking. She tucked her hand up under her arm as if it wasn't in death throes. "I run on cleaner energy than *food.*" With that, she stormed off, leaving Mae alone in the kitchen. The girl was so light her feet barely made the steps creak, and *everything* made this house creak. It was constantly settling, shifting, groaning, echoing with old footsteps that sometimes stirred her when she wasn't quite asleep yet.

Hard to tell if the kid was lying or genuinely believed she didn't need food. Hell, Mae couldn't tell, either. Dennie was five-five but couldn't weigh more than a hundred pounds at this point. Maybe an eating disorder, too?

Mae sat at the table, putting her head in her hands with a sigh. Her own mother had been so much to deal with. Pa passed so young, young for him, young for her, and that's when Ma stopped medicating. Mae had been an adult since she was eight. She was sick of it.

Little arms wrapped around her.

"You doing ok, Mom?" Januarius said. He actually

meant it, too. He really wanted to know. Damn it, that hug squeezed right around her heart. She bit back thirty years of sting, rubbing the back of his head.

"Just fine, son. You go play. I just need a minute. Your homework's done, right?"

He confirmed it was, then left the room, giving a little glance back as he passed the threshold. Mae busied herself with dishes until she heard his game start up, then slipped out the back door to call Sarah Lynn, who she hadn't spoken to in a few months, for no particular reason. Adults just sometimes lose touch for a bit, drifting in and out of each other's lives until accident or necessity draws them back together. This was the latter.

"Sarah Lynn, hey," she said, when her old friend finally answered. Mae had to call twice to get her. "I'm sorry for the trouble, but… if… I hate bringing this up, I'm sorry, but the man who helped your Bobby when he started having his troubles, could you give me his name? A phone number, maybe?"

"O'course, Mae," a tired voice crackled through over the din of sizzling meat. "Is it your daughter? Dennie?"

"How'd you know?" Mae's stomach twisted.

"My kids say she's been odd at school. Twitchy. Talking to no one. Sneaking off to dark corners, missing class, raving about nothing… I would'a called you first, but honey, I apologize, I thought you knew."

"Guess a mother's the last one to know when her kid's having troubles like this," Mae sighed. "Leastwise, the last to face it."

Sarah Lynn gladly coughed up the phone number. They made plans to get coffee on Saturday that neither would be able to keep, but they'd chat, reschedule, promise to make it work next time, and bail on that, too. They wouldn't see each other again until the funeral.

In the meanwhile, Mae had another call to make.

***

Everyone knew.
Everyone knew.
Everyone knew.

The house knew. It groaned and creaked every night. She heard the sounds of it knowing what she did, thumping with her sins. Hurting Grisham was an accident, but teach had been intentional, and every slam of that mallet down on her skull had been a judge's gavel sounding *guilty guilty guilty, go to jail and then to Hell, bitch.*

She was running low on fairy dust, rationing it. The Tooth Fairy didn't like Ms. Haggerty's teeth as much. None of them were broken, but three had fillings, two had cavities, and one was fake.

"Bad stock," The Tooth Fairy hissed from the dumbwaiter. "Bad teeth. Not cared for. Bad genes. Bad girl." He gave her so little. So very fucking little, each baggie was barely enough to coat her pinky finger three times, but it let her focus on her homework. On the one project she still actually had to do over break, at least now that the school said Ms. H's students didn't have to do any work for her courses to let them 'grieve properly.'

The house was full of cockroaches. Magic kept them away, but whenever it wore off, they came back, scuttling over her skin. She picked and scratched, trying to catch them, to kill them, but even when she pinched them between her fingers hard enough to tear the skin free, they slipped away from her. Everything hurt. All over. Her skin, her muscles, she was filled with their little bitey poisons, but her friend kept her safe.

Or had.
For a while.

She got lucky, but only a little. The day before classes

started, Jan told her he had another loose tooth. A canine. A fucking *canine*. A child's canine was pure gold to her friend in the walls, and he'd reward her handsomely for it. The kid said she could help free it, so she reached in his mouth, grasping it as firmly as she could. His mouth as so wet. It made her focus on how chapped and cracked her lips were, how her throat had turned to sandpaper, instead of on extracting her quarry. She tried the string-and-doorknob method but it doesn't work so well on the pointy little bone stalactites.

Dennie bit her lip. This was Januarius she was talking about. Her baby brother. But the roaches were scuttling in the walls. They were coming for her blood. She couldn't get into med school if they were draining her dry and trying to lay eggs in her skin. If she didn't get into med school, she'd never be able to cure diabetes. Or myocarditis. Or multiple sclerosis. She'd never be able to take revenge on evolution for all the ways it fucked her family over.

"Do you trust me?" she whispered, even though their mother wasn't home. "It might hurt a little, but loose teeth are... bad. They have to come out. They're dead in your mouth, you know, and if you don't take the dead out, it can poison you. And give you cavities, so you can't have any treats, even if you give yourself insulin first."

Jan made a face like he didn't quite believe her, but nodded anyway, so she told him to meet her in the bathroom. She went back to her room. Got the pliers from her drawer.

"*Don't do this*," they whispered. "*Not with him.*"

"You shut the fuck up," she told them. They'd gotten awful mouthy lately, but that was just the magic talking. They hadn't talked before the magic. The world had been so normal and boring before The Tooth Fairy gave her that first free bag of fairy dust. Every little bit brought her closer to his world, though.

He said so himself.

She returned to Januarius, ignoring how the pliers protested, and clamped them around his upper canine. He said something around the metal but she hushed him, beginning to pull. Her brother protested, trying to slap at her hands. Despite how they shook, how the little tool felt so impossibly heavy, she wriggled it loose, then managed to wrench it free. Ironic that pliers can wrench something.

A gush of hot, dark red spilled over the tiles, running freely from his mouth as tears rolled down his face. He sobbed, backing away from her as she loomed over, feeling every bit the dark side of fae lore—the child stealing, family ruining, flesh eating monster.

"I'm sorry, buddy. I know it hurt, but this…" She swallowed hard against the desert of her throat. "This is for the best."

Her brother curled in on himself, wracked with sobs. Against every instinct, she forced herself to put the pliers down, praying she could comfort him into shutting the fuck up before Mom got home. Jan tensed when she wrapped her arms around him, but soon relaxed, then, after a minute, hugged her back.

"I-I w-was trying to t-tell you," he sniffed. "You d-didn't l-let me t-talk."

"I know, Jan, I know," she whispered, struggling not to cry herself. She'd negotiate. Get a bigger dose of fairy dust for this. TF would pay up, big time.

"Y-you got the wrong one."

Her blood ran cold. Her bite-riddled skin tensed on itself, clamping around her muscles like a straitjacket, so tight it set them aching. The roaches came scuttling from the walls.

But she'd convinced him that dead teeth need to come out and lies need as much commitment as the woman who tells them, so she slipped him a fifty, then tore out the other one.

***

Dennie bounced her leg up and down against the floor, staring out the window. She sat in an office as pretentious as it was boring, the walls covered in frames degrees and the type of dull motel art probably meant to be calming.

It wasn't.

This art looked more like the shit an AI would generate if you told it to imagine the color beige as a landscape that was trying to teach me about the origin of the rowboat. It was also freezing. She'd wrapped up in her biggest hoodie but that didn't seem to help. Seemed like everywhere was cold these days.

"…and you believe this Tooth Fairy is communicating with you?" the doctor raised a fuzzy eyebrow. He had pale, cave fish skin that had never once been graced by sunlight, dull blue eyes that could've passed for pools of melted crayons, and a bulging gut that spoke of too many nights finding his own therapy in a bottle of whiskey.

In short, he looked like every other middle-aged White therapist she'd ever spoken to. He also sat in the most pretentious chair possible—a hair-backed armchair—and sat between her and the door.

"I don't *believe* shit." What the hell had her mother told this guy? "I gave him a tooth, he gave me a bag of fairy dust. 'nough said."

"Hm." He wrote something down, like an asshole. "When did you start hearing him?"

"Little while ago." Her mom made her come. Said she had to—said she'd cut off her cell phone, sell the clunker Dennie'd been driving since Mae still had the title in her name, all that usual parent shit. *For your own good.* Like parents always say when they don't fuckin' know shit about dick.

"And you believe fairies are real?"

"Ain't you a fairy?" she said, eyeing the pride flag on his desk, her face flushing. Oh, she hated saying that. She'd fuck any consenting partner with a pulse. Half her friends were under the rainbow somewhere. But this guy was being an ass and the corners of the room were so thick with mold she could see stalks of it wriggling, letting spores puff up into the air. Dennie could hear the lice biting into his scalp, instinctively scratching at her own.

"Just supportive," he said, but his eyes narrowed and lips pursed.

Liar.

"Why help this tooth fairy at all, though?"

"*The* Tooth Fairy. With 'the' and capital letters. I heard you say it lowercase, you fuck. Show a little respect," she snarled, prying her tongue against one of her back molars. It wiggled, just a bit. A lot of them felt loose. Would he pay extra for hers?

"Sorry. The Tooth Fairy." He held up his hands 'apologetically.'

"He... the fairy dust. It gives me his magic." A gnashing calm bit into the comforting electricity of her heightened nerves. "Need it."

"For what, if I may ask?" He leaned forward a little.

"Med school. Gotta get in. Gotta cure Janny, you know? Cure Dad. MS. Fix it." Relief sank its teeth into her. That junkyard dog whipped its head, ripping and tearing at the secrecy she'd so carefully established.

Shut up, shut up, she begged herself.

"So his magic will help you cure autoimmune diseases," he nodded, more to himself than to her. "The diseases that have taken family from you."

"Family from me, family from family, from family," Dennie sputtered, hugging herself. "Mom's mom had MS.

Dad's heart just stopped. Jan's had shots all his life. Not fair. Not fucking fair. If the magic helps me, it's worth it. Said it'll make me magical, too, if I take enough, then I can heal the whole world. I will. I'll heal the world. Just watch."

Her hands were shaking so hard she could barely hold herself. Most of her shivered. Tension. Nerves. Cold. Not enough magic. Without the magic, she couldn't hear how everything had a voice. Without it, the bugs came for her. Right now, she only had enough magic to hear the bugs, taunting her. She didn't know everything in the world could talk until TF gave her the magic.

The fat man's face betrayed every nuance as the rusted gears in his head began turning against her. She could see the suspicion, the accusation, the way she already decided she was rotten. The air shifted. She wasn't gonna like the next question.

"Have you hurt anyone to get this magic?" he met her gaze.

She looked away.

"No," she stared at the floor, on the verge of pissing herself. The carpet twitched toward her bouncing foot and she pulled away just in time to avoid the worms jumping toward it.

"I need you to be honest with me." His voice was so calm when telling her she was on the verge of getting locked up somewhere. "*You* need you to be honest with me."

Dennie bit her lip, watching the worms dance below her. Only a matter of time before they figured out how to climb up the chair. She just told him no again, realizing a bit too late that it was a more honest answer than she meant to give.

But he talked at her, she talked around him, and eventually, a year or so later, the hour was up, and the worms hadn't climbed her chair yet.

"*We'll eat ya soon enough, kiddo,*" they called out in a single voice. "*Starting with your eyes. You're gonna look real good with no eyes.*"

"Shut up," she whispered. The shrink definitely heard that, but only responded with asking when she wanted to reschedule. She picked a week, at his suggestion, because acquiescing to this shitbag seemed like a good way to escape. She was halfway out the door before noticing the letter opener on his desk, inches away from him.

"I look forward to seeing you next week," he nodded, without getting up. "I only want to help you."

Her hand lashed out, grabbing the letter opener, then slammed it through his throat. Literally through. She read enough textbooks and the shakes didn't stop her from hitting his carotid and trachea in one stab.

Beautiful, dark, arterial spray coated the wall before his eyes could even widen. A chorus of tiny squeals rejoiced as the worms danced in the crimson shower. Blood gurgled up his throat, pouring out his mouth as it also filled his lungs. He tried to cough it out but only coughed it all over her. He tried to get up. The doc's strength was already fading—must've been if she was able to shove him back.

"I want you to help me, too." A Cheshire grin split her face. "That's why I need your teeth. They're gonna help me just fine."

His chair was wide enough and she didn't need to be gentle. He tried to scream as she knelt alongside him, straddling him, a hand in his hair to yank his head back as she stabbed down into his face again and again.

She sheered flesh from the jaw, detached a lip, sliced through his gums, but that was his fault, his fault for squirming, for not making it easier on her. He could've just cooperated. Would've been less painful, but no, he was a bastard to the end. Dennie carved him to pieces, stabs and slashes, breathless and ecstatic, missed hard enough to take part of his nose off.

The whole time, he choked, drowning in his own blood, slapping feebly against her, trying to push her away. It obviously didn't work and wouldn't have accomplished anything if it had. In time, he stilled enough where his only movements where his eyes—pupils dilated, lids twitching, his gaze following her.

She didn't have pliers this time, so she cut his mouth Joker style, giving him a Glasgow smile and a closed casket to make sure he couldn't bite down on her fingers in some last-ditch attempt to piss her off. Then she sliced at his gums, stabbing where she needed to, then prying like a crowbar to pop 'em out.

One by one, the chicklets dislodged, and she snatched them up before he could try to swallow them as a final fuck you. It was harder, way harder, without the right tools, especially because of how slippery wet his face cavern had become. His dying body still jerked and spasmed with pain as exposed root hung from the new openings. She wondered if this was what he was like in bed: a blubbery spasm, then utter collapse.

She was probably doing his husband a favor.

Dennie made it sixteen teeth in before she realized the problem.

"I'm fucked," she whispered, her mouth somehow going even drier. "I... they'll know it was me. The appointment's in my name. There's security camera footage. Oh god. Oh, god. Oh, Tooth Fairy, help me." So she finished taking the rest. They were decent enough. A filling in one, but he had *big* canines, and TF loved them.

Maybe this would be enough to make her like him.

No. Not maybe. It had to be.

***

She snuck back into the house late. Her mom had taken Januarius out to dinner so he wouldn't ask too many questions about where Dennie was, though she had to imagine the kid would be asking even more questions that way, like 'Why didn't she come to dinner?' Ma probably just said Den was at school late.

"If you want to be like me," The Tooth Fairy's voice echoed to her down the dumbwaiter shaft, "then you owe me more."

"I don't have anymore!" she pleaded. "Please! I—I need to be magical, too! They're gonna catch me. Please, please help me."

"You do have more to offer. Don't act like you don't." His rasping voice ended each word with its own period.

Oh. Oh, fuck, of course she did. And they were all loose. Of course they were. This made perfect sense: the more the magic took hold, the more it prepared her body for the final transformation. The final sacrifice. She had to offer her own teeth. Then there'd really be no going back. She'd be fully magical.

She grabbed the pliers.

"No sense telling you not to. I know you won't listen." They whispered in their cold, click-clacking voice. *"So, I hope this is what you want. I hope it's what you're looking for."*

Dennie teared up, whispering a quiet thank you, then clamped them around her upper right incisor. This shouldn't hurt much. They were all loose. It wouldn't hurt much at all. She pulled, gently at first, feeling the pressure of her gums attempting to hold on tight, but as much as her hands shook, it wasn't enough to stop her from giving one solid yank, tearing the tooth free.

It hurt more than she could've possibly imagined. A bomb went off in her face, spreading napalm and lightning along her nerves. The pain shot down her neck, into her chest, her stomach, her hands. She almost dropped the tooth, it hurt so bad. Scarlet rivers flowed down along Dennie's hand and chin as she placed the prize in the open dumbwaiter. Her tongue instinctively prodded the new hole in its domain, flicking over exposed nerve root, forcing her to clamp a hand over her mouth to muffle her shriek.

The blood made this harder, just like it had with the shrink. She didn't stop.

Wouldn't.

Couldn't.

The alternative was jail, then death, with possibly some light whoring or gang activity in between, depending on how bad prison was. Did her state even have the death penalty? Wasn't worth finding out, so she grabbed the next incisor. She knew what to expect this time. Anticipating how much it would hurt made this easier. Knowing how worth it this would be made it much easier.

Every sequential tooth amplified the pain further. Her already-inflamed gums screamed louder and louder, already injured when the next tooth came free. The lower was even worse. She couldn't get a good angle and had to use both hands, pulling them straight up to free them, the way King Arthur once pulled a sword from a stone, or whatever.

She just imagined she was Ryu, or Ken, or Chun-Li, or any of those pricks. People get hurt during fights. People lose teeth during fights. If you stop fighting, if you get hurt and back down, it's all over. She wouldn't stop. She was a fighter. If she could double perfect motherfucking Akuma, she could easily rip out her own teeth.

Blood poured. It pooled. Her head spun. Pain lanced from her jaw through her entire torso. She clenched so hard she physically couldn't breathe. It took every ounce of strength left in her fading human form to not puke and fill her open wounds with vomit. But she did it. Eventually, she managed to extract the last anchors to her humanity and deposit them in the dumbwaiter, shutting the door.

She waited. The house groaned with fairy magic. Rope creaked as wood bowed and swelled at The Tooth Fairy's power. Dennie leaned against the wall, shaking harder than ever, her veins filled with ice. Her mouth hurt too much to close it; her mouth hurt too much to keep it open.

Then came the knock. She opened the door and found a substantial pouch of fairy dust.

"Ho' do I tack it no?" she groaned, hesitant to rub it on her raw, bleeding gums.

"The same way you always have."

The same way. With all the holes and exposed nerves. This was going to hurt like absolute hell, but every phoenix has to burn before it rises. She grabbed the bag, large enough to fill her palm—at least several ounces heavy—and upended it into her mouth.

Agony unfurled itself inside her, blossoming, a corpse flower in putrid bloom, but she clamped her mouth shut, swishing the powder around in blood until it made a fine pink slurry, soaking into her dry gums. They drank in her patron's magic, swelling with it, an April storm to her May flower, and she was the Spring now, the Source, could feel its power filling her with a *thump* so hard it rocked her body.

Thump thump, the magic *thump* so much more than *th-t-hth-thump* her skin knew how to control the wind *thump* she could feel pressure changes in her bones and channel storms with a wave of her hand *th-th-th.*

Dennie's vision blurred as her breathing slowed, yet her heart beat even harder. Wait, was that her heart? She gasped for air, gasped through the pain, gasped into the gale force winds blasting against her as she pressed her fingers into her throat. Her heartbeat came erratically, first there, then not, then five a second, then gone for three. Was her body rejecting the magic?

No. No, this wasn't rejection. Her human self had to die to set her free.

"I'll fiksh you," she said to the ether, thinking about Januarius. "Promish."

Dennie hit the ground, staring up at the ceiling. Magic sludge pooled in the back of her throat. It would've choked her if she was still breathing.

Overhead, the door to the attic opened. The ladder extended downward, letting a man crawl his way out. He looked like he'd been living in those clothes for months. No. He'd been living in their attic for months. Who the fuck was this? This wasn't a fairy. No magical being. He was just some guy, waving several sandwich bags of teeth at her.

"Thanks, kid," he grinned, nearly toothless himself. "That's good stuff, isn't it?"

Then, he left, cackling. The magic was gone. Dennie's heart sputtered to a stop.

The Misplaced Heart
James Patrick Riser

You hated how much of a stereotype you were. You owned a windowless white van with a stained mattress and shag carpeting. Thick glasses perched on your pinched mole man face. Your scalp has reclaimed space at the top of your head, like a mountain climber planting a flag on a conquered peak. Your whole life had been a battle against your body and your urges. Your body rebelled by aging and softening in all the wrong places. Your urges tore at you like a serrated knife twisting in your chest.

You didn't dare tell your mother.

She already told you the sins of your disgusting body. God made us disgusting so we'd want to rise out of the bodies we were cursed with.

Push everything down until it burns your throat like vomit.

It didn't make sense, but that's what you did.

Thank God she was dead. You sat next to her hospital bed listening to the steady rhythm of beeps and mechanical breathing. The doctor told you to talk to her. *Even though she looks like she's asleep, she can still hear you,* he had informed you.

You didn't say anything. You were there to watch her die. Nothing more. When she died, you didn't flinch. Didn't cry. You just thumbed the blade of her old pocketknife.

The van jostled as you drove, a combination between bad shocks and an unmaintained road. The neighborhood was a new hunting ground, but all you had to do was look for the streets with the potholes and lawns with uneven, yellow grass.

The sun bled into the horizon being slowly chased by a falling, folding curtain of blue, nearly starless, darkness. The afterschool programs for latchkey kids had already been let out. Some parents worked night shifts; the math worked out.

You didn't know any of this for certain, but if you ended up being wrong all you did was go for a drive. You could go back in the morning before school started, but that was riskier. Night comforted you. You looked better at night, in the reflections of windows car doors. Your gut wasn't as noticeable, and you looked taller, looked better as a shadow spilled out onto the sidewalk like an oily stain.

You turned a corner, and the headlights slid over the faces of houses. Their windows reflected the light like dull, lifeless eyes. Most of the windows glowed yellow with people moving like black cardboard cutouts. Some blue with the soft light of television.

You drove toward the end of the cul-de-sac planning on doing a U-turn and head back home to the studio apartment furnished with secondhand and inherited items. You would sit in front of the blue glow until you fell asleep.

Maybe you would jerk off. Maybe you wouldn't be able to cum and give up with chilly sweat beading on your big, furrowed forehead. The small child sized mannequins standing in your apartment would judge you with their faceless expressions.

As you were about to pull the steering well to the left, initiating the slow turn with tires crunching loose gravel like a cackling insect, you saw her. The pale white headlights clipped the side of a girl's face. The playful bounce of a ponytail slipped into the darkness. You turned the headlights off with a soft click and let the van roll to a soft halt against the curb.

You slowly shifted the vehicle into park. Every move you made sounded too loud. The noises punctuated the sound of your heart beating into your eardrums. A small surge of blood tingled your crotch. Your cock started to unfold itself like a waking baby snake. Don't get too excited.

You sat for a moment with your gaze concentrated on the passenger side-view mirror. The girl skipped around in one of the dry grass yards. She wore a black dress. The red bows on her shoes and her pale skin glowed in the deepening darkness. She seemed to skip in a circle and hummed a floating tune that seeped into the van despite the rolled up, tinted windows. After a few moments you gently pulled on the door handle and stepped out.

You winced as shoes crunched on the ground. Ignoring the sounds, you walked around the van. The girl didn't seem to notice. You stepped closer and stood with one foot on the curb. "Hey," you whispered hoarsely. "Do you live here?" Your voice felt thick in your throat, welling up like an avocado pit.

She skipped a few more rotations before stopping and jumping in the middle of her imagined circle. "No," she replied hands laced behind her back.

"Well, are you lost?" You fully stepped onto the sidewalk.

"No."

"What are you doing here?" You took a few steps toward her. The grass sighed under your feet.

"Playing." She didn't seem disturbed by your presence, and you continued to close in.

You stopped a couple of feet in front of her. She stood half your size, about five or six years old. The girl made hard eye contact, her blue eyes boring out of her pale, flawless face into your beady shit-browns. God made us disgusting.

She didn't flinch.

"Did you want to take a ride with me?" You knelt to eye level.

Her cool gaze followed you and her mouth became a hard line bordered by soft pink, plump lips. The girl's face looked like it was made from porcelain by a master doll maker. An image of an old man surrounded by scattered limbs and heads flashed in your head, a workshop. Your desired workshop. You reached out a shaking hand to her.

"Sure." She skipped to the van and turned around. A smile spread across her face as she cocked her head. "Can you open the door for me?"

You rose to your feet and your knees clicking and complaining. "Absolutely."

The girl stared at the van's featureless wall as she sat on the edge of the mattress. She swayed and bounced along with the road; her eyes transfixed on nothing. You reached your usual clearing in the woods and you killed the lights and turned off the engine. It clicked and settled. This was when they would start to cry.

She didn't cry.

The seat groaned as you got up. The indent of your ass slowly ballooned and hissed outward. You added the ripping sound of your jacket's zipper to the ticking symphony of car noises. You tossed your jacket on the passenger seat in a crumpled heap. The van rocked slightly as you made your way to the back.

The girl's eyes snapped up as if she just realized you had squeezed yourself between the front seats and slithered toward her like a fat snail. You licked your thin lips. The spiderweb cracks in your windshield became more noticeable.

"Are we going to fuck, or what?" the little girl asked, coldly, monotone, in a voice that didn't match her delicate features; like a doll being held in front of another, alien mouth, a shadow talking from somewhere behind her. Her head cocked slowly to the side, and she licked her lips with a small, cat-like pink tongue.

You halted and the van violently jerked. The words dropped ice in your guts. Whatever blood tingled in your crotch fled to the other parts of your body. Your fingertips tingled. "What?"

"Take them off," she reached for your belt, and you lunged back. "Let me see that little, button dick." She reached forward again, and the tips of her fingers found purchase on the reversible faux-leather belt you bought from Wal-Mart. The leather snapped and the loose, ill-fitting pants slid down to your thighs, stopping at your knees.

"I don't like the way you're talking. You know I'm going to kill you, right?" You tried to put some aggression in your voice and gnashed your teeth as you pulled your lips back in a menacing grin. The little cuts in your dry lips stung but the pain felt good; you smiled harder. You wanted to taste blood.

The girl smiled and made a low growl. A sound that bubbled deep from somewhere, but not her. She stood, and her shadow took up the entire van as an amorphous shape. You thought you saw a pair of floating yellow pinpricks behind her. "Let me see." She stepped toward you, but it wasn't a step. She glided.

You looked at her feet, but they were lost in shadow. She pulled off your underwear and the fabric split around your legs with a burping rip. You were flaccid, small. A button dick. It's something an escort called you once. A scar ran up your testicles like a thick white thread. Disgusting.

"It doesn't look like you're ready." She bit her lower lip and looked at his scar. "Mommy was right. You're impure. Evil. I like it. It's my turn now. Mommy's sweet little girl. Little disgusting girl."

She moved forward. A shadow flashed over your eyes. Your nose pressed into a faded brown stain of the mattress. Hands moved up and down your pimpled buttocks, but they were not her hands. They were big hands, cold with the texture of dry, wrinkled leather.

You tried to look back at her, but something faced you toward the mattress with alarming strength. The muscles in your neck seized and hardened. You felt yourself open. Something slid inside you and filled you up. All the muscles in your body clinched and you tried to straighten your legs to try to release yourself.

Something held you firmly in place. The thing inside you pulsed and expanded. Tears welled at the corners of your eyes, "Please stop. It hurts," the words squeezed from your throat.

"Too late. Your mommy told us who you are."

Bile bubbled its way from the corners of your mouth. The thing slid in and out of you, lubricated by warmth. A copper smell fills the van like a haze. You felt the gash in your lower back open and split. An electric jolt ran waved and shuddered up your back.

Your mouth opened involuntarily as something emerged from the back of your throat. It stretched and unhinged your jaw. Bones popped and grinded out of place. Something ice cold snaked its way up your body, tracing the widening gash. It caressed the side of your face and pulled its way up into your eye. A purple suction cup, like on an octopus' appendage, is the last thing you see from your right eye. More tentacles wound their way around your body as cold trails.

The member inside you swelled like a surgery balloon in and split you in half with the sound of rotten fibrous fruit being slowly torn by bare hands. Steam plumed from the remains that fell apart like two discarded husks of a molting insect.

The shadows shrank back into corners of the van as if they were being pulled into invisible drains. On the floor, nestled by the blood-soaked shag carpet, a misplaced heart beats.

When Dan and Lam Come to Visit
Dewey L. Yeatts

Tucker Theisen the Third ('Tuck' to his friends, and 'Tuck the Fuck' to the bitches he banged), had a perfect night planned. He had sent his latest piece of ass, Tiffany, out to party with her skanky friends, two of whom he had already fucked in the ass. Now Tiff, she had an awesome rack, but she was kind of clingy, and she never wanted to do anal.

So, what the hell, if she got drunk and blew some rando, he could give a flying fuck, because he had already lined up her replacement, had taken her out for a test-drive finger bang, and if she passed his blowjob test, (like M&Ms, Tuck comes in your mouth, not in your hand) he was ready to kick Tiff to the curb.

But tonight was about serious alone time, without Tiff winging about the place. It was about the lines of pharmaceutical grade nose candy on his black glass coffee table, and his dick in his hand, and a marathon viewing of his "special tape," until he came until he bled.

The special videocassette, obtained through a friend of a friend. This friend of a friend swore him to secrecy on even the tape's existence, much less that he had a copy, but that was peachy with him—as far as Tuck was concerned, this tape was for his eyes only.

He opened the secret compartment in his entertainment center and brought out the VHS tape. It wouldn't do for Tiff—or any of his bitches—to peep this tape.

He slid the tape into the VCR, snorted his first line, sat back on his couch, and gripped his member, already erect in anticipation. The first clip began.

It was a girl and a guy fucking, but this chick was heavy into her menstrual period. The guy was slamming his considerable organ into her, and every time he withdrew, it looked like his cock was being skinned alive, flecks of blood and uterine lining flicking over their abdomens.

When he was ready to come, he rose up, wiped his dick all over her face, jammed it into her mouth and ejaculated. The cum and the menstrual blood drooled out of her mouth in a pinkish froth.

The clips had a momentum to them; escalated as they went. He shot another line up his nostrils, as the tape cut to clip #2, and smiled as he saw the girl on the bed. She was a skinny bitch, and he could tell an addict when he saw one.

She was nude, strapped to the bed, arms and legs tied down. She was obviously doped to the gills, but still on the edge of consciousness, judging by the dull shine in her wide eyes. Her head slowly twisted, as she pulled at the restraints. She had a ball gag in her mouth.

A second girl entered the room, dressed in black latex, fondling a huge black strap-on. The camera zoomed in to show that the dildo was wrapped in barbed wire.

The girl crawled on the bed, knelt between the captive girl's thighs, gripped the dildo, and plunged it in. The damage was immediate and dramatic, as the barbwirewrapped dildo shredded her womanly parts.

It was all Tuck could do not to come right there, death grip on his cock, as he watched the drugged girl's eyes fly wide, and she screamed into the ball gag, teeth biting through it, one tooth breaking off.

She screamed, mouth wide, and her mouth began to tear at the corners. She vomited into the ball gag, some of it drooling out, the rest back down her throat, choking her. But she had problems other than aspiration, as the girl on top moved on to her other port of entry.

The girl with the dildo pounded away, blood spraying up between them. The cameraman got some good close-ups of the girl's holes being turned into bloody rags, and the blood spraying all over the latex woman.

It took a while for the girl to die. Tuck was almost ready to pop, but he had to hold out for clip #3, the piece de resistance. The threesome with a girl, and two racehorses.

As he stroked away, the clip started, and the sword sliced through his neck on the horizontal. It was a clean, surgical cut, so sudden there was almost no sound to herald its silver arc. Tuck's mouth dropped open, and everything was still.

And then all the blood vessels woke up to what just happened, and blood began to spew out, painting his torso. His head perched there for a moment, until the systolic pressure tipped it over.

His raging erection pointed skyward as his severed head fell straight down, and his cock went into his open mouth, spearing his head, full deep throat.

And he came, a terminal orgasm sending his cum through the bloody, still spurting, end of his neck.

Behind Tuck, Lam held his pose, sword parallel to the ground. He was splashed with blood over his protective gear. Lam was short, built like a cinder block, powerful. He was of no specific ethnicity. And right now, he was admiring his handiwork

Lam grunted, pointed at Tuck's head impaled on his dick. "You don't see that every day."

Dan stepped out of the shadows. Dan was lithe and petite. He moved like a cat through the living room, avoiding any of the pooling blood. He turned off the tape before the atrocities could continue. He popped the tape out of the VCR.

"True. But I bet he's been trying his whole life to get his lips around his own dick."

Lam smiled. "Now he's balls deep. Glad we could be of help." He flicked blood off the blade onto the shag carpet.

Lam sheathed his sword, took off his protective gear. Dan added the tape to his duffel bag. Lam stuffed his bloody gear into the bag, and Dan zipped it up. They moved very crisply, almost military in their precision. They had worked together a long time.

Lam said, "The stuff on that tape, there are some sick fucks in this world."

Dan noted that Lam was sporting a raging boner of his own, but he held his counsel. You don't get on the wrong side of a guy who can cut a man's head off in one swing. And what's wrong with enjoying your work? "Dumb shit never should have had this tape."

"Who else is on the list?" Lam's eyes glittered.

"We're working our way back. His buddy, next. We need to work him over, then we get the next name, and then the next name."

Dan would get the name, Lam knew without a doubt. Dan was the brains, and he didn't like to get his hands dirty, but he knew where to put pressure on a man. Pressure Lam was happy to exert. Their employer counted on them to work the chain, tie up loose ends, and cull this particular branch of sickos, before they put more misery out into the world.

What Dan didn't tell Lam, because Lam didn't need to know every detail, just needed to know whose neck needed to taste his steel, whose fingernails needed to be pulled, was that his boss had been paid a great deal of money to work up this particular sick chain, because one of the girls on this tape—that person was precious to the client, the man funding this cleanup.

They didn't need to take pictures to satisfy their boss, or the client, because this job would be all over the papers, and the Headless Wonder here had done their job for them, as with coke all over the place, it would look like a drug deal gone bad.

But the client would know. He would see the name in the paper, see the pictures, and know that one small bead on the chain leading to the men who had destroyed his daughter could be counted off.

And ole Tuck had been undone by his cleaning service, which found the tape, and popped it in, and word got to the people it needed to get to, and the cleaning lady, well she had iffy papers, so she shut up quick; no need to spill any blood there. Then the client had come to Dan and Lam's employer, a man who could get anything, provide any service. He put his best team on the job.

Like ninjas Dan and Lam padded away from Tuck's corpse, their exit as skillfully quiet as their entrance.

In the living room, blood continued to patter on the thick carpet. Tuck sat on his expensive Naugahyde sofa, head in his lap. His bowels let go, and shit flooded the floor, pooled around his feet.

With a wet plop, his head rolled off his softening dick and fell onto the glass top table with a hollow but forceful "*thunk*" and tumbled off the table and splashed into the pool of blood and shit.

Turns out Tiffany did blow another guy that night. They were married eight months later. It was about as happy an ending as anyone could have reasonably expected.

End

You Are What You Eat
My Wild Experience At Grafton's Gory Griddle: AKA How One Little Restaurant Changed My Entire Perception of Food
Gore-Mand Alastair Feasterback

Welcome back Boys, Ghouls, and everyone in-between to my humble little abode of horrifying dining deliciousness. As always, here on the Cannibal's Cuisine Guide, we're feasting on the flesh, sampling the sinews and gobbling down guts as I give you the finest recommendations on where to find your forbidden feasts.

From shady back-alley bodegas to the finest dining our world has to offer, I'll be there sampling all of the cannibalistic cuisine the world will allow so I can report back for all my aspiring entrants to this niche little community of entre enjoyers. You all must have some dark curiosity into this macabre world or you wouldn't be here in my little dark web den now, would you?

Well, let me leave you in suspense no longer and dig into today's festivities of flesh and muscle. I do warn you though, dear reader, this one is even darker than normal. We're headed to the very heart of New York City for a visit to Grafton's Gory Griddle. A quaint little establishment set right in the heart of Chelsea.

I will not disclose its location publicly as you never know who's prying eyes may be peeping. You know where to get the address if this text tickles those taste buds.

Right then, let's set the scene. I'm at the heart of a very busy intersection in one of the most upscale parts of New York City. I've traveled several hours on a very unpleasant flight full of noisy brats whose throats I could have easily ripped out and eaten to get here and now long for a bite to eat.

On all sides, I'm surrounded by fine dining restaurants, expensive hotels and a couple of nightclubs for the rich and famous. It's the most opulent block for quite a distance and now; I'm standing here drinking it all in like a fine wine.

I will not disclose the exuberant amount I had to pay to stay at a hotel nearby but let's just say I'm glad I have such generous benefactors backing my little venture. It's 5:30 PM so the crowds are starting to amass as they head for their boring overpriced meals or to flock into their resplendent rooms before another night on the town.

Mostly anyway, I do see a few businessmen running for the subway, the bus and hailing cabs hoping to make it to late meetings and nights of schmoozing potential clients. It's quite a breathtaking vista to take in. Nothing like the beating heart of a city to make one's pulse race.

I'm looking for a specific alley amongst this who's who of exclusive clubs and hotels; keeping an eye out for the slightest break in the façade. After a few seconds scanning the scenery, I find my entryway. Nestled between a hotel and a nightclub is an undiscerning little alleyway that leads into mystery.

There are no signs to point the way, no lights to guide the way. If you know, you know and will be led down the rabbit hole to where you want to go. Normally, you'd be told to stay away from lanes like this as you're likely to fall foul of vagrants and muggers but here, you'll find no such thing as there's an internal security force stealthily keeping the peace.

To any onlooker, it's a basic alley. To the trained eye, you'll find a manufactured sense of normalcy to keep the average passerby at bay. It's all perfectly positioned to look generic. A few trash bags here and there, a dumpster left against a wall, and a few pallets and boxes all paint a picture of calm, average goings-on.

Nothing untoward to draw in the unwanted eye. Even I found myself questioning if I had the right place despite knowing the full address. It's truly spectacular how they've managed to ape the quiet and non-threatening to their advantage. You'd never believe one of the highest-rated cannibalistic haunts is lurking at the end of this alley. The siren song of sinew is luring you toward the light.

After several minutes of traipsing down this silent tunnel to Salvation, I was eventually greeted by the most generic storefront I have ever seen. It looked like any normal store you'd see on any normal street. Nothing to scream gourmet gore or fleshy delights, not even anything to scream it's a restaurant.

The only denotation of business is a little wooden sign above a black-painted door that reads GGG. It doesn't even give the full name. You just have to know you're here. There are no windows and only one door set against bare brick. At a glance, you'd think you'd stumbled upon a storage unit or a tiny warehouse.

Once again, subterfuge seems to be the name of the game and I for one, love it. What better way to keep to oneself than by hiding in plain sight? It would shock very few of you to know some of the places I've sampled on this ravenous road trip have since closed down due to their décor. It is truly like Icarus flying too close to the sun when it comes to our brand of eatery daring to peacock its true colours.

We cannot be obvious. We cannot gloat and we absolutely cannot afford to draw anyone in that does not already want to be there. Well… unless you're the next course. It really is a breath of fresh air to see someone taking it so seriously. Not only are you risking our freedom by playing it fast and loose with your design but also bringing more attention to our part of society through your carelessness.

No, I will not come down from my high horse; it's comfy up here and too many of you end up behind bars because you can't keep your passions private.

Even further backing up my ideas on the owner's ideas of security was the fact I needed to give a password to get in. I'm not dumb enough to reveal it here. You're given your own when you make a reservation with the place. Once I'd uttered the correct phrase, I heard about six different locks click as the iron door creaked to life and a monster-sized security guard let me into the place, albeit after ensuring I had nothing but my trusty notepad, pen, and recorder.

I wasn't even allowed to have my phone to take food pictures this time. They really weren't taking any chances on their exposure. It had taken months of conversing with Grafton to even get the green light on publishing this review in the first place.

He was reticent to bring any notoriety to his joint but if anyone has a reputation for safety, security, and seriousness, it's me. I love my food and I would not want anyone to jeopardise it. Let alone myself. Turns out the security guard was a fan of my work, too, giving me a subtle little hint after frisking me.

The cold and stony demeanour dropping as he made light conversation. He seemed quite warm as a person despite the militaristic garb and exposed prosthetic leg. I'd have asked his story but I highly doubt he would eagerly tell it, even to little old me.

It is always nice to meet you lovely people out in the wild. I signed a little autograph and he assured me I was in for the experience of a lifetime tonight. I must say, I normally go in neutral but the reputation of the place and the fact that a stone-faced security guard who sees every customer and course could recommend it so highly, too, had me anticipating the best.

Once within the actual confines of the restaurant, I found myself in a sparsely decorated lobby of sorts. The iron door was bolted behind me with a security desk flanking it. The walls were a pleasant off-white, almost eggshell-colored, complimenting the culinary theme. The skirting boards and wall adornments were all a deep red with two equally crimson sofas for guests to sit at before their dining experience was to begin.

The floor was bare wood, immaculately clean, and free of dust. Another simple decorum to a very minimalist entryway to the gourmet. To some, it would be too pretentious and boring but to me, it struck me as an exact metaphor for our brand of food. It looks normal to the naked eye but once you see the bloody details, it becomes so much more intricate.

It's hard not to admire that attention to detail, even in such a dimly lit, non-essential space. I may have stared and gawked at the lobby for a bit too long as the security guard got a tad concerned and guided me toward one of the sofas, urging me to wait until Grafton was ready to guide me through a new level of cannibalistic cuisine.

Whilst I awaited my morbid maestro, I decided to take the time sunk into the cushion of a bloody plush couch to think of the best description for Grafton. Obviously, that's not his real name, it's the pseudonym that has kept diners haunting his doors for the past three years now.

Popping up in the world of gruesome gastronomy as the sous chef for fellow chef de decapitation Pierre Piercer, Grafton went from helping to prepare to opening his own unique abode focusing on a new type of fusion cuisine. Up until this point, I'd never even seen a picture of him, just heard of him by reputation.

Oftentimes quiet and unassuming, he has been surprising, shocking, and stuffing the greediest of gluttons with a host of unique and insane combinations of flavors in a way few would have thought to do. To call his food art would be underselling the ideas of what he brings to food.

Some make sculptures; we've all seen the serial killers who build statues, totems, sculptures and more from limbs and organs well. Grafton takes that and ups the ante. He takes bodies, be them living or dead and combines them to give us a fusion of essence and flavor like no other.

Ethnicities are morphed to become whole dishes and humanity becomes unified under a knife and fork. Many were traumatized by the idea of a Turducken, that Martha Stewart monstrosity. God have mercy on their delicate sensibilities if they see Grafton's meat grafts. Flesh stitched to flesh, grilled, seared, crisped, infused, smoked, and more then bound together to form a tapestry of tastes.

Nothing is off the table when it comes to Grafton's designs. He will live on in infamy for the feasts he has made from the unfortunate victims who end up on his plates. I've heard legend of what goes on in that kitchen and yet, I don't feel comfortable reiterating it here without the dining experience myself. Before you say it, yes, I know this is future Alastair writing but I'm telling a story, you impatient little cretin.

My thoughts were disturbed not long after as the serene silence of the lobby was broken up by the monstrous thud of heavy footsteps. I was convinced an entire army was coming to get me here given the din but alas it was one man who could easily fit the shadow of three.

It turns out Grafton is an absolute juggernaut of a man. I now understand why this restaurant is so cavernous as a man like Grafton requires that much space. He was pushing seven foot tall, wider than a shed and made of almost pure muscle. A flesh mask adorned his face, giving him a look between Leatherface and the Swedish Chef from the Muppets.

I'm not kidding, tanned leather was fused with fur and hair to create bushy eyebrows and an equally out of control moustache. Considering the imposing frame of the massive chef, I was taken aback by this comical and comedic approach to his face wear.

I do not doubt this was intentional. A slight bit of levity to put people at ease around his gigantic frame. Other than the unusual mask, he was wearing plain chef pants, boots with heavy metal decals, and a white shirt stained with blood, sauce, and missing the latter half of the sleeves.

It seemed a size too small as it was struggling against the mass of the chef. He looked more like a security guard than the security guard and carried with him an air of intimidation a dictator would wish for. Few people have made me feel concerned for my safety quite like he has (except maybe the unfortunate Elkswood Man Eater Festival incident where that contestant revealed he had Kuru and threatened to kill us all.).

He quickly made the distance between the dining area and the lobby in a few long strides and came to a halt in front of me. He towered over me and extended a hand for me to shake. I jumped out of the sofa crater I'd created and shook, meeting an iron grasp from a smooth, well-moisturised palm.

I hadn't known what to expect when it came to meating—sorry, meeting—Grafton but this wasn't necessarily it. His hands were the size of my head; I couldn't imagine the size of the utensils he must have to use or how someone so gargantuan could create some of the most intricate and delicate dishes I'd ever heard about.

As we broke off the shake, I noticed he'd tucked a similarly stained apron into the back pocket of his pants. He looked like a laborer over a chef but in this business I've learned to never accept appearances at face value. Some of the best chefs in our niche don't look like chefs.

Need I remind anyone of Eldmondo Ragatoni, the Italian Masterchef of Man-Eating who looks more like a neighborhood crack dealer with his gangly limbs, unkept beard, and occasional spasms? The same could be said of this hulking and humongous human looming over me right now.

Despite the nasty nature of his business and the apparent anonymity he was going for with the mask, he seemed sociable enough and possessed an air of gravitas few could muster. Either that or I was just fucking terrified but that's neither here nor there.

He beckoned me on and we slowly wandered down a corridor adorned in red paint and framed photos of food. To the naked eye, we were gazing at seared steaks, stir fries, and some other meal types from different ethnicities. Every food photo was lovingly printed and kept within walnut-colored frames arranged by style and complexity of dishes. From human foot tacos to human haggis to a less subtle dish with a human head at the centrepiece cut open and hollowed like a candy dish to show brains, eyes and bits of intestine floating in a spiced blood soup.

I only know it was spiced as I could make out leaves of thyme and sprigs of rosemary floating amidst the offal. It was bold, provocative but again, oddly tasteful considering some of the overindulgence I've seen from restaurant décor that less discerning and often lower quality chefs have decided appropriate for their diners and dives.

The bare wood of the corridor creaked slightly under my shoes as I walked, crying further in protest under the bulk of Grafton. The agonizing wood threw me from my rabbit hole of décor thoughts and snapped me back to reality.

I continued to browse the photos as I strolled, the conga line of cuisine near infinite, much like the corridor as we moved from the lobby through a tunnel of terror. Even the lights appeared to grow dimmer as I trudged farther on, struggling to keep pace with Grafton.

My silent traveling companion's excitement apparently grew as his gate became more animated. His imposing stature only grew scarier under the shadows. The hollow, bowl-shaped black lampshades seemed to nearly snuff out the struggling bulbs. We were heading deeper into hell and I could barely contain my excitement to feel the flames.

The corridor gave way to a curtained entryway. Pushing the curtain aside, I was soon standing in an audacious dining room. Grafton gave me the beckoning hand wave into a silent ta-dah as I stood dumbstruck trying to take in everything around me. The walls were that deep blood web, supported by ornate marble pillars.

The floor a deeply red and plush carpet. The cavernous

room was filled with elegantly decorated dark wood tables and chairs. All empty at the current moment as the venue had been exclusively booked for yours truly.

The tables were half covered with blood-red folded table covers. The bare dark wood left bare whilst the covers held delicate silver trays and multiple utensils of brushed slivers and golds. It was the full fine dining foray that reflected across all four walls thanks to a gigantic black chandelier that hung from the middle of the ceiling.

Everything was as you'd see within the most opulent establishments in the heart of the city. Grafton had taken what looked like a standard warehouse and turned it into the finest dining experience for our kind.

I hadn't even been seated yet and my mind was a whir of adjectives and descriptions to do justice to this room I now found myself in. Safe to say, dear reader, I still struggle now as I sit at my computer desperately putting words to screen.

It was almost dreamlike in its elegance. Grafton has crafted not only the finest of food but the finest of scenery to enjoy said food. The allure of blood-laced furnishings and decorum only elevated the food we were about to consume. My glee was becoming unstable. I needed to sample the cooking soon or I was going to explode.

Seating me at a table in the centre of the room, Grafton pulled out a chair and eagerly pushed me in. Again, he was surprisingly gentle for someone so massive. He refused to speak still as he presented me a singular menu explaining how the eating experience was to go.

It consisted of five courses taking me through the greatest hits of the restaurant. The first four were all classic ethnic dishes with a much more human touch. The first was described as a light bite, Human Foot Tacos with a salad of seasonal vegetables.

Course two was slightly more eyebrow-raising as it consisted of Chinese calf and thigh over fried rice. I couldn't be sure if the Chinese referred to the victim or the flavorings. My money was on the former. The third course was the Indian dish, a Madras made of cubed liver and kidney. That one was promising to be delectable and bring a nice level of heat.

I'd never had liver or kidney curried before so it would be a first time in more than one way. The fourth course and the last one with a full description was perhaps the most unusual. It was another light bite course made up of various ethnic jerky strips sewn together with veins and presented with skewers of various organs and muscle.

The full ingredient list not as available as it seemed to be determined by what was best from the corpse. The last course wasn't listed. It was shrouded in mystery claiming to be the ultimate meat. That one had me tantalized the most.

What in God's name could this ultimate meat be?

The fact it wasn't displayed for me to see made my mouth water. More pretentious play for sure but for a gentile like me, it's hard not to appreciate. I acknowledged his menu and signalled my pleasure with the offerings. He seemed to shake with as much excitement as I did, practically bouncing his way toward the double doors leading to the kitchen.

It's eerie, dear reader, to be left alone in a clearly abandoned dining room. To see the furnishings, placements, and usual make-up of a restaurant yet not see another living soul within it. I was alone in a sea of tables, chairs, and cutlery. The silence made me wistful and contemplative.

I couldn't help but wonder what was going into my meal. Who was going into my meal? I knew very little of where Grafton got his meat nor who he slaughtered for my delight. Perhaps he steals people as they leave the nearby hotels, drug people from the nearby clubs or perhaps he just nabs the homeless people who pollute the other areas of the city.

There's an endless supply of meat out there, I just hoped it came from well-bred animals. As if the cosmos was reading my mind and sensing my thoughts, my pondering was silenced by frantic and loud begging.

Grafton wheeled out a businessman, Caucasian, blond and brutish. An unfortunate soul who looked equal parts man and fish. He thrashed against the bonds that had him trapped in a wheelchair. It seemed comical to me to have him tied; Grafton could have probably kept him there with his bare hands.

That childlike Ta-Dah came out again, this time with a cleaver in his hand. It was there I noticed the chair had leg straighteners. One was expanded with a foot ready and willing to be severed at the ready. With an unceremonious swing, it was there no more.

A bloody gout stained the carpet as the foot was pulled away and deposited on a tray. That was to be the foot my tacos would come from. With that, Grafton wheeled his victim back to the kitchen, the screaming coming to an abrupt stop as they disappeared behind the double doors.

Fifteen minutes late, my first dish was served. Brought out on a small white plate, I was presented with two tacos with lovely browned and spiced shredded foot meat, guacamole, shredded lettuce, diced tomato and onion all lightly drizzled with lime juice in nice crisp shells.

The seasonal vegetables were various leaves and beetroot all drizzled and lightly roasted in aromatic oil and sprinkled with a blend of spices I couldn't quite make out. Definitely hints of Anise, Clove, and a generous dusting of

Coriander. It was all very delicately prepared.

The meat was delicious carrying a layer of pleasing heat amongst the earthy natural flavors of the cut. It had been minced and the soft meat barely required chewing. I could practically inhale it. Once combined with the whole structure of the taco I found myself embroiled in a war between soft and crunchy, sour and sweet, all flavors mixing on my tongue in bite after bite of pleasure.

I've never had such a pleasant Mexican experience and I've eaten at some of the best restaurants and street carts in this country. The businessman had made for an excellent opening course. I finished the whole plate in a few quick bites and almost lamented asking for seconds. Though with four other courses to go, one mustn't get too greedy. Feet hardly yield that much meat even when properly shredded.

This time Grafton didn't come out to retrieve my plate. A suited and booted maître d' came out through the double door with a tray of ice water and an array of fancy wines. He deposited the jug of ice water, a glass and three bottles of wine, one of each flavor on the table before taking my plate and swiftly pushing back through to the kitchen.

He didn't say anything, just looked at me cordially with gray tired eyes and a John Water's looking face. It seemed everyone in this place aside from the security had taken a vow of silence. No one would say a word to me, so I quickly recorded my thoughts on the first dish, scribbled down some notes and poured myself a nice glass of Shiraz. Red wine always goes best with red meat.

The second dish didn't have the pre-meal entertainment. No victim was brought out and killed in front of me much to my disappointment. Instead, the meal was brought to me with the face of the victim attached to it.

The same Matra-dee who brought the tray of drinks out came adorned in it, a freshly cut face leaking blood onto his skin. From the glance, I believe it to have been a Chinese woman. The meat presented to me was lightly coated in five spice and generously soaked in soy, sesame, and ginger.

Instead of the mince of the first dish, I was presented with seared steaks cooked medium rare. Both were generously proportioned with a texture similar to veal. From the delicate array of flavors coming through the spices and sauces, I could tell it had been tortured as much as a French speciality veal. The alluring first bite had me making noises close to orgasm.

The mix of soft fluffy rice with the sharp accompaniments of the sauces and soft texture of the meat was almost too much to handle. It was borderline otherworldly how incredible this meal had been made. Grafton was a flavor magician.

I could scarcely believe this was only the second course. The others were somehow going to be even better than this. The wine had paired nicely with it, giving me another level of complexity to my palate.

Again, my meal didn't last long as I needed to sample more and more. To see if each bite was as good as the last. I'd never had such well-cooked rice. It's often so forgettable unless it's truly unpleasant. Here it was on equal footing with the masterfully cooked meat.

It barely touched the sides before running out on me. I mopped my lips with the face left by the Matre-dee and placed it on the plate. A sign I was done and to prepare the next course. Something I was finding harder and harder to wait for. With food this good, impatience is always going to be prevalent.

With the next course still being prepared, I decided to try and relax. To do this, I recorded more thoughts and observations, trying to ignore the litany of bloodstains over the carpet. Whilst the red carpet hid some things, the blood was sticking to the fibres and producing crusts of discolouration.

They were everywhere.

The floor was saturated with old blood, my guess from the opening victim ceremony but I couldn't be sure. Maybe some customers were more unruly than others and ended up being a meal after eating a meal? The disturbing correlation between the location of the dried blood and the chairs of diners had me just a little on edge.

Blood is second nature in a place like this so why should I be squeamish when it comes to seeing it around tables? From bloody steaks to bloody executions, all had a place in this dining room, so it was only customary to see it here. Grafton clearly had an eye for the theatrics, especially when it came to showing where his meat came from.

How many businessmen's feet had been cut off in this dining room? How many faces peeled? There were plenty of rational explanations for the crimson deposits on the floor.

The downward spiral of my thought process was delayed by the entry of the next course. The smell hit me before the doors could even open. The scent of curry was mouthwatering. I could feel drool dripping to the table as the olfactory assault grabbed both of my nostrils by force.

It was like I was back in India, see the review of India's Flesh Pitta shop for more information there. The Madras was a luxurious brown and piping hot as steam rose to the ceiling. The dish was made up like a traditional curry, layers of Pilau Rice, Madras curry with generous lashings of meat and vegetables with a final layer of bay leaves, slightly wilted to release their flavors.

Yet again, I found myself blown away by the tender meat in the curry. I've had horrifically spongy liver and kidney before, especially when it comes to the human persuasion but this was near perfect. Their kidney was soft and flavorful, perfectly prepared and offering a slightly acidic twang to the spicy curry sauce burning my lips.

I don't know how Grafton knew this many flavors and cooking styles but the man was clearly a savant. The liver was just as nice but by now, we surely all know what liver tastes like. Thankfully here there were no fava beans in sight.

I'm so sick of people thinking we're all Hannibal Lecter. To taste something so close to Indian street food made with actual Indian organs was a divine experience. I could have eaten the whole pot and debated barging back into the kitchen to see if I could do just that. Alas, much like the other dishes, it was gone too soon despite more than generous proportions.

As if sensing my growing desperation for fine dining, my Waters-esque Matre-dee was back out within seconds of me finishing my meal to present me with a replacement bottle of wine and the fourth course. The light bite of flesh jerky was out, a tapestry of black, white, Asian, and more were all sewn together as a patchwork of food.

Different colors had been lashed together to make edible artwork and crisped to perfection. Normally, I hate jerky but again, I found today to be a day of many firsts. They were crisp, spiced and so full of tangy flavors. Some spiced, some smoked and some consisting of sticky barbecue and sweet chilli notes. Even the edible vein stitching was a fucking delight.

The saltiness was heavenly, too. I was in jerky heaven. In the nirvana of my dish, I almost neglected the other half of the dish, the kebabs. Three skewers lay next to the tapestry of flesh, each a unique concoction of limbs, muscle, and sinew. The trio also had a different sauce to go with it.

Cool mint for one, barbecue for a second and black sesame for the last one. They had a mix of intestine, various muscle and a tiny hint of brains. I know, I know it's taboo but hey, it's prepared properly in small doses. Your lovable scamp of a narrator isn't going to get Kuru from this little excursion.

Each bite was another small dose of food heaven. My vocabulary is running out of suitable adjectives to describe the succulent sensations this chef has subjected me to. Each course has upped the ante for me.

There was an uncomfortable delay between the fourth and fifth course. I'd been wined, dined, and treated to some of the finest meals to have ever come across my plate. Now, I grew impatient as my anticipation grew for whatever Grafton could quantify as the Ultimate Meat. He'd fed me four different types of cooking, countless variations on flavors and four dishes any chef would have heralded as the ultimate meat. I had to know, I had to know.

It was cracking into my skull like an unwelcome brainworm. Grafton's cooking had set a bar I don't think another restaurant will ever surpass. This mute giant in a goofy yet horrifying mask had nimbly, lovingly turned humans into something elevated.

Meals so good no price tag would make it worth it. He'd pushed the boundaries of everything I thought possible. I'd be making reservations here again now, without even having the final course yet. I was hooked now. I was a Grafton's regular. The Gory Griddle will be my Mecca. Just please, oh please give me this last course. Let me sample the Ultimate Meat. I must know.

The time dragged on until at last, a rumbling came from

the kitchen. I could barely hide my disappointment when Grafton came out with what looked like an operating table. I assumed it was going to be some live entertainment. That this monster was going to give me a live demonstration of how to properly butcher an animal before cooking it up.

I hoped he'd spare me those theatrics and just feed me. The confusion clouding my thoughts only grew though as I watched an army of Matre-dees come out with various cooking implements. There was a gas stove, a burner, pans and tongs all brought out by this suited service staff. They all converged on my table, staring at me in sullen silence.

Nobody said a thing, keeping me in suspense. What the hell was going on here? How did it play into this final course?

Grafton's hands were upon me in a second. He hoisted me up onto the table and began strapping me in. I was far too weak to resist that monster's grasp. An odd level of serenity came over me despite the circumstances. Maybe I was about to die?

I could die happy.

I'd tasted food heaven and now, I could potentially be a part of something equally as important. My limbs were lashed into the table and my trousers carefully removed, preserved for later use maybe?

I could feel the fear creeping into my limbs now. I was sweating and on the verge of struggling against the bonds. Some self-preservation instinct was kicking in, but I was doing my best to fight it. I didn't want to make it hard for the chef. Didn't want to ruin my meat. Some new diner was going to get to sample me, and I had to make sure it was as agreeable an experience as mine had been.

The cleaver was in his hand. That was the realization that nearly sent me over the edge. In the terror, I'd failed to notice that one of the service staff had applied a tourniquet around the top of my thigh, near the femoral. So I wasn't to die here. They wouldn't go to such lengths to preserve me otherwise. That took the edge off at least.

What sent my fear right back up to spiking was the cleaver sizing up the area below the tourniquet. Grafton was going to cut off my leg. I was horrified, but again, I couldn't help but feel some elation. The blow came hard and fast, because of the brute's strength, the leg was severed in one.

There was minimal blood, the small trickle coming through was flowing through a drainage system into a bucket below. The service staff immediately began to get to work preparing the meat, cutting the leg into parts, surgically removing bones and filleting it to the best bits. The gas burner was fired up, the pan heated with oil as I got to watch Grafton fry the meat.

Every piece was graciously seasoned with mystery spices and I looked on through the haze, ignoring the pain and trying not to go giddy. My vision kept fading in and out but the staff kept bringing me around. One injected me with something and from then, I was hyper-aware of every sound from the cooking to every scent.

The scent of myself cooking. Holy shit, I smelt delectable. I could see him finishing up on the first morsel of my meat and popping it on a skewer. He then held it to my mouth. I slowly ate it down, savoring every flavor of the ultimate forbidden fruit.

I… dear reader, I have no idea how to describe that moment. I know you come to me for the ultimate guide in the world of the cannibal and culinary but here I draw a blank. It was like nothing I've ever experienced before. The flavor profile was exquisite. For something so simple as a cube of meat from a leg, I'd never tasted something so good.

Every bite he fed me afterward was just as good, if not better. I could scarcely believe what I was experiencing. I was gorging on my own body. Savoring my own muscle and flesh. He even made a small broth of bone marrow. For the next hour, I lay on that table and sampled an absolute smorgasbord of nibbles made from my leg.

The staff diligently kept me going with damp cloths, water, and one more shot of the mystery drug that heightened my senses. In the end, the final part of my own dish was a wrap of mayonnaise, lettuce and tender muscle. I was properly full. My belly was happy even if there was a depraved air to the whole thing.

I'd just eaten my own leg. It had been brutally taken from me and cooked in front of me whilst I was forced to watch it all, unable to do anything. And I fucking loved it. I couldn't be happier about it.

So, dear reader, you must be wondering, what next? Well, after the meal, I was allowed to rest. Turns out before embarking on the culinary course, Grafton was a surgeon. That explains the stitching he can pull off. He silently fixed up my leg and fitted it with a prosthetic. I was able to walk out of that place on my own two feet, well with a little assistance.

I was escorted back to my hotel room a block away by two of the service staff and even given a little takeaway box of leftover goodies. Turns out Grafton is generous and gives you the extras for home. I hope he reads this and smiles to himself under that mask.

I couldn't be happier to have eaten at Grafton's Gory Griddle. Few restaurants had ever had that calibre of food before. Even fewer could give me that feeling of elegance whilst keeping the food grounded in reality. I got to enjoy the best street food of my life and some of the best ethnic cuisine around.

Grafton is truly a magician behind the grill. A man of vision. A man who will revolutionise the cannibal food industry. His food was free to me. Well, I paid a price but it's a price I'm willing to give. He took my leg and made it something so special. Be warned, you too will face the same thing should you go there.

What do you deem more worthwhile? The ultimate meal. The ultimate meat. It comes at the cost of a part of yourself. Not in the religious sense. I refuse to believe in souls. Just know, going to Grafton's will yield the best cuisine of your life.

Thank you for reading another episode of the Gore-Mand. We had a lot more on our plate than usual but it was so worth it. I will go back. I have another leg he can take. I've never tasted food so good and I'll never find food that good again outside of it.

Grafton's is the unachievable made achievable. Well, as long as I have limbs to spare. I do wonder what he can make with an arm. Until next time, reader, gored night and gored bless.

Witch boy
Daniel Rust

"What's the worst thing you've ever done?" Master Billy asks Beverly this as we stood at the top of the basement stairs in his home. We were watching the goblins violate and play with his mother's dead body at the bottom. I had only met my master three days ago, in a graveyard.

He had been chased into the woods by some other children and when they caught him, he was beaten and stuffed in a gap in a great big rotting tree in the long-forgotten graveyard—my tree. It had been in the graveyard six hundred and forty-seven years and was ghastly to behold. I've been out every few decades but somehow always end back up in that damn tree.

A master finds me and will release me, then they grow with power and cause havoc. They are found out and taken out by the other humans, balance restored.

It really is a sight to behold, the branches wilted and grayed like a sad old dog waiting to pass under a porch. The hollow of the tree, where the master had been stuffed, had been home to all kinds of beetles and spiders that didn't mind the aura my prison gave off.

I couldn't see him but I could hear him crying from the threats of the others, that if he left the tree before dark, they would beat him worse. After a few moments of him realizing he wouldn't be leaving the dead tree for a long time, it filled him with more tears and he kicked up the dirt below.

My heart quickened in pace as freedom became a possibility. He dug absently with the heel of his sneaker until something started to bump it. I licked my lips as he found a ruby—my ruby, my prison. As he picked it up, I felt his spirit through his fingertips and his soul through his blood.

I knew this boy had something dark in him, the pain and the anger and the humiliation was ripe, and then he did the best thing he could at that moment, he rubbed my ruby.

The wind blew harsh immediately, and the dead leaves drew together, as if magnetized. The ruby flew from his hand and out of the tree into the clearing just outside of it. The gem cracked and glowed before exploding in the whirlwind of leaves.

They spun faster and faster as I began to materialize. I clawed my way through the leaves; it was like swimming through jelly, and I fell onto the consecrated soil. My legs shook and my arms barely supported my attempts to right myself.

I was a fawn freshly born from the womb. I breathed heavily as I collected myself on the ground and peered around at the gray world. The master was whimpering, trying to hide himself deeper in the tree. I turned my head, having to push one of my ears out of my eye to get a proper view of my new master.

I stood and stretched my short limbs and watched as my skin rushed in color from gray to its normal dull green. My long nose felt as if it had been pressed down for a long time and was only now released to extend and breathe.

I took a great deal of pleasure cracking each one of my long fingers. I was nude, and the cold wind reminded me as it blew over my skin. The goose flesh tightened the skin of my arms and back as my nipples hardened. My belly stuck out and called for meat, but I'm sure the new master would be generous enough to feed his loyalist.

"Thank you for releasing me, Master," I said to him, bowing.

The master's blue eyes widened as he met my amber peppers. He dislodged himself from the tree but kept his distance. I could see the phrase "master" intrigued him. The wind blew around us and he had to push his wavy brown hair out of his face several times.

He was ratty, his blue jeans blood stained on the knee and his dark blue sweater torn and frayed at the collar and cuffs. It was two sizes too big for him. He had a light bruise around the left side of his lip as it slightly stuck out from swelling.

Yes his eyes were blue but they may as well have been black and red as I saw evil in him. It excited me and my heart quickened again.

"What are you?" he asked quietly.

"I'm a red cap and I'm your humble servant, Master."

He gave me a furrowed look, as if he didn't believe me. I explained the situation, as I've done so many times before.

"I'm a goblin, a red cap. I control the goblins for you. I've been trapped in that gem," I explained, pointing to the ruby, now dull and faded, "for a long time and now that you've released me, you may command the goblins."

It took a few moments of back and forth, talking about his mental state and the existence of goblins and creatures, but I could see it finally sunk in when he let himself fall to the ground and lean back on the old tree. I couldn't read his thoughts but his face wasn't trained in deception. His eyes bugged and rolled and his head shook and nodded with his internal debate. At last he smiled and let out a laugh.

"Fucking wicked," he let out under his breath.

His face dropped when we heard the other children come back to check if the master was still held captive. I hid behind a headstone and watched a tall boy sneer his ugly face as he saw the master reclined on the tree.

They appeared to have gone to a corner store and bought candies and soda as some chocolate was stained on a few lips and crushed cans were dropped from pockets of coats. The boy's nose drooped and his lips were constantly in a state of cringing. There were four boys and they strolled to the master. He looked at me, the fear on his face was comical now.

"Get rid of them," he whispered quickly at me.

I snapped my clawed fingers and six ugly green goblins fell out of the trees around the boys, slobber already oozing from their long unused mouths. They were only three feet tall, a full half foot shorter than me.

The children were surprised, then fearful as my creatures ran to them. They tried to turn tail and run but the goblins hooted and laughed as they gave chase. It was a short run as the goblins were able to jump and tackle the boys. They bit into the leader's nose and tore his ears off.

The others were brought to the dirt and savagely beaten and clawed. A goblin had a boy's neck wrapped around its arm and the boy's face changed three different colors as he cried for breath. One of them tried to swing his elbow on a goblin on his back, but it was caught and swiftly broken with maniacal laughter by my horde.

The ugly boy looked to the new master and screamed for help. He even cried. I was all smiles as I turned back to the master who shared an equally mischievous grin. He called to the goblins to finish the boys but they only laughed and beat their victims. The master looked to me and I explained that they don't understand human language, and this is why a red cap is needed.

Only I can speak both. He let out a sound of understanding, curling the corners of his lips and said those blissful words, "Tear 'em up."

The group choked on their blood as I gave the goblins permission to go all out. They had been waiting such a long time and the master seemed to be accommodatingly generous. After the mutilated corpses had been looted; watches, coats, shoes. The master shed one tear and smiled a lovely grin. This one, quite larger than the last.

Night had come and the master shivered against the cold, so I made one of the goblins give him one of the coats. The master nodded his thanks before I and the goblins fed on the meat. He watched but did not seem bothered by the gore. We stayed in the graveyard for a while longer as the master told me of his life and the times.

A sixteen-year-old boy, who wasn't a fan of education and spent many days avoiding school and walking around the woods. This was good, if we were going to become kings of this place, we would need no distractions. He informed me he was fatherless and that not all the bruises were caused by the other boys, but some by an iron knuckled mother when she found a fleshy magazine under his mattress.

He told me of a time she found ice cream in his room after he was told no; she was so enraged she locked him in the basement overnight, actually throwing him from the top of the stairs to the bottom. He said he was very young and he hit his head twice as he fell and was left alone in the dark. I could see that evil return to his eyes, and I gave him a smile, showing every needle tooth.

The master had grown tired and reluctantly made his

way home. A small ranch style home, far from another neighbor and plenty of deep trees surrounded it. The hour was late, so he insisted he had to climb in through the back window to his room. I was embarrassed for the boy, to be honest.

All this newly presented power and still fearful enough to crawl in a window like a punk. I'll change that. His room was a basic square with posters of music troops and movies. He had a collection of small paintings in his closet that he had done. They were mostly animals.

I assume he'd done them while staring out of the window into the woods. They used many dark reds and browns, making it look like they were painted in blood. He gave me a pair of boxers to wear, the master being uncomfortable with my nude form. They were black with red drops of blood on them, the droplets were in the shape of tear drops and also he bestowed a red beanie for me, a gesture to show I was truly his red cap.

He showed me a binder he had hidden in a vent in his closet. It contained photos of women tied up and enduring what I would describe as hard fetish acts. He also showed me another picture of a young woman. She was dressed as Jackie Kennedy sitting on the back of a 1961 black Lincoln Continental.

She laid across the trunk, stretching her long toned legs out and propping herself up with both arms. Her only clothes were a pink blazer with black trim leading to a pair of pristine white gloves on her hands. A pink thong pulled high mapped the area of her thigh meeting waist.

The smooth bronzed leg guided the eye to a pair of white high heels. Her face contrasted with her hair, her face being cool and seductive with a predatory smile. While her hair was wild twisters of chocolate haphazardly pinned down with a small pink hat. The pin-up would just have been a humorous joke if it had stopped there, but in that extra step into poor taste that gives you shameful arousal, the woman's face and lapel were splattered with a diagonal slash of red blood.

The high gloss made every hot color pop, the pink would almost hurt your eyes and her teeth melted into one bright white smile. The blood speckles are calculatingly imperfect on that ivory canoe.

The master told me if his mother saw this book she'd do a lot more than just take away his door again.

"What happened to your father?" I asked him while he flipped through the crude book of pleasure.

"He was the priest at the local church. The town never really found out but the older I got, the more I looked like the father and well rumors can kill a person. About four years ago, I rode my bike to finally confront him about it, but when I got through the woods across from the church, I saw him loading boxes into his station wagon.

I just watched him from the tree line as he strolled around to the driver's side door and before he got in, he noticed me. We held eye contact for years until he tightened his mouth and climbed into the car. He left town, shamed out actually."

The bastard son of a clergyman. This boy was destined to meet me.

He spent the night telling me his dreams of revenge and power. He even told me an ambitious and thrilling plan he had, but stated he had no means of execution, until now that is.

When I informed him of this, I saw this weight lift from his soul. This was quite an evil person who found me and I will raise him to be the king of my nightmares. He fell asleep around dawn as I heard his mother get her day started. She never came to check on the boy, but I did hear her faintly mutter curses with his name.

He hid me in a backpack as we left the house later in

the afternoon. He showed me the long trail behind his house in the woods. The trees were turning bare as the red leaves lay among their roots like skin falling away. After some time we stopped and he showed me a bow he kept hidden in the base of a tree. He was quite skilled with it, I must say. It was clear he spent a great deal of time out here practicing.

He would shoot arrows at rodents unfortunate enough to stumble upon our strategizing. I must say the boy had an amazing sense of humor. Eventually he stated he was hungry and didn't want to partake in the rodents like I did, so he took me to a small store where he bought cheap Mexican food and retreated back into the woods. He offered me a paper roll with a limp beige wrap in it. And after ingesting the contents, I must say, I prefer the paper. While eating, we heard a woman's voice.

"Seriously Tyler, stop!"

We quietly crept toward the sound and the master sent me to scout ahead. I saw a clearing, like a pit, full of dead leaves and large boulders. Pinned against one of those large rocks was a young woman, and she was held by a shaggy long-haired man with scrawny fingers.

He was holding her arms at her side and aggressively gnawing at her neck. Her face was pink from strain and tears. He would pull away and beg the girl to give it up. He sounded pathetic, even in the position of power. I could see she was trying to squirm away but the man was just slightly bigger than her.

She tried to kick her legs out, but her flared jeans found nothing but dirt. The scrawny man was pressing into her more as I could see she was starting to cry. His hands were tightening around her wrist and I retreated back to Master and recounted what I saw. His jaw tightened and he glanced around to see if anyone else was lurking.

We were alone and he gave his orders, I summoned

three goblins and they laughed gleefully as they ripped the man from the young woman. The master would tell me later he wished he could have seen the man's face when the goblins got him. One of them held her mouth shut as the other two tore him apart.

They ripped his beard off his face and quickly sliced into his belly to pull as much as they could out. They strangled him with his own intestines and ripped his genitals from his body before throwing them back into the woods. They held him tight against the ground as the master came from the hiding spot, having retrieved his bow.

The bloody man feebly struggled in the dirt, kicking debris into his wounds and his head twitched involuntarily. The master made eye contact the entire time and his pupils grew larger like a lioness who's wounded an antelope enough to give a final pounce with bloody claws.

He pulled back on the bow and put a bolt in the man's forehead. The body went limp and the only thing coming from his mouth now was blood. A goblin stood on his chest, drooling with glee, and listened to the death rattle, scratching his ass with a rib bone.

I had the goblins take care of the corpse and drag it back with them into the abyss. The master would only glance at the woman every few seconds. She had cried hard for a little bit but soon calmed down enough for the last goblin to retreat. She sank down to the ground and brought her knees to her face and hugged herself.

The master cautiously walked over to her; she flinched as he came closer. I watched closely, ready to summon my horde if things went all horses and men. The master spoke softly to the woman; I couldn't hear what he said but she nodded at him. She had long inky lines running down her cheeks, which she tried to wipe away.

Her hair matched her inky lines in color and length and

the master helped pick leaves and dirt off her hoodie. He turned his head to me and motioned for me to come to his side. I followed the order and he introduced me to the woman. She waved shyly and gave a small shaky thanks. I bowed courteously and gave her a toothy grin.

She worked at a record store with the scrawny man and the plan was for him to only walk her home. She told us her name was Beverly.

She walked back to the master's home with us to wash her face and get warm. She was taking the attack fairly well considering she knew the corpse, but I've found humans can be just as callous as a goblin. The master has proven that to me already.

They talked of misery and loathing for the world as I sat on the countertop, chewing a steak I found in the bottom of the fridge, it was quite juicy if you would like to know. The master gently moved his hand closer to hers and she didn't move it away and even gave him a small smile on one side of her face.

The master told her he had a plan with me about the world around them. Beverly looked puzzled as I felt the muscles in my face scrunch, and the master looked at me with a tiny smile. I knew what he was thinking and I shook my head, trying to signal this was not a good idea. He gave a small scowl and, against my objection, told Beverly our plan.

I stopped chewing the steak and got ready to call forth some help. She was blank in the face for a few moments and then asked the master to repeat the plan. I closed my eyes and grimaced as he did, and she did a foolish thing then, she chuckled. I shook my head and pinched the bridge between my eyes, as I knew this is what she would do.

He trusted her far too quickly, just because she had a pretty face. I spoke out loud at this point and told her not to laugh at the master and his plans. She gave me a curious look and returned her attention to the master. They held eye contact for several seconds and she pulled away from his hand.

She was turning fast. She rose and backed against the wall behind her. I sighed as the master came to a harsh realization that most boys must, just because she wears a black choker doesn't mean she's evil. Every time I'm released this happens, whether man or woman, they always want to share it as they think it'll strengthen a bond even if there is no bond established. I could see by master's judge of character that I may be back in that tree sooner than I thought.

Beverly stood back as far as she could and told the master he can't go through with this plan. She told him it was a horrible and wicked idea and the master looked wounded by her words. His face showed his confusion and worry and I couldn't take it anymore.

I summoned four goblins to let the woman know she was now a part of the plan. The master dropped his head in defeat then turned to me and looked apologetic. I nodded in understanding and snapped my fingers to tell the creatures to grab the silly girl.

The master left the room as I followed, leaving the goblins to make sure Beverly couldn't get away. We sat on the couch and the master looked nervous, hearing small yelps from the kitchen. He shook his leg and fidgeted. I consoled him, as a good second would, and told him nothing has gone wrong yet, we need only to keep the woman.

The master nodded and smiled a little when I informed him that if he planned to have a kingdom, then what's a king without a queen. After all, a royal marriage isn't based on love. We returned to the kitchen and laughed as one of the goblins was licking Beverly's face with a purple tongue, leaving blue streaks along her cheek.

She was on the verge of tears again as she apologized; she was sorry about her criticism of the master's plan. Another goblin was chewing on the cord of her hoodie as he put it on himself. She swore she would be with him as long as he made sure the goblins didn't hurt her. The master's smile widened and he graciously accepted. He pulled her away from the goblins by the hand and brought her closer to himself.

"I promise as long as you are with me, nothing will ever hurt you again. Not even them."

He brushed away the blue drool from her cheek and she peered down. She nodded in understanding. Maybe I had judged the master too quickly. I recommended the master take a bath to relieve some of the tension from the day's events. He agreed, and Beverly followed and helped wash the master with a few goblins, she made no fuss.

While dressing, the master's mother came home and let out an annoying screech. I suppose she saw the strange woman in her home, cooking a feast that *I* had suggested, with several ugly creatures swinging from the light overhead. I was pleased the master called upon me, because I was going to summon a group of my own volition.

She was quickly subdued and restrained to her bed with a sock stuffed in her mouth and head wrapped in plastic wrap. She was watched by four goblins as they stroked themselves over her crying body. The master showed no sign of caring, if he did at all.

I sat on the counter again as he paced wondering out loud what to do. Beverly looked worried and even tried to assure it would be alright. I suggested, simply, that kings aren't kings if their parents are around, they are only princes. The master stopped and locked eyes with me. I gave him a knowing look. He walked to his mother's room and was alone with her for a while. I was alone with Beverly as she checked on a roast in the oven and started peeling potatoes.

"It won't be as bad as you think," I told her, trying to make her transition as easy as possible for the master. "If you are betrothed to him, you may have accessibility to the goblins also. If the master wishes, of course. We could be your army, too."

Beverly's brow twitched at my words and she seemed to be in deep thought as she peeled away on the spuds. After the master returned, he sat at the table and tried to converse normally with Beverly. She had let him know she was no stranger to abuse and this was probably the reasoning for her easy adaptation to her new life.

The master told her all that stuff is in the past and she would never be subject to cruelty again. Her eyes went watery for a second, but she quickly wiped them and cleared her throat. Soon the three of us ate Beverly's roast; it was juicy. I'm sure the fear of what could happen to her caused her to be very mindful of the meat.

She made mashed potatoes and defrosted some green beans. She grew fearful as she told me there wasn't enough for all the goblins. I laughed and assured her the goblins took care of themselves in such matters. I didn't expect her to cook for all six hundred of the beasts. The master had opened three bottles of wine as we ate.

Beverly became more docile after she consumed a bottle by herself; she even gave a small smile when the master put his hand atop hers for a moment. It's as if she had forgotten the plans confessed to her earlier and the master had been given a second chance. The air was nice and the tension seemed to disperse.

However, Beverly was a few years older than the master, and it became apparent when he tried to keep up with her, the alcohol really hit him and he quickly had to be put to bed after dinner. I made sure Beverly was beside him as he slept. She disrobed and looked for a shirt to wear and when she looked in his closet, she found the secret vent.

Her brow furrowed as she noticed the binder hidden away. She looked back at master Billy to make sure he was still sleeping and then looked at me. I nodded to her, wanting to see what she thought of the master's fantasies. She quietly pulled the binder out and opened it. Her eyes went wide and a small gasp escaped her throat. I tried to hide a smile in the dark bedroom.

She flipped through the scenes and stopped on the Jackie Kennedy photo. She stared at it for quite a while and then turned to the master and I could have sworn, in this tiny moment, when she looked at the master, she bit her bottom lip and sucked in hard.

She returned the binder and seemed to remember she was only standing in her panties. She quickly grabbed a faded black T-shirt with a human skull with large horns protruding from its sides. She didn't look back at me as she climbed into bed. I watched for a long while to make sure she didn't try to run, but no, I believe she was even able to fall asleep in the master's embrace. Her head calmly rose and fell with the master's chest as she laid her head over his heart.

At around one in the morning, the master woke up when echoes of loud howls came from the woods. He laid back down and put his hand over his face. He noticed Beverly was still sleeping so he motioned for me to meet him outside the room. We stood in the hall as he explained the noise in the woods.

"It's fucking Nate and the lacrosse team from the college," the master told me. "After games they get drunk out in the woods all night. Sometimes they come up to the house and throw empty cans at my window. The cops always take their time and let those dicks get back to the woods, but they just come back and throw more cans after."

His eyes slitted, as he rubbed his chin. He gathered his jacket and hat and while putting on his shoes told me, "I want eight goblins here, four for Beverly and four to watch my mother. I want to see what a big group of you can do."

I followed his instructions with enthusiasm, and we were soon walking deep into the woods. We were led by a glowing bonfire in the distance. As it grew closer, the hollers of drunken celebration from the team and their friends grew louder. The master stopped before the fire exposed us and hid close to a tree. He watched as they passed balls back and forth with their lacrosse sticks while onlookers cheered. He looked back to me with an excited smile.

There was a gathering of at least fourteen people, most looked to be around Beverly's age. There were three large trucks with one of them sporting two large kegs in the bed. The party goers were wearing uniforms and shirts of silver and blue. Some even had stripes of the colors on the cheeks of their faces.

The master shook from cold and excitement as he relayed to me, "Alright, I'm leaving the amount up to you, but I want to know what exactly you can do in a crowd."

I was ready. I summoned forty of the creatures and they fell from the trees like hail, plummeting onto the party goers below. Hats were thrown off like can tops and teeth were sunken into the exposed flesh. We still kept our distance as we watched the fun begin. A large fraternity member was pushed onto his back as his ankle tendons were ripped from beneath him.

Several goblins jumped to his arms and held him down as three pulled his jaw from under his skull. The muffled yell turned to choking cries as the jaw was removed swiftly and gnawed on by the creatures. Lacrosse sticks were forced into rectal cavities and full cans of alcohol were shoved in the screaming maws.

The spray of foam and blood had the swarm rolling with laughter. No one was spared as the horde struck randomly. The women were violated and their breasts were chewed like the gristle of steak. Claws were used to slice openings if none were available to use. They even tore apart the large trucks like gremlins in the engines on a World War II plane.

Goblins started their own party that matched that of the team before. Skin was hung from tree branches like flags and the remaining blood and fat slid off like butter on a hot pan. The master nodded his head the whole time he watched. He saw what my creatures could do and what I could make them do for him. Eventually, everything that could be broken, was. And the flesh that could be devoured, was.

"That'll do," the master yawned, and it was time to return home.

Quite early in the morning, the master arose and got dressed. He wore his sweater from when we'd first met, he had let Beverly sleep in and put two goblins as guard to watch her. The master and I had gone out to the woods to retrieve his bow. Once we had returned, I called for his mother to be gathered.

The master then called for Beverly, and as she was collected I noticed some of the more mischievous members had gotten into the paint and created clown-like images on their faces and handprints on their bodies. Beverly was brought into the hallway to watch as the master stood at the top of the stairs leading to the basement.

She was still only wearing one of his shirts. She was held in place when she noticed a butcher's cleaver in the master's hand. His mother's face was a memory of the tears Beverly had just the other day. Her arms were bound in front of her breasts with an extension cord and electric tape cut into the sides of her mouth as it was wrapped around her head.

I summoned many goblins to watch the master assert his authority, they jumped and laughed and hooted in the extremely cramped hallway. Some were grinding their teeth as they peered at Beverly's exposed legs, knowing they were not allowed to touch her in such a perverted way. The master grabbed his mother's hair and leaned in. He stuck his tongue into the side of his cheek as he brought his arm back for a full swing.

"Hey Mom, you may have been right. Maybe I *was* a mistake."

All of his power went into the blow and the cleaver struck his mother's neck with a wet thud. He pulled the cleaver out with an obscene slurp. She tried to go limp but the master was able to hold her. She made funny hacking noises as she tried to breathe through her nose. So like a leader breaking ground, he took a starting hit and left the real work to his underlings.

He pushed her now convulsing body down the stairs and she fell in a most comical way. She even managed to bite through the electrical tape. The master jumped aside with a laugh as a wave of green meanies jumped down the stairs in brash excitement for a new plaything.

The master wiped away the long diagonal splat from his cheek. He turned his head to the last two goblins at the end of the hallway and motioned to have Beverly brought to him. She sucked in harshly when she saw the bloody woman at the bottom of the steps. The matriarch was unceremoniously slaughtered.

Her head was separated from her body with the same level of excitement as her other body parts. She was clawed, crushed and violated by the enthusiastic creatures in a lustful frenzy. Some goblins were even on the staircase sucking on the steps at her blood smears and eating the teeth that had been cracked and dislodged themselves from her tumble.

Some even slurped long strands of skin, reminiscent of a leather belt, like spaghetti. The master held on to Beverly's hand, chewing on his lip. He held on so tight, her fingers turned white. He had a grin on his face as he asked the question that you came in on.

"What's the worst thing you've ever done?"

She trembled and tried not to let her obvious fear be heard in her voice. I wasn't expecting her answer but couldn't help but give a small chuckle when I heard it.

"Meet you."

The master didn't respond, but I noticed his grip got tighter on her hand. A tear ran down her face, but I don't think it was the pain. He turned his head to me but only stared at the floor in front of me.

"Make sure everyone eats quickly. We have school today."

When We Were Dreamers
Brit Jones

"Imagine yourself naked, unclothed, floating on a warm cloud," the counselor said. "There is a slight breeze that ruffles your hair. You are at peace."

It was easy to buy into some of the bullshit. Marilou was certainly naked, the only one in the group, and the floor heater was providing a warm breeze, albeit too warm for comfort. She felt sweat popping out of her pores.

"What are you feeling right now?"

"Hot. And I don't mean the good kind. Like an idiot for agreeing to be a part of this bullshit. At the moment I think I'd prefer the fire hose. Whatever nimrod sets the HVAC in this compound needs to be replaced. After a couple of these "warmth" sessions."

Gillian, the counselor, let a flash of irritation, quickly as the ghost of electricity, mar the bones of her face.

Christ, Marilou thought. *When it's Dylan things are likely to get bad.*

"Sisters," Gillian said placidly, "would you please go help in the gardens while Sister Marilou and I have a private word?"

There was a murmur of assent as the six others, all in their brown smocks, rose to leave. Marilou couldn't help but notice the undercurrent of excitement. It was always present when one of the girls stepped out of line, but with Marilou there were bound to be fireworks.

"Who put you up to it this time? Strickland? Power corrupting absolutely and all that? That pit bull he drags around on that chain hasn't been fixed. One word, one jerk on the chain, and that thing's a killing machine."

"Beasley's as gentle as a kitten. Unless he's provoked. You seem to take a great deal of pleasure in provoking anything or anybody around you."

"Bitch, you know I didn't choose to be here. Given the choice between waterboarding and having a shiv driven between my ribs is really no choice at all."

"Sister, at the end of the day we are all responsible for our own choices."

"Lesson received. Can I please put my clothes back on now?"

The placid, serene Sister Gillian was gone. She had been replaced by a feral animal, poised for violence and barely hanging on to her self-control.

"Put on your fucking clothes. Believe it or not, Strickland's going easy on you. Why on earth he's chosen to is an utter mystery to me as well as the other sisters. Third strike for you, Marilou Barton. Most guests don't get past two. The little girl in question is expected to live, although she may not ever walk again. A car wreck? Really?"

There was a pause. A pause in which Marilou almost seemed poised to say something self-recriminating. The moment passed.

"At least the child molesting dad is in the morgue. I'll send flowers or some shit."

"You really are a monster, aren't you, Marilou?"

"For every action an equal and opposite reaction. For every act of kindness, you get one of me. Says something good about human nature and we're always way ahead of schedule."

"Waterboarding. Four hours. If I had it my way it would be eight,"

"Good thing you're not in charge."

***

Marilou almost made it. She didn't start to gag and groan for mercy until after the three and a half hour mark. The fact that it was a pyrrhic victory was not lost on her. It simply meant the next session would be longer and more brutal. But such victories had become a central tenet of her personality since the rape. At four months along pregnant, this mousy, unassuming school teacher had tracked down her rapist (something the police seemed uninteresting in doing for a young, poor black school teacher) cut off his balls with a dull, rusty knife and duct taped them into his mouth until he suffocated to death in agonizing pain.

She lost the baby. Guiltily, she was relieved. There was no way she could have loved a child conceived in such a way. Something broke in her when the doctors told her she could never bring a pregnancy to term.

Sympathetic friendly witnesses and cops who had seen too much in their time contrived to only have her sentenced to two years of felony probation. She had, of course, lost her job, but an outpouring of grief and outrage sparked a swell of #gofundme, #metoo and #patreon pages, very few operating under the purview of what the organizations were founded for. Nobody seemed to give a second look and Marilou found herself in no need of cash.

That was when they found her.

***

They asked could she do it again. Could she do it to a stranger, someone she had never met and probably never would?

Absolutely not, she said. It made her vaguely sick to her stomach that she had done it once. They told her it was this or a women's home. Basically a halfway house where she could be in danger every moment. She demurred.

That all changed when the brother of the man she had killed kidnapped and killed her parents, her sister, and her niece. There would be no more running away. There were monsters in the world. They needed to be exterminated. She was one of the few who existed with the motivation, the drive, and the stomach for the work.

She excelled at her training. Some of her instructors expressed concerns that she was overzealous. She was supposed to bring them in. Beat to hell, sure. Being fed through a tube for the rest of their lives, fine. But dying or already dead in truly depraved conditions was off the plantation. All the kings horses and all the kings men couldn't keep such extravagances from legitimate law enforcement agencies finding out.

So they gave her harder jobs. And she thrived. They subjected her to soft interrogation methods. She got better. Her body count grew. The fact that her victims were certainly guilty, who had walked on technicalities, carried little water where habeas corpus was concerned. The ones in charge, the ones with the most to lose, decided she needed to be discretely dealt with.

***

"Strickland, sir, why do I get the impression you don't want me around anymore?"

"What do you mean by that, sister?"

"Oh, cut the bullshit. You're Steve and I'm Marilou. Just like always. Pulled from the field. A real juicy one at that."

"You're spiraling out of control, Marilou. Drugging a man, tying him to a chair, and burning him alive is outside the purview of our mission."

"That man was kidnapping infants and eating them. The fact that law enforcement couldn't turn up shit when I could, pretty easily at that, speaks volumes about law enforcement in this city."

"You should have turned your information over to the police."

"And watch the fucker get away with it? Even if they gave him life inside, he'd still be walking around breathing while those children never got the chance."

"Nevertheless. I'm pulling you from the field. You are obviously in need of some down time."

"You'll regret this, Strickland. Very seriously regret it. Not a single one of those idiots out there can find their assess with both hands. I'm the only one who gets results."

"It's your results I find alarming. I'm putting you on interrogation for the time being. That should satisfy some of your blood lust."

"Nothing short of hearing the pieces of shit beathing their last will satisfy my blood lust."

"Interrogation, sister. Do a good job, don't kill any of the subjects, and we'll reassess in a few months. Mess this up, Marilou, and I don't need to explain the consequences to you."

"Fuck you and fuck your consequences. When do I start?"

***

"Put the electrodes on his balls."

"Sister, we're supposed to put them on his nipples."

"And, *sister,* I say put them on his balls. Do you want to go soft on this murdering rapist? It won't kill him. But he'll sure wish it would."

The sister obsequiously attached the electrodes to the naked man's testicles.

"Please," the man begged. "I didn't do anything!"

Marilou said, "Sister Katherine, give him a jolt,"

Sister Katherine turned the knob on the generator to two. The man howled.

"Please," he gasped when Sister Katherine shut the generator off. "I didn't do anything! Why are you doing this to me?"

Marilou walked over to the generator and slapped Sister Katherine hard across the face.

"When I say a jolt, bitch, I mean a *jolt,*"

Marilou cranked the knob to eight. The man shrieked as though he were burning in the fires of hell. Smoke rose from his crotch. Sister Katherine, holding her face, ran from the hut.

Producing a stiletto from her smock, Marilou walked over to the chair the man was strapped into. She placed it gently below his chin, and then gradually began to apply pressure.

"Please, please," the man gasped. "I didn't mean to. I just couldn't help myself. With any of them."

"We're talking here about Emily White, your last one, although the fact that there were others makes this easier. Tell me, what were Emily White's last words?"

"Please," he gasped. "Please stop this."

"Her last words, or yours, little man?"

She pushed the stiletto farther into his throat.

"Mine! Mine! I don't remember what she said. What any of them said! Just the screaming!"

"Well, boyo, think real hard about what you want yours to be, because in about five seconds I'm going to slit your throat and it'll be too late."

Strickland's voice rang out from the door of the hut.

"Merilou, stand down!"

She shoved the stiletto into the man's neck. He gurgled as he died.

"Hmm. No last words after all."

"This is the end, Marilou. You've been given more chances than you deserve,"

Strickland's pit bull slavered at the end of its chain.

"So, what, me verses the beast? Do I get a sword or anything?"

"In spite of your fondest wishes, we're not so barbaric here. While what happened to you was a tragedy beyond imagining, it has turned you into a predator, and predators have no place here. You will be confined to your hut until the council decides what to do with you. As they say, live by the sword, die by the sword.. For you, it will be something much worse."

"Screw you, Steve. What can you possibly do to me that's worse than has already been done?"

"Give the council time. I'm sure we'll think of something. Until then you'll be locked in your hut. No visitors. One meal a day."

"And if I'm really good, do I get a puppy for Christmas?"

"Take her away."

***

Marilou lay on her cot in the darkness. Dim moonlight filtered in through the windows set high in the walls. The stick girl crouched in the shadows of the corner.

"It's been a long time, my love," she said.

"It's been a long time since I needed you."

"And what now, little dove? What has happened?"

"I was too good at my job, so they decided to kill me for it. And I don't mean softly."

"Well, we certainly can't have that happen," the stick girl said. "What would you have me do?"

"Kill them. Every last one."

"Tonight? It can be done."

"No, one at a time. One each night."

"Have you a name for the first?"

"Sister Gillian first. Make it grisly. Set an example."

"It will be done," the stick girl said. And then she was gone.

***

In the morning Marilou's door slammed open, waking her.

"What the hell did you do, Marilou?" Strickland yelled. "What the fuck did you do!"

Beasley, sensing impending violence, snarled at the end of his chain.

"What are you talking about," Marilou said sleepily. "I was locked in here all night. You locked me in. Remember?"

"Sister Gillian was murdered last night. Tortured and murdered. Dismembered. She was stacked like cordwood with her head on top."

"Horrible. Simply horrible. Forgive me if I don't shed a tear."

"Listen, you little *bitch*! I don't know how, but I know you had something to do with this. Well, it'll all be over soon. The council meets tomorrow morning. Your story will be over by tomorrow night."

"Threats come so easily to you with that beast chained at your side. I could have you begging for death in five minutes given the chance.

"I guess we'll never know. I suggest you spend your last hours in contemplation. Come to peace with the things you've done."

"You wouldn't happen to have a copy of *Moby Dick* laying around, would you? I never got around to reading it."

Strickland slammed and locked the door.

***

The stick girl was back that night.

"Did I do well, sweetling?"

"You nailed it. You always do."

"And, so, which one tonight?

"I need five tonight. The members of the council. Sisters Antoinette, Roseanne, Margot, Eunice, and Marilyn. Make it look like a mass suicide. That should put their panties in a twist."

"A large request, my love, but doable. You must know, little dove, that, when this is over, there will be a price. I've always loved and protected you, and always will, but an undertaking of this size requires it."

"I'll pay any price to see them all suffer."

"Very well, child," she said, and was gone.

***

The five sisters were found hanging in the council chamber. There was no note. It was agreed that they had hung themselves. No outsider could have pulled off such a stunt. While there were a great many cries of dismay and tears from the remaining assembled sisters, Strickland expressed nothing but rage.

He burst into Marilou's hut and shouted, "I guess you think you dodged a bullet. I've got news for you, *sister*, I don't need the council to do what needs to be done. These others will do as I say!"

Marilou grinned.

"I guess that depends on how many you've got left."

That night the stick girl said, "Strickland is the most dangerous. Shall I take care of him tonight?"

"No, I want Strickland for last. I want him to see everything he built crumble before he dies."

"Very well, sweetness. Have you a name for me?"

Marilou did.

***

And so it continued. Sister Katherine's body was found, but her head never was. Sister Marie was found nailed to a tree with her eyes gouged out. Sister Sharon was found in her cot, a huge wooden splinter piercing her neck. No one could explain where a splinter that size had come from.

Sisters began disappearing from the compound. The handful remaining assumed they were leaving on their own accord, out of fear, but a few assigned a more sinister fate for the missing girls.

After two weeks only Strickland and his loyal dog remained.

"Tonight it's Strickland," Marilou told the stick girl. "I want his dog Beasley to kill him. And this time I want to watch."

"As you say, little dove. It will be done. This will be the last of it. The price must be paid."

"Let's just get this over with."

***

That night at sunset Strickland and Beasley came for Marilou. He let her out of her hut and stood off, regarding her coldly. She couldn't blame him. She was filthy and she stank. Off under the shadows of an oak tree she could see the stick girl.

He said, "Well, I can't pretend to know how you pulled it off, but you've managed to destroy everything I built here, *we* built here, out of what? Spite?"

"You were going to torture me to death, asshole, or did you forget that part? And, as far as you need to know, I just wished this would happen."

"Marilou, sometimes the most dangerous wishes are the ones that come true."

"Oh for crying out loud, enough with your platitudes. You brought this on yourself and deep down you know it."

"You'll take the fall for this. Multiple homicides. I know enough about you and what you've done that I don't need to end you. The law will."

"If anyone takes a fall, Strickland, it won't be me. I was locked in a hut the whole time. Not that it matters. This will be over for good in a matter of minutes."

"Do you know why I built this place? I and the others had a dream of a place where traumatized women could come and, to whatever degree possible, recover. Sometimes that entailed kidnapping those who caused that trauma and forcing confessions from them before turning them over to the police. That dream became a beautiful reality and we thrived. Until you came along. We underestimated your pain, your rage, your desire for vengeance. Locked in a hut or not, you would have destroyed this place."

"And this great dream of yours entailed torturing and

murdering me?"

"That was never the plan. Of course, we wanted you to think so but, seeing what you've seen here, did you really think we would do something so medieval? We kept a dossier on you, on all the sisters. Yours is especially incriminating. We were going to turn you over to the police and let justice be done."

"I think I've heard enough of this pious bullshit. So, what do you intend to do now?"

"I'm going to unchain Beasley and let him do what he's best at. Self-defense if it comes to that. Just an out-of-control dog that got loose if it doesn't."

Marilou looked over at the stick girl.

"Are you ready?"

"Of course, my child," the wind seemed to whisper.

"Kill him."

"Who are you talking to?" Strickland asked, suddenly panicky.

The stick girl snapped her wooden fingers.

The chain holding Beasley broke and the dog leapt viciously up at his master, tearing at him with his fangs.

"Beasley, no!" Strickland screamed. "Down! Down!"

Beasley ripped Stickland's throat out and the screams abruptly ended. The dog stood over his fallen master, breath heaving, gore dripping from his muzzle.

"Is that all, my dove? Everything you wished for?" the stick girl asked.

"Everything and more."

"It pleases me to please you, sweetness. I have loved and protected you since your first time of need. But what Strickland said about wishes is more than just a platitude. I will always love you, but I can't protect you anymore."

"Wait, no…"

The stick girl snapped her wooden fingers again and Beasley lunged for Marilou's throat.

OTHER HELLBOUND BOOKS
www.hellboundbooks.com

VHS Nasty: The Video Nasties

We are proud to present our very first non-fiction "coffee-table" book! A fascinating expose of the 1980's video nasty phenomenon that gripped Britain and led to some of the most draconian censorship the country had seen for decades.

VHS Nasty: The Video Nasties is the definitive, full-color guide to the halcyon days of the 1980s, when the British government and its nanny state, headed by the self-proclaimed and totally unelected "Protector of Public Morals," Mary Whitehouse, decided it would dictate what the viewing public could-and, more specifically, couldn't-watch in the privacy of their own homes.

The fight to control the voracious, countrywide spread of video players brought about the much-maligned Video Recordings Act 1984, which came complete with a list of "video nasties," horror movies deemed much too disturbing for the delicate sensitivities of the British public, and which were not to be viewed on home VCRs. And, not only were those films banned, producers and directors were prosecuted, video stores were raided by the police, and video cassettes were burned (*Fahrenheit 451* anyone?).

Naturally, the act not only blighted the whole video/home entertainment revolution but it also inadvertently created the cult underground movement and a huge collector's market for the iconic films, many of which still change hands for phenomenal sums of money!

I Spit on Your Grave, The Driller Killer, Cannibal Holocaust, Xtro, The Texas Chainsaw Massacre, and *The Evil Dead* were just a handful of the initial 72 titles that made the "must-see" list of the 1980's horror aficionados, all of whom moved heaven and hell to get their hands on a copy!

Tony Newton and David Bond lead us through the history of those dark, draconian days with an engaging, conversational style that makes for simply terrific reading. They also provide a comprehensive, title-by-title list of each and every one of the banned and prosecuted films, along with comments and memories of some of the producers, directors, writers, and actors responsible for creating the whole video nasty phenomenon.

With insightful contributions from: Lloyd Kaufman, Taylor Sprow, Ramsey Campbell, Graham Masterton, Barbie Wilde, Nicholas Vince, John Thomson, Ruggero Deodato (*Cannibal Holocaust)*, Steve Wright, Terry M. West, Richard Stanley, James Cullen Bressack (*Blood Lake*), Mark Miller (Seraphim Films), Colin McCracken, Eric Weston (*Evilspeak*), Glenn Criddle, Max Weinstein, John Penney (*The Return of the Living Dead 3, Hellgate*), and many, many more.

Anthology of Splatterpunk Volume II

splat·ter·punk
noun
informal
noun: splatterpunk

Definition: "A literary genre characterized by graphically described scenes of an extremely gory nature."

Welcome once again, fellow gore lovers, to HellBound Books' second foray into the deliciously bloody, innards-strewn world of splatterpunk!

Death, dismemberment, and destruction abound within these pages, as we bring to you nineteen perfectly ghoulish tales of terror that are definitely not to be read while eating!

Go on, we dare you!

You have short tales from: Shannon Blake Skelton, Juan Ozuna, Sarah Moon, Seaton Kay-Smith, S.C. Vincent, S. Michael Wilson, Carson Demmans, Diana Parrilla, Michael Errol Swaim, John Schlimm, P.J. Verfall, Karly Foland, W.L. Lewis, Caleb James K., Brian J. Smith, D.J. Tuskmor, Terry Grimwood, Dave Davis, and Paul Allih.

Anthology of Creature Features

Come on, admit it, we all love a gripping tale of our fellow creatures gone bad. Think *Jaws, The Rats, The Crabs, Pede, Them!* – the list is practically endless (hell, they even made a movie about killer bunny rabbits! *Night of the Lepus*, 1972, anyone?).

There's just something so inherently terrifying about the animals we see every day and take for granted are going to stay in their dens, burrows, nests, swamps, and crevices going on a murderous rampage of mayhem and outright slaughter against us poor human beings. Knowing what they are truly capable of has us keeping one wary eye on the critters, that's for sure.

And so, gathered within the pages of this skin-crawling, nerve-jangling anthology, you'll discover a collection of the most horrifying examples of Mother Nature gone psycho we could unearth. We have killer goldfish, a murderous mantis, a hellish giant arachnid, giant lizards, turtles, something altogether indescribable with tentacles, and so much more. Heck, there's even a tale of butterflies we guarantee will chill you to your very soul!

Featuring zoological tales of terror from: *Tim Newton Anderson, R. D. Tyler, Chad Barger, Seaton Kay-Smith, Milan Kovačević, Julien Jayus, Robb White, Serena Daniels, Rose Strickman, Janna Layton, J. Neira*, and the amazing *Cliff McNish.*

The Last Customer

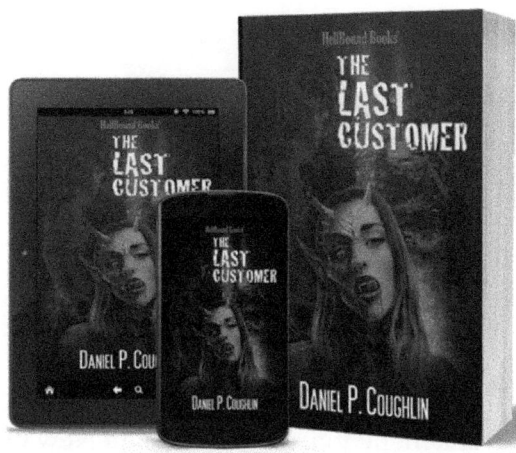

One hot August evening in the small town of Dodge Junction, Wisconsin, Win and Garth Gasper close their family-owned liquor store for the night.

When the demons Sammael and Jezebeth show up in search of Father Leslie Gardner—the priest that many years ago exorcised Sammael—the Gaspers are forced to confront the most terrifying customers they have ever experienced!

Up the hill from the liquor store, Father Gardner senses he is being challenged by the demons. Unable to ignore their foul presence, he makes his way to where the demons have kicked off their destructively sinister plans for the evening.

Now, Garth, Win, Gardner and three unexpected armed robbers must fight their way out of the liquor store where their flesh and souls are being shredded by the denizens of Hell.

Father Gardner must revisit his terrifying past and renew his faith to defeat the nastiest demon he's ever encountered and protect the lives of his neighbors against the last - and by far the worst - customer of the night.

And Then You Die

Following a drunken, hedonistic night out in New Orleans, highly successful businesswoman and sexual deviant, Claire Jepson, accidentally soils herself in her car. The resulting excrement comes to life as a sardonic fecal spirit, and not only dishes out a gruesome death to Claire's unfaithful, gold-digging fiancé, but also thwarts a kidnap/murder plot by her employees. It then introduces Claire to a world of depraved pleasures beyond her imagination.

A year later, the errant spirit has spiraled wildly out of control - its insatiable appetite for perverted sex and human flesh and has destroyed Claire's life. Then, to her horror, Claire discovers the fecal spirit must consume her unborn child to attain immortality; she must return to the seedy underbelly of the Big Easy in a heart-pounding race against time to confront the spirit's creator - a high priest of an ancient, deadly order, who is the only one who can put a stop to the spirit's murderous intentions.

A wicked, fast-paced story laced with tongue-in-cheek, dark humor, which is at the same time incredibly erotic and stomach churning. Most definitely not one to be read whilst eating!

Anthology of Bizarro

Welcome to the wonderfully horrific world of Bizarro - that dark, forbidding corner of the horror genre where absolutely anything goes and one may delve into the farthest recesses of the authors' warped imaginations.

Prepare yourself, dear reader, for a journey into the unknown reaches of terror, from which you can only hope you will return with your sanity intact...

Enjoy 16 outstanding stories from:

Scott McGregor, A.L. King, Garvan Giltinan, Keith Kennedy, Robert Prescott, T.M. Morgan, Lee Rozelle, John W. Leonard, A.L. King, Matthew McKiernan, Aron Beauregard, Ken Goldman, Victor Marrow, Ryan Woods, and Stephen Daultrey

**A HellBound Books Publishing LLC
Publication**

www.hellboundbookspublishing.com